SWALLOWTAIL

Also by Emily Ross

Half in Love with Death

Swallowtail

EMILY ROSS

galiot press

For David, Thomas, and Julianne

Chapter One

July 12, 1994

THE CITY OF Quincy opened up on summer nights for me and my best friend, Bridget McGann. Sometimes we'd cruise the streets in her cousin Barb's black Camaro, Barb up front holding the wheel with one hand, a cigarette in the other, Bridget next to her, pulling down the vanity mirror to check her makeup, while I hunkered in the back seat. Other times we'd join a pack of teens and roam the city on foot. We'd end up downing cheap beer at the quarries, in the woods on Piney, down the Mount, on the Neck, at the Rock. I can still hear Bridget's husky voice as she recited the names of these drinking spots we'd discovered with the soles of our feet.

But that night she had other plans. A light rain fell as we walked down her slippery front steps to the street across from the ocean, me in powder blue pumps with a blue rose on each toe, her in red stilettos. When we reached the bottom, she glanced up at her house in the Hough's Neck section of Quincy, worried her father was at the window scouring the darkness for us. He'd told her she couldn't go to the party, with a slam of his fist on the table and a "shut up if you know what's good for you." I would have been happy to stay in and watch *Edward Scissorhands* again. With his sad porcelain-mask face and knives for fingers, Edward—destined for heartbreak and loneliness—never failed to make me cry. But Bridget insisted we go to the party. We'd waited until her dad was too drunk to notice us sneaking out.

The party was being held in honor of Devon Ford, the love of her life. Bridget acted as if he were a golden-haired god sent down to Earth to save her from Quincy. But Devon hadn't descended from heaven. He'd moved here from Montana to study surrealistic painting with my father at the Blackwood College of Art. He and a select group of my father's other students often gathered at our house for dinner and drawing critiques while Bridget and I lurked at the edge of their impassioned conversations.

My dream was to become a surrealist artist like my father. He barely acknowledged me around his students. But Devon took an interest in my work. He said my art had potential and he'd love to paint me with my raven hair and spectral blue eyes. I read far more into his attention than I should have. It was Bridget he noticed most, with her long legs, fluffed up blond hair, and a hard smile that said, *Just try it, I dare you.* She became his muse, his model, his everything.

The contest was my father's idea. "Take a myth and give it a twist," he'd said, pointing to a painting he'd done of my mother as an example. It was a variation on Dante Gabriel Rossetti's Persephone—full lips, sad eyes, wavy russet hair cascading down her long neck, her hand curved around a pomegranate—but in my father's version my mother held a snow globe with a tiny snow-covered town inside.

"You can try, too, Samantha," he'd added as an afterthought. I did try, but Devon won the contest with his painting of Bridget as the nymph Daphne, complete with a laurel crown in her hair. Now, it was on display at the college, and the Epoch Gallery in New York was giving him a show later in the week. He was taking Bridget to New York with him after the party. All she could talk about was how he was her ticket out of Quincy.

As we waited on the deserted street for him to pick us up, the wind howling off the ocean made me shiver. I clutched my thin sweater tight while a buoy bell tolled in the distance. Hough's Neck wasn't safe at night. Bridget told me not to worry—she could take anyone. But I sensed her tensing beside me as she fussed with the laurel crown she'd insisted on wearing.

A white car emerged from the fog, long and sleek with a gold grill gleaming with rain. Bridget dashed up to the driver's side, heels clicking on the wet pavement. She tugged her short silver-sequined dress down over her butt, leaned in the window, and chatted with someone I couldn't see.

"Come on." She smiled at me. "He's taking us to the party."

She slid onto the front seat. I sat down next to her. The boy wore a black hoodie pulled down low over his face. He reeked of Cool Water cologne and cigarettes. I figured he was someone Bridget knew from the Neck. As he rolled the windows up against the wind, David Bowie came on the radio singing "Let's Dance," and Bridget bobbed her head to the beat. He handed her a flask. She took a swallow and passed it to me. I wiped off the top with my palm and drank.

The locks clicked.

* * *

Detective Brian O'Neil found me in a couple of inches of water at the bottom of a ravine hidden in the miles of wooded wilderness near Quincy, known as the Blue Hills. I had no idea how long I'd been lying on my back, too frightened and in too much pain to move. When his freckled face peered down at me like the moon shining through darkness, there was a comfort in his brown eyes. His voice was pure melody as he called out, "I found her. She's alive."

As the EMTs carried me past the crime scene in the woods, Brian covered my eyes and said, "You're going to be all right, Samantha. Just don't look."

But it was too late. I'd already seen her. My best friend. The stab wounds in her chest like slits in a piecrust, the laurel crown in her hair, a yellow swallowtail butterfly placed on the ribbon of blood that separated her head from her body.

Chapter Two

Twenty Years Later
July 12, 2014

PIA, THE LONG-HAIRED chihuahua, wouldn't sit still for her portrait. We'd tried the white leather sofa, a red kitchen chair, her dog bed. Nothing worked. We decided to try the yard. Linda Tran had a big yard for Quincy—a veritable sea of green.

I pointed to some pink roses climbing the fence at the back of it. "How about over there?"

Linda held Pia close and smiled. It was sweltering, but Linda looked as calm and cool in her white capris and crisp linen shirt as someone in a deodorant commercial, even with a squirming dog in her arms. "You're the artist, Samantha. Whatever you say is fine with me."

"It's nice to be called an artist instead of Detective Star for a change."

Linda's dark eyes met mine. "You *are* an artist. You should do more of it."

"I wish I had more time." I surveyed the yard through the camera on my phone looking for the right backdrop for my painting of Pia. I was focusing on some rose petals scattered on the green grass when a flash of yellow caught my eye. A leaf? My chest tightened. A yellow butterfly? I zoomed in. A dandelion.

"Sam?" Linda was saying.

"Sorry." I turned to her. "I'm just a little preoccupied. It's the anniversary."

Twenty years since Bridget's killer had left that yellow swallowtail at the crime scene, and he was still out there. Twenty years since Detective Brian O'Neil had rescued me from that ravine.

Linda drew her brows together. "I completely forgot. If you don't want to do this today, I understand."

"I want to do this. It takes my mind off things," I said, and she nodded sympathetically. She knew how difficult it was for me to get through this day.

She placed Pia on the brick patio. The dog looked up with big, dark eyes. From the intensity of Pia's gaze I was pretty sure she took herself quite seriously. But when she began running madly in circles, a platinum mop on spindly legs, it was a relief to laugh, given how deadly serious I felt right then.

Linda clapped her hands. "Pia, stop." The dog scampered off into the yard and she said, "I am many things. A dog trainer isn't one of them."

"It's fine. She'll tire herself out." I dug my hands into the pockets of my jeans and waited until, sure enough, Pia plopped down in front of the roses—right where I wanted her.

As I ventured onto the lawn, the air had a sweet, suffocating smell. It was quiet here for Quincy, no sirens, no rumble of trains or traffic noise—nothing but the faint hum of bees buried in the folds of flower petals. The freshly mown grass felt spongy and strange beneath my feet, like with one misstep I'd be swallowed up. I tensed, always vigilant, listening for a footfall, the crunch of leaves. *For him.*

Pia looked up as I approached. I knelt so I was eye level with her and held out a treat. She cautiously ate it from my palm and then stared at me expectantly, her eyes as black as the shiny beetle inching along a rose behind her. I raised the camera and snapped a burst of pictures before she ran back to Linda.

"I'll have a painting for you in a couple of weeks," I said. Linda scooped Pia up and summoned me back into the kitchen for iced coffee.

"Beverly is going to love this. Between SAT prep and the dance team, she works so hard. I want to show her some appreciation." She stirred condensed milk into the coffee and poured it over glasses filled with ice. "What do I owe you?"

"Nothing. You're always there for me when I need you to drive Corinne to dance team events. That's more than enough." I swallowed some of the sweet Vietnamese coffee the wrong way and couldn't stop coughing.

Linda pushed her chin-length black hair behind her ear. "Are you okay, Samantha?"

"I'm fine, just getting used to the single life, and working a lot," I said, when I could finally speak.

"That must be hard on you and Corinne." She eyed me with concern. "And that terrible stuff you deal with on your job, I don't know how you do it." I frowned as she went on. "I bet you could make decent money with your art, and you might be happier."

I stiffened. "I didn't suffer through being a beat cop for years to leave now that I'm a detective," I said, more sharply than I'd intended.

She sipped her coffee. After an awkward silence she said, "I love the dance Corinne and Beverly are doing for States."

"Me too. Maybe the team will win it all this year." My phone buzzed, and O'Neil's name popped up on the screen. "Fuck, Brian. It's my day off," I said. Linda raised a perfectly shaped eyebrow, but I forced a smile. "My partner doesn't understand I have a life, though maybe I don't. I have to go."

* * *

Patrol cars were pulled up in front of the twinkling green lights of the Good Luck Shamrock, the convenience store where my mother, Eva, used to buy the flour for the Irish brown bread she always insisted on baking on St. Patrick's Day. I lived just up the street from the place and it always reminded me of her.

"Sorry to bug you on your day off," Brian said as he led me through the crowd of onlookers.

"Corinne and I have our special dinner tonight." I frowned. Brian pushed up his mirrored sunglasses and his warm brown eyes met mine. He knew I always took this day off and that I deliberately filled it with distractions, ending with the special dinner my husband, Jeff, used to make to celebrate the fact that I survived. Now that Jeff and I were separated, it was just me and Corinne. "I have to stop at the store," I said. "This better not make me late."

"It won't take long." The fine lines around his eyes sharpened when he smiled.

"So why am I here?" I asked.

"OD, but this one's a little different." Brian eyed me. "When I saw the body, I wanted you to take a look, too."

I followed him to the trash-filled vacant lot behind the store. An officer at the scene came up to us and said, "The guy who found him stopped for a Quick Pick and noticed the smell. Thought it was from the dumpster and found the body. Not his lucky day. Not the victim's lucky day, either."

I edged closer to the big guy splayed out in the weeds next to a crushed Bud Light can and an empty pizza box. There was a purplish tinge to his lips and nails, and he was wearing a Celtics jersey, baggy jeans, and sneakers.

The officer pointed to the torn flesh at his throat. "His head was almost chewed off. Probably coyotes got to him or raccoons."

Brian glanced at me. "A little like what happened to Bridget, right?"

I inhaled the foul-smelling air. "Maybe." It had been twenty years, but we still searched for a connection whenever a crime scene even remotely resembled the old case.

Brian went on. "He's from down the end of Hough's Neck. Name's Walter Blair. Does it ring a bell?" I shook my head. That was near where Bridget used to live but I'd never heard of him.

"Just another loser," the officer said.

Brian flashed him a glance. "So many ODs lately. Could be anyone's father or brother."

I sighed. Brian's younger brother had died of an overdose years ago. My mother had overdosed, too. One night, when I was ten, she left with a man who always wore a backward baseball cap and made her laugh more than my father ever had. The next time I saw her, she was in a coffin. I used to look at my father's painting of her and imagine her lost somewhere in that tiny snow globe town. Gone.

Brian turned back to me. "You mind taking a closer look? It might jog a memory." He knelt in the dry grass and groaned. "Hurt my knee in a pickup basketball game last week."

The officer cracked a smile. "Getting old, O'Neil?"

"Speak for yourself. Still a few years before I hit the big five-oh." He eyed me expectantly as I crouched beside him. "What do you think?"

I breathed in and out slowly to relax and waited for the gruesome scene to whisper dark secrets from my past. But as I looked from Walter's bloated face to his Celtics jersey—the same jewel green Edward Hopper used in his bleak urban paintings—and then to his hands clasped on his huge belly, I saw only the obvious. The ragged wound on Walter Blair's throat had to be from animals. It wasn't from a knife, like the cut that went across Bridget's neck. "The scene isn't arranged to make a macabre statement the way Bridget's was," I said. "I think it's an OD."

Brian nodded. "You see the article in the *Sun* today?"

"Not yet."

He handed me his phone open to the article they published every year on the anniversary. This year, Alice Crane, the *Sun*'s Arts and Culture reporter, had written it. I tensed as I read:

Twenty years ago, the brutal murder of sixteen-year-old Bridget McGann rocked the small, working-class city of Quincy. Today, a new development project promises to revitalize its dying downtown, but the person who murdered McGann and abducted her friend, Samantha

Star (née Flynn), still hasn't been found. Star, now a Quincy detective, is the only one of this serial killer's victims to survive.

McGann, a lifeguard and hometown hero who saved a toddler from drowning at Wollaston Beach, was also the model for artist Devon Ford's prizewinning painting of Daphne, a figure from Greek mythology. But McGann's promising future was cut short when she became the first victim of the person dubbed the "Butterfly Killer." In letters to Star, he described his crime scenes as works of art inspired by myths from Ovid's Metamorphoses. *A far more accomplished artist than this deranged killer, Star has devoted her life to solving this case.*

The article ended with a plea for leads to stop this vicious murderer who silences women the way they are silenced in the myths.

There was a faint pulsing in my left eyelid, like a hummingbird beating its wings—a gift from falling into that ravine twenty years ago. I handed Brian his phone.

"Nice touch, mentioning you're an artist," Brian said. "Working on anything new?"

"A portrait of a chihuahua." I tightened my ponytail. "Am I done here?"

"Almost." Brian ran his hand through his silver-flecked red hair. "You know someone named Kerrilyn Sloane?" I shook my head. The name was familiar, but I couldn't quite place her. "She's Walter's girlfriend. They lived down the Neck together. She completely lost it when we showed her his body. Not surprised. She doesn't believe he overdosed but wouldn't tell me why. She wants to talk to you about it."

I followed Brian down the block to where Kerrilyn stood in front of an empty storefront. She was a good head shorter than me, with blond corkscrew curls. She wore a skimpy camisole and, though it was closing in on 90 degrees, cute suede boots over tight jeans.

"It's been a while, Sam," she said with a cautious glance, and I remembered seeing those same curls when she sat in front of me in tenth-grade geometry.

"Sorry to meet again under these circumstances," I said. "Do you know how Walter ended up behind the Good Luck Shamrock?"

She tugged on a curl. "He went out last night and didn't come back. I figured he'd run off. He did that sometimes, but he always came home. We have two little girls. He was good to them."

"Were you aware of his drug problem?" Brian asked.

"Yeah." She ran a finger anxiously around the tattoo on her shoulder—a flower in a spiral of leaves. "Every time he left and the phone rang, I'd think it was the call." Her eyes had a frozen, startled look, as if she were fleeing into someplace deep inside herself. "I should've checked on him, but I didn't want to know."

When she finished telling the rest of her sad, familiar story, she looked at me. "Sam, remember us?"

"I do," I said, though the reality was there was no *us*. I barely knew her. She had been a wide-eyed hanger-on, more Bridget's friend than mine.

"I saw Bridget's cousin down by the marina a couple weeks ago, but she acted like she didn't know me." Kerrilyn sniffled and wiped a hand across her nose. "Guess Barb's too good for me now."

"That's just how she is," I said. Even before Barb married Max Delaney, a big developer in Quincy, and became all high-and-mighty, she rarely gave me the time of day, let alone Kerrilyn.

"It makes no sense that Bridget saves that boy's life and a year later she's dead." Apparently, she'd read the article in the *Sun*, too. She rubbed her palms on her jeans. "Walter was in recovery. He turned his life around and now he's dead. That doesn't make sense, either." She eyed me. "I don't think he overdosed."

I raised a brow. "Why do you say that?"

"I saw a yellow butterfly this morning." She twisted her hands together. "A swallowtail. It felt like a sign."

My mouth went dry. "Where did you see this butterfly?"

"In my yard. I've never seen one there before, but I saw one today. It's the anniversary and Walter's dead. It has to be related."

I took a long breath. "Is there something specific you know that makes you think Walter's death is connected to Bridget's murder?"

She shook her head. "It's just a feeling."

"Sounds like a coincidence," Brian said.

She stared at me. "You understand it's not a coincidence. I know you do."

"I think it's a coincidence, too," I said, before she drove herself mad connecting random things to explain what was staring her right in the face; her boyfriend fell off the wagon, took a fatal dose, and someone dumped him here.

She pressed the heels of her suede boots into the dusty ground and then locked her eyes on mine. "We should catch up sometime."

I told her, "Yes," though rehashing the past with her was the last thing I wanted to do.

"Sorry for ruining your day," Brian said as he walked me to my car. "But I wanted to be sure this was just one of those crazy tips we get on the anniversary."

"You can be sure," I said. Lots of people on this planet had probably seen yellow butterflies today, but only two people were predisposed to see that as part of a larger pattern related to Bridget's murder—Kerrilyn and me.

Half-moons of sweat showed on his shirt as Brian leaned against my car. "You going to be okay today?"

I smiled. "I'm fine. I got my dinner with Corinne to look forward to."

Chapter
Three

Before

August 1993

AS WE SPREAD our towels on the burning sand and sat down, Bridget pointed to some kids playing at the ocean's edge and said, "Look at those little fools." I gave her a questioning glance and she went on. "They're probably hunting for those periwinkles that look blue underwater and turn ordinary when you take them out. When I was little, I kept hoping to find one that stayed blue. But I never did. They disappointed me. Just like everything here."

She brushed some sand off her red-painted toenails and frowned. "Being a lifeguard is so boring. If I didn't need the money to get out of Quin-zee," she said with an eye roll, "I'd quit. Everything here is boring. These fries we got on the boardwalk are boring. They should call it Bored Walk. The boys are boring."

"Even Frank?" I smiled, trying to humor her. Frank was her latest.

"Oh my fucking god, he's just another boring punk pretending to be a gangster. I can't take him anymore," she said, so loud it would have been embarrassing coming from anyone else.

"But he loves you." I smirked and we both laughed because love was something we desired and derided at the same time.

"It's my boobs he loves, Sam," she went on. "I can't stand the way he begs me to let him touch them."

Her breasts were full, pale, perfectly shaped—goddess-like. At nearly five eleven with the chunky highlights in her blond hair, soft full lips, and long tanned legs, she was a goddess.

I was lean and almost flat with ghost pale skin, long black hair, and light blue eyes I emphasized with smoky eye shadow. Though the latest boy I wrestled with when we were drinking in the woods on Piney told me a handful was enough, I was no goddess.

"Everything's so boring now that Barb's with Max all the time," Bridget said. "It's like she's forgotten I exist."

I smoothed the edge of her towel. "No one could forget you exist."

"You really think so?" She gave me a look so hard it could grind you into dust. "I don't even care about love anymore. I just want to feel something, even if it hurts."

"Me too," I said, though deep down inside I was a prude with a Disney princess idea of love—cartoon lips kissing, no teeth or spit or bad breath, bluebirds of happiness circling my true love as we clasped hands.

She crumpled the grease-spotted bag that held the remains of our fries. "Can you throw that away for me? My shift is starting."

I took it with an eye roll. She liked ordering people around, but I put up with it because she was not boring. She dragged her feet across the sand toward the plump acne-spotted girl who had the shift before her and climbed languidly up to the lifeguard chair.

The ocean shimmered like a mirage on the highway. Hardly anyone was swimming. The sign said Wollaston Beach wasn't pol-luted today, but no one believed that. It would have been easy for her to stop paying attention, but Bridget kept her eyes trained on the water. I grabbed my sketch pad and started drawing her sitting up high in her chair—but I couldn't concentrate. The sun blasting down had almost lulled me to sleep when I heard her shrill whistle and saw her race past the kids we'd seen earlier and run through the water toward something I couldn't see. Moments later she emerged, cradling the limp body of a little boy, and began CPR. Watching her pushing down on him with her big hands made me worry she'd break the little bird ribs in his thin chest. But she wasn't about breaking him. She was about saving him.

The boy's mother was so busy talking to some dude, she hadn't even noticed he was missing until she saw Bridget holding him. Now she was screaming at her for letting it happen. Bridget paused only long enough to look at me and say, "Shut her up."

I went over and said calmly, "I know you're scared, but let her do her job and everything will be okay."

The guy beside her smelled of weed and beer. "Just be quiet, Helen," he said, and she pressed her thin lips together and frowned.

When a little water spurted out of the boy's mouth and his eyes opened, the look on Bridget's face said it all. I'd never seen her so happy. The EMTs were there now, and she let them take over. As they put him on a stretcher, she squeezed my hand. "I saved him."

While the boy's mother headed for the ambulance, the guy who was with her came up to us. His long pants were rolled, he was barefoot, with sun-bleached hair, and his Hawaiian shirt was unbuttoned all the way down. He was nothing like a Disney prince but for a second, he made my legs weak. From the bag in his hand, he grabbed some green grapes that were the same color as his eyes and said to Bridget, "I am truly thankful for what you did." As the two of them stared at each other, it was like I wasn't even there.

The local news showed up a few minutes later, and Bridget was in the center of everything, being adored—just the way she liked it.

"Sammy," she said when we were leaving. "Remember this day. I saved a boy and it's going to change everything."

Chapter
Four

I MADE A left at the light and drove past the block of stores that looked ready to fold, the perpetual line of cars at the Wendy's drive-thru, the mini-mall with a Dunkin' Donuts and a Chinese takeout place, and the Marshalls that was my fashion destination. I made another left into Stop & Shop. I needed blood oranges for the special salad I was making for Corinne. Jeff always made it for her, and I wanted to get it right. They had navel oranges, tangerines, tangelos—all the usual suspects, but no blood.

I finally found them in a bin next to the avocados. A woman stood in front of them, taking her time to decide. As I reached past her, she snapped, "Ever hear of saying 'excuse me'?" I reflexively returned her hard stare, and she backed away. I was putting some oranges in a plastic bag when "Let's Dance" came over the sound system. The memory flashed through my mind: Bridget opening the door of the white car, that song on the radio, the locks clicking. As Bowie crooned, "Put on your red shoes," I broke into a cold sweat, my heart beating hard. An electric buzz tickled the back of my head. The plastic bag slipped from my hand.

Someone raised a knife and brought it down on an orange. Blood spurted everywhere. "Do it like this, baby," Bowie sang. Only it wasn't

Bowie. It was someone in a white Mardi Gras mask with green glitter around the eye holes.

I felt a searing pain in my arm. The next thing I knew I was on the floor with my fists pressed in my eye sockets, and a man in a purple Stop & Shop shirt was saying, "Are you all right, miss?"

I stood up, and looked at my arm—no blood, just an old scar from my abduction. I showed the manager my badge, told him I was fine, bought my oranges, and got out of there.

* * *

I took an orange from the bag, dropped the rest on the kitchen counter, grabbed a knife from a drawer, and rushed upstairs. I needed a Xanax. But when I dug the bottle out of my dresser drawer, it was empty. I'd had episodes like this ever since Bridget and I were abducted, but not in a while. They were all I remembered of what happened to me between the time we got in the car and when Brian found me. My first therapist chalked up my localized amnesia to the trauma, the ketamine the killer had given me, or both. She gave me the PTSD diagnosis when I was seventeen. Over the years I tried medication, meditation, cognitive therapy, talk therapy, hypnotism. Nothing helped me remember. And in my episodes, the man always wore a Mardi Gras mask.

Peter Reynolds, my current therapist, assured me a memory of trauma can't remain submerged forever. No matter how much you wanted to hide from it, the memory would rise to the surface like a drowned person, sometimes in pieces. Eventually all the fragments would come together, and I'd remember what happened that night, and feel whole again. He encouraged me to draw my episodes, said art might be a better way into the blacked-out part of my memory than words.

I had to record what I'd seen in Stop & Shop before it faded. The messy drafting table set up in our third bedroom was covered with drawings I'd done in the margins of newspapers, on envelopes, on anything within reach. Just looking at all the things I'd started and never finished was exhausting. As I cleared a space for my sketchbook, the knife, and the orange, I pushed aside my father's critical voice in my head telling me I wasn't good enough. Now wasn't the time to worry about what he thought of my work; I needed to get down the details of my episode. But as I turned to a blank page in my sketchbook, the printer on the desk next to my table started up, and the door creaked open.

Anton Koslov stepped in softly and ran a hand over the black bandana holding back his blond hair. He was on the dance team with Corinne—one of the only boys. They'd been friends ever since he'd come here from Russia when he was nine and he was often at our house, practicing with Corinne, escaping his father's dark moods. He was usually so quiet I'd forget he was there. But when he danced, he was unforgettable.

"Mrs. S.! I'm sorry. I didn't mean to disturb you." He tugged on the neck of his T-shirt with *Real Men Dance* written across the front. "My bird, Percy, is missing. We're making flyers."

"Oh no," I said. "Sorry about Percy."

His gaze went from the orange and the knife to my blank page. "Thinking of a painting?" I nodded and he said, "Is it like a dance? You start with nothing, feel hopeless, but then you see it right before your eyes?"

I swiveled on my stool. "I wish." I glanced at his eyes that never quite met yours. The color shifted between silver and blue like the inside of a shell. He gave me a quick smile, scooped up the fliers from the printer, and backed out the door, leaving it open. When I went to close it, I smelled smoke from Corinne's room. "Jesus Christ," I muttered, and went in. Nina Crowne, Shannon Delaney, the team captain, and Shannon's sidekick, Lane, were there with Anton.

Nina flicked her cigarette out the open window behind her when she saw me. Corinne looked up from petting Ginger Rogers, our sweet and absurdly laid-back King Charles spaniel. "Mom, haven't you heard of knocking?"

"This is a no smoking zone." I turned to Nina. "You should know better. You're a dancer."

She stretched her swan-like neck. "We weren't smoking."

"This is also a no lying zone." I shook my head. Took brass balls to lie to my face.

"Okay, Detective Star." Nina slid one long slender leg over the other and shared a smirk with Lane.

"Mrs. S. is right." Shannon smiled. With her round face, upturned nose, and rosebud mouth, she looked like a cherub except for the fierce intensity of her green eyes. "My mom says I have to be extra careful because I've had rheumatic fever and smoking's bad for your heart."

"At least one of you understands." I could fault Bridget's cousin, Barb Delaney, for many things, but she was devoted to her daughter.

Corinne stared daggers at me. Usually she hung out with Linda Tran's daughter, Beverly, a homebody like Corinne and a perfect friend in my opinion. Beverly was probably at SAT prep right now, while Corinne was with the stars of the dance team trying to impress them. I decided not to embarrass her any more than I already had and turned to Anton. "How did you lose Percy?"

"I lost him," Shannon said. "I had him at my house and he flew out a window someone left open. I feel awful about it. I love that little tweety bird so much." She ran her hand through her short blond hair as she straddled the arm of Anton's chair.

"It's not your fault," he said.

She leaned over and kissed the divot-like scar on his forehead. "We'll find him."

According to Corinne, Anton got that scar when he fell while he was dancing on a beach in Russia and smacked his head on a sharp rock. The injury left him with recurring headaches and was one more reason his father, Vasily, didn't like that he was a dancer. Neither did some of the local boys. They called him the Russian creeper, among other even less generous, names. But Anton shrugged them off. Nothing could stop him from dancing.

I eyed the tattoos of roses and flames winding up his arm as he handed me a flyer and said, "Could you put this up at the station, Mrs. S.?"

As I studied the photo of the parakeet his father had given him from his exotic animal store, I caught my breath; the bird was the same soft ethereal blue that the artist Della Robbia had made famous. I gave him back the flier saying, "I'll put it up at the station, but your best bet is to call the animal shelter or put this on one of those Facebook pages about lost pets."

Corinne swept her chestnut hair off her shoulder. "We know that."

Nina thrust her sharp shoulders back as she studied a flyer. She was exquisitely thin, but Corinne assured me Nina wasn't as delicate as she looked, and she was an even better dancer than Shannon, albeit less showy. She was also Anton's most recent ex. Or was that Megan O'Hare, another dance team star? It was hard to keep track, but apparently, he was with Shannon now. Corinne kept me up to date whether I wanted to know or not, all the while insisting she and Anton were just friends. I worried sooner or later she'd end up hurt.

She sucked on the tip of a green glitter painted nail as I grabbed another flyer. "I love that color," I said. "Can I borrow some?"

She tilted her moony face toward me. "I thought you couldn't wear polish at work."

"I can wear it when I'm not working." I smiled. As she handed me the bottle from her dresser, I saw the *South Shore Sun* open to the article. "Did you read that?"

"Yeah." She pushed my hair from my face—she was always fussing with me as if I needed fixing—and gazed at me with calm concern. "Does he still write to you, Mom?"

"No," I said.

"My mom says he does." Shannon set her piercing eyes on me.

I frowned. This was obviously one of Barb Delaney's deeply held, misguided opinions. "Your mom doesn't know everything."

There was an awkward silence. Lane walked languidly to the

dresser, perused the article, and said, "I didn't know Bridget was a model."

"My mom told me she was really beautiful." Shannon flashed me a look.

Lane furrowed her brow. "Who *is* Daphne?"

"She's a girl in a myth. Apollo, the god of the sun, burns for her but she doesn't burn for him." I smiled. "He chases her and is closing in when she's saved by being turned into a tree." I paused. "Though *save* isn't the right word."

"He must have been pretty hot if he was the god of the sun," Shannon said.

Lane smiled slowly. "Maybe he just thought he was hot."

Nina raised her pointed chin. "All boys think they're hot."

Anton cracked a smile. "You mean I'm not?"

Shannon leaned into him. "You have nothing to worry about." She nodded at the others. "We should go to practice now. We can hang up the flyers and get pizza after."

I eyed Corinne. It was the anniversary, and she was almost sixteen, the same age I was when it happened. My fears were irrational, but I had to say something. "Don't stay out late. States is tomorrow and we have our special dinner tonight."

Shannon turned to me. "I'll make sure she gets home early. We could win it all this year. And not just States. Scouts from *Wish Upon a Dancer* will be there, and they're picking someone to audition."

"*Wish Upon a Dancer*?"

Corinne gave me her death-glare. "You know, the show I watch every week, Mom?" Her voice rose. "This is the biggest thing that ever happened to us." *Shit. I'd forgotten.*

"They'll pick Megan," Nina said sourly. "She always gets what she wants."

The color flared in Shannon's cheeks. "No way they'll pick her." She hooked her hand in Anton's. "My dance is way better," she said and they left, with Ginger Rogers padding faithfully after Corinne.

* * *

I raised the knife up over the orange on my drafting table, but I couldn't bear to bring it down the way I'd seen in my episode. I sliced it carefully instead and sketched a mechanical hand holding a knife. I turned the orange into a wheel with white spokes and filled in its crimson flesh with a colored pencil from a mug on the table, all the while trying to ignore the voice from my episode saying, "Do it like this, baby."

As I drew the mask and dabbed Corinne's green glitter polish around the eye holes, it was all I could do not to call and beg her to come home. But I reassured myself she was at practice with her friends. She was fine.

I went over to the paintings stacked against the wall and pulled out the one I always returned to whenever I had an episode. It was the first painting I'd done when I got home from the hospital after Brian rescued me. It showed me at the bottom of the ravine, almost completely submerged in black water. I kept hoping I'd remember something and be able to fill more in, but I still had nothing to add. I swiveled my stool as I stared at it. Then I reached for the mug full of colored pencils, fished a key from it, and took a locked metal box out of a desk drawer. The original letters were in the case files, but I kept copies here.

The first letter had arrived in a cream-colored envelope lined with gold, two weeks after Bridget was murdered. I thought it was a party invitation until I tore it open. I swallowed hard now as I reread it.

Darling Samantha,

I hope you enjoyed my latest work of art: Deceitful Daphne.

My golden girl thought she could escape, but I am the sun, the one you can't outrun. The bark seals her lips. The tree holds her still. If I can't have her no one will.

Nothing is as blue as a lost blue rose, remember?

At the time I wanted to tear the letter up, but I shared it with Brian. The last line convinced him the letter was the real deal because the rose from one of my shoes was missing, and they hadn't made that detail public. He entered the letter in evidence, but they never figured out who sent it.

Because Devon's painting of Bridget as Daphne resembled the crime scene, my father and Devon were suspects early on. But they had alibis and I was certain Devon wasn't the guy who had picked me and Bridget up in the white car, so they were eliminated as suspects. Some people, including Barb Delaney, were convinced I was in on it. I'd introduced Bridget to Devon—still the prime suspect in their minds. I was the last person to see Bridget alive, and I escaped. Was there a reason the killer had let me go? I asked myself that same question, too.

On the news they called Bridget's murderer a sick artist. In the months that followed, I worked on that painting of myself and one of Bridget. My father discouraged me from painting her, said after what happened to me, it might be too upsetting. But I didn't listen. I painted her perched on her lifeguard chair in her red bathing suit, smiling at the calm sea and holding a lustrous blue periwinkle on her palm. If you looked hard you could see a few insignificant brushstrokes of red nestled in the distant hills—the murder scene. I added a hand reaching up from the ocean, only it didn't belong to the little boy she saved from drowning. It had knives for fingers like *Edward Scissorhands*. When I showed my painting to my father, I told him I'd merged the day when she saved that boy with the horror that came later and made time meaningless—like the melting clock in Dalí's *The Persistence of Memory*.

"You should explore the experience of memory more in your work," he'd said with a cryptic smile. I told him I wanted to but still couldn't remember a thing from that night. "Create a new world," he'd insisted in his quiet way. But I couldn't do that, either.

A year after Bridget was killed, eighteen-year-old Laurel Brown was found murdered in Vermont, dressed in a red sequined G-string and pasties and covered with white feathers, a white butterfly on her throat. I received another letter. He called his new work of art *Lascivious Leda*, his take on the myth of Leda and the Swan. The following year Crystal Gould was found dead in the woods in New Hampshire, wrapped in a cocoon of multicolored thread, with a black-and-white swallowtail where her tongue should have been. In his letter he called her *Silver-tongued Philomela*. He wrote, *Unheard melodies are sweeter, right?* But Philomela didn't go unheard. In the myth, she reveals the story of her rape in a tapestry. The lovely language of the myths made it easy to forget that they were about raping and silencing women. But I couldn't forget the monster who mutilated and murdered his victims in the name of the myths and called it art. I decided to paint Crystal and Laurel—not as victims, but as the people they might have become.

I got a couple of paintings into a group show at a small gallery in South Boston. My father came to the opening. As I stood with a plate of orange cheese cubes and crackers, he said, "You're making some progress." I forced a smile, grateful for any praise from him.

I sold a painting and felt my artistic career beginning. The gallery owner said I could sell more paintings if I dove deeper into the darkness. But a month after the show closed, I got another letter. All it said was: *flesh and blood is the best medium to work in.* It felt like a threat, and I stopped doing paintings of murder victims. With Brian's encouragement I joined the force and set aside my artistic dreams for a job that involved going into actual dark places where I could make a difference. I was determined to find Bridget's killer, but as the years passed, I never got another letter from the killer, and as far as we knew he hadn't committed any more murders. Now when I painted, which wasn't often, I was happy doing occasional pet portraits.

*   *   *

The salad I'd made with arugula, pistachios, and honey mustard dressing looked delicious except for the blood orange slices on top.

The baked ziti I'd bought was in the oven and the tiny eclairs from a French Vietnamese bakery Corinne and I both loved were in the fridge. Everything was ready and she wasn't here.

As I was checking on the ziti the doorbell rang. I raced to get it, hoping it was her and she'd forgotten her key as usual. But it was Brian. He raised up a bottle of the Bulleit bourbon that was my drink of choice and said, "I come bearing a gift."

I smiled and put two glasses on the coffee table in the living room. He sat down on the couch and filled them to the brim. I sat in a chair opposite him. He handed me a glass. "I thought you might need this tonight," he said.

"That's an understatement." I took a long swallow and waited for the bourbon to work its magic.

He took a healthy sip of his and said, "Where's the star of the show?"

I gave my phone an anxious glance. "Out with friends. She's late but she has the dog with her so she can't get into that much trouble. She'll be home soon."

"I'm sure she will. She's a good kid." He cupped his hands around his glass and asked the inevitable question. "How are things with Jeff?"

I shrugged. "The same. Corinne's here for the weekend. I get to have dinner with her and I'm taking her to States tomorrow. Next week she'll be back with Jeff." I set my eyes on him. "It's my fault. I've been pushing him away since the day I said, 'I do,' and I finally did it for real."

He gave me a small smile. "Not for nothing, but he did cheat on you, Sam."

I frowned. "How are things with Mary Ann?"

"I'm seeing her later tonight." He fiddled with his sleek, stylish gold watch.

"That new?" I asked.

"I won big in a poker game. I couldn't decide between the watch and this silver and ebony pool cue. It was gorgeous but the watch won my heart."

I smiled. He always used his winnings for extravagant purchases. For someone who fancied himself a hard-ass, he was a sucker for all that glittered. But I understood what it was like to lose your heart to every beautiful thing. I was an artist. "You want some dinner?" I asked. "Looks like Corinne has deserted me, and I made a lot of ziti."

"Smells great, but Mary Ann and I are grabbing something at the Adams Tavern later." He pressed his gently freckled arms on the table. "So, other than me making you look at that OD and your daughter blowing you off, how's the rest of your day off going?"

"Fine," I said.

He fiddled with his watch some more. His sad, serious expression made me uneasy. "A manager from Stop & Shop called," he finally said. "He told me you had an incident there. Were you going to tell me about that, Sam?"

I forced a laugh. "Here I was thinking you were here because you're secretly in love with me."

"That will always be true," he said.

"The incident at Stop & Shop was nothing," I shifted in my seat. "Just an episode."

He shook his head. "Took some convincing to get the manager to let it go."

"In case you're interested," I said, "I saw a man slicing an orange and it bled. He was telling me how to use the knife and then he cut me."

Brian's brown eyes met mine. "But no one cut you. And if you'd drawn your gun, we'd be having a different conversation now."

"That didn't happen. And it never will."

He leaned forward. "Did you see the man's face this time?"

"I would have told you that." I paused. "The episode feels like a memory from the night Bridget was murdered, but I don't understand it."

"Maybe Peter can help you with that." He eyed me with concern. He was the only person on the force I'd told that I saw a therapist. He understood the importance of that, and I trusted him not to tell anyone else.

"I'll make an appointment right now," I said and called Peter and left a message.

Brian took another healthy swallow of his bourbon. I drank more of mine and we slipped into the conversation it felt we'd been having ever since he'd interviewed me when I got back from the hospital. We kept talking even after the interviews were done. I was sixteen and he was twenty-five, but it was as if we could tell each other anything, except for what I didn't remember. He encouraged me more than my father ever had and convinced me to join the force. Now he shared that he worried Mary Ann was trying to control his life but maybe he needed her to control his life. I shared my worries that Corinne was hiding her feelings about my separation from Jeff, and that sometimes she acted like she didn't care about things, because I cared too much about my job.

"We both care too much, Sam," he said.

I tipped my glass back again, feeling the warmth that was always just beneath the surface between us, though we rarely acknowledged it. Then, because I couldn't stop myself, I checked my phone again and ruined my good mood. I turned to Brian. "I'm driving myself crazy today over Corinne. I wish she'd just show up already."

He smiled. "She's a teenager. Making you miserable is her mission in life."

"Yeah, but tonight of all nights?" I thrust myself back in my chair. "It's been twenty years but what happened then is still right there inside me."

He let go a slow breath. "When I found Bridget in those woods, seeing her like that tore a hole in me. It lets the darkness in, Sam, and no matter what I do, it won't go away. What that man did to you was much worse." He kept his eyes on me as he said, "That case will always be here with us. But I don't think about it all the time. Neither should you. That's how we survive."

"It won't always be this way." I went to the window and pushed aside the curtain. As I stared into the grainy dusk willing Corinne to appear, Brian rested his hand on my shoulder. Something inside me settled softly and there she was, coming up the street carrying the poor exhausted dog.

Brian greeted Corinne on his way out. Ginger ambled to her bowl. Corinne collapsed on the couch and kicked her tan sandals off onto the rug, where'd they'd stay until she realized days later that she couldn't find them. I took a moment to savor the incredible relief I felt and brought us bowls of ziti and salad to eat in front of the TV.

"You got my bloody oranges, Mom," she said with a grin, adding, "But the ziti isn't as good as Dad's."

"Of course it isn't. I bought it frozen from Emilio's," I said.

Between bites she told me they hadn't found Percy yet, but they'd practiced a lot. "*Wish Upon a Dancer* is on tonight. Will you watch it with me?" she said, as we each ate exactly one tiny eclair. A few minutes later, we were watching a bright-eyed dancer tell the judges her mother had sacrificed everything so she could audition. I sighed. I hadn't done that for Corinne, though admittedly she was way past wanting me to lacquer her bun in place with hair spray. As the dancer did swift turns across the stage, Corinne clutched my hand and exclaimed, "Pay attention. That could be me, Mom."

Chapter
Five

PETER CALLED FIRST thing in the morning saying he could fit me in. States didn't start until noon, but the team had to be there early. I swung by the dreary street where Elle's Dance Studio was wedged between a check-cashing place and a coffee shop and dropped Corinne off to grab a ride with Beverly.

I braced myself as I sat down in Peter's office, not far from the dance studio, and said, "A thing happened. You know, one of my episodes."

He tugged at the cuff of his gray-green shirt printed with tiny gold flowers. "Tell me about this one." After I explained it, he said, "Must have been frightening to have that happen in a public place."

"Not my first choice for where to lose my shit." I brushed at the dog hair I'd noticed on my black jeans as soon as I'd sat down.

"Did you feel threatened, Samantha?" he said in a soothing voice.

"Yeah, and embarrassed."

He leaned forward. "Did you draw this episode?"

I showed him a photo of the drawing on my phone and said, "What do you think it means?"

He smiled. "You're the artist. You tell me."

I shrugged. "If I knew I wouldn't ask."

He pointed to the hand. "It's mechanical. The orange looks mechanical, too. Why?"

"To distance myself from my feelings?"

"Do you want to distance yourself?" he asked, as if we hadn't discussed this many times.

"The orange looks like a sweet fruit, but when you slice it open, it's a machine that bleeds. Like me."

"Don't be so hard on yourself." He drew his brows together. "Perhaps it's easier to witness an orange being cut than your friend."

"So seeing Bridget as an orange is my way of coping?"

"Maybe." He gazed at me calmly. "This isn't the first time you've painted an orange."

How could I not have seen it? "Right." I sighed. "The painting I did for my father's contest."

He nodded. "Tell me about that again."

I'd rehashed a lot of my past with Peter, but this was not an event I liked revisiting. "I chose to do Persephone as a still life, different from the painting my father had done of my mother. It seemed unfair to me that eating a few pomegranate seeds doomed her to living in two worlds forever, so I gave her a different ending. I loved Degas, so I made her a dancer. I didn't have a pomegranate, so I used an orange and waited until it rotted. I painted her pirouetting in a pink tutu and tights into the rotten darkness of the orange and coming out the other side with wings painted with gold glitter glue. I thought it was a brilliant twist on the myth."

Peter propped his chin on his clasped hands. "Was it?"

"My father didn't think so. He invited his students to bring their work over for a last crit before the contest. Everyone gushed over Devon's painting of Bridget as Daphne. My father said mine was an intriguing juxtaposition of death and over-ripeness, but he didn't believe my happy ending. He laughed at me and suggested I make the dancer emerge as a skeleton with gold leaf sticking to her tiny bones. He and everyone else including Devon went on discussing my father's mastery of gold leaf as if I wasn't there."

Peter winced with sympathy. "This sounds like your father's pattern of cutting you down."

My shoulders tightened. My father knew exactly how to cut me down. After Bridget died, while I didn't believe he had played any role in her murder, I thought he knew something. But he refused to talk about what had happened and said it was unhealthy to dwell on the past. When he moved to Vermont for a new teaching job, he asked me to come study with him—so he could help me become a *real* artist. But I told him I was staying in Quincy until I solved the case. Now we talked occasionally on the phone, he visited on Christmas and Thanksgiving, and that was it.

I eyed Peter. "I don't want to talk about my father anymore."

"I understand. But consider this: your father was a teacher, but he didn't teach you the way he should have. The man in your episode was telling or teaching you how to hold a knife." His eyes searched mine. "Could the episode be related to your anger toward your father for literally cutting you down?"

"I guess." I bit my lip. "But you told me my episodes would help me figure out what happened that night, and when I put the pieces together I'd be whole again. I don't see what my feelings about my father have to do with that. I just want to understand my episode."

He rested his palm on his cheek. "Your episodes aren't puzzle pieces. They're parts of the trauma you can't cope with. Understanding your feelings about all of this, including your father, will help you become whole." He leaned forward. "Did your episode help you make any progress with your painting of you in the ravine?"

I shook my head. "It's still just a cliff with me below, covered in black water. I wish I could remember more."

He nodded. "Don't worry. You'll get there. Remember, your happiness is what matters most." His look of intense concern made me uneasy. "Are you doing the meditation exercises I gave you?" I said I was, though I wasn't. He smiled. "Keep at it."

I got up to admire the calming seascapes on the wall—photos of sunrises and sunsets on Wolly Beach with inspirational quotes like *Believe in Tomorrow* written on the sky above them, a sleek sailboat resting on water as still as glass beneath the word *Breathe*.

"Not bad for photographs," I said.

"Vera gave them to me." He smiled. The one time I took the liberty of asking about *his* personal life, he'd told me he'd started dating her. He looked at his watch. Tick tock. Session over.

I cleared my throat. "I could use more Xanax."

His expression grew serious. "Just ten, Samantha."

* * *

I made it to the competition without a minute to spare and searched the auditorium—far nicer than the one at our shabby high school—for the team's black satin jackets with *Fearless Flyers* embroidered in lavender on the back. I waved to Linda, but there were no empty seats in her row.

To my surprise, Barb Delaney called out my name; I spotted her in the crowd, patting the empty seat beside her. I shimmied down the row and sat down uneasily. When we first met, Barb lived across the street from Bridget in a little house with dingy siding and an *I Love America* sign on the door. Like most people from Hough's Neck, she was suspicious of outsiders, let alone someone with a weird artist for a father. These days, she lived in a mansion with Max, but she still seemed like she was peering out the window of that little house, sizing me up.

I brushed again at the dog hair on my jeans. She ran a hand through her platinum hair that matched her nail polish and said, "I was saving that seat for Max, but lucky for you he couldn't make it."

"Max can never make it," Megan's mother, Gloria, chimed in from the seat beside me, and Barb frowned.

Max's brother Jay leaned in from Barb's other side. He never missed a single one of Shannon's performances. He pointed to the television scouts from *Wish Upon a Dancer* in the front row and said, "A friend of mine who's a TV producer arranged for them to be here." He touched the silver stud in his ear. "Winning States wins the team a place in Regionals, but the real prize is being chosen to audition.

Means a lot to me to give Shannon that chance." He caught Gloria's fiery glance and added, "To give the whole team that chance."

About halfway through the competition Elle, the team's coach, stepped on stage in a tight, low-cut gold dress and high heels. Her blond hair was gathered in a high ponytail, secured with a rhinestone hair tie. As she pressed her long-fingered hands together and introduced the team, she still looked like the Las Vegas showgirl she used to be. She was that rare bird: someone who had left Quincy and come back. Some people complained her students danced like strippers, but that didn't bother me.

The youngest dancers went first, followed by group numbers and duos. Corinne and Beverly's duo was a tap dance the program listed as "Paris in the Rain." They wore blue-sequined costumes with tulle skirts and wide-brimmed hats and carried parasols as they tapped across the stage. Corinne was tall and long-limbed like me. Beverly was a head shorter, sturdy and spritely. Together they were graceful and perfectly synchronized. I clapped hard for my girl.

This was a team competition, but it all came down to the solos. Nina went first in a frothy white tutu, with white feathers pinned in her red hair. She did a ballet number and held her head high as she fluttered and whirled away into a white blur.

Megan strode on stage next, thin and taut as a wire in a shimmering red costume, fishnet tights, and red patent leather boots. She burst into motion to Lady Gaga's "Starstruck" and did one sharp jazz dance turn after another, her red fringed skirt whipping around her and her boot heels banging on the stage with exquisite fury as Gaga sang about blowing her heart up.

Anton did a breakdance ballet in torn white jeans and a thin white T-shirt. His face was painted white with blue circles around his eyes. He looked like he was wearing a mask. I smelled my own sweat as I stretched my arms on the back of my seat. There was something ghostlike about the way he moved, rippling his arms, doing spinning headstands and dazzling leaps, one step flowing into the next.

Shannon strutted out last in high heels and a sequined purple leotard cut as high as it could go. Her back was bare as low as it could go. The room exploded with "Poker Face," and I smiled—yet another Lady Gaga. But this one was different. It was impossible to look away as Shannon marched forward like a diabolical robot, rolling her shoulders, punching the air, and swinging her hips to the relentless, pulse-pounding beat, as Gaga sang about getting him hard. Her face was flushed and glistening with sweat as she took a bow and blew the audience a kiss.

Megan O'Hare's solo took first place. Shannon took second, and the team placed first overall, earning a slot in Regionals. As Linda and I waited in the lobby while the team met with the *Wish Upon a Dancer* scouts, she leaned close and said, "I don't care who they pick. Our girls are the best." I smiled. Though I hadn't even started, I told her I'd be done with her painting soon.

Megan came out first. She pushed her curly black hair from her face, revealing the thick eyebrows Corinne told me Megan hated. "They chose me," she shouted and hugged her mother. Shannon looked downcast as she came out with the rest of team. Barb frowned, but Shannon laughed and said, "Gotcha. They picked me, too."

Elle gathered everyone around her, pumped her fist in the air and said, "Congratulations Fearless Flyers. We're going on to Regionals." Then she raised up Shannon's and Megan's hands saying, "Special congratulations to these two who will be auditioning for *Wish Upon a Dancer*."

Shannon said, "I'm so grateful."

"Grateful?" Barb snapped. "You should have beaten Megan for best solo. It was your idea to dance to Lady Gaga. She copied it." She fixed Gloria with the same hard stare she'd given me on Hough's Neck years ago.

Megan's dark eyes widened. "I didn't copy it. 'Starstruck' is my favorite song."

"That's the truth, Mom," Shannon said. "And if one of us wins the whole team wins." Jay wrapped his arm around her. Barb set her lips together, still upset. For her, anything less than perfection wasn't good enough—just like my father. As I hugged Corinne and told her how proud I was of her, Anton walked toward us, complaining about losing his phone.

Shannon smiled at him. "I found it backstage. You lose everything, babe," she said and handed him the phone from her pocket.

He brushed her sweaty bangs from her face. "Thank you." They locked eyes and he said, "I hope I never lose you."

She blinked away tears. "You never will."

I shook my head. *Oh lord, the drama.*

Chapter Six

One week later

I THOUGHT BRIAN'S call was part of a dream, but his "Good morning" had the ring of reality. The blurred digits on my phone came into focus—three a.m. The next thing he said woke me all the way up. "Some teens on Piney found a body by Blacks Creek." My chest tightened. Piney was an outcropping of evergreens in the marsh that became an island when the tide was high. It was a perfect spot to drink, because Quincy's finest didn't like to get their feet wet. It was near the neighborhood where I had grown up and where Bridget and I used to hang out. Now Corinne's friends did. I waited for Brian to say it was one of the homeless people who sometimes slept near the creek. All he said was, "Meet me there. I'm on my way now." *Click.*

I hurried into a T-shirt and jeans and checked on Corinne. She was sound asleep. I left a note on her nightstand telling her I had to respond to a call. She knew the drill. She was not to leave the house and if she had any questions she should call me or Jeff.

It was still dark out and deadly quiet, the moon a chalk crescent. I floored it down Quincy Shore Drive, past Wolly Beach and the shuttered restaurants and bars on the boardwalk, and made a right. My old neighborhood was alive with patrol cars and folks in bathrobes angling for a look. I pulled my car up behind the others, got out, and ducked under the yellow tape stretched across the main entrance into the area around the creek.

Brian was already there. "Where's this body?" I asked.

"She's in the Sailors Home Cemetery," he said.

"She?"

"I just got here myself. I don't know any more than you. Come on."

I put ugly plastic covers on my shoes, and then we followed the dirt road through the park to the graveyard tucked at the back of it. The creek was beyond it, a lovely vista for Quincy sailors who had served in the Civil War to have for all eternity. The rusted gate was open, the lock broken. It had been that way for years. This wasn't exactly a popular tourist attraction. We stepped inside and walked through the tall grass, skirting fallen tombstones and tattered little flags. Up ahead officers and techs were gathered beneath a tree, illumined by portable lights.

Janine Brown, the ME, knelt beside the body of a young woman who wore a short red dress with skinny straps. Her torso was twisted to the right with her arms over her head, and her legs were bent to the left. Branches were tangled in the halo of black hair around her face. Her eyes were shut beneath dark eyebrows. I knew those eyebrows.

"Megan." Her name caught in my throat.

"I heard about her big win." Brian gave me a grim glance.

Janine turned to us. "The kids said this was how they found her, but you know, kids. Can't be sure." She gave me a sympathetic look. She had a teenage daughter, too.

I knelt down. There was a flower on Megan's throat, but when I held the flashlight from my phone over it, it wasn't a flower. It was a blue butterfly. "Bri?" I said.

He squatted next to me with a groan. His knee still bothered him. "Interesting."

"This is interesting, too." Janine moved the bodice of Megan's dress aside, baring a familiar pattern of stab wounds on her chest.

I went pale. "You think?" I said, unable shake my uneasy sense of my past and present colliding.

Brian eyed me. "Too soon to think anything yet." His mantra was don't start coming up with a story until you've walked the whole scene. Let the evidence speak to you. I focused on how the branches appeared placed in her hair, the uncertain red line on her throat, how clean her hands were, how haphazard the scene was, like the work of an amateurish artist who didn't know what they were doing—anything to fight the black wave threatening to engulf me.

Janine gently lifted Megan's head. "I'm thinking this is what killed her." She pointed to where the back of her skull was smashed in, that place where her thoughts and dreams resided now a gaping hole.

An officer stepped forward and said, "The kids who found Megan are waiting on Piney to talk to you." He paused. "Some of them are on the dance team."

My stomach lurched. Brian told him we were heading there right now. I looked skyward. As gray clouds sailed across the dark sky, I could swear I felt Megan slipping away, as quietly as the exhalation of a breath.

*　*　*

My feet sank in the muck as we walked along the land bridge that was one of two ways to get to Piney without a boat. The other was a path from behind the Manor Apartments by the marsh. Both paths were almost flooded out at high tide.

"If whoever killed her used this path to carry the body to the graveyard, someone might have seen him," Brian said. "Or her killer could have pulled his car into the woods by the park after dark." He scratched his head. "Or someone brought her body in by boat."

A little past Piney, there was an inlet where small boats were moored. There was also a park on the other side of the marsh where people sometimes launched rowboats to go fishing. The creek was in the middle of it all. I paused, drinking in the green silence, listening, watching, *for him.*

Brian turned to me. "This is a nightmare. Too many ways in and out."

It was a nightmare. My parents' old house was a few blocks away, the college where my father taught just beyond it. We stepped onto Piney and walked past gnarled, stunted pine trees to a clearing where an officer stood in front of a dying fire in a trash can with Shannon, Lane, Nina, and her boyfriend, Nick Fleming. I dug my heels into the soft pine needles, thankful Corinne wasn't here, and turned uneasily to Shannon. "How are you doing?"

"Oh my god, Mrs. S.," she said and dissolved into tears.

"Do you know who did it?" Nina asked in a barely audible voice.

"We're hoping you can help us figure that out," Brian said.

"Can we go home? I have early practice. My mom keeps texting me," Nick said. He was the star forward on the high school basketball team. I sighed. It would be awful if Megan's parents found out she was dead via text.

"When I say so." Brian glared. "And put the phone away." Nick frowned. He was Mary Ann's son. She was recently divorced and Brian was reluctantly adjusting to stepparenting him.

We spoke to each of them separately. None of them wanted a parent present, and they all told the same story. Nina, Nick, and Lane arrived at the island around eight p.m. Shannon and Anton got there an hour later. Anton left early. Other kids came and went before they found the body. We got the names of everyone they remembered seeing.

Shannon told us she and Megan had been practicing for the audition at Shannon's house. Megan left around three p.m. Anton came over around five p.m. They drove to the beach, grabbed dinner at the Clam Shack, and went to Piney. Megan was supposed to come, but she never showed up.

"Do you know where Megan went after she left your house?" I asked.

"She had her car. I figured she was meeting her boyfriend."

I asked if she knew how to get in touch with Megan's boyfriend, and she shook her head. "Megan wouldn't tell anyone his name." She choked back a raspy sob. "I should have called her when she didn't show up," she said, and sobbed some more. I gave my phone a quick glance. No texts from Corinne. I needed to tell her about this, but I decided to let her sleep and not know the horrible truth a little while longer. When Shannon stopped crying, she told us Anton had left around midnight and gone to his cousin Dmitry's because he felt a migraine coming on.

"Did he see the body?" I asked.

She shook her head. "He took the path through the Manor Apartments, the one that doesn't go by the graveyard. I left with Nick and Nina sometime after midnight. We took the other path because Nick was parked near the graveyard." She twisted her hands together. "We were goofing around there when we found Megan's body. Nick called 911."

We told them we'd be in touch and the officer took them to their parents. Brian and I headed back to the crime scene. The creek was blue now, the soft glow of dawn bleeding through the clouds. A bird spread wide its black wings and rose from the spectral silence of the water. I nudged Brian. "An eagle."

"A couple of them have a nest around here," he said. "They mate for life, you know."

I gave him a sympathetic nod. He'd never had a relationship that lasted and now, apparently, neither had I. As we approached the graveyard, there was rustling in the long grass followed by a juicy cough. A man stood up unsteadily and lurched toward us.

Brian raised his gun. "Stay where you are."

The man brushed some leaves from his paint-spattered T-shirt and jeans, gave us a terrified glance and took off. He didn't get far before Brian tackled him to the ground.

"What are you running from?" Brian yanked him to his feet.

"You." The man looked at us.

"Nothing to be afraid of," I said. "We just need to know if you saw anything going on here last night."

"Didn't see anything," he said. He told us his name was Eric Daniels and he often crashed by the graveyard. He had been out cold the whole night. Brian asked him to empty his pockets. Eric pulled out a wad of cash, a syringe, a small plastic packet with a white residue in it, and a bracelet.

"Where'd you get all that money?" Brian asked.

He glared at us. "I worked for it."

Brian eyed the bracelet. "Where'd you get that?"

Eric muttered that he found it on the ground.

"On the ground?" Brian said. "Sure you didn't find it on a dead girl?"

Eric shook his head. "I don't know what you're talking about."

"Maybe your memory will be better when you're at the station." Brian bagged the bracelet and handed it to me. It was gold, set with multicolored glimmering stones. Something about it was familiar. I could have seen Megan wearing it. But it reminded me of something else, something from my past that I couldn't quite remember.

Chapter
Seven

I FOLLOWED THE feeling that my past was creeping up on me and crossed the street to canvas my old neighborhood. The small Cape I had grown up in looked surprisingly ordinary for a place that used be filled with my parents' artist friends and parties. The purple clematis that wound around the lamppost was still there, but the purple pansies my mother had planted along the front walk had been replaced by the pink impatiens you saw everywhere here. My mother would have hated them. The day we had planted the pansies she'd cupped my face in her soft hands and said, "Such a deep purple, almost black. No one else has these. They're special. Like me and you."

I let go a slow breath. My mother had called herself special, but different (and not in a good way) would have been a better word. Back then she told me that she was a free spirit who no one understood. The truth, which I'd figured out later, was that she was impulsive, reckless, unreliable, and got caught up with drugs and local criminals. My father said she was a rare wildflower, and he was compelled to rescue her. Obviously he hadn't.

I rang the bell to my old house. A young couple came to the door and introduced themselves as Tim and Bethany Sullivan. I recognized Tim. He'd been a high school football star until he tore his

ACL and fell in love with coke. Bethany reminded me of one of those blondes I would see at parties back then, pink chipmunk cheeks, cute forgettable face—handed round from one boy to another until she married one of them. I showed them my badge and explained about the murder. They already knew about it. They hadn't seen or heard anything unusual the night before.

I told them I'd lived in their house years ago and Tim stammered, "You're Samantha, the one who . . ." I nodded. He looked a beat too long at me and I felt like my mother must have. Different.

I got their permission to search their backyard, the same yard I used to let my friends run through when the police chased us off Piney. From there, we'd cut through all the way to the beach and run along it under the big starry sky—free. Whoever killed Megan might have cut through here, too, and dropped something. But I didn't find anything, not even a cigarette butt or a beer can. I rubbed my forehead, feeling like a fool for wasting time here.

I left the backyard and knocked on more doors, but no one else on the street had noticed anything unusual the night before. The world was waking up as I emerged from my old neighborhood. Traffic was heavy on Quincy Shore Drive. The marsh was a deep, sun-soaked green, and the creek a milky mirror of the clouds overhead. I took a moment to call Corinne. I'd forgotten to take my phone off silent and I felt sick when I saw her missed calls and texts. When I got through to her, she already knew. Her friends must have told her. She was crying so hard I could barely understand her. Jeff got on the line. "I had to go get her, Sam. She was all alone," he said reproachfully. I told him I was doing the best I could and shoved my phone in my pocket.

I met up with Brian at the entrance to the Sailors Home Cemetery. I told him no one in my old neighborhood had seen anything unusual. He said no one who lived by the creek had, either. Techs were tracking down the folks who moored boats there and looking for a weapon. Officers had spoken to some of the other kids at Piney that night. They all claimed they'd seen nothing. He dug his hands in his pockets and said, "I caught up with Anton at his cousin Dmitry's.

Anton told me he'd spent the day working for his father and then drove to the beach with Shannon in his father's van. He left Piney about midnight because he had a headache, just like Shannon told us. He claimed he didn't go anywhere near the graveyard and was with his cousin for the rest of the night. Dmitry's mother backed up his story. He didn't know Megan was dead until Shannon called and told him." He cocked his head. "He's a bit unusual."

"In the best way," I said. "He has a tough home life but he's a great dancer."

Brian winked. "Better than me?"

"No one's better than you. But he's just as good, only different," I said.

*   *   *

When I got back to the station, Brian was with Chief Wilson. I was lightheaded from not having eaten so I grabbed a buffalo chicken salad from a place down the street and brought it back to my desk. As I devoured it, hoping to stop the feeling of a tsunami heading for me, I read through the background check on Eric, the guy we had found near the crime scene. It told a story I'd heard many times before: numerous drug arrests, stints in jail and rehab, no known address, the degree in business he'd received before his life had gone south.

I was picking at the dregs of my salad when Brian pulled up his chair. "What did you get me?"

"Nothing," It was all I could do not to swat his hand as he grabbed a handful of my chips. "Any news?"

"An officer already talked to Megan's parents." He let out a loud sigh. "Her dad's at the morgue identifying her. Her mom's in rough shape. And Max and Barb Delaney are all over the Chief about solving the case. They think Shannon's in danger. Jay Delaney called from New York, where he's at a work conference, to tell us that, too."

"The whole team could be in danger," I said. "Including Corinne." For a second, I couldn't breathe.

Brian nodded. "Shannon and the other kids who were on the island are saying the Butterfly Killer is back. Chief wants us to make an arrest and put that rumor back in its cocoon before this all blows up."

"But what if our guy *is* back?" I asked.

Brian helped himself to more of my chips. "You have a reason for saying that?"

"The bracelet feels familiar, like it's connected to the old case, but I don't know why. If Eric is involved, it has to be a copycat crime. He's way too young." I handed him the background check. "You like him for this?"

He gave it a quick read. "He was at the scene, but he'd have to be pretty stupid to sleep near Megan if he killed her. A crime like this, there would have been a lot of blood. There wasn't a speck on him. He could have found the bracelet on the ground like he said or stolen it off Megan. We don't even know if it belongs to her." He finished off my chips and tossed the empty bag in the trash. "But Eric's the best we've got right now, and he might have seen something. Let's talk to him, and then the O'Hares."

* * *

Eric eyed us warily as he told us he had a job painting a garage all day, finished up around five, and went to Nostalgia, a bar across from the beach. He left around midnight and crashed at the Sailors Home Cemetery because it was too late to get a bed at Father Pat's homeless shelter.

"I like sleeping in the graveyard," he said mournfully. "Dead men are quiet."

Brian leaned forward. "You had almost a thousand dollars on you. That's a lot of money for painting a garage."

"It was a big job." Eric folded his arms across his chest. "When am I getting my money back?"

"When we figure out if it's yours," Brian said. He asked if Eric had seen or heard anything unusual at the graveyard. He insisted he hadn't. Brian showed Eric a photo of Megan and asked if he knew her. He gave the photo a wistful glance and said, "She's pretty, but I've never seen her before."

When we mentioned the bracelet, he still insisted he had found it on the ground. When I asked where exactly he said, "Sparkling by the edge of the creek."

"Sparkling in the dark?" I said.

"In the moonlight," he replied solemnly.

Chapter Eight

THE O'HARES LIVED in a small bungalow on a street of other small bungalows packed so tightly you could hear your neighbors disagreeing about what to have for dinner. Teddy bears, stuffed bunnies, and bouquets of flowers were already piled around the dogwood in their well-cared-for front yard.

Gloria sat stiff and straight on a red velvet sofa in a sleeveless dress, with her curly hair gathered into a tight bun. Her husband, Joe, sat next to her, his dark hair swept back on top and shaved on the sides, his muscles swelling beneath his white shirt. Brian and I settled onto a loveseat opposite them. We offered our condolences and Brian said, "Hate to trouble you during this difficult time, but we have to ask you a few questions."

"Whatever you need to get the guy who did this to my daughter." Joe gave us a hard stare. I'd gone to high school with him but hadn't known him well. He'd been one of those boys on the wrong path, liked by some, feared by others. After meeting Gloria, he'd turned his life around and gotten a plum job at the Department of Public Works because he was a friend of the mayor's. Now he was a pillar of the community, though he still had a reputation as a brawler, someone good to have on your side, someone you didn't cross, and there was still some fire in his dark eyes.

Megan looked down on us with those same dark eyes from a painting of her in a red tutu that hung above the sofa.

"You like the picture of my beautiful daughter?" I heard the pride in Gloria's voice.

I nodded. My father would have called it a sentimental caricature, but I wasn't about to tell Gloria that. I went over to the fireplace mantle crowded with framed photos of Megan posing in dance costumes from preschool to the present—so many triumphs. Megan's younger brother, Matthew, appeared in only one, smiling self-consciously and clutching a basketball. They'd had some trouble with him, typical boy stuff: throwing tennis balls at cars, vandalism, drinking. He always skated on the charges because of Joe's connections. If Matthew had ever won anything, there was no evidence of it. Must have been hard to be him around here.

More photos of Megan were spread out on a coffee table in front of Gloria. She moved them around like playing cards. "I need to choose some of these for the wake." Her fragile composure shattered as she spoke that last word and she broke down crying.

I waited until she stopped. "I'm sorry, but I have to do this. Can you tell me when you last saw Megan?"

She pulled a tissue from a pack on the table, wiped her eyes, and pressed her palms on the couch. "The last time I saw her was when she left for practice in the morning. She went to Shannon's after practice to help her with her dance for the audition."

I wrinkled my brow. "She wanted to help her when they were both competing for a spot on *Wish Upon a Dancer*?"

"Barb Delaney has a problem, but the girls don't," Gloria said. "They're a team. One of them wins, they all win. That's how Megan saw it."

"Where were you while Megan was at Shannon's?"

"I was home with her brother, Matt. Megan called around lunchtime to tell me she was going out later with her friends, like she did most Friday nights. When she didn't stop at home for dinner, I figured she drove straight there with Shannon."

"Drove straight where?" I asked.

Gloria frowned. "You know where, Samantha—Piney. Megan usually drove because she didn't drink."

Brian leaned forward. "We're looking for her car. A navy blue Honda Civic, right?"

Gloria's voice shook as she said, "We gave it to her for her sixteenth birthday. She took great care of it, drove carefully. She wasn't one of those kids who take things for granted."

"When did you notice she was missing?" I asked.

"I fell asleep watching TV after dinner and woke up around ten. She wasn't home yet so I called her. Her phone went straight to voicemail. Sometimes she turns it off when she doesn't want me to find her. You know kids . . ." Her anguished eyes met mine. "I should have called again, but I wanted her to have fun for a change. There's so much pressure on her. Matt was at a friend's house, so I asked him to call her, figured she'd pick up for him, but she didn't answer him, either."

"Can we talk to him?" I asked.

"He's at his grandmother's. I'll call him." She fumbled for her phone.

"No need right now," I said.

Brian turned to Joe. "How did you spend your day yesterday?"

"I went to work at the DPW, had dinner at home, and went to Champions to watch the Sox." He folded his arms across his chest. "When I was at Champions, I didn't know Megan hadn't come home. That one there didn't tell me." He flashed Gloria a look.

"I didn't want to upset you," she said. "You know how you get."

"How does he get?" I asked.

She stiffened. "Goes from zero to sixty in an instant." She turned to him. "I'm sorry, Joe, but that doesn't help."

"When did you leave Champions?" Brian asked.

"Around eleven. If Gloria had told me Megan hadn't come home, I would have driven all over this city until I found her." He glared at her. "When I got home, I wanted to call the police, but she said we should wait a little longer."

She twisted her hands together. "I didn't want to get her in trouble. If the folks at *Wish Upon a Dancer* found out she got caught drinking in the woods, it could have ruined everything for her."

Joe stared at the red oriental rug. "I'd say everything's ruined for her now."

Gloria winced and turned to me. "Megan hates when I call her friends, but I was so worried I called Shannon after Joe got home. When she said she hadn't seen her all night, I called the police. They said they'd look for her, but she'd probably walk in any minute." She shot Joe a glance. "I did my best."

Brian fiddled with his gold watch. "I need to show you something." He put a photo on the table. "Do you know this man? His name is Eric Daniels."

Joe shook his head. Gloria did, too, and said, "She never mentioned anyone named Eric. Do you think he's involved with this?"

"Not at liberty to say," Brian said.

Joe shoved his arms forward on the table. "Level with me. Max Delaney told me you had some homeless guy in custody. Is it Eric?"

"I can't tell you that, either," Brian said.

"You can't tell us nothing." Joe drew himself up. "My daughter is dead, and if that guy Eric had anything to do with it, you better arrest him or I'll take care of him myself."

Brian fixed his eyes on him. "You want us to get the person who did this, stay out of it, Joe."

Joe thrust himself back against the couch with a disgusted sigh. I went on. "Some of the girls on the team say Megan had a new boyfriend. Could that have been Eric?"

Gloria gave her head a hard shake. "She'd never date someone like him. Honestly, she didn't have time for a boyfriend."

"What about Anton?" I said.

"She broke it off a few months ago. He kept begging her to change her mind. It was hard for her to tell him no, but she had to focus on her dancing. She practiced every single day. Stayed in every night doing her homework." Her lower lip trembled.

"Did Anton stop begging her?"

"I assume he did eventually."

Joe grumbled, "I never liked that shit-weasel."

"Why do you say that?" I asked.

Joe frowned. "A girl breaks it off, you let her go. You don't come begging."

Brian put another photo on the table. "Do either of you recognize this bracelet?"

"I've never seen it before," Gloria said. Joe hadn't, either.

"Could someone have given it to Megan without you knowing?" I asked.

She looked at us. "Boys sometimes gave her things."

"They did?" Joe grunted.

"She was a pretty girl," Gloria snapped. "What do you expect? But I never saw her wearing that bracelet. She always wore the Minnie Mouse watch I bought her years ago at Disney World. She said it was good luck."

"She wasn't wearing the watch when we found her," I said.

"I know she was. Wait a minute." She went upstairs and came down a few minutes later looking distraught. "I can't find it. But I found this when I was cleaning her room a couple of weeks ago." She held out a small white leather box containing a pair of teardrop-shaped blue earrings with the ghost of a star in each one. "They look like sapphires, I have no idea where she got them."

"From a new boyfriend?" I said.

"I told you. She didn't have a new boyfriend." Her mouth tightened.

I asked if we could take the earrings as evidence and she told me yes. I said, "Her friends say she kept her boyfriend secret. Could she have kept him secret from you?"

"She would have told me. She tells me everything."

Brian clasped his hands around his knee and leaned forward. "Sometimes kids tell you things in other ways. Did she seem stressed or afraid lately? Had her behavior changed? Were there any signs she was using drugs?"

Gloria's eyes darted uncertainly about the room. "No, but she takes an antidepressant and Valium for anxiety. She was stressed about the dance team. She got into these black moods. Her medication saved her life."

"Right." Joe snorted. "She didn't need those drugs. She needed you to lay off for once." He pounded his fist on the table and swept the photos onto the floor. Gloria's face looked about to crack into pieces. And then it did. She began gasping, choking, and wailing as she crouched over the photos. Joe gave us an agonized look and put his hand on her back. "I'm sorry. God, I'm so sorry," he said.

* * *

I stopped at Nostalgia to check out Eric's alibi on my way home. The bar, which used to be a popular spot in the nineties, wasn't far from where Megan was found. As I pulled into one of the many empty spots in the gravel lot, my phone pinged, a text from Corinne: Mom where are you? Every other mother on the team was with her son or daughter now, and I wasn't with Corinne when she needed me most. I felt the cold rush of my anxiety, tipped my bottle of Xanax onto my palm, swallowed one dry, and texted, Will call soon.

The bar was still painted chalk green, with a green awning over the outdoor seating and two sickly potted palms by the door. The interior was still decorated in a tropical island theme with a dusty mirrored disco ball hanging from the ceiling. Back in the day they had gotten some name bands, but not anymore. I was amazed it was still in business. I ordered a whiskey sour because I used to like them. When the bartender put it down in front of me I said, "Can I ask you a question?"

He wasn't bad-looking. Longish brown hair, and a lemon twist to his smile. "Name's Hank and, yes, I'm single."

"Good try. I had another question in mind." I pushed a photo of Eric and my badge across the bar. "Did this guy come in here last night?"

"Yeah, that's Eric." He shook his head. "He comes here sometimes. Last night he came in around six."

"How long did he stay?" I asked.

Hank stroked his chin. "He had one beer and left around seven."

"Any idea where he went?"

He stroked his chin some more. "Are you investigating the murder by the creek?" I nodded and he leaned close. "I overheard him talking to someone about heading to the Hat Trick. He was probably looking to score drugs there."

"Does the bar have surveillance cameras?"

"They used to, but they broke a couple of months ago."

Everything here was a used-to-be. My drink was too sweet and weak, not as good as it used to be, either. The sour taste of dread came up my throat as I remembered the time Bridget and I came here. My phone buzzed. Another text from Corinne. Mom? The sky already had the soft blue tint of dusk, and night was creeping in around the edges. It was time to go.

Chapter Nine

Before
January 1994

IT WAS ALREADY snowing when Bridget and I left my house that January night. My father was too busy painting to question our story about going to a party down the street and then a sleepover at Bridget's. I wore a slim black coat with a fake fur collar over a flowered dress. Nostalgia was just a short walk away, but my black suede boots were soaked by the time we got there. I was worried that I looked nothing like the picture on my fake ID, but Bridget wasn't worried. She looked older than sixteen. It wasn't just her tight dress and spike-heeled red boots. It was the assured way she moved, running her hand softly along the backs of chairs, and smiling at everyone as we made our way to a table.

The first whiskey sour went down easy. As I licked the sweet foam off my second one, Bridget turned to me. "Are you happy yet, Sam?"

I nodded with a sloppy grin. She gave me a friendly shove. "No, you're not. You won't be happy till you've tried it." She was always trying to make me happy, as if I was her personal self-improvement project—only the answer was always drugs. Now she was on my case about trying ecstasy. I liked alcohol and weed, but I was hesitant to try something new. I maybe told her to shut up, but when Bridget wanted something there was no denying her. She grabbed my arm so hard it hurt, yanked me up from my seat, and waved to someone I couldn't see. Between the whiskey sours and the beers we'd had before we'd come, I could barely feel my feet as she pulled me across the crowded room. As I rubbed my sore arm, there he was: a lazy blond curl on his forehead, skintight jeans that showed a hint of something I didn't want to see.

He glanced at Bridget and said, "So this is Samantha." She fluffed her pale hair and gave him a knowing nod.

"Just like a kitten in a basket." He nodded at me and added, "You get my seal of approval." The way he said this—like he was sizing me up for something I wanted and didn't want at the same time—stuck with me. When he gave me the little white pill, I took it. I would have taken anything from him.

I lost track of who I danced with, but I felt close to everyone. I was tingling all over and my heart was going full speed ahead. Bridget was right. I hadn't known what happiness was until now. We ended up in the parking lot. The air was thick with snowflakes like lacy flower petals drifting down from some magical tree that wouldn't stop blossoming. Bridget scooped snow into her green-and-black striped gloved hands and pelted me with snowballs. I ducked, laughing so hard my throat hurt, and hurled more right back at her. We were ridiculously and absurdly happy and then we were in a car with the handsome guy taking curves too fast and fishtailing in the snow.

* * *

The next morning, I woke to Bridget shaking me. "Thank god," she said. "I thought you'd never wake up." A smile quickly replaced the worry on her face. "But I fuckin' saved you."

I sat up in my sleeping bag on the floor in her cold attic room. "My head is pounding, my mouth tastes like dog shit, and I feel like I've been hit by a bus. Honestly, I'm sorry I woke up."

She ran her tongue over her lip. "You just have a little happiness hangover."

I asked her what the handsome guy's name was. "Don't even think about him," she said. Her expression grew serious. "He's mine."

She held a glass of water to my lips. I guzzled it down, I was so thirsty. "Feel better now?" she asked. I nodded, though the happiness was already a distant memory. I never felt that way again.

Chapter
Ten

"YOU WANT SOMETHING to drink?" Jeff pushed his hand through his unkempt curly black hair as I stood awkwardly in the apartment he was renting. He was wearing baggy jeans and he was barefoot—his usual work attire when he was home coding instead of at the office.

"I definitely need a drink," I said, as Ginger jumped all over me like a long-lost friend. I turned to Corinne. "I'm so sorry for not being there for you today."

"I understand you had to do your job, Mom." She pushed a strand of hair that had snaked its way out of my ponytail behind my ear, still trying to fix me. We stared at each other a moment and then tears ran down her cheeks. It always surprised me how easily she cried, when I seemed to have forgotten how. "Yesterday at practice Megan did twenty fouetté turns without stopping," she said through sobs. "And now she's dead."

"Oh, hon," I said, and pulled her in for a hug.

I didn't want to let her go but she stepped back. "I'll be all right," she said, trying hard not to cry more.

"How are you doing?" Jeff tipped his head to the side as he handed me a glass of bourbon.

"Haven't slept much or showered, but I'm okay." I took a long swallow, trying to find some semblance of normal in my drink and the fading calm of my Xanax.

He pushed his hands in his pockets. "I'm making blintzes for dinner. You're welcome to stay for some." I breathed easier at the kindness in his voice and told him I'd like that.

I glanced from one end of the long, narrow living area to the other. He'd been here a few months, but it still looked like he'd just moved in. Papers, empty soda water cans, and dirty plates were stacked next to his laptop on the coffee table. The cramped dark space was damp and musty from the ocean which was close by. I figured it was his penance for cheating on me. He'd apologized almost immediately when he had a brief fling with a coworker, said it was over and meant nothing. He offered to tell me more, but I didn't want to know. I hadn't forgiven him, more because of what it said about my own flaws than anything else.

He made the blintzes one at a time, flipping them with his usual aplomb, and sliding each perfectly folded one onto a plate. It was an involved meal for such a stressful day, but cooking helped Jeff relax. His mother was Jewish and had passed this recipe down to him. Jeff wasn't religious, but he liked cooking food from what his mother called the old country—said it was a way to bring the past to life in the present. I'd prefer not to have my past in my present, but my past was different. I wasn't religious, either, unless you counted our endless discussions about whether god was real according to evidence beyond my understanding, or a quantum entity as Jeff insisted—or both.

We barely fit around the card table he'd set up in the tiny kitchen area, but the blintzes were lightly browned to perfection as always and the pot cheese filling had just the right touch of sweetness. When we finished eating, I turned to Corinne and said, "Get your stuff and we can go back to my place." She exchanged a cautious glance with Jeff.

"It's best if she stays here for a while," he said. "You have your work, and it will be safer."

I felt sick inside, but he was right. Until we caught Megan's killer, Corinne wouldn't be safe anywhere. The case required my full attention. It felt like the wrong time but there would never be a right one. I had to ask. "Did you see Megan after practice yesterday?"

"No. I went to Beverly's and then I had dinner with you." She gave me a puzzled look.

"Did Megan ever talk to you about being afraid or bothered by anyone?" She said no. I took a breath. "You told me Anton broke up with her. Are you sure of that?"

She stared back so hard I thought her eyes were going to pop out of her head. "Yes, I'm sure."

I persisted. "Did Megan have a new boyfriend?"

"Oh my god. Why are you asking me these questions now? If she had one, I don't know who he is, okay?"

I ignored her glare and showed her a picture of the bracelet we'd found on the homeless man by the creek. "Have you ever seen Megan wearing this?"

She calmed a little as she looked at it and said, "No, Mom. I've never seen it before."

Jeff's dark eyes widened. "Why are you showing her that?"

I leaned in. "Between us, we found that on a suspect."

"You have a suspect?" he said.

"Not a great one, but it's a start."

Corinne glanced at her phone. "My friends are saying the person who killed Megan is the same one who killed your friend Bridget."

"Why do they say that?" I asked.

She chewed on her lip. "Because there was a butterfly on Megan."

"We have no evidence it's the same killer," I said.

Jeff stared at me grimly. "Are we in danger?"

"We need to be careful until this gets sorted out." I gave Corinne a firm look. "Don't go anywhere without telling me or Dad and never go out alone. Even if it's just to CVS. Understand?" I expected her to protest, but all she said was, "Okay," before going to her room. I pushed away the papers on the couch and sat down. As I watched TV, Jeff paced as he often did when he was thinking, not even noticing when he bumped into the coffee table and sent an empty soda can flying into my lap.

"Sorry, Sam," he said, putting the can back on the table. "I'm so stressed with all this and I'm working on this recursive function that's making my head explode." He tugged on the neck of his worn T-shirt with a constellation of little holes on the chest. I shook my head—brilliant, chaotic Jeff always in disarray.

"Oh no, not recursion. I hate it just from listening to you talk about it." I smiled. "No matter how many times you explain it, I still don't get it."

"It's just this little thing, that's the start of everything. If you keep going back to it over and over again, it's very efficient. But if you mess something up you never get out of the loop." He stared at me. "I hate recursion, too, but at least I understand it. What I don't understand is a world where someone kills Megan."

"There's a reason." I said. "I can't see it yet. But I'll keep looping through the evidence until I do. I'm going to get the person who killed her." As I stood to go, he pulled me close. Through my thin shirt, I felt him press on the spidery scars the killer had carved on my back. His hand circled the scar on my arm as he said, "You can stay if you want," but I told him I had to leave.

* * *

The next morning, the AC was barely working in the incident room. Brian looked positively wilted as he stood in front of us and said, "We've confirmed Eric, the suspect we found sleeping near the crime scene, spent the day painting a garage and then went to Nostalgia. He said he was there until midnight, but the bartender told Detective Star that Eric left for the Hat Trick around seven p.m. We need to check that out. We're still looking into whether a bracelet Eric claimed he found on the scene belonged to Megan. For now, we're holding him on a drug charge. We've subpoenaed Megan's phone records, and techs are going through her laptop."

Brian mopped his brow with a tissue from his pocket. "Let's hear from Janine now."

Janine smiled demurely in a white dress and kitten heels as she went through the autopsy report. She told us Megan died from blunt force trauma to her head. The nature of the fracture suggested a blow from an object with a hard edge like a golf putter.

She pointed to a photo of the crime scene and explained that the butterfly was a Mexican Bluewing, not native to here, and that it was stuck to her throat with Krazy Glue. The cut on her neck was barely more than a scratch. There was no evidence of defensive wounds. She pointed to the piecrust-like slits and said, "The cuts on her chest start out tentative, too, but they get deeper. The tissue is torn outward at the end which suggests they were made by a knife with a hooked or curved point, possibly a gut-hook hunting knife."

Brian said, "With any luck we can track down someone who bought that type of knife recently. Ditto for the butterfly."

Janine went on. "There's evidence the body was moved. Full rigor had set in when I examined it at three a.m., which puts time of death sometime on Friday before eleven p.m." She paused. "There's no evidence she was sexually assaulted. The basic tox screen showed diazepam, but not enough to be the cause of death. I'm awaiting the results of the full tox screen. Any other questions?"

"We're good." Brian wiped his face some more and turned to Chief, who sat at the front of the room. "It sounds like we're dealing with a copycat, but we'll know more soon."

Chief frowned. "Unless you have evidence that points there, I don't want to hear a peep about the old case, understand? The mayor doesn't want rumors flying around about the Butterfly Killer when Max Delaney kicks off his development project for downtown Quincy next week. And the DA wants good news to announce at his press conference tomorrow. Got it, O'Neil?" Brian nodded and the Chief said, "I've brought in Detective George Price from the state police to help you out. Stand up, Price. Don't be shy."

He stood up and gave us a polite nod. His dark hair was slicked down so hard it couldn't be out of place if it wanted to. His white shirt was pristine, and he was handsome in a tight-lipped way, if you went for that.

"Welcome to the team." Brian smiled at him.

"Wonderful. The Staties are taking over," I said as we left the room.

Brian sighed. "We always work with them on homicides like this. Honestly, we could use the help, and we lucked out with George. He helped convict Junior Black last year." I nodded. I was grateful that Quincy's most notorious gangster and local legend was finally in jail, thanks to George and others. Brian went on, "You know the story about George's sister, right?"

"Yeah," I said. "She was injured in a car accident with a drunk driver. She survived with a head injury, and he takes care of her now. He's a living, breathing saint."

Brian went on. "He's a stand-up guy, and he won't push us around. Give him a chance."

* * *

The Hat Trick was wedged between Patriot Liquors and Diego Chang's Chinese Palace on a treeless street of triple-deckers and bleak storefronts in West Quincy. Inside it was bathed in a perpetual twilight, infused with the smell of stale beer with hints of vomit. A rusty Budweiser sign hung above a discolored mirror, and its bathroom with a shower curtain for a door was legendary. The few grizzled regulars at the bar had their eyes fixed on a flat-screen TV tuned to reruns of *Everybody Loves Raymond*. And there was keno.

Brian and I commandeered two stools at the bar. He wore a lavender plaid shirt, jeans, and polished loafers. I had on clean jeans without dog hair and a stylish blue shirt, sleeves rolled. We were conspicuous, but all we got was curiosity-soaked silence. "One benefit of the stools being bolted down is they don't wobble," Brian said with a smile.

"Adds to the ambience," I replied.

"It's a carryover from the old days when they might get thrown around," the crinkle-faced man sitting beside me informed us.

Brian greeted Vince, the bartender, like they were old pals. They probably were. He ordered a club soda. I got a Diet Coke.

The crinkle-faced man cupped his hand around his mouth and said, "Good choice, the Bud draft is a little chunky."

Vince fixed his pug-like eyes on us. "I assume you're not here for the ambience or the beer?"

Brian pushed his badge across the bar, along with a photo. "Did this guy come in here on Friday night? His name is Eric."

Vince straightened, giving us the full benefit of his bulked-up physique. "What's this about?"

"We're investigating the murder of Megan O'Hare." My bag slipped off my shoulder, and I retrieved it from the unspeakable darkness beneath my feet.

"The dancer?" The crinkled-faced man said. "I read about her in the paper."

I nodded, and the entire room turned our way. Apparently, we were more entertaining than *Everybody Loves Raymond*. "Eric said he was here that night."

Vince paused to count on his fingers. "Now that you mention it, the last time he was here *Cheers* was on. He asked me to put on the Sox game, so must have been Friday."

Last time, I thought. He was a regular. "What time did he get here?"

His bulging eyes lingered on my breasts. "Around seven thirty."

"What time did he leave?"

The corner of his mouth crooked up. "He left when the game ended. About eleven."

The crinkle-faced man jumped in again. "What about when he stepped out during the game?"

Vince looked around as if someone could be listening in. I doubted it. Every fly on the wall was dead. He leaned close. "Completely slipped my mind. Eric took off for a while around eight thirty. He came back about an hour later and bought a round for everyone."

"How did he get the money?" Brian said.

Vince smiled. "He didn't share that with me."

Brian handed him his card. "If you think of anything else, call me."

I handed him mine. He studied it a moment. "You were kidnapped with Bridget McGann, right?" I nodded, and it was like someone turned the volume in the room down. "Bridget's dad used to stop by here for a drink now and then. What a tragedy." He leaned closer. "She came in here with this guy a few times, asked me not to tell her dad, said he would kill her if he found out."

I stiffened. "What's the guy's name?"

He gave the water-stained ceiling tiles a wistful glance. "Don't know. All I remember is he had blond hair, was full of himself, went on about what a great artist he was. Bridget tagged along like a puppy. He said jump and she jumped. Last time they came in they had a fight about his greatness. He got a little rough with her, and they left. A week later she was dead."

I tried to swivel the stool, but it didn't budge. Bridget had told me the Hat Trick was crawling with drug dealers and to avoid it, but she had been here.

Brian ran his thumb over his gold watch. "It took you twenty years to tell us this?"

Vince knuckled away a faux tear. "You never asked."

* * *

George was waiting with subs in the break room when we got back. "I grabbed dinner for you." He looked at his sub mournfully. "Not enough pickles. Only counted two."

"That's what you get for ordering a veggie. A crime if you ask me." Brian unwrapped his tuna sub, oozing mayo—a crime in my book. I hate mayonnaise.

George handed me mine. "I heard you'd go for buffalo chicken."

"You got that one right." I smiled. A Statie who went for veggie subs—now that was different.

"So, where are we?" George asked.

Brian clasped his hands on the table. "Megan's parents didn't recognize Eric or the bracelet we found on him. We confirmed he was at the Hat Trick most of that night with an hour unaccounted for. That's on the other side of the city from the Sailors Home Cemetery. Unless he managed to murder her and get her there in an hour, he's a liar and a junkie, but probably not our killer. And we have no obvious other suspects. Max Delaney was at his office that day, Jay was in New York, Barb was home with Shannon all day and with Max that night. Elle confirmed Shannon was helping Megan prepare for the audition. Anton and the other dancers have alibis, too. So do the O'Hares." He eyed George. "Please tell me you have something for us."

"My resources are examining Megan's phone and computer, but nothing so far." He nibbled on a pickle.

I leaned forward. "Shannon Delaney told us Megan had a secret boyfriend. Look for a number Megan called a lot. That could be him."

Brian tapped his fingers on the table. "Gloria told us Megan didn't have a boyfriend."

I shrugged. "Sometimes mothers are the last to know."

"She also told us Anton had problems letting Megan go. Maybe he was jealous of her new guy."

"According to Corinne, he broke up with Megan and he's dating Shannon. Why would he be jealous?" I bit into my sub.

"Either Megan lied to her parents or Anton lied to Corinne," Brian said in a clipped voice.

George plucked a lettuce shred off his shirt. "Why is Chief so concerned about the Butterfly Killer rumors?"

"The Butterfly Killer is the kind of local myth that never dies," I said. "It's not exactly good publicity for Max Delaney's plan to reinvent the city."

George nodded. "Do you think the Butterfly Killer is back?"

I glanced at Brian. "Nothing so far indicates that."

"If I may offer an opinion," George said. It took all I had not to roll my eyes. "Megan's murder scene is a bad copy of Bridget's. The cause of death is different. Bridget's throat was cut. Megan died from a blow to the head. The knife wounds on her chest are similar to Bridget's, but they're more hesitant. Megan was left under a tree with a butterfly on her throat, but it was blue not yellow and wasn't a swallowtail like the ones found on his other victims. The crime scene doesn't have the same mythic quality as Bridget's. Right?" He eyed me and I held his gaze. The guy had done his homework.

I took a bite of spicy chicken and said, "The old crime scene was like the work of a traditional painter. Each detail was carefully planned, right down to the hollow tree and the green leaves on her fingertips. It reflects the so-called artist's need for control. Megan's crime scene is a careless sketch, done in a hurry."

"I agree," George replied. "But there's more to it. Bridget's crime scene suggests a killer who takes sadistic pleasure from domination and inflicting pain. Megan's looks like the work of someone who killed her in a fit of rage or jealousy, read the article about the anniversary, and tried to put the blame on the old killer by copying his work, but rushed the job."

"I like your sloppy copy theory, George." Brian said. I frowned, not surprised he'd given George all the credit. "But Finny wants a suspect now. Let's give him Eric. Finny can announce we have a person of interest in custody at the press conference. That will make Max Delaney and the Chief happy and buy us time to keep looking for more suspects."

George tipped his chair back. "I'm glad to hear Tom Finn's the ADA on this case. He's a good guy. We go back a ways." I let go a slow breath. *Of course they did.*

Brian looked at me. "You with me on this, Sam?"

"Yeah, but . . ." I shifted in my seat uneasily. I had to say this. "If everything points to a copycat, what about the bracelet?"

George set his dark eyes on me. "What do the bracelet and our copycat theory have to do with each other?"

I swallowed hard. He didn't miss a thing. "The bracelet feels like something from the past that I can't place. My instincts could be wrong. But if the crime is a sloppy copy, it makes no sense that Eric would have a bracelet related to the old case or that it would be at the scene."

"You're right. It makes no sense." Brian gave me an exasperated look. His phone buzzed. He answered it and turned back to me. "This has been tough on you, Sam. Go on home now. George, you can leave, too. I'll hang out here a little longer. That was Mary Ann. I got a date with her later."

"Mary Ann?" George said.

"Mary Ann Fleming. His latest." I turned to Brian. "Third time's a charm, right?"

George raised a brow and Brian said, "My first wife was perfect, totally blew my chance for a white picket fence and snot-nosed rug rats with her. My second was another kind of perfect. I blew that, too." He shrugged sheepishly. "What can I say? I can reel them in but can't keep them." He tapped his fingers on his desk. "One more thing. Max is having his summer fundraiser for Road to Redemption tomorrow night after the press conference. Mary Ann was supposed to go with me, but she just bailed on that. We should all go."

George looked up. "Glad to be there for a worthy cause."

"I'm in, too," I said. I wasn't a member of the Max fan club but the counseling center his brother, Jay, ran helped a lot of people.

Brian smiled at me. "I'll pick you up on my way there."

"It's a date." I smiled back, shut down my computer, and headed out. The station lot was nearly deserted when I left. As I tucked a loose strand of hair back in my ponytail, there was a *click* like someone dropped a penny. I turned. The lot was dark except for the faint glow of a streetlight on the black asphalt.

Chapter
Eleven

Before
February 1994

AFTER MY MOTHER died, Bridget began her quest to make me happy. She brought me to church in an effort to save my soul, and we baked chocolate chip cookies in her cramped kitchen. I ate dinner at her house more than at my own. She took me clothes shopping and brushed my hair into different styles as if I was her very own doll. In middle school we shoplifted lipstick together at CVS, running till the air burned our throats, and laughing hard after. She gave me my first beer. In high school she was a goddess roaming the halls, and I was her dark-haired sidekick. Even after she and Barb wrote *slut* on my forehead in lipstick once when I was passed out drunk, I still believed in the special bond we shared. It was like a blood oath, only forged with stolen lipstick and alcohol.

But after that night at Nostalgia, everything changed. Bridget stopped coming around. I figured the blond guy had all of her attention, or maybe they'd broken up and she was too miserable to talk to me. I was too miserable myself to think about her. I caught a cold that settled in my chest and wouldn't let go. Around that time, Bridget's friend Debbie Duggan died of a drug overdose, and I felt too depressed and sick to go to the memorial. Bridget didn't speak to me again that winter, and I assumed she was mad at me for not going. I gave myself to art like a nun to her calling, dreamed of being Degas, of building up layer upon layer of soft pastel to capture dancers in their pink tights and gauzy tutus, bending, leaping, arching, and pirouetting off the page, more beautiful than life itself. Occasionally, my father offered opinions, but mostly he left me alone.

One afternoon I came home from school, and a man was sitting at our kitchen table with my father. He was so handsome that I froze. He said, "Who is this lovely young lady?" I was lost the minute he set his blue-sky eyes on me.

"That is Samantha," my father said with a laugh. He introduced Devon as one of his most talented students and asked me to join them. I plunked my bony butt on a chair, agonized by the scrape it made against the floor when I pulled it up to the table. I was wearing jeans ripped at the knee, a black crew neck sweater with frayed cuffs, earrings along the rim of my ear, and I'd hacked off my hair so it hung in jagged points to my shoulders. The flowered dress I'd worn to Nostalgia was hanging in the closet, never to be worn again.

"Nice ink." Devon traced his fingers over the black crow tattooed on my forearm.

"Crude, but it has some artistic merit." My father eyed the image of the crow in flight that gave me hope during that dark winter.

I listened while they talked about their work, mute as a stone about my own. When my father asked me to make dinner, I dumped leftover beef stew into a pot and grew frustrated when the sticky dumplings wouldn't drop easily from the spoon. They devoured it, but I picked at mine, too nervous to eat. After I finished clearing the plates, Devon reached his smooth muscled arm across me and set down a paint sketch he'd done. "Here's my take on Botticelli's *Birth of Venus*. The goddess of love born from the sea," he said. The image of a naked girl standing on a giant scallop shell seemed a little weird, but as Devon whispered, "I'd like to paint you sometime," a flush came to my cheeks.

I pointed to the green snakes coiled around her ankles. "Are those in the Botticelli?"

He shrugged. "No. But this is more than a copy. Those snakes came to me when I was doing the painting." He placed his hand so it was ever so lightly touching mine and said, "To be a real artist you must follow wherever the darkness leads you," and I believed him.

"I taught him well," my father said.

Devon smiled. "I'm lucky I found him. If I was in Montana I'd still be painting wheat fields, cows, and wildflowers."

Each time he came over after that, I waited for him to say, "It's you I came for," but it was always my father. He said he'd make Devon's reputation and taught him as if he were his own son. But sometimes I caught Devon looking at me out of the corner of his eye.

One day when my father wasn't home, I finally showed Devon my sketchbook. He told me my drawings of dancers were skillful copies of Degas, but I hadn't found myself yet. When I told him I didn't know how, he said, "First you need to show me who you are."

"Fine," I said, surprising myself. "Let's go."

I took him all over Quincy and showed him the places where I hung out with my friends. I saved the quarries for last. As we stood at the edge of one, I said, "Kids jump off these cliffs. Someone drowns here almost every summer. The mob dumps bodies here, too."

He gave the green scum on the murky water far below a bored glance. "You should paint these places," he said. "Show the violence lurking beneath the surface." He smiled as he pressed his thumb into the crow on my arm, and I didn't want to be Degas anymore. I wanted to be Devon. As he pulled me close and kissed me, his lips were soft and gentle, and I believed he was the only person in the world who saw who I really was.

Chapter Twelve

"WHO DO YOU really like for this? No wrong answers," Brian said as we drove past the sign welcoming us to Starlight Bay. Years back, Max Delaney had turned this desolate stretch of mudflats, gnats, and seagrass into luxury condos, a marina, and a boardwalk flanked by fancy people walking fancy dogs past fancy shops and restaurants. Now he had the same vision for Quincy center.

"Anton, maybe. The new boyfriend, if he exists." I pulled down the mirror and checked my lipstick.

"The new boyfriend is probably married or older. A bad boyfriend, for sure." He turned down a street lined with sherbet-colored town houses.

I tugged at the tight black dress I'd put on for Max's fundraiser. "I've been thinking about what Vince said about Bridget fighting at the Hat Trick with a blond guy who was full of himself and into art. It was a week before she was killed. That could have been Devon." I inhaled sharply. "Sounds like he was a bad boyfriend, too."

"Your first love was into art and full of himself, but that's not a crime." He winked at me. "And he had an alibi." One night when Brian and I had had too much to drink, we moved on to the topic of exes, his many, my few, and I'd shared the painful details of my teenage crush on Devon. I'd always regretted it.

Brian parked behind the line of cars in front of the peach-colored mansion Max had built for Barb on a bluff overlooking the bay, and we stepped out of the car. He looked good in a new blue shirt and jeans that fit him just right. The heat rose up the back of my neck as he pushed up the thin strap of my dress.

The party was in a high-ceilinged room as big as the whole first floor of my house. I went straight for the bar and got an old fashioned. Barb Delaney sidled up and reached past me for her Malbec. "Just awful, isn't it, Samantha? I feel so bad for Gloria and poor Megan." I nodded and chewed on the orange rind that had been floating in my drink. Her fingers closed around the stem of her glass. "You don't really think it's a copycat, do you?"

"I can't comment on a case."

She sipped her wine. "Where are Jeff and Corinne tonight?"

I stiffened. "At Jeff's new place."

Barb ran her free hand over her blond hair, which was slicked back into a low bun. Cold little diamonds sparkled in her ears. It was a different look from the days when she and Bridget wore their hair in loose blond curls with baby bangs and ringed their eyes with black mascara. They'd looked like twins then, though Barb was two years older. She gave me a pitying look. "Must be hard. With your job, you already miss so many precious moments. And now this."

"Come on, you have lots of social obligations. It's no different." I rested my glass on a coaster and picked up a miniature peach-colored mansion from the sideboard. "Is this a model of your house?"

She nodded. "It was a wedding present from Bridget. That guy, Bobby something, who made the Christmas village at the Crust and Crumb café . . . He made it for her, but she never got to give it to me." She sighed. "Her mom gave it to me after Bridget was murdered."

I put the little house down. "Bridget and I went to the Crust and Crumb to see the Christmas village every year. The last time, she couldn't stop talking about your wedding and the house Max was building for you."

She leaned so close I smelled her stale wine breath. "She was as excited about my wedding as I was. But I was so busy planning it, I couldn't spend as much time with her as I wanted to. And she was always with you." She gave me a hard look.

I thrust my shoulders back. "She didn't spend much time with me that winter, either, Barb. She was unhappy and I didn't understand why. I know you've been asked this before, but do you have any idea what was bothering her? Was she seeing someone new?"

"Like I already told Brian, if she was, she didn't tell me. I tried to set her up with Jay, but she thought she was too good for him. Honestly, she seemed fine to me, Sam. It wasn't until you introduced her to Devon that everything went to hell." Her gaze lingered and I felt the snake of her recriminations uncoiling. She lowered her eyes to her empty glass and said, "Time for a refill."

I needed more than a refill to get through this night. I needed a Xanax, but Brian caught up with me before I could take it, and we descended on the raw bar.

"Don't be greedy," he said as I helped myself to the plump oysters and jumbo shrimp languishing on ice. His own plate was heaped far higher than mine.

George joined us and helped himself to some shrimp. "No oysters?" I said as we grabbed a table.

He smiled wanly. "Not for me."

"Your loss." I tipped one into my mouth and swallowed it.

As he tore the tail off his shrimp, Alice Crane, the reporter from the *Sun*, sat down next to him and flounced out the skirt of a polka-dot dress that made her look like an overgrown child. "I need to talk to you," she said to me.

I smiled. "Here I am."

She tugged on a round black earring, like an escaped polka dot. "I'm writing an article on the Butterfly Killer's victims. As the only one who survived, I'd love to interview you for it."

"I don't do interviews," I said.

She smiled slowly. "This is your chance to tell your story for yourself and his other victims."

"I don't remember anything. I don't have a story." I folded my arms across my chest.

She pursed her lips, painted an unrelenting shade of red. "Must be hard seeing this happen again, knowing you didn't catch the guy who did it the first time."

Brian leaned in. "We're following up on all leads. If you have one, Alice, let us know." He stood up. "Anyone want another drink?"

Alice asked for an Absolut martini, very dirty. When he left, she turned to George. "I don't believe we've met."

I rolled my eyes. "This is Detective George Price. He's with the state police."

"Hope you don't mind." She helped herself to one of his shrimp and said, "Are you the same Detective Price who helped put that monster Junior Black in prison?"

He nodded. "That would be me. The world is better place with one more serial killer off the streets."

She swallowed an oyster. "I thought he was a gangster, not a serial killer."

George pressed his arms on the table. "A gangster, who kills multiple people, including women, and doesn't feel a thing, is a serial killer. It's just easier to romanticize him if you call him a gangster."

"Interesting perspective." She leaned so close her lips almost touched his cheek. "What's your gut? Is the guy who murdered Megan the same person who murdered Bridget?"

He sat back. "If I knew I couldn't tell you." He sipped his vodka on ice. "I read what you wrote in the *Sun* about the killer silencing his victims like in the myths. I get that Bridget's killer silenced her, but in the myth of Daphne, she's running from some handsome dude who has the hots for her and is saved by being transformed into a tree. That doesn't sound so bad to me. I've seen a lot worse."

"A Statie who reads myths. Now that's something," Alice said. "But you got it wrong, George. Daphne has to spend the rest of her life as a tree soaking up golden rays from Apollo, the god who was after her. Connect the dots. He silenced her—because he raped her."

"Just because Apollo chases after her doesn't mean he's a rapist." He eyed Alice. "Some women like to be pursued. And he didn't strangle her and bury her in cement in a basement, like Junior Black did."

I couldn't take it any longer. I turned to George. "You have to see through the pretty language in the myths to get to the truth. You don't run from someone as if for dear life unless they're threatening you. Being turned into a tree isn't all that different from being buried in cement, right?"

"Point taken." George dipped his shrimp in cocktail sauce.

Alice set her eyes on me. "You really should speak out on this. I could get the *Sun* to put a photo of one of your paintings in the article, maybe a new one?" I leaned back. A dog portrait from my languishing Etsy page wasn't what they wanted. They'd want another murder painting and to shine a new light on my old ones. I could just imagine the questions they'd ask, the pressure I'd feel to talk about my own rape, something I couldn't even remember.

Alice went on. "It could be an opportunity to get a gallery's attention."

As I loosened an oyster from the shell, my knife slit the soft belly and blood poured from the tender flesh. My throat tightened. When I looked again it was hot sauce. I didn't need the kind of attention the *Sun* would give me. What I needed was a Xanax right now. I stared at her coolly. "A young girl is dead and I'm trying to find her killer. That's my opportunity."

Brian returned with our drinks. Alice took hers without a thank-you and left. Jay Delaney came by, but when Brian offered him a seat he declined, saying, "I'm heading up there. I'm the guest of honor." He touched the gold RTR monogram—short for Road to Redemption—that dangled from a chain on his neck and took his place at the front of the room along with Max, Barb, and Shannon. Max said a few somber words about Megan and some hopeful ones about the new Quincy before handing the mic to Jay.

He went on as he always did. "The road to recovery is not paved with gold. It's paved with hard work and faith . . . Recovery is not someone else's problem. There but for the grace . . . with all the love in my heart I ask you to open yours and give what you can . . ." He wrapped it up by hugging Shannon and saying, "In memory of Megan O'Hare, the folks at *Wish Upon a Dancer* will match whatever we raise."

As they took pledges, I headed to the bathroom to take that Xanax, but Jay waved me over. He was with my therapist Peter, Barb, and Shannon. Barb averted her eyes when she saw me. Jay clapped Peter on the shoulder and said, "You know this guy, Sam?" I nodded and he said, "We go way back. He's my friend and he just made a hell of a donation."

"It's the least I can do when something so awful has happened." Peter gave me a polite smile as if we were merely professional acquaintances and added, "This must be hard for you, Detective Star. I hope you're okay. I speak for all of us when I say we are grateful for what you're doing."

I met his calm gaze. "I don't think anyone's okay right now, but thank you."

I sucked up the last of my old fashioned as Jay went on about Road to Redemption. Anxious to make an exit, I made an excuse about refreshing my drink, rushed past two waiters refilling trays of hors d'oeuvres in the kitchen, went into the bathroom, and washed a Xanax down with water from the faucet. Through the thin door I heard the waiters talking.

"'New Quincy,' right," one of them said. "The Dirty Q is still crawling with junkies. Nothing's going to change that."

The other said, "Kathy was mugged at knifepoint behind Diego Chang's last Friday night." I stiffened. Diego Chang's was near the Hat Trick.

"Kathy Lamb?" the first waiter said.

"Yeah, she's real messed up about it."

When I opened the door, they stopped talking and hurried out of the kitchen. I stepped onto the patio to wait for the Xanax to kick in. Soft lights dotted the boats on the bay far below. As I stood on the dry grass on the edge of the bluff, a hand touched the scar on my bare shoulder, and I almost lost my balance.

"Sorry to startle you." Max kept his hand on my scar. The sea breeze rifled his silver hair. "If you're ever looking for a good plastic surgeon to take care of those, I can recommend someone." I stepped away. My scars were no secret around here, but his touch was too much.

I narrowed my eyes at him. "Thank you?"

Brian texted, *I'm leaving if you want a ride.* I answered yes and got out of there.

* * *

I sipped a bourbon as I sat on my bed scrolling through the Quincy PD crime log from last Friday on my laptop. There were a few break-ins, some vandalism, the usual fights after the bars closed. And then I saw it.

Katherine Lamb was walking down Ames Street around 8:30 when she was robbed. Ames Street ran behind the Hat Trick. Eric, our person of interest, was guilty of something, but it probably wasn't killing Megan.

I let go a long breath and set my laptop aside. As I undressed and put on a big T-shirt, I glimpsed my scars in the mirror and cringed thinking of Max's hand on my shoulder. The first time I'd undressed in front of Jeff I wanted the lights off, but he wanted to see all of me, and so I showed him. He ran his fingers over my scars and told me they were beautiful and I was beautiful. I'm not the sort of woman who needs compliments or candy and flowers. It was enough that Jeff didn't want to change my scars the way Max did.

Maybe it was the Xanax and the bourbon, but tears came up my throat. I forced them down. The night when I told Brian about my crush on Devon, he'd said, "And then Jeff swept you off your feet." It was more like he'd scraped me off the floor, but I didn't share that.

When I was in the hospital, they'd done a rape kit. Brian had told me they'd found DNA but the sample was too degraded to use. I told him I didn't remember anything. We never talked about it after that. A few years later when I told Jeff about it, I asked him not to bring it up again. He said he understood. But that night long ago, when I'd let him come closer than anyone else ever had, there was a knot inside me that wouldn't untie. It was still there now.

I was drifting off to sleep when a thought stopped me cold. I opened my laptop and returned to the police report to see what had been stolen. It listed cash, two credit cards, and there it was: a bracelet. There was a picture of it. I compared it with the photo of the bracelet logged into evidence from the murder scene. There was no mistaking those shining multicolored stones. It was the same bracelet we had found on Eric. It wasn't Megan's and it wasn't connected to my past.

We released Eric the next day. He'd robbed Katherine in a drug deal gone wrong. But she wasn't pressing charges. The fact that we no longer had a suspect was all over the news. That afternoon Brian gave me a weary glance and said, "We need a new suspect. Let's focus on finding Megan's new boyfriend."

Chapter Thirteen

"MOM, YOU HAVE to see this YouTube," Corinne said, passing me her phone. I took it, eager to share every moment of this day with her. She hadn't stayed with me since Megan's murder and wouldn't have been here now if Jeff hadn't needed to go on an unexpected work trip. We'd gone to the mall earlier and I'd bought her a sundress at Forever 21 and makeup at Glamora, her favorite store. We stopped at Stop & Shop on the way home to get ingredients for a pavlova, a complicated dessert involving meringue. Jeff had recently shown her how to make it and she wanted to show me. As she'd beaten the egg whites and folded in the sugar, I'd marveled at what a careful and intuitive cook she was, just like Jeff.

She peered over my shoulder now as I held her phone and watched as Anton came up behind Shannon and ran his hands down the length of her, as close as he could without touching. They wound around each other to New Age music full of bells and anguish, he in white, she in black, on a stage covered with white petals.

"Their new dance is called Whispers," she said breathlessly. "Anton choreographed it. They're going to perform it at the *Wish Upon a Dancer* audition. Shannon chose him to replace Megan. Nina was mad she didn't pick her, but he is the best dancer on the team." She paused. "I think Megan would want them to go on with the audition and win."

"I think so, too." I said, finishing a slice of the pizza I'd ordered for dinner because I hated cooking.

She looked up hesitantly. "Dad wants to go to Grandma's house by the lake for a vacation soon. Can you come?"

I exhaled slowly, thinking of the lovely place where we spent two weeks' vacation around this time every summer. "I wish I could go," I said. "But I can't with this case."

Her face fell. She got up from the couch saying, "I need to make the whipped cream for the pavlova," and went into the kitchen.

I was about to put her phone aside, but I stopped. Whoever murdered Megan could have watched the YouTube video. I scrolled through the comments on it but didn't find anything suspicious. It wouldn't make sense that her murderer could be in contact with Corinne, but anything was possible. I looked quickly through her recent texts. Nothing stood out, but I checked her recent calls, too. They were mostly spam, but when I scrolled back to the night of Megan's murder, my stomach sank.

"Voilà," Corinne said as she placed the meringue heaped with whipped cream and strawberries on the coffee table. She watched expectantly as I took a bite and said, "What do you think, Mom?"

"This is heavenly," I replied. She seemed so proud, I didn't want to say anything else but I had to. "Did Anton call you the night Megan was murdered?"

She drew her brows together. "Why are you asking me that?"

I handed her back the phone. "There's a call in your phone from him at around four a.m."

"Mom," she exclaimed. "You snooped in my phone."

"I wanted to make sure you were safe," I said.

She studied her phone. "He called to see if I'd heard that Megan was murdered. He thought I might know more about it because, you know, you're my mother." She glared at me. "I wanted to ask you, but you weren't home. He was crying. We both were. Everyone called me that night. I'm sorry I didn't tell you, but I had a lot on my mind, and it didn't seem important."

Her eyes widened in alarm as I took the phone back. "That's illegal search and seizure," she said, echoing things I'd taught her.

"Not between parents and children," I said calmly. When I found calls from Shannon and Nina around three-thirty a.m., I breathed a sigh of relief. "It's not important, if that's all it was."

"Mom, that's all it was." She grabbed her phone and Ginger, went up to her room, and slammed the door.

I stared at the pavlova drowning in a pool of wilting whipped cream. She'd eaten hardly any of it. Of course, her friends had called to tell her Megan was murdered. I hadn't been there to tell her. I'd left her alone and hadn't even answered her calls. I hurried upstairs to smooth things over with her but stopped at her shut door. She was talking on the phone. I flinched as I heard her say, "My mom snooped on me. I can't believe it. My own mom. I don't even know who she is anymore."

I took a long breath. This had been my chance to connect with her and I'd broken her trust.

Chapter Fourteen

I'D ARRANGED TO have the next morning off, too, so I could take Corinne out to breakfast at IHOP, before Jeff came to get her. I hoped to win her trust back with some silver dollar pancakes. But Jeff came by early. It was raining out and, as he stood dripping on the carpet, I suggested we all go to breakfast together. He glanced at me and then at Corinne. She wouldn't meet my gaze as she said, "I asked him to come, Mom. I don't want to go to IHOP. I have practice later. I can't fill up on pancakes." She turned to Jeff, "Let's go now." It felt like someone was wringing out my heart as they left.

I didn't feel ready to go to the station, so I made a fresh cup of coffee and took it upstairs. When my feelings were all tied up in knots like this, painting was one of the only things that could untangle them. I brought the photos I'd taken of Pia up on my laptop and chose one to work from. As I sketched the dog on a canvas board, I heard my father saying, "What a waste of your abilities." For him, any art that wasn't "high art" wasn't worth doing. He'd called a few days ago to make sure we were all okay. And now he was back in my head, but I pushed his voice away. He'd failed me and I worried I was failing Corinne in the same way. I'd ruined our time together by scrutinizing her like a detective instead of being there for her as her mother—but I could fix this. And I would. Much-needed calm descended on me as I painted. I filled in the darkest values first: Pia's nose, her ebony eyes, then more darks and lights, the grass, the tufts of hair in her ears, and the beetle creeping along a rose petal behind her.

It was almost noon when my phone buzzed. I thought it might be Corinne, but it was an email.

I lay the girl in red bare and crack her skull like an egg on a saucer. In the black mirror of her eyes I see the beginning of time and the end, what was, what is, and what is to be. Though the wind rustles the little butterflies in her hair, my tiny dancer will always be still. If I can't have her no one will.

I exhaled slowly. He was talking about Megan. It took everything I had to not hurl my phone against the wall.

* * *

I shook the rain off my jacket, hung it on the back of my chair, reached into the box of Munchkins I'd bought because I craved something sweet, and grabbed a glazed one.

"Is this your idea of lunch or are you just trying raise my blood sugar?" Brian asked and helped himself to a powdered sugar one.

"It's whatever you want it to be," I said. "We're cops. We like donuts. We eat them all the time, right?" George pressed his chin on his palm and stared at me skeptically.

"Is something wrong, Sam?" Brian asked.

I told them about the email and brought it up on my laptop. "It's similar to the first letter I got," I said, as he and George crowded around for a look.

Brian raised an eyebrow. "You think this is for real?"

I cradled my dark roast in my hands. "He knows Megan's skull was fractured. That detail wasn't made public."

"The letters have never been a secret. Someone could have leaked

Megan's cause of death." Brian frowned as he brushed powdered sugar from his shirt.

"I'll see if the techs can figure out who sent it," I said.

"Unfortunately, it's easy to make an email impossible to trace." George's hand hovered over the Munchkins like it was the decision of the century.

"Geez. Just pick one already." I smiled.

George kept studying them. "What makes you think this isn't a hoax?"

I tipped my chair back. "The end of the first letter mentioned the rose that was missing from my shoe when Brian found me. That convinced us the letter was genuine because that detail was never made public. The line at the end of this one is similar."

Brian pressed his thumb on my laptop. "So this line, 'the little butterflies in her hair,' is trying to convince us he's the real deal?"

"Yeah. It must have something to do with me, but I don't know what he's referring to."

George finally settled on a glazed Munchkin. "Maybe you don't know because it really is a hoax, and whoever wrote the letter made that detail up and was just copying the pattern."

I frowned. "It's possible, but I have a feeling about it."

"Hold that thought. We have something else," Brian said, as he and George exchanged a glance.

George popped the Munchkin in his mouth. "My resources found multiple calls from Megan's phone to a burner in the weeks before her murder and on the day of. We can't figure out who owns the burner, but they're still determining where it was located when she called it."

Brian turned to me. "That burner could belong to Megan's new boyfriend."

"There's also this," George said. "Ten minutes after Megan called the burner on the day of the murder, there was a second call to it from Shannon Delaney's phone."

I sat up straighter. "Maybe Megan's boyfriend isn't a mystery after all. I'll talk to Shannon."

Brian's brow creased with concern. "George and I can handle that."

"I might have better luck. She trusts me."

His mouth tightened. "She's Corinne's friend. That's a conflict of interest."

I frowned. "That doesn't matter when it suits you."

"True," Brian replied. "But Barb Delaney has been insinuating you're involved since day one. It's better you don't interview her daughter."

"Jesus." I started to get up.

He motioned me back down. "Focus on figuring out who sent the email, Sam. He could be the same person who owns the burner phone and Megan's new boyfriend."

After they left, I gave the email to the head tech at the station. He said he might have an answer for me in a day or so. Given all the folders piled haphazardly on his desk, I wasn't optimistic. I decided I had to do my own digging. If I could figure out the reference to the little butterflies, that could lead me to who sent the email. The light over the stairs was out, and I was literally descending into darkness as I went down to the evidence room in the basement and signed in. The evidence from the old case was stacked on metal shelves near the back.

I grabbed the box that held the artifacts from the worst time in my life: Bridget's silver dress stiff with blood, her red stilettos, my bloodstained blue dress. Most of the blood on my dress was mine, but some was Bridget's. I swallowed hard, imagining us clutching each other in fear. My blue shoes were in a bag beneath the dress, a rusty dot on the toe where the rose was missing. I inspected Bridget's crystal earrings, my silver star ones, the laurel crown I'd bobby-pinned into her hair—bits and pieces of my nightmare all neatly bagged. My chest tightened as I remembered how we had fought about Devon that night and headed down the steps in the rain barely speaking to each other.

I turned to the crime scene photos of the killer's so-called work of art: Bridget in the hollow of a fallen tree, the rips in her sequined dress baring the wounds on her chest, her legs smeared with dirt and bark, the green leaves shoved beneath her fingernails. Her head rested on a gold circle made of wood, like the sun with twisted gold spikes coming out of it. Her blackened eyes were shut, and her lips were sealed. Her hair was full of leaves and branches and shiny things. Flecks of gold leaf—like my father sometimes used in his paintings. Not little butterflies. My eyes moved down to the yellow butterfly on the bloody place where her throat had been cut. The killer had left just one butterfly on each of his victims. No little butterflies.

Next, I took down the boxes that held the hundreds of pages of interviews Brian had done with me. I had a vague memory of mentioning my hair in the first one. I might have mentioned little butterflies too. The interview transcript wasn't hard to find. I skimmed through it until I found the place where I told Brian that Bridget must have known the guy who picked us up. She wouldn't have gotten in a car with a stranger. I didn't get a good look at his face, but he was a big guy and maybe in his early twenties.

When Brian asked how I could be sitting in the same car as him and not see his face, I said he wore a hoodie and that when he held us captive he'd worn a mask. He asked if the guy had said anything to us in the car. I told him Bridget had said something like, "Doesn't her hair look pretty?" and he'd replied, "Yes." I mentioned that the way he'd talked without looking at me was weird.

I pressed my palms on the metal table. This had to be the mention of my hair I remembered, and it meant nothing. I kept reading. Brian asked if Bridget was afraid of anyone. I said one time at the beach she took off to meet someone and came back with a bruise on her cheek. I'd assumed someone must have hit her.

He asked if I knew who hit her and I told him it was probably Devon because they fought sometimes. He asked if Bridget and I ever fought and I told him no, too embarrassed to admit I'd ruined the last few good moments we had together that night because I was jealous.

He went on and asked, "Could Devon be the one who picked

you up?" I told him I would have recognized him. He said, "But you couldn't see his face and he wore a mask later, so it could have been him, right?" I told him no again.

I ran my hand over the line in the transcript where he'd said, "Are you lying to me, Samantha?" Those words, coming from him, still stung even now. When I insisted I wasn't lying, ever logical, he'd replied, "It makes no sense that he would put on a mask after you'd seen him."

I'd said, "A white Mardi Gras mask with green glitter on it is one of the only things I remember from that night. I have nightmares about it."

As rain pattered on the dust-filmed basement windows, I realized how illogical I sounded. Had I been lying then without knowing it? Was I lying to myself now? All I knew was that in my nightmares, a snake wearing a mask wove back and forth, studying me with a cold, clinical gaze that made me feel like I didn't exist. In my sessions, Peter suggested there might have been no mask at all. It could be my way of coping with what I was afraid to see. But Peter was wrong. Brian was, too. The man had worn a mask.

Brian had shown me pictures of my father's students at the art college and mug shots of criminals in the area. I couldn't identify any of them as the man in the car. He had shown me photos of white cars, but I hadn't recognized any of them, either. I read through more of the interviews, but nothing jogged my memory. There was one more place to look.

Some girls save prom corsages, withered flowers on velvet wristbands, a program from the movie they went to on a first date, but I had none of that romantic trivia. After Jeff had made a few failed attempts at flowers, I scared him off from trying again. My only romantic keepsakes were letters from a killer, typed on stationery with a creamy satin finish, held together by an elastic, and they were stuffed in a plastic evidence bag. I had copies at home that I reread occasionally, but I was here now. I read through them again hoping that, like a talisman, the feel of the original smooth paper might help me to see something I'd missed—but I found no mentions of little butterflies.

* * *

Later, in the incident room, Brian said, "We had an interesting chat with Shannon."

George clicked his pen. "She said Megan was worried about screwing up the audition, and she helped her get her confidence back."

I propped my feet on the table. "The O'Hares told us Megan was the one helping Shannon."

George went on. "Shannon said Megan didn't want her parents to know she needed help, that she acted like everything was fine even when it wasn't. That could also be why she told them breaking up with Anton was her idea."

"Yeah. Teens rarely tell their parents the whole story. You have to worm it out of them," I said, thinking about Corinne. "What about the calls from the burner?"

"I was getting to that. Shannon said Megan got an upsetting call and ran into the bathroom crying. Shannon assumed it was from Megan's new boyfriend. Only a boy would make her act like that." George smiled. "While Megan was in the bathroom, Shannon got the number of the last call from Megan's phone and called it from her own phone to find out who he was, but he hung up when he heard her voice."

"Do you believe her?" I asked. "Her explanation is pretty convoluted."

He kept clicking his pen. "It's the only call from Shannon to the burner. All the other calls on the burner for the past month are to or from Megan."

Brian leaned forward. "The techs confirmed the burner was used in downtown Quincy, but that doesn't narrow it down much. It was turned off after the call from Shannon and hasn't been used since."

He eyed George. "Let's swing by the O'Hares' tomorrow. Maybe Megan told her brother about the boyfriend."

George slid his pen in his pocket and turned to me. "Did you learn anything about the email?"

"Nothing yet." I dropped my feet to the floor. "But as you suspected, the little butterflies were a waste of time." If he was gloating he didn't show it. I was thankful for that.

Chapter Fifteen

I MADE SPAGHETTI with sauce from a jar and added wine and oregano, along with microwaved meatballs. Jeff would have scoffed, but I ate every last bit of it and took a glass of bourbon upstairs with me. Wind-driven rain was whipping against the house. As I settled in under the covers, I heard a *thunk* from Corinne's room.

Her window was open, and a gust of wind had knocked her philodendron off the sill. She called it her rescue plant, because it was half dead when she got it from the bargain table at Home Depot. Now it lay in a mess of soil and broken crockery on the floor. I grabbed the broom from the bathroom closet and began sweeping it up.

When I stretched the broom under her bed, I hit something hard. It was one of the black leather portfolios of my father's drawings that I kept in the attic. Corinne loved the drawings of magical animals, rabbits with wings, and birds with cat faces that my father had done for her when she was younger. I figured she'd brought them down to look at them.

But this portfolio didn't contain drawings of animals; it contained drawings of Bridget. After she was murdered, the police confiscated Devon's artwork as evidence. They returned his winning painting to him right away. But by the time they returned the drawings of her, my father was teaching in Vermont, and Devon had moved to

Maine, so they left them with me. At the time, my father told me Devon didn't want them back. When Jeff and I moved here, I stashed them under the eaves in the attic. I'd never shown them to Corinne.

My stomach soured as I flipped to a black-and-white sketch of Bridget lying on the grass. Her skin looked like polished marble. There was a butterfly on her forehead, branches entwined in her hair, and her head rested on a sunflower. I remembered the next one. I'd been there when Devon had done it. She was half naked, eyes almost shut, a blissful smile on her face. I'd watched for a few minutes while he worked on it, with my stomach tied in knots. At the time I was too upset to notice what he'd actually included in the image, but now I took a closer look. He'd added color to this one. Green leaves sprouted from Bridget's fingertips as they had at the crime scene. As in the first drawing, she rested her head on a sunflower. But the butterfly was on her throat, not her forehead, and it was blue. Blue. Like the one we found on Megan. As I looked through more of the sketches, I could see that Devon had made small changes, ultimately settling on an orange-and-black monarch butterfly in his winning painting, instead of a blue one. Bridget's killer had obviously copied Devon's painting. But he'd changed the color of the butterfly from orange to yellow, the sunflower to a spiked wheel, and he hadn't painted her. He'd murdered her.

Uneasiness spread through me as I looked again at the blue butterfly in the old paint sketch. Had Megan's killer somehow seen this sketch? I couldn't stop staring at it. A car pulled up outside, hip-hop blaring, jolting me from my trance. Too upset to do anything else, I closed the sketchbook and gathered up Corinne's dirty laundry, which she'd left carelessly scattered on the floor. There were more dirty clothes in her closet—tights whose feet were stiff with sweat, a pink leotard, a flowered dress balled in a heap, and something else, stiff like the tights. Only it wasn't stiff with sweat. It was a T-shirt, covered with blood, the words *Real Men Dance* barely visible beneath the red-brown stain. I'd seen Anton wearing that shirt before. My heart sank. I wanted to wash it or throw it away, but I couldn't do that.

I finished my bourbon and went downstairs for another. The rain had stopped and everything was painfully quiet. As I sipped my drink, I told myself it wasn't possible that Anton was involved in Megan's murder and that Corinne knew. But it actually was possible. I took a deep breath and called Jeff.

He sounded half asleep when he answered. I told him I needed him and Corinne to come over, it had to do with the case. No one was in danger, but we had to talk.

"Now?" he said incredulously. I told him it could wait until morning, and he replied with a weary, "Fine."

I carefully repotted the philodendron, and put it on the kitchen windowsill, a curling green tendril dangling over the edge. Behind it the black sky was dotted with stars, like a page out of a children's picture book. This was our home, a place where everything was supposed to be safe. But now the snaking vine of my past was slithering into the present.

* * *

The next morning I brewed a pot of coffee and spread grape jelly on my English muffin, burnt the way I liked it. Jeff and Corinne showed up with Ginger as I was dumping the jelly-smeared half I couldn't finish down the disposal. I poured them some coffee and offered to make them breakfast, but they'd already eaten.

Corinne looked put upon as she sat down. Jeff exchanged a knowing glance with her. They'd probably been talking about how unhinged I was. I set my eyes on her. "I found some things in your room while I was gathering up your laundry."

"Jesus, Mom, first you snoop on my phone and now you're snooping in my room?" She glared at me.

I ignored her outrage and pulled the plastic bag with the bloody shirt in it out from beneath some newspapers on the kitchen table. "I found this."

"That's Anton's," she said, as if it were nothing.

"Can you explain how it got in your closet?"

Jeff looked perplexed. "It was in her closet?"

"Corinne?" I wanted to shake her and hug her at the same time. "Tell me how it got there."

She ran a finger around her coffee cup. "Like I already told you, he called around four in the morning to tell me about Megan. He was crying. I was crying. He asked me to meet him in the backyard."

"He was in our backyard at four in the morning?" I said.

She sighed as if having to explain this was simply too much. "Anton comes over at night sometimes when he can't sleep, and we talk. There was blood all over his shirt from a bloody nose. He didn't want to wear the shirt to Dmitry's, so I gave him one of Dad's shirts."

"How did he get a bloody nose?"

"He tripped and fell when he left Piney."

I inhaled long and hard. "How come you didn't tell me about this?"

"I . . . I just . . . couldn't . . ." She kept pulling on her sleeve. If she could have turned herself inside out, she probably would have. "I believed what Anton told me, but I knew nobody else would. He gets blamed for everything, and I didn't want to get him in trouble. I didn't know what to do with the shirt. I hoped it would all go away. I'm sorry, Mom."

She was right about no one believing Anton. There are people who come into this life with instant credibility. Others raise doubts with their first step. With Anton being Russian in a very Irish Catholic city, a dancer, and having those eyes that never quite met yours, he was the latter. Corinne sometimes faced that, too, because Jeff was Jewish. I figured it had brought her and Anton together.

I sighed, remembering the time some kids had slashed tires along a street near us. They blamed Anton for it, even though he'd been at practice with Corinne when it happened. That night he'd shown up at our house with a bloody nose, too. He wouldn't tell me what had happened at first, but after an hour of me asking him and handing him fresh ice packs, he admitted that his father had blamed him for the tires and given him a beating. I offered to speak to Vasily, but he said he didn't need my help because he'd never let his father do it again. Later, I got the tire-slashing charges thrown out. But though I suspected Anton knew the kids who'd done it, he never gave them up.

I wrapped Corinne's hands in mine and said, "The good thing is you're no longer hiding this. Whether Anton is telling the truth or not is for me to figure out."

"Mom, he didn't do anything." She yanked her hands away.

"He was covered with blood." Jeff's voice rose. "How can you say he didn't do anything?"

She flinched. He never raised his voice at her. "He had an explanation."

"And you believed his explanation? I thought you were smarter than that. You could have gotten yourself in a lot of trouble." He turned to me. "I guess Corinne and I won't be taking vacation anytime soon."

"Right," I said.

He frowned. "What happens next?"

"She'll give Brian a statement and we'll take it from there." I turned to Corinne. "There's something else. I found Devon's sketches under your bed."

"I think they're cool so I showed them to my friends. Is that a crime now, too?" She looked about to exit in a huff, clearly not comprehending how serious this was.

"When did you show them to your friends?"

"The day you barged in on us. We were talking about the article, and I thought they'd be interested."

My stomach sank. Anton had seen the blue butterfly before Megan's murder. "Did Anton say anything about the blue butterfly in the sketch?"

She ran a strand of hair between her fingers. "None of us even noticed a blue butterfly. We were too busy looking at Bridget."

"Who was there?"

"Lane, Nina, Shannon, and Anton." She gave me a worried look. "The butterfly on Megan could be a coincidence, right?"

"Maybe," I said. It was suspicious that she hadn't told me about the phone call or the shirt, but if Anton had done something wrong, she probably didn't know. Corinne was so trusting, too trusting. I turned to her. "Tell Brian what you told me, and you'll be fine."

She gave me a frantic look. "Why do I have to talk to him? Anton didn't do anything."

"If he didn't do anything, he has nothing to worry about." I hesitated and added, "Not a word about this to any of your friends."

"Mom, stop it," she said and told Jeff she wanted to go home. *Home.* That word really hurt.

Chapter Sixteen

I PULLED A chair up opposite Brian and George and told them about finding the shirt, what Corinne had said about Anton's falling on the path, and the bloody nose. There was a long silence. "Anton was right in my backyard the night Megan was killed," I said. "He lied when you asked him what he had done that night, and there's more. A week before Megan's murder, Corrine showed him a sketch Devon did of Bridget with a blue butterfly." Brian studied me with concern. I swallowed hard. "When do you want to talk to Corinne?"

"As soon as she can get here," he said. I phoned Jeff and told him to bring her in. Brian ran a finger over his watch. "We have news that could be related. None of the O'Hares recognized the burner number. But Megan's brother, Matt, said when he and his friends went to look for her at Piney, they ran into Anton around midnight on the edge of the island. When Matt asked if he'd seen Megan, Anton told him no and took off toward the graveyard." He eyed me. "Anton told us he hadn't gone anywhere near the graveyard."

"Right. He lied," I said. "But how come Matt and his friends didn't look for her there?"

"Matt claimed they didn't think of it." George frowned. "Typical bonehead kids."

"Shannon, Nick, and Nina all said Anton didn't go anywhere near the graveyard. Are they lying, too?" I asked.

Brian shrugged. "Friends don't rat on friends around here. But if we get one to crack, they all will."

"Let's start with Nina," I said. "Anton dumped her, and Shannon picked him over her to audition for *Wish Upon a Dancer*. She's probably mad at them."

Brian leaned forward. "George and I will talk to her. Now that you've found evidence in your own home, it's even more important to let us handle these conversations."

I exhaled loudly. "You're dating Nick's mother and he's Nina's boyfriend. But if you don't trust me to do this, fine."

George tugged at his shirt cuff. Ninety degrees out and he was wearing a button-down. "I'm okay with you talking to Nina, Sam. She's more likely to open up to you than to a life-of-the-party guy like me." He smiled. "I'll have the blood on the shirt tested and talk to Shannon again. We have to be BFFS by now."

"My god, George, you actually made a joke," Brian said. He turned to me. "We'll talk to Nina after I interview Corinne."

When she arrived a half hour later, I watched the interview through the one-way mirror. Corinne never wavered, even as Brian tried to confuse her. I was proud of her, but when we crossed paths in the hall, she paused only long enough to say, "I hate you," before Jeff whisked her away.

* * *

There are two parts of West Quincy: the part where the buildings are so small and mean you can almost feel the sweaty hand pressing them down, and the part where Nina Crowne lived with pink rhododendrons as tall as trees, and cozy houses nestled in yards as rich and soft as the green velvet that lined my grandmother's fancy silverware case. Bourgeois crap, my mother called it. I thought it was pretty.

The Crownes' charming but tiny gray Cape was across from a

park that was a back entrance into the miles of scenic woods and hiking trails known as the Blue Hills. Bridget's body had been found off one of those trails by someone who stopped by the side of a road and went into the woods to take a piss.

"Tell me about Nina," Brian said, as we walked up to her plum-colored front door.

"Die-hard perfectionist. Likes to be in control. Corinne says Nina and Anton were doomed from the beginning. But Nina's not as frosty as she seems. When Anton broke up with her she was suicidal, but her mom got her some help. Then Anton dumped Megan for Shannon and Nina met Nick. Now she lives for ballet, though she's practically starving herself to death to get into the Boston Ballet School next year." I smiled. "Aren't you glad I'm here now?"

"I'm always glad you're here." He let the brass knocker drop.

* * *

"Why do you need to talk to Nina?" her mother, Miranda, asked as we sat in her tidy kitchen with cheerful wallpaper patterned with tiny red apples.

"We're talking again to everyone who was at the scene. Nothing to be concerned about." Brian gave her a quick smile. Of course, they were friends. Brian probably brought Mary Ann and Nick here for backyard barbecues.

She set a box of cookies and mugs of coffee on the table and turned to me. "This must be hard on Corinne and Jeff."

"It is. Murder is hard on everyone." I frowned as I took a sip from a mug that was the same shade of red as the apples on the wallpaper—all part of some decorating scheme.

Nina slipped in wearing a white shirt and matching shorts. She wound herself around a chair and swept her auburn ponytail over her bony shoulder. She was thinner than the last time I had seen her, if that was possible. She gave the impression she might vanish with a breath.

Brian helped himself to a shell-shaped cookie. "How's Nick doing?"

"He's fine." She set her doe-like eyes on him.

"He's a good athlete and a good kid." Brian pushed the cookies her way. She stared at them like they were poison. He smiled. "Come on, take one. You know you want it." She plucked one gingerly from the box. "Look, I'm not an expert in the romance department, but Anton dumped you for Megan and then he dumped Megan for Shannon, am I right?" She gave him a painful nod. Brian ate his cookie. "He sure gets around. You're lucky to have Nick."

Nina blushed. "Nick and I are happy. I'm glad Anton is, too. I don't blame him for anything." She gave her mother a cautious glance. "Megan's one of those girls who take what they want without thinking about anyone else."

Brian raised a brow. "You know anything about her new boy-friend?"

"No. I'm sorry she's dead, but to be honest I didn't care who she was dating." Nina lowered her eyes.

I drew in a breath. "Tell me again how Anton left Piney that night?"

"He took the path through the Manor Apartments." She stretched her swanlike neck. "Why are you asking about him?"

"We're trying to understand where everyone was that night in case someone saw something." I chose a cookie filled with apricot jam. "Did Megan's brother, Matt, come looking for her?"

"He came with his friends after Anton left."

"You and Anton used to be dance partners, right?" I said.

"Sometimes." She held her cookie between her thumb and fore-finger.

"It's pretty amazing that he and Shannon are doing a dance together for *Wish Upon a Dancer*, don't you think?"

She put the cookie down. "They are?"

I widened my eyes. "Shannon didn't tell you? They're doing the Whispers dance. You must have seen it on YouTube. Everyone's raving about it."

"I saw it." A sharp line appeared between her perfectly shaped eyebrows. "The moves are simple. It's nothing special."

"They asked Shannon to choose a dancer to fill Megan's spot, and she chose Anton. It should have been you. You're the best dancer on the team." I leaned forward. "Anton broke up with you so he could date Megan. He didn't choose you. He chose her. And then he chose Shannon. And now she's chosen him for the dance. Is Shannon one of those girls who takes what she wants, too?" I set my eyes on Nina and she stiffened. "Why are you covering for Anton when he treats you this way?"

She thrust her bony shoulders back. "I'm not covering for him."

Brian shook his head. "That's funny, because we have witnesses who saw him heading toward the graveyard."

Miranda gave us a startled glance. "Witnesses?"

"Yes, ma'am." Brian turned to Nina. "You certain about what you just said?"

She knotted her delicate fingers together. "Yes."

"First Anton leaves you for Megan. Then he gets that audition. It must be hard never getting what you want." Brian helped himself to another cookie. "These sure are good. I'd hate to see you deprive yourself for nothing." He looked directly at her. "But if we find out you're lying, you can kiss your ballet dreams goodbye."

The overhead light buzzed. Miranda set her red mug down with a thud. "Your future is more important than covering for your friends."

Nina studied the nest of her knotted fingers for a long, terrible moment. She finally looked up and said, "When we found Megan, I said I thought it was weird Anton hadn't called us. He must have seen her body, too. Shannon said he left through the apartments so he couldn't have. I told her I thought I saw him leaving the other way. She begged me to say he took the path by the apartments or he could get in trouble." Her worried gaze met mine. "I'm sorry for lying, but he's my friend. I didn't want to get him in trouble."

"Thank you, Nina," I said. "I know this is hard, but you've been a big help." She gave me a faint smile. She was staring at the cookie when we left.

As we stood in front of her house, Brian nodded at the sun-dappled woods across the street. "Hard to believe the place where we found Bridget is just a short walk through there." He turned to me. "We were ready to give up on finding you when I saw your shoes under some brambles near the scene. They were pointing toward the ravine, like you were showing me where to look."

"More likely I took my shoes off because it's hard to run in heels." I dug my hands into the pockets of my jeans. "What Nina told us is pretty damning for Anton."

Brian gave me a grim nod. "I'm glad she spoke up."

"You didn't have to torture her with the cookie," I said.

"She'll get over it." He adjusted his mirrored sunglasses. "We do what we have to do, Sam." I supposed we did, but I knew how it felt to struggle with something that wouldn't let go. I'd spent too many nights obsessing at three a.m. about how I'd pushed aside my dream of being an artist and my own family for my job. When I turned back to her house, Nina stood like a paper doll pressed against the window, watching us.

Chapter Seventeen

ANTON CAME TO the station the next day and gave us fingerprints, blood, and DNA samples. He said he had nothing to hide. We got a search warrant for the small bungalow where he lived on a street near Wollaston Beach, with its long stretch of shoreline and views of Quincy Bay. Years ago, this neighborhood was mostly Irish Catholic. Statues of the Virgin Mary could still be found in some of the tiny yards, and you could catch a brogue here and there. But now red-and-gold Chinese lanterns swayed on a few front porches. Anton's family had come here from Russia. The Siberian tiger painted on the side of his dad's van seemed to bare its fangs at the onlookers gathered around his house as we headed inside.

Vasily was at work, and Anton was at the dance studio. His mother, Irina, was the only one home. She had the same light hair, high cheek bones, and pale, deep-set eyes as her son. She gestured to the officers tearing apart her house and said to me, "Why are you doing this to Anton?" I told her we were just doing our job, and she frowned. I'd dropped Corinne off here many times, but she and I had rarely spoken. She was reclusive and almost never attended Anton's performances or left the house. Anton said she had been a dancer back in Russia and he'd inherited his talent from her.

Except for the posters on the wall of Nureyev mid-leap, and

Channing Tatum in *Step Up*, Anton's messy small bedroom was typical for a teenage boy: dirty socks on the floor, a fifth of vodka stashed under the bed, a film can of pot in a desk drawer, cigarette burns on the coffee table, Acqua di Gio cologne on the dresser, and one empty birdcage. Apparently, Percy had never come home. I ran a finger over the metal bars of the cage, remembering how gentle and patient Anton was with Corinne when he taught her dance steps. I wrapped my arms around myself. She hadn't spoken to me since I'd found the shirt and it was killing me.

Brian held up a photo of Anton with his arm around Shannon. "She stood by her man when George talked to her, but I bet she'll change her tune now."

"Never underestimate the power of love." I took in Shannon's hopeful smile, thinking about the danger she might be in. When I'd first met Devon he was so beautiful with his creamy skin and muscled arms, like Botticelli's Venus rising from the sea, I would have done whatever he told me to do.

We met up with George in the driveway where the techs were searching Vasily's van. So far, they hadn't found any evidence of blood. George pushed up the sleeves of his spotless white shirt and peered inside it. "What kind of business is Anton's father in?"

Brian pointed to the Siberian tiger snarling beneath the sign on the van that read: KOSLOV'S EXOTIC ANIMALS AND ANTIQUES. "He sells rare animals and other things, not all of them legal."

"Lizards, snakes, exotic cats, birds, and collectible insects." I smiled. "Want me to spin by there?"

"Vasily knows you. George, you swing by and pretend to be a collector."

George smiled. "It's always been my dream to go undercover."

Brian shot him a look. "Yeah, undercover butterfly collector. Get yourself a net."

After George left, Brian and I went to check on the search at Anton's cousin Dmitry's. He lived a block away in a house that suffered from an excess of flowered wallpaper, chintz upholstered furniture, and cute knickknacks. At over six feet, with a hulking frame and sullen eyes, Dmitry didn't match the décor. Except for the officers swarming the place, he was the only one home. He told us the same story he'd told Brian earlier. Anton came over around midnight and spent the night there. When Brian pressed him about the exact timing, Dmitry said, "I do not check the time every second. It was late. That's all I know." When I asked if Anton had blood on his shirt, he told me no. When I asked if he was sure Anton had been there the whole night, Dmitry told us he was.

He took pleasure in showing us the pool table, flat-screen TV, and video games in his boy cave in the basement. He also kept a set of fancy knives here. He took pleasure in showing us them, too.

Brian admired a knife with an ornate mother-of-pearl handle and a curved blade. "You must have paid a lot for these."

"Vasily gave them to me."

"Are they just for show?" Brian raised an eyebrow.

Dmitry laughed. "We play games with them."

"What kind of games?" Brian asked.

"We throw them." He grinned.

"Anton, too?" I asked.

Dmitry rolled his formidable shoulders. "Sometimes."

Brian pointed to an empty slot in the suede case. "There's one missing. What happened to it?"

"Someone broke in and stole it a few months ago." Dmitry frowned. "That one was just for show. A gut hook knife." When I asked if he'd reported it stolen, he told us no.

When we were done with Dmitry, I exchanged a glance with Brian and we stepped outside. "Does he really expect us to believe someone broke into his house and stole a knife that matches the murder weapon? The kid is either incredibly self-destructive or stupid or both," he said.

I shrugged. "Or he doesn't know it was the type of knife used on Megan."

"I need a smoke," Brian said. We walked to the end of Anton's street and across Quincy Shore Drive to the beach. He cupped his hand around his cigarette to light it and said, "You think Anton is guilty?"

I stared at the waves fanning out on the sand. "No blood found in his house or in the van or at Dmitry's yet. The story he told Corinne about the bloody nose could be true. But Dmitry lied about Anton being with him from midnight on. I wonder why."

He leaned on the breakwater. "Would be nice to find the missing knife."

I shrugged. "It's probably out there in the bay."

"Always a glass-half-empty gal." He smiled. "You want to know what I think?"

"No, but you're going to tell me anyway."

"I think he was at the graveyard around midnight, and we need to figure out why. He had blood on his shirt. The test results will tell us if it's his or Megan's. Maybe he lied to Corinne. Maybe he didn't." He shot me a look. "But he was at your house at four a.m., and he and Dmitry both lied about that. We need to find out what Anton was really doing between midnight and four a.m."

I inhaled the rank seaweed smell. "He had a migraine that night. Maybe he stayed in the van until he felt better."

"But why lie about that? And why are you defending him?" He narrowed his eyes at me. "You really want your daughter hanging out with someone who could be a killer?"

"That's the last thing I want. But I'm looking at all the angles because we have to get this right." He gave me a reluctant nod and sucked on the last of his cigarette. "You need to quit smoking," I said.

"You've only told me a thousand times." He handed it to me and said, "You know you want it." It had been years since I'd had a cigarette, but I did want it. I took a drag and handed it back. He looked from one end of the beach to other. "Anton drove somewhere during the time gap before he got to your house and doesn't want us to know where. Too bad the city has dragged their feet on putting up surveillance cameras here."

I felt rain in the air as we walked toward the red umbrella of a lifeguard chair that loomed ahead. "That used to be Bridget's chair," I said. "I sat in it once when she asked me to cover for her. Because she had to meet someone during her shift. I assumed it was Devon."

Brian raised a brow. "She left her post?"

"Yeah. It was strange. A few weeks before that, she'd insisted on teaching me how to save someone from drowning. She dove into the water. When I tried to save her, she grabbed me and dragged me down. She was so strong I was sure I was going to drown, but she let me go and we both shot up to the surface. She screamed at me for not doing what she taught me. I didn't blow my whistle. I didn't throw the ring. I didn't make sure I was safe before saving her. She shouted, 'People who are drowning can kill you.'"

"She's right about that." He stubbed out his cigarette.

I went on. "The day she left her post, she came back with the bruise on her cheek I told you about when you interviewed me." Brian nodded. "What she said next stuck with me. She made me promise that no matter what happened, I'd save myself first like she'd taught me, not to count on anyone else to do it. I assumed she was being melodramatic because she'd had a fight with Devon. Honestly, I was too jealous to ask what happened."

"Don't blame yourself. You were just a kid. And Bridget was tough, gave as good as she got." He paused. "We got called to her house a few times when her dad slapped her mom around, and her mom gave it right back. When you grow up with that, sometimes you end up in the same kind of relationship." He pushed the sand around with his toe. "We thought she might have fought with Devon at the beach, but he denied it. He had an alibi for the night she was killed so we stopped investigating."

He rubbed his chin. "It might not have been him at the beach. But that arrogant guy Vince told us about who came into the Hat Trick and talked about art and was rough with Bridget sure sounds like Devon. An artist with a violent side. Anton could be like that, too," he said. I tensed, remembering how Devon had told me that to be a real artist I had to follow wherever the darkness led me. I'd believed him—right up until when Bridget was murdered.

He gazed at the thunderclouds gathering on the horizon. "Let's head back to Dmitry's." My phone buzzed. Jeff. I told Brian to go ahead, I'd catch up with him later, and called Jeff back.

"What's up?" I said when he answered.

There was silence and then, "I have a production release tomorrow night. These damn companies, they think they own you. It could go all night, and I don't like leaving Corinne alone that long. You know teens."

"I do know teens," I said.

"I was hoping I could drop her off with you around six and pick her up in the morning?"

I waited a moment to make him sweat and said, "See you then." As the clouds grew even darker, I wanted to jump for joy. Because I was getting to see Corinne. I put my phone in my pocket and looked down Quincy Shore Drive, thinking about surveillance cameras.

Chapter Eighteen

BY THE TIME the rain started I'd gone past Dmitry's all the way to the intersection at the other end of the beach. From there Quincy Shore Drive went on toward Boston. If you turned left, you headed toward my neighborhood. If you turned right, the road ran past blue water running into brown marsh, the entrance to Starlight Bay, and ended up in Squantum, another peninsula that jutted into the sea like Hough's Neck, only more upscale.

I went into the Dunkin' Donuts across the street and ordered a frozen coffee. As I sipped the decadent sugary drink, I showed my badge to the manager and told him I was investigating a murder and needed his surveillance footage from last Friday night.

"You need a subpoena for that." He crossed his arms across his chest. "Rules are rules."

I fixed my gaze on his name tag. "Do you really want to be that person who let a killer get away because you were afraid to bend a rule, Fred?"

He huffed and uncrossed his arms. "Fine," he said. "But just this once."

* * *

Back at the station Brian and I went through the footage. Anton's van didn't appear in it, but something more interesting did. Around 1:00 a.m. a dark blue Honda Civic turned right and disappeared down the road toward Squantum. It was Megan's car, driven by a light-haired man.

We found the car off the road, behind some trees, stuck in the mud by the marsh. While the techs combed through it, Brian and I searched the long marsh grass for evidence but came up empty.

He lit a cigarette by the water's edge. "You think Anton ditched the car here?"

"Maybe."

He squinted at the sun rising over the mudflats. "My little brother, Kevin, and I used to dig clams here and smash them on the rocks."

"I used to collect them. My father told me the white shells were fairy wings."

"That's the difference between us. Your father helped you find pretty shells. Kevin and I smashed shells and my father smashed him. Your father taught you about art. Mine taught us the power of the closed fist."

I dug my hands into my pockets. "There's more than one way to screw up a life."

He glanced down the road. "We lived in the part of Squantum without an expensive water view, four kids in a five-room house. Kevin was trouble from the start, the kind of kid who made friends everywhere and grabbed at every shiny thing."

"Like you?" I said.

"Yeah, but I have impulse control, Sam."

"I know." I smiled. "But everyone here is your friend. They don't call you a freak because your father is a weird artist. Your father might be a bastard but he's one of them, like you. I never will be."

"Count your blessings. Being an insider here is overrated." He frowned. "Kevin was using by the time he hit high school. Dad would come home from work like a mad dog that broke his chain. My mom tried to keep the peace, but all it took was for the conversation to turn to Kevin and everything went to hell." His cigarette glowed red in the soft gray dawn.

"You tried to help him," I said. It never got easier hearing him tell this story.

"Yeah." He gave me a woeful glance. "I bailed him out of jail, got him into rehab over and over again. But you know how that went." I nodded. "I don't know what else I could have done. But it wasn't enough." He looked out over the marsh. "When he graduated high school, I told him I didn't want to find his body behind some Quickie Mart, that he should get clean and enlist. For once he listened." He paused. "When he came home on leave that Christmas, I shouldn't have let him out of my sight, but my mind was on other things. Isabel and I had just gotten engaged and I was over the moon. She was the most beautiful girl I'd ever seen." He eyed me. "I suppose I've told you that too many times."

"You have," I said.

He looked up at the amber-tinged clouds. "My mom had Christmas Eve dinner ready. We waited and waited while the roast got cold and finally went on without Kevin. Isabel said everything would be okay." He shook his head. "But everything was not okay. I still can't believe that foolish kid bought himself a present, a dose he wasn't used to, and that was it. Sometimes the world doesn't make any sense, Sam." He flicked his cigarette into the bronze water. "I didn't save my brother. But at least I saved you." I felt almost shy as his eyes skated over me.

We were about to leave when I glimpsed something bobbing in the reeds. We took off our shoes and waded over to a little beige Gucci knockoff bag with black trim and a thin black strap. It was open and some of the contents had spilled out. We knelt down in the shallow water. Brian retrieved a comb from the slippery mud and stood up with a groan. He muttered, "If I need surgery on this damn knee, I'll shoot myself." Not far from the bag, beneath a thin layer of silt, I found a phone in a mermaid case. The screen was smashed.

* * *

The next morning, George had croissants for us and coffee from the only Starbucks in Quincy. As I grabbed a chocolate croissant he said, "My sister, Casey, made those. She's really into baking lately."

Brian bit into a plain one. "This is amazing, George but . . ." He frowned at his dark roast. "You should have gone to Dunkies."

He smiled. "I thought you were ready for a new experience."

"Fine." Brian put his usual four Equals in his coffee along with a boatload of cream.

As I attempted to eat my croissant without getting chocolate all over myself, I told George about finding Megan's car and the bag and phone by the marsh.

"That's huge." He paused. "I have news, too. I went to Anton's father's exotic animal store. Vasily told me he had a Mexican Bluewing, but when he went to look for it, he couldn't find it. He claims he misplaced it."

"Go figure." Brian threw him a look. "Speaking of missing things, a knife like the one used on Megan happens to be missing from Dmitry's boy cave. He claims it was stolen. You should have seen the set, mother-of-pearl handles inlaid with lapis."

George gave him an appreciative nod and flicked croissant flakes from his fingers. "I also got the lab results on Anton's shirt. The blood on it is his and Megan's."

"Wow, way to bury the lede, George." Brian smiled. "He was at the scene and he lied about it. His father sold the same kind of butterfly that ended up on Megan, and it's missing. It would be nice to find the missing knife, but we don't need it. If the techs can connect Anton to Megan's car or the phone or bag, we got him."

George turned to me. "What about the email?"

"The techs can't trace it. And I can't see Anton writing it."

"It has to be a hoax," Brian said.

"It doesn't feel like a hoax to me." I pulled my ponytail tighter.

Brian sighed in frustration. "Why are you fighting this, Sam?"

I sucked in a breath. "I don't fucking know, okay?"

George apologized for having to go into Boston for a meeting. The head tech called later that afternoon and told us they were still checking out the bag and the phone. The interior of the car was wiped clean, but they found a bloody fingerprint matching Anton's on the outside door handle.

Brian laid his hand on mine. "Do you think we have enough evidence now?"

I forced a grim smile. "Let's do this."

*　*　*

Vasily Koslov came to the door wearing a black leather vest over his bare chest, black jeans, and engineer boots. When we told him we were there for Anton, he turned back toward the house and yelled, "You got company."

The place wasn't in bad shape considering the techs had tossed it the day before. Anton was stretched out on a mushroom-colored sectional. He wore a sleeveless basketball jersey and shorts. Shannon sat under his long hairy legs, clicking through channels on the flat-screen TV. She tugged her hot pink tank top down and pulled out from under him when she saw us.

Anton swung his legs onto the floor, stood up, smiled uneasily at me, and said, "Hello, Mrs. S." His smile vanished when I didn't reply. He looked from me to Brian and stammered, "What's going on?"

Brian stepped toward him saying, "You're under arrest for the murder of Megan O'Hare." He read him his rights and handcuffed him.

Irina gave us a fierce look. "We want a lawyer." Her voice rose. "Vasily, call a lawyer."

He frowned. "Lawyers cost money."

"If you can't afford one you can get a public defender," I told them.

Shannon focused her green eyes on me. "Why are you arresting him? You know he didn't do anything." She turned to Anton. "I'm calling my father. He'll take care of this."

Anton spoke calmly. "You don't need to. I'll be okay."

"If she's offering help, take it," Vasily said. "You've cost us enough already with your dance lessons because your mother thinks you're so talented." He glared at Irina.

She glared right back. "How can you say that about your own son?" She turned to Anton. "Take Shannon's help. You need a good lawyer."

He stared at his parents. "I don't need your help. You can get out of my life now."

As we ushered Anton into the squad car, Shannon stood on the cracked cement step talking on her phone. She turned to him and mouthed, *I love you.* A moment later, Irina came running out crying and begging us not to take him away. Brian went over to speak with her.

I turned round to Anton in the back seat. Light flickered from the silver crescent moon dangling from his ear. As he slouched, withdrawing into himself, I thought of the boy who had come to our house so many times and the dancer he'd become. Maybe it wasn't professional, but I leaned close to the mesh between us and said, "Anton, it might feel like all is lost but that doesn't have to be the case." He set his lips together grimly. "Remember how you told me when you make up a dance you start with nothing? It feels hopeless but then you see it. Can you tell me more about that?"

I didn't expect an answer, but after a pause he responded. "Sometimes music or a feeling grabs me and I swim down into the Black Sea. It's all darkness but then I see the dance."

"What do you mean by the Black Sea?"

He chewed his lip. "When I had my accident on that beach in Russia, I was dancing on a rock. Next thing I was on the sand, blood all over me, and that cut on my forehead. I didn't know how I ended up there and couldn't remember anything in between. Kind of like you."

He frowned as Shannon disappeared into Jay's silver Mercedes and turned back to me. "When I asked my mother what happened she said, 'It's all in the Black Sea.' I told her I didn't understand, and she said, 'Everything dies at the bottom of it. Nothing ever leaves. It's all there.'"

He leaned closer. "Part of me is always there. It's the place where my dancing comes from."

I thought of the painting I'd done of myself in the ravine under the black water, the things I couldn't remember. His pale eyes, luminous as a phosphorescent sea creature's, met mine. A touch so light as to be indescribable, no stronger than the breeze off the water, passed between us.

Chapter Nineteen

ANTON SAT OPPOSITE us, wearing a white T-shirt and jeans, in the steamy interview room with olive drab walls, broken AC, and a plastic fan valiantly trying to make a difference. He leaned forward with an imploring look. "Why did you arrest me, Mrs. S.? You know I'd never hurt anyone."

There was nothing I wanted more than to learn something from him that would change my mind, but I couldn't say that. "We followed the evidence," I said instead, keeping my voice steady. I asked if he wanted his parents or a lawyer present. He said no. I explained we were recording this and asked him to start by telling us what he'd done when he left Piney.

He pressed his hands on his knees. "I felt a migraine coming on, so I left before it got worse." He eyed me. "May I have some water, please?"

I got a plastic bottle from the vending machine in the hall and handed it to him. "What did you do next?"

"I drove to Dmitry's."

"What time was that?"

"Around midnight. We played video games and went to bed." He rubbed at a round scar near the rose tattooed on his wrist.

I stared at him with concern. "Are you sure? Because Corinne told me you were in my backyard at four a.m."

His gaze shifted away. "Sorry, I forgot that. Between everything I had to drink and the migraine I was pretty messed up. I fell asleep in the van and woke up when Shannon called and told me about Megan. She was crying, said it was horrible, and not to go near there. I didn't know what else to do, so I went to talk to Corinne and then I went to Dmitry's. I guess it was later than I thought."

"It was a lot later," I said.

"Yeah. My memory of that night is fuzzy." He rubbed his wrist some more.

"Let me refresh your memory." Brian put a photo of the shirt on the table. "This is the shirt you were wearing that night, the shirt Detective Star found in Corinne's closet. See right there?" He pushed his thumb down on a dark stain. "That's blood. How did it get there? Think hard. You want to get this one right."

Anton gave the photo a quick glance. "I tripped on the path and got a bloody nose."

Brian frowned. "How come you didn't mention the bloody nose earlier?"

He shrugged. "It was just a bloody nose."

"If that's all it was, why did you ask Corinne to get rid of your shirt?" Brian said.

"I didn't ask her to get rid of it. She gave me another shirt, and I forgot to bring mine home."

Brian smiled disdainfully. "Did you forget to tell us about being in the graveyard that night, too?"

"I wasn't in the graveyard. I left on the path that goes through the apartments."

Brian planted his elbows on the table. "Then how come Matt O'Hare says he saw you heading toward the graveyard?"

"He must have seen someone else."

Brian wiped sweat from his brow. "If you weren't there, how did Megan's blood get on your shirt?"

Anton looked grimly from me to Brian and took a long painful breath. "I ran into Matt and his friends when I was leaving Piney. He asked if I'd seen Megan. When I told him no, they got into it with me, called me a creeper like they always do, and shoved me down. That's how I got the bloody nose. I would have said something earlier, but Matt was drunk. He can be a jerk, but I'm not. I didn't want to get him and his friends in trouble. I took off through the graveyard . . ." He closed his hand around his water bottle. "I found Megan under the tree. When I checked her pulse and saw that she was dead, I ran."

Brian shook his head. "Let me get this straight. You didn't call 911. All you did was run away?"

He turned to me as if for support. "When I saw the butterfly on her, I knew the man who killed your friend was back and I had to get out of there I . . ." He paused. "I hugged Megan and left. That must be how her blood got on my shirt."

"You hugged her?" Brian said.

Anton looked up. "I hugged her goodbye."

Brian sighed. "Something else bothers me. You said you thought the man who killed Bridget was back, but he used a yellow butterfly. The one on Megan was blue."

"What difference does the color make?" Anton said.

Brian arched a brow. "A big difference. Corinne showed you a sketch of a blue butterfly before Megan was murdered, and the killer just happens to choose the same color? How do you explain that?"

Anton eyed me hopefully. "Maybe he saw the sketch somehow and it's his way of telling us he's back?"

Brian leaned in. "Did you send the email to let us know he was back, too?"

He appeared confused. "What email? I don't know what you're talking about."

"Of course you don't," Brian said. "If you thought the Butterfly Killer was back, why didn't you call the police or warn Shannon? Why did you wait for her to call you?"

Anton clenched his fists. "I'm not a fool. I knew what it looked like, me with my dead ex-girlfriend. I'm the one people always blame, the one they call the creeper. I didn't stand a chance, so I didn't say anything."

"Why do they call you that?" Brian pressed his arms on the table.

"I don't know." The tendons in his neck stood out as he clenched his fists tighter.

I leaned forward with a kind smile so he would trust me. "Anton," I said. "Everyone in Quincy loves Brian. He doesn't understand like we do what it's like to be different in this city, to always be on the outside looking in, to know that even when people act like you're included, they're pretending. But it doesn't have to be that way. I'll listen to you and if the evidence supports what you tell us, I'll make sure you're treated fairly." He rubbed some more at the scar on his wrist. I squinted and saw more round scars among the roses and flames tattooed on his arm. "What happened there?" I pointed to them.

He shrugged. "An accident. I fell asleep with a cigarette."

"Those don't look like accidents. Looks like someone put a cigarette out on you," I said.

"Nobody did. I'm careless."

Brian gave his arm a look. "Boy, you're covered with scars."

Anton flashed me a glance. "Just like you Mrs. S."

"The person who gave me my scars was a killer." I held his eyes in mine. "Are you sure you can't tell us who gave you those scars?"

"It was an accident," he said again.

"What happened next?" I asked.

"I drove to see Corinne."

"But you told us you left Piney around midnight, and you didn't get to our house until around four a.m. What were you doing all that time?"

He glanced away. "I rested until my headache was gone and then I drove around a while."

Brian shook his head in disgust. "Come on, you weren't driving around. You were ditching Megan's car. We found your bloody fingerprint in it."

He exhaled slowly. "When I was going to the van, I noticed her car in the lot by creek. I might have touched it, but I didn't drive it anywhere."

Brian waited a beat. "You saw Megan's car in a parking lot and all you did was touch it? You didn't tell anyone you'd found it? You really expect us to believe that? Do you think we're stupid?"

"I don't think you're stupid. My head was killing me. I wasn't thinking straight."

"Jesus, you have an explanation for everything." Brian pulled out the photo we'd doctored from a picture of a knife we'd found online. "Have you seen this before?"

He studied it. "Looks like one of Dmitry's knives."

"It's not just any one of his knives, is it?"

Anton's eyes rounded. "You found the one that was stolen?"

Brian shook his head slowly. "No, but you know it wasn't stolen. It's the knife you used to cut up your pretty ex-girlfriend."

"I didn't cut Megan up. How can you even say that?"

"Anton, this is the time to tell us where the stolen knife is, because we're going to find it and then things will get even worse for you."

Anton rolled his neck from side to side. "I have no idea where it is."

Brian let that settle and went on. "You and Dmitry like playing with knives. Did Megan like it, too? Did it turn you on, cutting her up?"

Anton set his mouth in a hard line. "We threw the knives. No one got hurt and I did not cut her up."

"Did she break up with you because she didn't want to play those games anymore?"

He glared. "She didn't break up with me. I broke up with her."

Brian tapped his fingers on the table. "Really? That's not what her mother says."

"Her mother doesn't know everything. I broke up with her because I was in love with Shannon."

Brian gave him a withering look. "Do you and Shannon play with knives, too? How about we ask her?"

"Leave her out of this." Anton's voice rose.

Brian smiled. "We're not leaving her out of this. We're going to ask her why she's covering for you. And when she hears what you've done, she's going to dump you." Anton lunged across the table toward him but Brian grabbed him by his shirt. "I'm not some little girl you can push around. Is that what happened? Megan pissed you off and you shoved her, and she hit her head." He flung him back down. "We got you lying. We got your bloody shirt. We got the car." He leaned forward. "And there's a blue butterfly missing from your father's store. How do you explain that?"

"Someone stole it like they stole the knife." He picked at the label on the water bottle.

"Anton," I said sharply. "You understand what could happen to you, don't you? Life in prison. Stuck in a room smaller than your bedroom at home for the rest of your life. The way things look, you murdered her. But if you tell us the truth, things could go easier for you." I kept my eyes on him. "Was it an accident and you didn't mean to kill her? Or maybe the person who gave you those scars did it, and you're covering for them?"

"I didn't do it. I'm not covering for anyone," he said.

"Detective Star is one of the only friends you got left in this world. You should listen to her," Brian said.

"Stop. Fucking stop." Anton buried his face in his hands, sobbing. The door to the interview room opened and his public defender stepped in, leaned close to him, and said, "Don't say anything else. We're done here."

Chapter Twenty

I WAS LOOKING forward to having Corinne stay with me while Jeff was working, but her accusations spilled out in a tear-filled torrent as soon as we sat down to eat our Thai takeout for dinner. She insisted Anton wasn't a killer. I shouldn't have arrested him. She twisted her shirt in her hands. "Shannon says the Butterfly Killer did it. Everyone does."

"The Butterfly Killer has nothing to do with this." I kept my voice even.

She glared at me. "You don't know everything."

"Corinne, you need to face reality." It was the wrong thing to say to a teenage girl under any circumstance, let alone this one. "I understand this is painful for you," I said. "It's painful for me, too, but we had no choice. The evidence points to Anton."

She turned her tearstained face my way. "I'll find new evidence if you need it."

A chill went through me. "That's my job, not yours. There's nothing more you can do for him." I reached for her hand, but she wrenched it away.

"Why can't I have a normal mother who doesn't arrest my friends?" she said and pounded upstairs sobbing. The hurt from her words churned inside me as I ate. But Anton couldn't come anywhere near her now, and I had to keep it that way.

I gave Corinne an hour or so to cry it out and tapped gently on her door. She let me in with a disapproving glare.

Ginger was splayed on Corinne's blue spread patterned with dancers and doves. I sat down next to her. "I'm sorry you have to go through this," I said.

Corinne turned from observing her tear-blotched face in the mirror over her dresser. "Anton's my friend. He couldn't have killed Megan."

I kept my eyes on her. "It's hard to lose a friend to murder, even harder to learn another friend may have done it. I like Anton. But the evidence tells a story. It might not be the whole story. We might find something that tells a different one. But it's the story we have so far, and it contains enough evidence that we had to arrest him. I can't change that, but I promise to do everything I can to get to the truth of what happened to Megan."

She fiddled with a shirt button, studying me. "You really will, Mom?"

"I will," I said. Technically this wasn't entirely under my control, but she was my daughter, my Corinne, and I had to say what she needed to hear.

"Do you think he could be innocent?" she asked.

"It's possible." Her gray-green eyes met mine and I pulled her in for a hug. We stayed like that a moment, and I felt how far away I had been from her, and how much she needed me to be there for her now. Then she gathered my hair in her hands and fastened it back with a tortoiseshell clip from a basket on her dresser. "That looks so much better," she said. As we stood in front of the mirror, something in the room shifted ever so slightly and I heard Bridget's husky voice in my ear. "These will look as nice as my laurel crown," she was saying as she pulled back the loose strands with blue clips. I could see them—little butterfly clips, smaller than Corinne's tortoiseshell one. You squeezed the plastic wings together and they opened up. They clamped shut when you let them go.

* * *

Jeff was late picking her up the next day. He apologized, saying things had taken longer than expected because they had to back out the production release. There was a problem in his recursive routine, some edge case that hadn't gotten tested, and he hadn't figured it out yet. He and Corinne were about to leave when the news of Anton's arrest came on the TV. A clip of him dancing in the Whispers video flashed across the screen, as the announcer said *Wish Upon a Dancer* had dropped him and Shannon from the auditions. As Corinne fought back tears, I realized how easily the fragile connection I'd forged with her could be broken.

* * *

That afternoon at the groundbreaking ceremony for the new Quincy project, Max Delaney gave a stiff speech, snipped the yellow ribbon, and poured champagne onto the torn-up municipal parking lot from which his glittering condos would rise.

"Max Delaney could make the discovery of extraterrestrial life boring," I said in the incident room later that day.

"I've heard he's paying for a fancy lawyer for Anton," Brian said.

"Shannon gets whatever she wants." George smiled as he held out a bag of salted pumpkin seeds.

"No thank you. I'm not a bird." Brian snapped.

I helped myself to some and chewed them slowly, thinking about how I'd told Corinne I'd do everything I could to get to the truth. The timing wasn't great. They'd probably think I'd gone off the deep end … But I had to tell them. "I figured out the little butterflies reference in the email," I said. Brian and George turned my way. "Last night while I was with Corinne, I remembered Bridget putting these things we called little butterfly clips in my hair when we were getting ready for Devon's party. They were popular then."

"There were no clips in your hair when I found you," Brian said.

"The killer probably took them out." I gave him a firm look. "Brian, I remembered them and that means the person who sent the email knew me back then. He could be Bridget's killer and could be working with Anton." I paused. "Or Anton could be innocent."

George leaned in. "Did you ever mention the clips to your daughter?"

My stomach knotted. "I don't know. Maybe."

"She could have told Anton. Or . . ." He gave me a concerned look. "Are you sure it's a real memory?"

His question nearly unraveled me, but I plowed ahead. "It's possible it's not real. But what if it is? Don't you think we should look into that?"

"Nothing's off the table," Brian said. "But right now let's concentrate on building a case against Anton. Here's how I see it. He left the blue butterfly on Megan so people would think the old killer was back. But the old killer used a yellow one. Anton chose blue, because he saw it in the sketch Corinne showed him. He stole a knife from Dmitry and a blue butterfly from his father's store. He killed Megan sometime on Friday while he was working for his father. Maybe he called her from the burner phone. He dumped her body at the graveyard, picked up Shannon, hung out on Piney, and returned to the scene of the crime for some reason and got her blood on his shirt. He ditched her car and went to Corinne's. He changed his shirt and went to Dmitry's. What do you think?"

Compared to this overwhelming evidence, the little butterflies felt ridiculous. "It makes sense," I said.

George turned to me. "I'm glad you've seen the light."

"Thanks for believing in me, kids," Brian said as he dug his hands in his pockets. "Chief invited us to celebrate the arrest over at Finnegan's Wake Saturday night. Make an appearance."

* * *

Finnegan's Wake was as lively as ever on a Saturday night. Half the force was there. My green silk shirt clung to me like a soft breeze, my jeans fit just right, and I was sipping an old fashioned. I was feeling good. Alice Crane came over in a pleated plaid skirt and white blouse. Her pigtails completed the Catholic schoolgirl look, but I didn't hate it. She raised her martini. "Congratulations on arresting the dancer. Not surprised it turned out to be the ex."

"Nothing is certain yet. But he's not getting out anytime soon. Bail's set at half a million." I clinked my glass against hers, trying to convince myself I wasn't worried about him.

"At least celebrate the moment with something special for you, other than that." Alice nodded at my glass. "I'd still like to do that article with your paintings."

I lowered my drink, a near perfect old fashioned except for the anemic-looking mangled maraschino cherries at the bottom. "Not interested."

George and Brian sidled up. George was wearing a blue-and-white pinstripe shirt—a radical look for him. He stepped forward and said, "Drinks on me. What'll it be?"

"Another one of these." I pointed to my old-fashioned.

"I'll have what Sam's having, only make it a double," Brian said. He waved at Mary Ann who was seated at a nearby table. She pushed her dark brown hair behind her ear and gave him a lovely smile.

Alice turned to George. "Another martini, please, very dirty."

George came back with the drinks a few minutes later. He narrowed his eyes at Alice's martini as he handed it to her and said, "Tell me. Is it dirty enough?"

She chewed on the olive contemplatively and held out the glass. "Have a sip and find out for yourself."

He shook his head. "I don't drink those. I like my vodka plain, on ice."

"Maybe you could learn to like them." She licked her lip. "I'd love to hear more of your thoughts on the girl buried in cement."

George eyed her dispassionately. "There's a picture of her in a Catholic school uniform, kind of like what you have on only she wasn't pretending to be a schoolgirl. She actually went to Catholic school. She was wearing these little round glasses. The big grin on her face gave no clue her stepfather, Junior's right-hand man, was assaulting her. A few years later she was on the streets, taking drugs, getting into trouble, and talking too much. That was a problem for her stepfather and Junior. They took care of her—buried, silenced her, whatever you want to call it." He straightened. "Law enforcement protected them because their information was more important than a little girl in round glasses. The cover-up went all the way up the chain, but a few of us fought back. So, there's your silencing myth. Only it's not a myth. It's real."

Alice pressed her lips to the rim of her glass. "We really should talk more about this sometime."

"Call me," he said and made an excuse about having to go find the chief and ditched us.

Brian rested his hand on my shoulder. "Mary Ann's giving me the evil eye so I must leave you two as well."

Alice smiled and asked me to come to the restroom with her.

*　*　*

As I stood in front of the mirror, pulling my long dark hair into a ponytail, I caught her hungry eyes sneaking a look at the scar on my shoulder. "Like what you see?"

She shrugged. "You have nice hair."

"It's okay if you were staring. I'm used to it." I waited for her to pitch her article again, but she leaned over the sink, ran red lipstick over her soft mouth, and asked if George had a girlfriend. I told her not that I knew of.

"Good, 'cause I think he's sweet."

"Sweet is not a word I'd use for George," I said. "Stickler maybe, know-it-all, rule follower, dogged, kind of a dork." I eyed her. "Though his heart's in the right place."

Alice said, "In other words, better than most guys," and we both laughed. It felt good having her beside me as if we were any two girls getting drunk and talking about a guy. I was applying peach lipstick when I heard a buzz, like a silver-tongued mosquito.

The email came from a different address this time.

Sleek, smooth, and white as snow. How clumsily her hoof writes her name in the sand. How greedily she devours the apple from my hand. Candy apple red, understand?

I fumbled my lipstick back into my bag, bolted past Alice to where Brian sat with Mary Ann. I tapped him on the shoulder and said, "Hey."

He turned to me. "What's going on?"

"I need you. Now."

Mary Ann's pretty smile turned sour. He apologized and followed me to a table where George sat nursing his vodka, alone.

"I got another email." I handed them my phone.

Brian's frown deepened and he said, "Either some bastard's messing with us, or we've got a problem."

Chapter
Twenty-One

WE STAYED AT the station past midnight checking missing persons reports, hoping to find his next victim while she was still alive. Nothing fit. I called Jeff and was relieved to learn Corinne was home and her friends were home, too. When we spoke to Anton the next day, all he did was plead with us to keep Shannon safe. The techs had no more luck tracing this email than the last one.

"There has to be a clue in this somewhere," I said as I brought the email up on my phone. I showed it to George and Brian again. "It's the story of Io. He's never done that myth before."

"Io?" Brian said.

I gave him the SparkNotes version. "Io, the daughter of a river god, is raped by Zeus the god of all gods, and Zeus turns her into a white heifer, so his jealous wife won't know he was screwing around." I chewed on my nail. "If we don't figure this out soon, another girl could end up dead."

Brian peered over my shoulder. "Clue's always near the end, right?"

"Yeah, it has to be the apple, but I don't get it," I said.

George peered over my shoulder, too. "Does 'candy apple red' mean anything to you?"

"Not that I remember." I looked at the email about Megan again.

It described her in red, like her dance costume, with black mirror eyes, like those shiny dark eyes in the painting of her in her living room—details from her life. I'd seen apples somewhere recently, too, and not in the grocery store. My throat constricted. "The wallpaper in Nina's kitchen has apples on it."

I called Nina's mother, Miranda. When she told me Nina was out with Shannon and Nick, I sighed with relief, but she called back a few minutes later. Nina wasn't answering her phone. She'd called Nick and he and Shannon hadn't seen her. I told her we were on our way.

Miranda stood on her front steps with her husband, Gabe, her hands tucked in the sleeves of a thin sweater she didn't need in this heat. She explained she had spent the day painting the guest room upstairs. Gabe had been golfing. That morning Nina had told her she was meeting Nick and Shannon near the beach for lunch. She didn't hear her leave, but the AC was on, it was hard to hear anything. She didn't worry until I called. Brian reassured them we'd search the area out of an excess of caution, but Nina would probably walk in any minute.

The only road in and out of Nina's neighborhood forked into two roads that curved around and met in the middle—Cedar (Nina's street) and Skyline Road. You generally didn't end up here by accident. Someone would notice a person or car that didn't belong. Officers were canvassing the neighborhood, but so far no one had seen anything unusual.

We met up with Shannon and Nick at the beach. She told us Nina was supposed to meet them at the Clam Shack, but she wasn't surprised when Nina didn't show up. Nina had been moody lately. Nick gave us an agonized look as he said he thought Nina was mad at him for something he'd done, though he had no idea what. Then Shannon started to cry, and we told them to let us know if they heard from her.

No one at the Clam Shack recalled seeing Nina, though they had seen Shannon and Nick. We joined George and the other officers searching the Blue Hills. It was past two a.m. when Brian and I returned to her house empty-handed. I thought of Nina's face pressed against the window a few days ago, her sitting on the sill in Corinne's room, a cigarette between her pale lips. Nina wasn't as delicate as she appeared, but compared to *him* she was as fragile as the fuzz you blow off a dandelion.

"Time to call it a night." Brian looked as exhausted as I felt, but I wasn't ready to leave.

"You go along," I said. "I'll poke around here a little more."

He drew himself up. "Go home and get some sleep. That's an order."

"I'm not giving up yet. He can't have her. I won't let him." I folded my arms across my chest.

"We've done everything we can. They're bringing in search dogs. If they find anything we'll come back."

"We leave now, it's over. You know that." I dug my heels into the ground. "She could be in any one of these houses. She could still be alive."

Brian pushed his sweaty hair from his forehead. "We already talked to everyone who lives around here. No one saw a thing."

I glared at him. "You found me alive when everyone else had given up. I'm not giving up now."

Brian sighed. "I'll cruise down Cedar again. You take Skyline. You see anything suspicious, call me before you go in."

I followed Cedar up a sharp curve to where it met Skyline Road. Some of the houses here had views all the way down to the woods across from Nina's house. Whoever had written the apple line in the email had to be a friend or someone who'd seen the inside of her kitchen some other way. I went into the yards of the houses behind Nina's to see if any of them had a view of her kitchen. A small Cape with a swing set and playhouse in the backyard had a view obscured by trees. There was a run-down Colonial next to it with a towering pink rhododendron in the front yard. I walked down the long driveway that wrapped around behind it. Sure enough, you could see into her kitchen from there. With binoculars you might be able to see the pattern on the wallpaper.

When I called Brian to give him the address, he told me officers had already checked the place; it was vacant. I told him I was going to double check. He said to wait until he got there. He was on his way. But if Nina was in there, every second counted. The door was locked. I took the small screwdriver and lock pick I kept in a pouch on my belt and got the door open. I stopped in the foyer, listening. It was your classic center-entrance Colonial, stairs up the middle. Light from a streetlight illuminated a living room on one side, sparsely furnished with a couch, worn oriental rug, and two wing chairs. The dining room on the other side was empty. The kitchen at the back was, too.

I paused on the second-floor landing. Not a sound. I turned a black porcelain knob and walked into a bedroom with my gun raised. I opened a closet door, bare except for rusty hangers. A cool breeze teased the back of my neck, and I turned. A window was open. Through it I could see Nina's backyard, the kitchen, and into the upstairs bedrooms—the perfect spot for watching and waiting for the right moment to grab her. I went through the other bedrooms and checked the attic. Empty, like the officers had said.

Sticky cobwebs clung to me as I walked down the basement stairs past granite walls and a window cloudy with dust. I preferred my basements finished, with a wet bar and a flat-screen TV. At the bottom of the stairs it felt like electrical charges were misfiring in my brain. I sometimes felt that way before an episode. But this time I sensed his presence, was certain he'd been here. Something white flashed at the corner of my eye. A Mardi Gras mask? As I whipped around, the room disintegrated into black flecks and I gritted my teeth—not now. A knife sliced an arm open. Blood sprayed every-where.

The black tide left me gasping for breath. When the room reas-sembled, the mask was nothing but a white sun hat hanging on a hook. I searched the rest of the cellar. No one. I went out through a back door and stared up at the stars sprayed across the sky. "Let me save her," I whispered, "you owe me that much."

I walked to the edge of the overgrown backyard and looked down into Nina's yard. Her windows glowed yellow in the darkness. There was a faint rustling of leaves, nothing else. No one in the toolshed to the right of the abandoned house. But as I latched the wooden door, I caught sight of a neglected greenhouse almost hidden by the tall grass and weeds.

The air inside was moist as a steam bath. With the flashlight from my phone, I made out glass walls filmed with moss. Vines and plants crawled over wooden tables and crept across the floor. I moved forward cautiously. He could be crouching in the shadows. He could be anywhere. A leaf tickled my ankle and I stiffened.

She was on a vine-covered table, beneath a blanket of white rose petals.

I put on gloves, pushed the petals aside, and felt for a pulse—nothing. A butterfly with iridescent wings that looked green from one angle, black from another, rested on the deep gash in her throat. She was naked, her body spray-painted white. An apple painted glossy red was shoved in her mouth. It felt like it was made of stone. Her lips and cheeks were smeared with glossy red, too. The word COW was carved into her chest, and her ankles and feet were bound with black electrical tape—like hooves.

A whisper of night air came in followed by footfalls on the damp leaves. I turned toward Brian. His grim face met mine.

"The paint on her mouth looks like some kind of high-gloss enamel," I said and leaned closer. Black horns protruded from her spray-painted hair. I choked back the scream rising inside me. I was supposed to save Nina, but this man had mutilated her, humiliated her, and made her look like a monster. The strong yet delicate girl was gone.

Chapter
Twenty-Two

AS I GLANCED down the quiet street, I braced myself for the conversation I was about to have and rang the bell. Jeff and Corinne were seated at the card table eating waffles Jeff had made—his way of coping with this nightmare. He insisted on making me one. I forced myself to take a bite as I filled them in on what I could about Nina's murder. It wasn't much more than what they'd already heard on the news, which was for the best. When I finished, Jeff flung his arms out exclaiming, "This is awful. That poor girl," and knocked his waffles onto the floor. Corinne's eyes widened in alarm as he wiped up the sticky mess with paper towels while shouting about what a terrible world this was and how we had to do something, or she could be next. He almost never lost it like this. Even Ginger lost her cool and was barking her head off.

After I helped him clean up, I said, "I'm going to catch whoever did this. Until then I'm putting a police detail out front, and Corinne shouldn't go anywhere alone." She stared back at me in horror. I took her hand and held it, unable to find any words to make this better. The blue-violet polish on her perfectly manicured nails gleamed. "What color is that?" I asked as I let her hand go.

"Jazzberry." She gave me a puzzled look. "Mom, why are you asking me about nail polish now?"

I told her I just liked it, glanced at my phone, and said I was sorry but I had to get back to the scene. I assured them everything would be okay. "Dear god, I hope you're right," Jeff said. I did, too.

I met Brian in front of the house where we'd found Nina. He told me the ninety-year-old owner had passed away three years ago, and her one living relative had paid no attention to the house. Now it was the old, abandoned house everyone complained about and a place neighborhood kids broke into so they could drink. His shoulders fell as he went on. "Janine says the cut on Nina's neck was what killed her. She bled to death, which means she wasn't murdered here. There would have been more blood at the scene if she had been." He dug his hands into his pockets. "Janine hasn't determined the time of death yet. But we know Nina was murdered sometime between Saturday morning when her mother last saw her and just after two a.m. when you found her. The way I see it, he either left her body here before we started looking for her and nobody noticed the greenhouse, or he waited until after dark and left her there while we were out searching in the Blue Hills."

I hesitated and added, "I thought I saw a Mardi Gras mask when I was in the cellar. Turned out to be a hat. It sounds crazy, but I had a feeling the man who abducted me had been there not long before I was."

He gave me a probing glance. "It's not crazy. Something here could have sparked your memories of that other time. Or maybe he really was here. But we need concrete evidence to find him." He was right. For all my feelings, I hadn't saved Nina. He gestured to the techs scouring the scene. "They determined it was a marble apple. That's something."

"It is." I pressed my feet into the soft ground "I'm pretty sure the killer painted Nina and the apple with nail polish." I put on gloves. "Let's take another look around."

The air smelled of rotting weeds and death as we stepped into the murky twilight of the greenhouse. There was a red drop on the edge of the table where Nina's body had been placed and another on the dirty floor below. I ran my finger over the smooth surface. It felt like polish. I brought up the crime scene photos on my phone. Her nails were the same shade of red. A chill went through me, picturing him painting them with the tiny brush that came with the polish. I turned to Brian, "He killed her someplace else but added some last touches to his masterpiece here and he was sloppy." As we searched through the decaying overgrown plants, something gleamed beneath a monstrous succulent. I knelt down and pulled a bottle of polish from the moist soil.

I held it up. "Candy apple red, like in the email." I felt my throat closing, coughed to force air down as I said, "From Glamora. It's a chain. There's one in the mall. Corinne and her friends love it."

"George can confirm if it's the same type of polish used on her. With any luck we'll get a fingerprint from the bottle, too." He loosened his collar. "Discarding the polish so near the scene is a careless move."

"Maybe he wants us to find him this time," I said. "Every artist wants credit for his work."

* * *

That night I woke from a nightmare. Bridget with her shiny red lipstick mouth, pink powder on her face, and bouncy blond hair floated toward me like a parade balloon. When she got too close, I screamed and sat bolt upright in bed.

I tossed and turned but I couldn't get the nightmare of Nina in the greenhouse and the one of Bridget out of my head. Jeff cooked to deal with stress, but I was no cook. I popped a Xanax, and watched a baking show on TV to distract myself, but like a black hole, my past pulled me right back in.

Chapter
Twenty-Three

Before
June 1994

THE WORLD WAS drowning in green when Bridget came back into my life. I was heading to the Crust and Crumb café after school for an iced coffee when she came up to me. It was now June, and we hadn't spoken since Debbie Duggan ODed in February. She hiked up her flares and said, "Can I get a coffee with you?"

I eyed her warily. "Sure."

She ordered a frozen mocha and I got one, too. We sat down at a round metal table. "Sorry for being such a ghost." She fiddled with the lace strap of her peach crop top and smiled. "You're glowing."

I touched my cheek. Did it show? "I met someone."

Her eyes widened. "Has he got a name?"

I hesitated. "Devon."

She dipped her finger in the whipped cream. "How did you meet him?"

I leaned forward. "He studies art with my father and he's teaching me how to find my artistic vision." She rolled her eyes, but I went on. "He told me to paint landscapes with violence in them. I did one based on the myth of the sirens who lure sailors to their deaths, only in mine a sexy mermaid sinks a Cadillac with a gangster in it beneath the scummy green water of a quarry."

"He can hang out down there with the girls he murdered." She set her lips together. "Is Devon teaching you other things. too?"

A hot flush came to my cheeks. My first kiss with Devon had been followed by more, but we never went further than that. "Yeah, but we're going slow because I'm sixteen and he's twenty."

"That's dumb," she said. "I've dated guys older than twenty."

I stared at my wilting whipped cream. "I'm sure you have. How's your friend from Nostalgia?"

A shadow crossed her face. "That's over."

"Too bad. He was cute." I sucked up the chocolate syrup on the side of my glass with my straw. "Hard to believe the last time we were here was Christmas. You seemed so happy."

"Yeah." She glanced away.

In the past, I wouldn't have said more, but I couldn't let this go. "All these months I thought you hated me."

"I don't hate you. I was helping Barb plan her wedding." She looked away uneasily. "She didn't want you around."

"And you went along." I put a five on the table. "I'm out of here. Keep the change."

"Don't." She put her hand on mine. "We just thought you'd be bored because seriously, Sam, you're not really into picking out china patterns." She examined my crow tattoo. "I like that. It suits you."

I glared, not wanting to give her the satisfaction of winning me over that easily. "It fits my mood. Until I met Devon, all I wanted to do was fly away."

"I haven't been in a good place, either." She tore at her napkin with the point of her red polished nail. "I did something terrible."

That got my attention. "What?"

She sucked on her lip. "I don't want to talk about it."

I pressed my chin on my hand and stared. "You brought it up. I think you do."

She shredded her napkin some more. "Remember when Debbie Duggan died?"

I tipped my face to the side. "That was so sad. I'm sorry for not going to her memorial, but I had the worst cold."

Bridget lowered her voice. "I was with her the night she overdosed." She glanced anxiously around the café. "When I was little and my dad beat on my mom, I used to hide in my room and pretend to be asleep so he wouldn't come after me. That's how I saved myself. After Debbie took all those pills, she looked so peaceful . . ." She ran a finger over her lip. "I thought I was saving her from this awful world by letting her sleep. But then, no matter how many times I tried, I couldn't wake her up, and I got scared and left her. I didn't save her, Sam. She died. Everyone calls me a hero for saving that boy, but I don't save people. I hurt them."

I'd heard stories of friends who ran out on friends when they overdosed, because they didn't want to get in trouble. I let her suffer a moment before saying, "Debbie was the one who took the drugs. You can't blame yourself for that."

"Yeah." As if a switch had flipped, her lips parted in a smile. "I'd love to meet this Devon guy who's got you all hot and bothered."

"My dad's doing a demo for his students at our house later. Devon will be there. If you don't mind watching, you can come."

*　*　*

My father gave the demo in his studio. We pulled up chairs around a table with a bowl of cherries on it. Bridget stared at her nails as he showed me, Devon, and a few of his other students how to build up a glossy surface with oil paint. He described each brushstroke as a soft caress, lovingly creating translucent layer upon layer of color. Then we each did our own painting of cherries. My father said to be original and make the cherries shine. Devon did a painting of blood spatter as cherries. Another guy did a night sky with cherries for stars. They talked over each other as they discussed "the surrealistic still life." When I got frustrated with my painting of a black cat with cherries for eyes, my father told me to slow down, that it took a lot of patience to create a lustrous crimson. I didn't listen and ended up with red paint on my face—though my painting wasn't bad. When we were through, Devon dipped a rag in turpentine. I held my breath so I wouldn't inhale the noxious fumes as he rubbed the paint off my cheek.

Bridget came up behind us, startling me as she said, "She's a slob. And you must be Devon. I'm Bridget."

He brushed a blond curl from his wide forehead. "You're even more beautiful than Sam led me to believe."

"Come on. I told my father we'd make salad for dinner." I nudged her but she didn't move.

He went on. "How come you didn't do a painting?"

She smirked. "I'm not talented like Sam. I only paint my nails."

He studied her fingers and said, "Cherry red?"

She shook her head. "Candy apple."

He smiled slowly. "I'd say you achieved a perfect shine."

* * *

"No offense, but Devon seems pretty full of himself," Bridget said as we smoked a joint in my backyard. I sighed with relief that she was already kicking him off his pedestal. In the kitchen as we made the salad, she put a lettuce leaf on her head and did a model's walk across the room. We laughed as if this was the funniest thing in the world. I was glad to have her back in my life.

As I bit into a slice of pepperoni pizza, my father announced a contest to do a painting of a myth with a new twist. He turned to Bridget. "We have a goddess right here if anyone needs inspiration." I stiffened.

He went on to tell us that the Epoch Gallery in New York would offer the winning artist a show. He'd had a show there himself once. He pointed to his painting of my mother as Persephone as an example of what they'd like. He blinked away a tear. "She's still my muse."

Devon smiled at Bridget. "You can be my muse," he said, and there went my appetite.

I frowned. "I'm going to do Persephone for the contest."

My father gave me a troubled look. "I don't think that's a good idea."

"I don't care." I folded my arms across my chest. Everyone was silent. No one crossed my father—ever.

"You're welcome to try," he finally said. "But right now, please get us some dessert from the kitchen." I grabbed a bowl of leftover cherries from the fridge and put it on the table. I ate cherry after cherry and piled the pits on my napkin. When no one was looking, I filled a glass with wine and sank lower and lower in my seat as I drank it down.

I told Bridget I wanted to leave and find something else to do. She said, "In a minute," and cleared the table the way she always did at her house. Devon followed her into the kitchen. As I carried the bowl of cherries in, I paused in the doorway. She was leaning back with her palms on the counter, and he stood in front of her. I overheard him say, "I'd love to paint you for the contest."

"Oh my god, I'd be honored," she said in her husky voice. As he held her hand to his lips and kissed each finger, all the breath went out of me. Only my fear of being discovered kept me from throwing every single last cherry at them.

It felt like the end of the world, but in the next few weeks I still sat on the beach with her while she covered her lifeguard shift. We still went out on Friday nights with friends sometimes, but she was with Devon a lot. She told me she'd given him the idea to paint her as Daphne for the contest.

One day I went along when she posed for him in the small apartment he shared with another student. I sat down on a couch that looked like he'd pulled it off the street on trash day and propped my feet on the glass coffee table. I flipped through an art magazine, but I was too curious to concentrate. I hovered in the doorway to the bedroom he also used as a studio, transfixed as he raised her arms over her head and pushed the loose neck of her dress down so you could see her breasts. As he whispered, "Your skin is like silk," I coughed. "Samantha, leave, now," he said. His voice cut through me. He didn't want me there. He didn't want me at all.

Bridget took me aside later. She had this dreamy look as she said, "When I pose for him, it's like he's touching me all over, my boobs, my stomach, between my legs." I rolled my eyes. Bridget always gave too much information. "It's the most beautiful feeling. He makes me shine."

I winced. "Why are you telling me this?"

She gave me a sleepy smile. "Because someday you'll feel this way about someone, too." She'd conveniently forgotten how I felt about Devon. But I focused on what she'd just said about me meeting someone new rather than on her betrayal. As the day to submit to the contest approached, I worked furiously on my painting. I might not have won at love, but I was determined to win at art.

Chapter
Twenty-Four

BRIAN GRIMACED AS he sipped the coffee I'd gotten from Starbucks. "They didn't have Equals, but I added four Splendas. Give it a chance," I said.

He took another sip, still grimacing. "We now have a new murder. It's similar to Megan's murder but obviously not the same killer."

"Does this mean you don't think the two cases are related?" I asked.

"No, it means everything just got harder. We need to look for a connection to Megan's murder, but Nina's killer is still out there. We have to find him first." He put another Splenda in his coffee and frowned. "It still tastes like paint thinner, Sam."

"I like it," George said and turned to me. "The polish on Nina and the apple is a match to the bottle of Glamora candy apple red you found. We checked it for prints. No hits in the system." He sipped his coffee, no sugar or cream, nothing but darkness. "But Nina's crime scene is more elaborately arranged than Megan's. It suggests the work of a sadistic, controlling killer similar to Bridget's."

Brian looked up. "Good to know, but we need an actual clue."

"I might have one," I said. "Bridget used candy apple red nail polish, and Devon knew about it. We should look at him for this."

"You have proof of that?" Brian asked. I told him it was a memory. He let go a long breath. "We need more than a memory, Sam."

George's dark eyes bored into me. "Memory is fallible. We can change our own memories without even knowing it which means we can't trust them. We need physical evidence that ties Devon to the crime."

"There are things I don't remember, but the things I do remember are clues. I use my intuition to follow them like an artist, not a robot. That's what works for me." I glared at George. "I'll start by looking at the evidence we already have: the nail polish and the marble apple. I'll find something."

"In the meantime," Brian said, "George and I will see if Nina's parents know anything about the polish."

After they left, I brought up a photo on my laptop of the red marble apple from the crime scene. It was as lustrous as the cherries we had painted in my father's studio. The hurt from Devon was still like a stone lodged in my throat, but George was right about one thing. I needed more than a memory. As I examined the photo of the apple, I remembered how many layers of paint it had taken to make the cherries shine. Polish was streakier than paint. When I did my nails, it was frustrating how many times I had to go back over them. It would take a ton of polish to cover a marble apple. I needed to look for customers who bought more than one bottle.

I created a list of all the Glamoras in the US and began calling them for information on customers who bought candy apple red. An hour later, I hit pay dirt—someone bought a lot of bottles at a Glamora in a mall in Portland, Maine. Devon lived not far from there in Livingston, Maine.

I used to search for news of him obsessively, at first at the library, and then on the internet. Now I only googled him once in a while, hoping for bad news, his untimely death, a scathing review of his paintings, but he was maddeningly successful. It didn't take me long to find a recent exhibit he'd had near Livingston. He still painted mythological scenes with a heavy hand, women as broken statues—a limb here, a torso there, flowers blossoming from broken skulls like macabre planters. In one painting, a young woman pressed her face through a silver stocking. Everything was monochrome except for her glossy red lips—like Bridget's mouth in my dream. I caught my breath. The blurb stated it was mixed media, gouache with lipstick, and nail polish.

I called the Glamora in Portsmouth again and said I was a journalist doing a piece on local artists who use cosmetics in their work. I'd heard Devon Ford bought his signature candy apple red polish there. After a few tries, I found someone who told me Devon came in often. He'd talked to her about his paintings. *Of course.* About a month ago he'd bought ten bottles of candy apple red. My mind raced to the obvious conclusion. I could barely sit still, I was so fired up, but I forced myself to slow down. Devon had an alibi for Bridget's murder, and I was sure he wasn't the man who had picked us up in the white car. Any of my father's students or Bridget's friends could have known she wore candy apple polish. Brian told me that initially they thought whoever killed her might be a student at the college because the crime scene was a copy of Devon's painting. But they never found enough evidence to charge anyone. Nina's killer could be copying Devon again, or he might have been Devon all along and his alibi was a lie. I needed to find out more. I compiled a list of students who had been in the college at the same time as Devon and called Brian.

"Devon bought ten bottles of that polish," I said. "I'm driving up to Maine to talk to him. Meet me there."

There was a long pause. "We're done talking to Nina's parents. They don't know anything. Wait until I get back."

* * *

It was a three-hour drive to Livingston. I kept my foot heavy on the gas, my hands tight on the wheel. I was so tense I almost plowed into the car in front of me when it stopped for a red light. Brian called when I reached the state liquor store on the Mass. border.

"Jesus Christ, Sam, I told you to wait." he said.

"You know I couldn't." I rolled my shoulders.

"Lucky for you, I'm already on my way. And, Sam . . ." There was a pause. "Don't go in until I get there."

"I'm not some damsel in distress. I can take care of myself," I said and hung up.

Devon's house was at the end of a winding dirt road off a main drag. It was white with a black door, like a stark Georgia O'Keeffe. No color except for the green yard dotted with yellow daisies. I walked up and rang the bell.

"Samantha?" Devon's big-sky eyes went wide. The sleeves of his plaid shirt were rolled, showing the gold hairs on his thick forearms. A silver-and-turquoise band circled his wrist. He still had that arty look, though now a potbelly hung over his tooled leather belt, and his face was craggy. Not as handsome anymore. Check. "It's been a while," he said uneasily.

"Twenty years." I showed my badge. "I need to ask you a few questions."

He nodded. I followed him into an ornate living room with a chandelier dripping with amber crystals and sat down on a blue velvet Victorian sofa. He settled into a moss green brocade chair.

I put my phone on the glass coffee table. "If you don't mind, I'd like to record our conversation."

"Go ahead. I have nothing to hide." He brushed away the blond curl falling over his forehead—a last vestige of his handsomeness. Check.

I showed him a photo. "This is Nina Crowne, the dancer who was murdered in Quincy this past Sunday. Do you know her?"

He raised an eyebrow. "No, but I heard the news about her. It's very upsetting."

"It sure is." I pressed my palms on the table.

His eyes took me in. "You're looking good, Samantha."

I smiled. I was wearing a clean lavender shirt with a denim jacket to cover my gun, and black jeans with no dog hair. Check. I *was* looking good. "Remember how we thought Bridget's killer might have been inspired by your painting?"

"I'm not responsible for what some sick person takes from my work." He gave me an affronted sniff.

"I understand." I handed him the list of names on my phone. "Could one of these students at the college have copied your painting for the crime scene—maybe someone with a grudge against you or a crush on Bridget, or an overzealous fan."

"The police went over this with me years ago." His jaw tightened. "Why are you asking again?"

"Because we're looking at the old case again in relation to Nina's murder."

He examined the list. "No one rings a bell. None of them had any real talent. Your father was an excellent teacher, but the college was second-rate." Deep lines dug into the sides of his mouth as he grinned. "I do recall one fan, though. You thought I walked on water."

"You don't?" I smiled and slid a photo of Anton onto the glass coffee table. "You know this guy?" He shook his head. "You sure? That's Anton Koslov. We arrested him for the murder of Megan O'Hare. I have reason to believe you do know him."

"That's ridiculous." He narrowed his eyes at me. "Am I a suspect?"

"We're just talking." I stood up. "I'd love to see what you're working on now."

His cowboy boots clacked on the wooden floor as he led me to his studio at the back of the house. Cool light poured through a wall of glass that overlooked a patio at the edge of a wildflower-strewn meadow. Devon stood beside me. "Meredith and I have coffee out there in the morning and listen to the birds." He pointed to a large painting like the one of the girl with a silver stocking over her face I'd seen online. In this one she pressed her red lips through a green stocking. "That's her." His mouth twitched into a smile. "My homage to Man Ray. Seeing a girl emerging through that veil is so sensual, don't you think?"

"I think it's suffocating." I paused. "It's great how you always manage to find a new muse."

He frowned. "She poses for me but she's also a talented artist.

She made these." He gestured to white marble boxes with nothing in them arranged on a shelf. "She calls them experiments with emptiness."

"Emptiness indeed." I sighed. "Where were you last Sunday?"

"I was here with Meredith. I did some painting. She worked in the garden, and we went on a hike."

"What about Sunday night?"

He gazed at me calmly. "She made dinner, and we stayed in watching TV."

I asked for her contact info and he gave me her card. I walked around the studio looking for a painting that resembled Nina's murder scene or sketches of Megan or Nina, but I didn't find any-thing.

"You still have the winning contest painting of Bridget?" I asked.

He shook his head. "I sold it to a collector years ago, but there's something else I want to show you." He led me to a drawing on the opposite side of the room and said, "My first muse." The paper was yellowed and one corner drooped from the wall. Bridget was clutch-ing the seat bar of a roller coaster, head tipped back, screaming, her hair snaking in the wind behind her. "I took her to the carnival after we met at your house painting those cherries, remember?" I gave him a tight nod. He rubbed his thumb across her open mouth. "I can still hear her scream, part thrill, part terror. She said she loved pushing herself to the edge of death, that it was the only time she felt really alive. That was the night she first told me she wanted to get away from Quincy."

"Did she say why?"

"I assumed she was running from someone. Maybe her father." His eyes ferreted out mine. "Or maybe she just wanted to spread her wings. Did she tell you why?"

"No. But she thought going to New York with you would solve everything."

"Not a day I don't regret failing her." He lowered his eyes. "I've had other muses, but she was my best one."

I frowned. "If she hadn't been your muse she might have a life of her own today."

He stroked his chin softly. "I hear you, Sam. I often wonder if she'd still be alive if I hadn't done that painting and given that monster the idea. But she was so like Daphne—fearless, strong, and untouchable."

I gave him a skeptical look. "Why the butterfly?"

"A symbol of what she could become. Daphne ends up trapped in a tree. In my version, she takes flight."

I frowned. "We all know how that turned out."

He ignored my remark. "Do you still paint?"

I bit the inside of my cheek. "Yes."

He smiled slowly. "You were good."

"Thanks for telling me now," I said.

"I told you many times. Your father did, too, but you never listened. After Bridget's murder, he told me he didn't know how to reach you. I'm sorry you two are estranged. He loves you dearly, blames himself for not being there when you needed him most."

Not being there was putting it mildly. Whenever I tried to talk to him about what had happened, he'd tell me to stop obsessing and live my life, as if that were easy. As I frowned thinking about this, I saw the jar of linseed oil, like my father used to use, right there on the table. It glimmered like poisonous honey, next to a sea of nail polish bottles—blue, green, pink, and seven bottles of Glamora candy apple red. There was a row of glossy painted apples on the table behind them. I turned to Devon slowly. "You must really like that color."

"Meredith carves the apples out of marble. I tried different shades of red. Candy apple works best. I paint them with layers of polish to achieve the perfect shine."

I raised a brow. "Like when we painted those cherries?"

"Exactly." He handed me one. It was heavy. "Feels delightful, doesn't it?"

"Feels like you could kill someone with this."

"I call them Snow White apples. I sell them at my open studios. Mothers buy them for their daughters." He snatched the apple from me.

I stepped back. "What did you fight about with Bridget that day when she left her post on the beach to meet you?"

He stared at me quizzically. "I don't know what you're talking about."

"A week before your party, she left her post and came back with a bruise on her cheek. Did she tell you she loved someone else, so you hit her? Is that what happened?"

"I never hit Bridget." He sounded outraged.

"I think you did," I said. "Did you ever go to a bar called the Hat Trick?"

"I've never heard of it," he snapped.

"I think you have. The bartender there remembers you." I smiled.

He glanced away. "I may have gone there once or twice. Why do you care?"

"I think you know. You paint violent things, but sometimes painting them isn't enough, right? Sometimes you hurt the people you love. Sometimes you kill them."

"How can you say that? I loved Bridget and I also loved you, Samantha." His mouth twisted. "And I had an alibi. I bet Bridget got mixed up with some abusive lowlife from that bar. That's who you should be looking for."

"Then tell me his name."

"I don't know his name." He edged closer. "What happened to you and Bridget was a terrible tragedy, but we have to go on with our lives." He breathed in and out slowly. "I hear you have a beautiful daughter. Corinne, right? I'll give you one of my apples for her." He slid his rough thumb down my cheek. "You were a sight with the red all over your face from painting those cherries. It looked like blood." He reached past me for something silver on the table.

"Drop it," I said.

He stared back with glassy eyes and the room went dark. I was trapped in the darkness and couldn't move. Gold curls showed at the edge of the mask coming at me, weaving back and forth like a snake. "Choose, you bitch, you whore," he shouted as the knife flashed through the air.

I seized him by the throat and slammed him onto the floor. The knife bounced out of his hand. His terrified face looked up and the hole that was his mouth shouted, "Stop." I jabbed my gun into his forehead. It took everything I had not to pull the trigger.

"You're making a mistake," he whimpered. I told him to shut up. As I jammed my foot in his chest, I glimpsed the knife on the floor. Only it wasn't a knife. It was a slender hammer with a delicately shaped silver head.

The room became excruciatingly still. My head felt stuffed with cotton, my skin clammy. My heart thudded in my chest. I kept my gun aimed at him and told him to stay put until my partner got here. Brian arrived a few minutes later with two other officers.

"She tried to kill me," Devon said to him.

"He attacked me with that." I pointed to the hammer.

"You're lying. I was going to nail that drawing back up." He glanced at the picture of Bridget curling off the wall.

I banished a sliver of doubt. "Bullshit. You murdered Nina Crowne and used that polish." I gestured to the bottles on the table.

Devon turned his bloody face to me. "I don't know Nina Crowne. And I don't understand what nail polish has to do with this."

"It's the same polish you painted on Nina's body." I jerked my chin up. "You like painting on dead girls?"

"I work with mixed media. I don't paint on dead girls." He wiped frantically at the blood trickling down his cheek. "This is a misunderstanding."

I gestured to the apples on the table. "Are these a misunderstanding, too? 'Cause I'd sure like to know how one ended up shoved in a dead girl's mouth."

"I have no idea what she's talking about. She's out of her mind." He gave Brian an imploring look.

"You can tell us all about it at the station. You're under arrest for assaulting an officer." As Brian cuffed him, Devon went on about how he was going to bleed to death. He didn't shut up until an officer bandaged his head and they took him away in a squad car.

Brian gave me a concerned look. "What happened in there?"

"He attacked me with the hammer." The doubt in his eyes ate at me. My own doubt did, too.

Chapter Twenty-Five

WE CHARGED DEVON with assault on an officer, and he was released the next day with a mild concussion. He was a well-known artist, an upstanding member of the community. He had no record. The judge didn't consider him a flight risk. Meredith paid his bail and backed up his alibi for Nina's murder.

Brian gave me a baleful look. "She's a fool for covering for him. She could be next."

"I'm sorry for rushing things. I should have waited for you." I drank some bitter coffee. "And I shouldn't have lost it on him."

Brian moved his chair closer. "Look, no one better than you to send him to his maker, but I'm glad you didn't pull the trigger. The evidence you found implicates him in Nina's murder. We just need more."

"But he has an alibi for her murder," I said. "Just like he had one for Bridget's murder."

"We'll get a warrant and find enough evidence to arrest him for Nina's murder, alibi or not," Brian said.

"What about Anton?" I asked.

"This doesn't change the evidence we have against him for Megan's murder." He kept his steady gaze on me. "What you went through with Devon must have been hard on you. Take a day off. Talk to Peter if you need to."

The fact that Devon was a person of interest in Nina's murder as well as in a decades-old case was all over the news by the time I got home. I called Jeff and reassured him the end of this nightmare was in sight. I expected him to say he didn't believe that, but all he did was ask if he could drop Corinne off with me in the morning as he had back-to-back meetings all day, and she had a special practice to work on a dance in memory of Nina and Megan. I told him that would be fine.

The next afternoon I drove Corinne to the studio and pulled up behind the patrol car Elle had arranged to be stationed there. When I asked Corinne if I could come in and watch, she shot me down with a harsh, "Mom!" As she walked away, holding herself erect, her shoulder blades showing between the thin straps of her leotard, I thought of how much I missed her and the danger she could be in—the things I tried not to think about because it was hard to do my job if I did. I asked the officer in the patrol car to call me if anything seemed wrong, and I left.

While I waited at home to pick her up, I called Peter. He was on vacation, so I made an appointment for when he got back. I sat down to paint my episode, but I put a different image on the drafting table instead: my unfinished painting of me in the ravine. Though I still felt trapped beneath that dark water, I remembered what Anton said about how nothing in the Black Sea ever leaves and I decided to try again. I found Corinne's old compass from math class, dug the point into that darkness, and inscribed black flowers in the water covering me. Then I swallowed hard, picked up a brush, and painted a black shadow at the top of the cliff. Maybe it was Devon. Maybe not. But I was certain it was the murderer looking down at me.

Barb called a little later to tell me she was having the team and parents back to her house after practice, for a gathering in memory of Nina. Corinne was already there. I put on a black dress and a black sweater to hide my shoulder holster, fed poor Ginger, who didn't want me to leave, and was heading out when Brian called. "You sitting down?" he said.

"Not exactly."

"The prints on the bottle of polish we found near the crime scene are Devon's." I caught my breath. "Sam, you there? You were right. It's him."

"I'm here," I said.

Brian went on. "George and I are driving up to bring him in."

"I have to go to a thing at the Delaneys with Corinne, but I can meet you there later."

There was a long pause. Brian said, "It's better you sit this one out."

I was going to miss this moment I'd been waiting for all these years, and I had no one to blame but myself.

* * *

Barb's little gathering was far from small. There were platters of cold cuts, bite-size meatballs, cocktail franks, plenty to drink, and make-your-own sundaes for the dance team. I grabbed a glass of prosecco and let the bright bubbles break on my tongue. I was chatting with Elle when Max announced that Jay was going to say a few words about Nina. Couldn't have a gathering at the Delaneys' without a few words from Jay.

"First we lost Megan and now we mourn the loss of Nina—a glimmering girl sparkling with promise," he intoned like a preacher. "Their loss will never leave us but . . ." He drew himself up. "A new beginning rises from the ashes of our sorrow. What doesn't break us teaches us to fly."

I frowned. Nina and Megan were dead. No amount of overwrought words about learning to fly eased the pain of that. When Jay was through, he strode over to us and said, "How are you doing?"

"Been better." Elle looked as elegiac as an El Greco as she pressed her long-fingered hands together.

"I've faced my share of grief, too. It never gets easier," he said. Everyone knew Jay had a thing for Barb for years before he finally married a woman named Marie. Their little girl drowned in their backyard pool when she was three. Their marriage didn't survive her death. He became addicted to oxy, redeemed himself, and had been saving others ever since.

Elle touched the black lace at her creamy throat. "I worry about the team. They had the best practice today. They need each other, but I'm going to have to close the studio for the summer. It's not safe."

Barb came over with Shannon, Corinne, and some of the other dancers. Jay pulled Shannon into a hug, saying, "My best girl." He gestured to the others. "I meant what I said about learning to fly. Mark my words. This is the moment when the Fearless Flyers will take off." He grinned at Shannon. "I talked to my friend from *Wish Upon a Dancer*. They'll let you audition alone. How does that sound?"

She smiled demurely. "I love it."

"I bet you do, darlin'." He ruffled her hair and sent her and the other girls off to the patio to make sundaes. He turned to Elle. "That should get you some good publicity, help you stay in business."

"Thanks," she said. "But I still can't afford the cost of the added security I'd need."

"We can pick up the tab, right, Barb?" He smiled at her and she nodded. "And you need to get Devon off the street and put him away for life," he said to me.

"I can't believe you let him go," Barb said.

"Wasn't my decision." I checked my phone for news from Brian. Nothing. I had a few more drinks, a few meatballs, talked to a few people I didn't want to talk to, and went out to the patio to see if Corinne was ready to go. She sat with Beverly, Shannon, and the rest of the team around a white wrought iron table strewn with rainbow sprinkles and gummy bears drowning in pools of melted ice cream. Music blasted from outdoor speakers.

"Wish you'd brought your hot partner with you," Shannon said. She went to stand but fell back into her chair.

I sniffed a red cup that stank of fruit punch and rum and asked if they'd been drinking. Hands went to mouths giggling.

Shannon slurred, "Not me," and sashayed to the edge of the bluff. She rose up on her toes, spread her arms wide saying, "Time to fly," and gave me a backward glance.

I reached out my hand and spoke calmly. "Come on over here, hon."

"Don't worry. I won't jump." She stumbled into me. I slung her arm over my shoulder, feeling relief and sadness. But as I guided her to the patio, she reached for the gun tucked in my shoulder holster. I swatted her hand away.

"Jesus Christ. I just wanted to see if it was real. Never touched a real one before." She smirked and pointed a finger at me. "Bang you're dead."

"Guns aren't a joke," I said, looking quickly at the rest of the girls.

"Whoa sorry." Shannon flopped into a chair. "A gun's the best way to end it all if you ask me." Her piercing eyes challenged me to deny it.

I lowered my voice so the others couldn't hear. "Shannon, there's no shame in asking for help. This is a lot to handle. I can find someone for you to talk to."

"I'm fine. Fine. Fine." She gave the starry sky a mournful look. "And I have someone to talk to. He told me if I fill my heart with love all the darkness will be washed away."

"Who told you that?"

She waited a second and replied, "Uncle Jay."

"Wise words," I said.

Her eyes searched mine. "But Megan's dead. Nina's dead. I wonder if anyone up there is looking out for us. Do you think so, Mrs. S.?"

I took a breath. "It would be nice."

"I don't know. I'm probably next." She stabbed a gummy bear with a toothpick and popped it in her mouth. "Might as well enjoy myself before I die."

I eyed her. "That's not happening to you." I turned to the others. "Or anyone else on the team."

"If you say so." Shannon wiped a tear from her blotchy pink cheek. A song with a pounding beat came on. She waggled her fingers saying, "Let's show Mrs. S. our dance for Megan and Nina." Corinne hesitated and Shannon said, "Come on. You're my best girl." The others followed and they twisted, spun, whipped their hair around and joined hands precariously along the bluff, like a string of paper dolls, the Fearless Flyers, a breath away from flying into the wind. I was about to yell, "Stop," when Shannon snapped her fingers, and they collapsed in a heap on the grass.

She lay on her stomach with her chin propped on her hands. "You like it, Mrs. S.?" I told her I did and she said, "Are you going to let Anton go now since he's innocent? We need him on the team." She gave me a pointed glance.

I knelt so I was level with them and said, "That's not up to me, but I need you all to pay attention." I scrolled through my phone and found a photo. "This is Devon Ford, the guy who's a suspect in Nina's murder. Have any of you seen her with him or heard her mention him?"

They crowded around Shannon as she examined the photo. "Nina was in love with Nick," she said, handing it back. "She'd never be with a creepy old dude like that." I felt their eyes on me, including Corinne's, as they repeated, "Never," like a refrain, and followed Shannon into the kitchen.

Jay was standing at the counter drinking coffee. "Come here, my sweet girl," he called out as he enfolded Shannon in his broad arms. He eyed me. "Not an easy time for the team."

Corinne exchanged a nervous glance with Beverly and said, "Let's go, Mom. She needs a ride, too." I was about to leave with them when Brian called. I told them I'd be right back and stepped onto the patio to take it.

He got straight to the point. "Devon's dead."

My heart ground to a halt. I'd killed him after all. "Was it the concussion? I didn't hit him that . . ."

Brian cut me off. "It's nothing you did. He shot himself. He knew we were on to him and took the easy way out." I looked down from the bluff. "Sam?" he said. Everything below was small and oddly inconsequential. "You saw what all of us missed, and you acted. That's no crime."

"I'm just glad I wasn't the one who killed him." My voice trailed off.

"I need you to take a look at something here," he said.

I dropped Beverly at her house and Corinne at Jeff's and drove up to Maine. Brian showed me a plastic evidence bag when I walked in the door. He wanted to know if it looked familiar. My mouth went dry. It was the mud-stained blue leather rose missing from the shoe I'd worn that night.

"Serial killers keep trophies," George said, as if this was news. "We found this, too." He showed me a Minnie Mouse watch, like Megan's—the one Gloria O'Hare had said was missing.

"Between the blue rose, the print on the polish, and the watch, we have a connection to Bridget's, Megan's, and Nina's murders," Brian said.

"Do you think Devon got the watch from Anton?" I asked.

"We have to figure that out. For now, Finny will keep him in jail." Brian eyed me. "There's more I need to show you," he said, and we went into Devon's bedroom.

Iridescent eyes gazed at me from peacock feathers in a vase beside his bed. Devon lay on a blood-soaked mattress, red splatters on the white wall behind him worthy of Jackson Pollock, an artist Devon and my father despised. The right side of his head was gone, but blond curls still clung to the edge of his masklike face.

"Looks like suicide, but the techs will tell us more. Wanted to give you a chance to view the scene before they take him away. Anything jump out at you?"

"It's an odd way to exit this earth for someone who freaked out about a tiny cut on his head." Devon was lying on his side, his left arm bent under him. "Which hand was holding the gun?"

"Right," Brian said. "Gun powder residue on his right hand, too. We're checking if he's right-handed." I said I was pretty sure he was. He paused. "There's one more thing." I swallowed hard, always one more thing. "He left a note. Want to take a look?"

I sighed. "Do I have a choice?"

He shook his head and handed me an envelope from an evidence bag. *My last letter to you* was scrawled across the front. The note inside said:

See you on the other side, Persephone.

George looked at me. "You're Persephone—his last myth."

Brian drew his brows together. "Persephone?"

I inhaled slowly. "She was kidnapped by the king of the underworld and became his queen. She escaped. But like a violent abuser he still had a hold on her. She had to split the rest of her time between the living and the dead."

"Reminds me a little of you." George narrowed his dark eyes at me.

"Thanks for the compliment." I frowned. "He laid out everything we need to close the case. It feels almost too good to be true."

"That doesn't mean it isn't true. I've been waiting for this moment a long time." Brian put his hand on my shoulder. "At least act like you're happy, Sam. As far as news goes this is as good as it gets."

"Depends how you look at it." I'd been waiting for this moment for years, too, but I still couldn't see behind the glittering mask. Now that he was dead maybe I never would.

Chapter Twenty-Six

THE NEXT AFTERNOON we met with Meredith at a coffee shop in Maine. She dabbed at her delicate red nostrils with a tissue as she told us how on the day he died, she and Devon had breakfast on the patio. Then she went to her studio. He headed to a physical therapy appointment. He promised to call later but never did. The PT was for a shoulder injury that was interfering with his painting. It didn't make sense he'd be worried about that if he was going to kill himself.

She assured us Devon had never met Anton or Nina and that he was with her on Sunday when Nina was murdered. She set her red-rimmed eyes on me. "He wasn't giving up. He cared too much about his art to take his own life." She paused. "He was doing another painting of me. I was his muse."

"A muse is a fool who lets someone else use her instead of making art for herself," I said. "But, hey, at least you make those boxes."

She sniffed. "Yes, my experiment with emptiness."

I nodded. "I do dog portraits. My experiment with barking."

She frowned. "You don't understand. I become someone else when he paints me."

"You're lucky you didn't become dead," I snapped.

* * *

That night Devon's suicide was on the national and local news. Brian and I were portrayed as heroes who caught the man who murdered Nina Crowne and might be the long sought-after Butterfly Killer. I was cautiously hopeful that this nightmare was almost over. I had the next day off, so I took Corinne out to lunch, eager to spend time with her. I planned to drop her at practice afterward and go to my appointment with Peter. She decided on the Clam Shack. Fried seafood on the boardwalk was fine with me. We snagged a table out front beneath a red-and-white striped awning.

"You got a birthday coming up soon," I said. She was turning sixteen, the same age I was when I was abducted, but I tried not to dwell on that. "It's a big one. We need to plan a special party."

She gave me a reproachful look. "Dad and I already planned it. We're getting pizza, but no one will come."

I swallowed my guilt for forgetting to help her plan this key life moment and put my hand on hers. "Your friends will come because you're awesome. I'll pick you up a Funfetti cake from Gemelli's. That's still your favorite, right?"

"Yeah." She stirred her Diet Coke with her straw.

"Have you decided what you want for your birthday?"

Her eyes met mine. "I want us all to be happy."

It killed me that she knew I was unhappy, and now she was unhappy, too. I tightened my ponytail to keep the strand that always snaked out in place. "You might feel like you'll never be happy again, but you will be," I said. "You get through sadness and you move on."

"Seriously?" Her appalled look told me I'd never really moved on.

"How about I give you some money and you can go to the mall with Beverly to pick out a gift?"

"Sure, Mom." She gave me a miserable glance as she picked at her Greek salad wrap.

I dug into my tiny paper cup of coleslaw. "What you're going through isn't easy. I know how it feels."

She looked up slowly. "You don't. Shannon and my other friends all think it's our fault that Anton was arrested, and they hate me for that. I hate myself. He was my friend."

"They're wrong. If they're really your friends they'll figure that out. Just like they did when they accused you of killing Jesus because Dad was Jewish and you told them you were a Jewish Catholic Wiccan heretic." I smiled.

"I remember." Corinne chewed on her lip. "Was Bridget really your friend?"

"I thought she was, though there were things that made me wonder . . ." I took a bite of fried shrimp. "Like the time she invited Barb and me for a sleepover. We stole liquor from her parents and got drunk." I raised up my hand. "Don't even think about doing that," I said and she let go a smile. "I woke up to them writing 'slut' in lipstick on my forehead. They'd drawn all over me with it. Bridget said, 'Now we're artists like you,' and they laughed at me. That really hurt."

"She called you a slut? How could you have stayed friends with her?" Corinne said.

"Everyone used that word then. We didn't talk for weeks. Bridget finally said she meant it as a joke and she was really sorry. She begged me to forgive her and I did." I paused. "She sometimes hurt people, Corinne, but she couldn't help it. She had a hard life. Your friends are hurting now. They want to blame someone, but if they're really your friends, they'll realize their mistake just like Bridget did." I pointed across the street. "We first met right over there."

She tilted her moony face. "I know."

I'd told her before, but I told it again. "The summer I was nine, there was a rock concert over there every Saturday night. Your grandma Eva took me to one. She wore the prettiest skirt that night. I can still see it—long and black, printed with tiny red flowers. She wore it with a wide red leather belt studded with brass stars and ankle boots."

Corinne said, "I wish I'd gotten to meet her."

"I do, too. Addiction is a sickness, and it can be fatal. Like they tell you in school. Don't ever do drugs, Corinne."

She rolled her eyes. "You sound like the DARE officer, Mom."

I smiled and went on. "My mom and I grabbed a spot along the seawall. A rock band was playing Irish music. This girl with long legs and blond hair was dancing in front of them. She stole the show. You would have appreciated what a good dancer she was. She waved and asked me to come on up with her, but I froze. My mom was smoking a cigarette and laughing with some guy. She shoved me and said, 'Go on. Dance.'"

I squeezed my napkin in my fist. It wasn't just any guy. It was the guy who had picked my mother up the night she left for the last time. I turned to Corinne. "I was nervous, but the band launched into my favorite song 'Shoals of Herring' and that worked its magic. It felt like it was just me and Bridget dancing. I forgot anyone was watching and I was really dancing." I blinked away the unwanted tears that stung my eyes. "We never would have found each other if a news photographer hadn't snapped a photo of us dancing for the *Sun*. The next day she called me up, said since we were both famous, we might as well get to know each other. She wasn't perfect, Corrine, but she really was my friend." A stiff breeze came off the water and I grabbed our napkins before they blew away. "I'm looking forward to seeing all your friends at your party."

"Me too," Corinne removed a piece of lettuce from her wrap and chewed it slowly. "Dad wants to have it at his place but it's so small and messy, it's embarrassing. Can we have it at your place? Dad can come." She eyed me. "I just want things to be the way they used to be."

"I understand that." I met her gaze and added, "If you ever want to talk more about your dad, I'm always here to listen, okay?"

"Mom, I have practice."

"Right. Come on, let's go," I said.

* * *

"Vera and I got back last night," Peter said. "The Vineyard is lovely, but it's nice to be home." He rolled the sleeves of his dark blue patterned shirt up over his tanned forearms. "I assume you're here to talk about Devon's death."

I shifted in that uncomfortable chair I always sat in and blurted it all out. "I had an episode when I was talking to him as part of our investigation. He reached for a hammer. I thought it was a knife and I came close to killing him, but I didn't. Turns out it didn't matter since he killed himself."

A line formed between his chestnut brows. "He killed Bridget. He threatened you. Why didn't you kill him?"

"Because I'm not a killer." I leaned back against the stiff mesh of the supposedly comfortable ergonomic chair. "And if he died, I'd never get the answers I want. But it happened anyway."

"You made the right choice in a situation where someone else might have lost control." He smiled sympathetically. "But you still don't have your answers. How do you feel about that?"

"I can live with it." I tucked my hands in my armpits.

Peter, ever patient, said, "Did the episode show you anything new?"

"I saw his blond hair. I never saw anything but the mask before."

He tipped his chair forward. "Devon was blond. Seeing his blond hair could be your mind's way of telling you that you were right about him. Did anything else stand out?"

"He asked me to choose, called me a bitch, a whore, and raised a knife."

He stared at me calmly. "Do you have any idea what the choice refers to?"

"No." I picked at the nubby fabric of the chair.

"Did you paint it?"

"No. I worked on my unfinished painting instead." I showed him a photo of it on my phone.

His gaze went from the black flowers on the water to the shadow on the cliff. "The veil has lifted a fraction."

"Almost twenty years and all I get is a fraction?"

"You put a figure on the cliff. That's new. Is it Devon?"

"The evidence points to him but I'm not sure." I crossed my legs. "I still feel trapped in that darkness."

"You've solved the case, but the trauma is still inside you. Don't be so hard on yourself. Now could be the time to let yourself move on." He blinked those green eyes of his, wanting, I supposed, to get me to come over to the other side where people were actually happy.

"I've been trying to figure this out for twenty years. It's not easy to stop." I heaved a sigh. "I worry I don't have any real memories because of the ketamine. I was sure I remembered a bracelet from that night and it didn't even exist."

"Interesting." He propped his chin on his folded hands. "But you have fragments of memories. If you'd never formed them you wouldn't have those."

"I guess it could all still be there, like in the Black Sea." Peter gave me a questioning look. "Shipwrecks, blue shoes, a bracelet, a knife. The lack of oxygen deep below the surface preserves everything that has the misfortune to end up there."

"I'd never heard that before, but it's an excellent analogy." He pointed to the water inscribed with flowers. "Is that the Black Sea?"

I raised a shoulder. "I don't know. Maybe they're just dark, creepy flowers." I leaned forward. "I want to try to remember one more time. Could you hypnotize me?"

He frowned. "We've tried that before, and it didn't work. But if it's what you want, I'll do my best."

"Just don't make me quack like a duck," I said.

He gave me a faint smile and explained he'd do a guided meditation. It would help me go under if I told myself a story. When I was fully relaxed, he'd ask me questions about what was happening. If I felt unsafe I should say the word "duck." That made me smile. I stretched out on the couch.

He said in a soothing voice, "Imagine going down the steps into a pool, only this one has no bottom."

The stairs were cold and wet beneath my feet, the way they had been that night. My chest tightened, but I kept going down until there were no more stairs and water rose up around me.

"Underwater." My voice sounded muffled.

"How do you feel?" he said.

"Okay," I said, though I couldn't tell where I ended and the water began.

A voice said to go deeper and deeper, to find the things I had left behind, the things I had never left, to let the darkness enfold me. Something cool brushed the top of my head, and it felt like my mind was expanding into boundless space. Images flew out of the ghostly silence. A blue bird landed on my shoulder and squawked, "What do you see?"

"A mask." A pale shape drifted toward me, blond curls rippling along the edge.

The bird's voice grew firm. "Take his mask off."

"I can't." My voice was breathy as a child's.

"Don't be afraid. Devon can't hurt you anymore." The bird sounded kind. "You were only sixteen. Surround that frightened girl with love. She's been waiting for you all these years. Take her hand and tell her she can do this." I reached for the mask, ready to see his face, but it vanished. I heard Bridget saying, "Wake up," in a strange soft voice, felt her cold hand caressing my forehead. And then she was right there, cowering in her silver dress and crying, "Help me," but I couldn't move. A man shouted, "Run," and I ran through branches that tore at me like fingernails. I managed to say, "Duck," and came out of hypnosis gasping for air.

"Samantha, are you all right?" Peter's voice was full of concern.

"I didn't see his face, but I now know I ignored Bridget's cries for help and I ran." I paused for a painful second. "I left her behind to die." I couldn't stop the tears from coming.

Peter looked at me with more caring than my father had ever

showed me, handed me a box of tissues, and said, "You chose to live. There's nothing wrong with saving yourself."

"I can't forgive myself for that," I said.

He leaned forward. "I realize that's how you feel, but the voice saying to run could be telling you you're ready to put your nightmare behind you. You don't have to be trapped by the past your whole life. You have the power to be happy."

I stared into his calm green eyes. If what I experienced under hypnosis was a real memory, it meant Bridget's killer had let me go. But I still didn't know if it had been a strange act of kindness or because I helped him. I ran a finger over the crow tattoo on my arm. I wanted to leave my nightmare behind and be happy. Corinne wanted me to be happy, too. I had to try.

Chapter Twenty-Seven

"I'M GOING OVER the evidence we have against Devon one more time." Brian pointed to the place on the whiteboard where he'd written, *Nina: his fingerprint on the polish, he made marble apples like the one found in her mouth. Megan: he had her watch. Bridget: he had the blue rose from Samantha's shoe.* He rubbed his chin. "What we don't have is any other evidence connecting Devon to Megan's or Bridget's murders, no evidence he knew Nina or Megan, no weapon, and no motive."

He stepped back. "Devon's dead so technically no more case but we need more evidence that he killed Nina, so we can be sure her killer isn't still out there. If we find evidence that ties him to the other murders, all the better."

"I'll track down who bought the butterfly as that seems to be my area of expertise." George smiled to himself as he looked down at his phone.

I propped my feet on the table. "I'll talk to Meredith again, see if I can get her to poke a hole in Devon's alibi."

Brian nodded. "See if Devon has an alibi for Megan's murder, too. The evidence points to Anton, but Devon had her watch. There must be a connection between them. We just haven't found it yet. I'll look into who attended Devon's open studios. Maybe one of them knows something useful. Any other ideas?"

George kept smiling at this phone.

Brian raised a brow. "George why are you smiling like that? You're making me nervous. Is something going on?"

George looked up from his phone, still smiling. "I think I have a date."

I leaned forward. "A date? You?"

He frowned. "Alice wants to meet for a drink. She's interested in my perspective on the Junior Black case."

"She probably wants to pick your brain about Nina's murder," I said.

Brian gave me a sidelong glance. "George excels at keeping lips sealed." He turned to him. "It's about time you had some fun."

I went back to my desk and called Meredith. She stuck to her alibi for Devon for Nina's murder and insisted she had been with Devon on the day Megan was killed. They had gone to a local restaurant called The Sea Hut that night. They went there every Friday night for their seared scallops in honey bourbon sauce. The restaurant backed her up. I called Devon's physical therapist to confirm he had kept his appointment the day of his suicide, but no one picked up, so I left a message. It was maddening. Even though we had all this evidence, his alibis for Megan's and Nina's murders seemed solid. But there was one more thing I wanted to look at: his alibi for the night of Bridget's death.

I read through the details in the old case file. Devon said he had stopped at Patriot Liquors in West Quincy on the way to pick up me and Bridget. Two men mugged him as he went to his car. They took his money, beat him up, and slashed his tires. His car was towed. He called my father for a ride from the repair shop around ten p.m. Then they drove to the Neck. When we weren't there, Devon assumed Bridget was mad at him for being late and that we were at her house. My father called the police when I didn't come home the next day. The police never found the muggers, but the repair shop backed up Devon's story. I told them he wasn't the man who picked us up, and he and my father were cleared as suspects.

It didn't occur to me to question his story then because I was naive and had a crush on Devon. But now it bothered me. I was reviewing a map of that West Quincy neighborhood when Brian came by and pulled up a chair. "I got a list of people who went to Devon's open studios. I've contacted some of them. So far none of them have a connection to Nina or Megan, but I'm still looking. How about you?" He grabbed a pen from the purple Fearless Flyers mug on my desk.

"Devon's alibi for Megan's and Nina's murders holds up." I shrugged. "But something about his alibi for Bridget's murder doesn't make sense."

"How so?" He clicked the pen.

"He said he stopped at Patriot Liquors. That's nowhere near the Neck. Why go so far out of his way to buy booze unless he was doing something else?" I pointed to the map. "That liquor store is next to the Hat Trick. Vince said Bridget came in with a blond guy sometimes. Devon admitted to me he'd been there before. If he stopped there that night, we need to find out why."

He raised a brow. "Not to be a dickhead, but why do we care?"

"Because it's all we've got." I grabbed the pen from him and put it back in the mug where it belonged.

* * *

Business was slow at the Hat Trick. *Everybody Loves Raymond* was on the TV to an audience of none; the bolted-down barstools were empty. Vince tapped his forehead and said, "Wait. Don't tell me. Club soda and a Diet Coke. Am I right?"

Brian frowned. "Unfortunately, yes."

When I explained why we were there, he said, "As fate would have it, I was working here the night Bridget and you were snatched by that dirtbag. You don't forget where you were when something like that happens. Just like I'll never forget being stuck on the Southeast Expressway when the first plane hit the towers." He handed us our drinks.

"Did this guy come in here that night?" Brian slid a photo of Devon over to him.

Vince twisted his mouth in thought. "I remember a lady who wore spurs on her cowboy boots and a dude with a bald eagle tattooed on his bald head coming in." He studied it some more. "That's the guy who offed himself, isn't it?" Brian nodded. "Now that I think of it, a blond guy who looked like him did come in with another guy. Things got heated, the cowgirl told them to chill, and they left. He came back a while later, said someone had beaten him up and his car was trashed. He was afraid he was dying, thought I would care. He used the pay phone and he was out of here."

"Do you remember the time?" I asked

He sighed. "It had to be after eight when my shift started."

"Can you tell us who he was with?" Brian said.

"It might have been this dude we called Wally the Whale."

I smiled. "Did he have a real name?"

"Don't know it, but he was a muscle guy who sold illegal substances."

"Last time we spoke," I said, "you told us Bridget came in with a blond guy. Was that Devon, too?"

Vince leaned his meaty arms on the bar. "The guy who came in with Bridget was wound tight, ready to blow, the type of guy you don't cross. Definitely not that chickenshit Devon."

"Can you give us his name?" I asked.

"Like I told you the last time you asked, princess, I don't know it." His gaze shifted away. "Now, if you don't mind, I got work to do."

I glanced around the empty bar. "Really?"

"Dishes to wash. Promises to keep. The usual." He cracked a smile.

* * *

"Princess. You think?" I said as we walked to the car.

"Obviously." Brian's certainty was touching. "Sounds like Devon had an alibi, only not what we thought it was."

"And he lied about it." I looked down the block of storefronts and triple-deckers, one of many scenes here worthy of Edward Hopper—right down to the acid green Astroturf in front of a hardware store. With each breath, I inhaled car exhaust and hopelessness. As I slid onto the hot vinyl seat, Devon's physical therapist returned my call. It was all I could do not to heave the phone out the window as he spoke to me. But I jammed it in my pocket and gave Brian the bad news. "Devon broke his right shoulder a few months ago. It healed, but he was still having problems with numbness in his right hand from nerve damage. He could barely grip a brush, let alone kill Nina and get her body into the greenhouse."

"Or hold a gun in his right hand to kill himself." Brian pounded the steering wheel. "His suicide must have been staged. The whole thing was a setup, the guy we're looking for is still out there, and we don't have a fucking clue who he is."

"And I walked right into his trap," I said. Everything had been so easy when I thought Devon had done it. I was off the hook for almost killing him and happiness was within reach. As we drove back neither of us said a word. I always found the moment when a case falls into place a beautiful reassurance of order in the universe—the moment when it falls apart, not so much.

*   *   *

The next morning, I stopped by Gemelli's on the way to the station and picked up the Funfetti cake for Corinne's birthday and impulse-bought blueberry muffins. I stashed the glorious rainbow-sprinkled cake in the breakroom fridge beneath a sign saying, *Eat this and you die, Love Sam*, and set the muffins on my desk.

Brian helped himself to one. As George and I stared at him grimly, he said, "Painful as it is we must think this through again. On the bright side the evidence is still the same. It just doesn't point to Devon." He bit into his muffin. "The way I see it, Nina's killer went to Devon's open studio, somehow got Devon to leave a fingerprint on the polish, stole it and the apple to make it look like Devon was guilty. Then he staged Devon's suicide and left evidence there to frame him for Bridget's murder, Megan's murder, and Nina's murder."

George carefully removed the paper from his muffin. "This guy went to a lot to trouble to frame Devon. Why?"

"The obvious reason is he killed all three of them, he wants to get away with it, and he really wants to get back at Devon for something." Brian brushed at his blue shirt cuff. "Damn I got blueberry on this, and it's new."

"At least it's blue." I smiled. "That makes sense, but why would he frame Devon for Megan's murder when we already arrested Anton for it?"

Brian tipped his chair back. "Either the killer is his accomplice, though we have no evidence of that, or Anton really is innocent. It's possible. The case is circumstantial."

"But even if Anton's innocent, why wouldn't the killer just let him take the blame for Megan's murder?" I said.

George eyed us cooly. "Because this guy is a psychopath who thinks he's an artist. He takes pride in his work and wants credit for it."

"Maybe." Brian shook his head. "But none of this speculation tells us who he is."

"I can help with that," George said. "I looked into the butterfly. The yellow swallowtail that was found on Bridget is from around here. The Mexican Bluewing on Megan isn't native, but it's not that rare. Anton's father sold them, and you can buy them online. But the butterfly on Nina was a Luzon peacock swallowtail. They're native to an island in the Philippines and they're endangered, not easy to get." He showed us a butterfly on his phone that looked like the one on Nina. "You have to wonder why he chose such a rare one."

I stared at the black wings threaded with iridescent green and gold and then it hit me. "In the myth, Io is guarded by Argus, a hundred-eyed giant—kind of like a private eye, only private eyes." I looked up with a smile. "When he dies his eyes are placed in a peacock's tail."

"Jesus, you're fucking brilliant, Sam." Brian winked at George. "Why can't you be more like her?"

George smiled. "You can't buy a peacock swallowtail on Amazon. You can't buy them anywhere legitimately. You have to find a black-market distributor. We find out who bought the butterfly, we'll have our guy."

"If he's Anton's accomplice, maybe Anton's father sold him the butterfly," I said.

George nodded. "I already gave Vasily a call. He told me if I could afford it, he'd find me one."

* * *

Koslov's Exotic Animals and Antiques was in North Quincy, otherwise known as the Downs. When I used to go there with Bridget, the Downs was mostly pizza joints, sub shops, and Irish pubs. Now it was Asian restaurants, bubble tea shops, nail salons, and tattoo parlors. Vasily's store was flanked on one side by a cell phone store and on the other by a dive bar called the Irish Rover—a last vestige of the way the Downs used to be.

George went on ahead into Vasily's, but I stopped in front of the cell phone store.

"Thinking of upgrading?" Brian said.

"Just thinking." I turned to him. "This used to be the Crust and Crumb café. Bridget and I came here around Christmastime for hot chocolate and this sweet bread that had some spice in it. Cardamom, I think."

"I liked that bread, too." He pressed his hand on the window.

"They set up this miniature Christmas village every year. Tiny houses, tiny lights, hills with white glitter for snow, a little train running up and down them. We went there for the last time the winter before she was murdered. I remember looking through a window of her favorite house with her. The detail was incredible: oriental rugs, china patterned with roses, a tree with ornaments, there were even

173

stockings on the mantel. She said her 'love bunny' was giving her a real house like that someday, better than the one Max was building for Barb. I almost fell over laughing that she called him her 'love bunny.' She got mad and refused to tell me who he was." I stared into the shadowy reflections in the store window. "She actually took me to see the real house a few weeks later. It was snowing and we could barely see a foot ahead. She led me down this dirt road into the Blue Hills. When we got there, it was a one-room cabin littered with beer cans and empty pizza boxes. It looked like just another place where kids came to drink, but she assured me her love bunny was going to make it beautiful. I felt kind of bad for her."

"All of her boyfriends that we knew about had alibis." Brian rested his hand on my shoulder. "Come on."

Inside Vasily's shop, George was eyeing a set of pink Depression-glass dishes he thought might be valuable. We tore him away and went over to where Vasily stood with a parakeet perched on his arm. It looked like Percy, except it was green rather than blue. "To what do I owe the honor of a visit from Quincy's finest?"

George introduced himself and said, "We spoke on the phone. You told me you could help me find a Luzon peacock swallowtail."

"First you wanted a blue butterfly and now a peacock one?" Vasily frowned. "I'm sorry if I misled you, but I don't sell those. They're endangered."

"We're not here to bust you," Brian said. "We just want to know who you sold it to."

"I never sold one of those." He gave the bird a love peck and turned to me. "Samantha, when are you letting Anton go? You know he's innocent."

I met his gaze and said, "Your best bet for clearing Anton is to help us find the man who bought one of those butterflies."

He shook his head. "I haven't sold endangered butterflies for years, not worth the trouble, but I know people who do." He wrote a name on a piece of paper and gave it to me. "Don't say you got this from me."

Chapter
Twenty-Eight

RENEE MARCHANT OWNED a gift shop called Birds, Bees, and Butterflies, about an hour away in the small coastal town of Mattapoisett. Brian called and told her we were a married couple interested in adding some rare specimens to our butterfly collection. She agreed to meet us that afternoon.

"Wife?" I said when he hung up. He smiled. "A man can dream." I told him I'd be his worst nightmare.

Renee's shop was in a mini-mall along with Totes and Tea, Umbrellas Etc., and a store devoted entirely to bird seed. Birds, Bees, and Butterflies sold collectible insects and butterflies along with china, jewelry, mugs, and other gifts on a creepy-crawly theme. I picked up a glass paperweight with an iridescent beetle trapped inside and looked into its bulging black eyes. A woman wearing an orange linen dress and necklace made of amber beads came over as we hovered over a display case of butterflies. "Excuse me, are you Brian?" she said.

"Yes, ma'am. You must be Renee." He smiled. "This is my wife, Betty." I wanted to punch him, but I smiled. Brian told her we were looking for a Luzon peacock swallowtail.

She stiffened. "I'm sorry but we don't have any of those."

Brian reached for his wallet. "What a shame. We were counting on one, even got a special display case made for it. You sure you can't find one for me? I'll pay cash." He hooked his arm around me, and I really wanted to punch him.

Renee touched her dragonfly earring. "I can't you get a peacock swallowtail, but I have some like it." She led us to a room at the back and showed us photographs of various green butterflies.

Brian shook his head. "Darlin', if I may call you that."

She pursed her lips. "You may call me Renee."

"Renee, I have it on the word of a close friend he got one of them peacock butterflies from you. Showed it to me. Why should I settle for second best?"

Her cheeks flared. "Those are very expensive."

Brian grinned. "How much?"

"They start at ten thousand."

"Put it in writing and we have a deal." Brian loved playing the high roller.

"It may take a week or more to get it," she said.

"No worries." He studied the invoice she gave him and pressed his badge on the table. "Trafficking in endangered species is a crime. But you already know that, darlin'."

She twisted her necklace around her hand and her face crumpled. "You have to believe me. I've never done anything like this before." I was surprised at how quickly she admitted it, but this was probably her first foray into crime. "My husband made some bad real estate deals. He owes people money. He's received threats. We had no other choice."

"Looks like you made the wrong one, and it's not the first time," I said.

She managed some tears. "I promise not to sell any more. Please don't arrest me."

Brian and I stepped aside and pretended to confer. When we came back, I said, "If you help us out, we'll look the other way, but we need the contact information for anyone you've sold a peacock swallowtail to in the past year."

"We only sold one." She clicked away on her laptop and looked up after a moment. "His name is John Smith. We spoke over the phone." She passed a Post-it with his phone number to Brian. "He said it was a gift for his daughter's birthday, that she'd be thrilled to add such a rare specimen to her collection. I delivered it to him on July 30th, but I don't have his address. He sent a money order up front and told me to leave his package on a bench in Shipyard Park at ten that night."

Brian stroked his chin. "That's a lot of hoops to go through for a butterfly."

"He was a bit paranoid about the transaction, as was I. He sounded like such a nice man. Has he done something wrong?"

"We just want to talk to him. Did you get a look at him?" I asked.

"No. We did everything over the phone. He told me to put the package on the bench and leave. Frankly, I couldn't wait to get out of there."

I asked if she had an invoice for the transaction. She printed it out. As I reviewed it, I caught my breath. "He bought more than one butterfly."

"Yes, a red glider. Another gift for his daughter."

I took a moment to digest the possibility he had future plans and pointed to another item on the invoice. "What's this?"

She smiled. "He also bought her the cutest pink jade earrings, saw them on our website."

"Can you show me them? It's my daughter's birthday today." I tensed. I'd almost forgotten I needed to be home in time for her party.

She showed us a pair of delicate ballerina earrings in a case out front and said, "He told me his daughter was a dancer." It was as if a vacuum cleaner had sucked all the air out of the room. She asked if I wanted to buy a pair. I stammered, no.

Brian set his steady gaze on her. "John Smith could be dangerous. If he contacts you again let me know."

* * *

As I sat in the suffocatingly hot car, I thought of Corinne getting ready for her birthday party while I was here, and my anxiety came crashing in. I breathed in and out into my cupped hands to calm myself.

Brian glanced at me as he started the car. "You okay, Betty?"

"I'm fine. But the next time I'm your wife please call me Giselle or Olivia, not Betty," I said.

He drove down the sleepy main street lined with quaint houses with overflowing window boxes and pulled up opposite Shipyard Park. The park had a gazebo and a view of the harbor. It was deadly quiet for a summer afternoon. I suspected it always was.

"I'll do my best, Olivia." Brian smiled. "July 30th is a week before Nina was murdered so the timing is right. I doubt his real name is John Smith. He probably used a burner." He set his mirrored sunglasses on me. "He went to a lot of trouble to conceal his identity."

"And he bought another butterfly." I nodded at the restaurant with a screened porch across the street. "Someone dining there might have noticed the deal going down."

"Or we can start here." Brian pointed to the surveillance camera at the traffic light right before the park.

It was a slow afternoon for the Mattapoisett PD. Every afternoon probably was. When we told them we were looking for surveillance tapes from the night of July 30th, an officer explained we were in luck. The surveillance camera had only been there since the beginning of July. Traffic wasn't usually a problem here, but kids were drag-racing in front of the harbor.

I shot Brian a look. "Probably racing Mommy and Daddy's Porsches."

"Still haven't caught them," the officer said, "but they stopped racing. That's what matters." He paused. "You're not after those kids, are you?"

After Brian explained we were investigating a murder, they found the tapes quickly. We watched the ones from nine to ten p.m. There were almost no cars. But around 9:45 a white Audi stopped in front of the park. "Get a load of Renee's new wheels," one of the officers said. I shook my head. Apparently, she wasn't in such dire straits. She got out of the car, left a package on the bench, and drove off a little before ten. "You looking for her?" the officer asked, and we told him no. A few minutes later an older-model brown sedan pulled into her spot. I could make out the blurred image of a tall man who went into the park and came back holding a box. He walked briskly to his car, made a U-turn, and drove back toward the camera. We couldn't see enough to identify him, but we had something better. The camera got his license plate—twice.

* * *

The brown 2001 Buick Century was registered to Robert Michael Concannon, 32 Briar Lane, Lakeville, Massachusetts, about a half-hour drive from Mattapoisett. Brian went to start the car so we could head there and stopped. "What is it?" I asked.

He reached his phone from the center console. "His name was familiar and now I know why." He pointed to the name Robert Concannon in a list of guests who attended the open studios. "He was there."

There was a lake around every bend. Brian took the curves so fast I was sure he'd send us into one. As we got closer, he called for backup. The house was hidden behind a wall of arborvitae. The front porch needed painting, and the hanging planters were full of dead petunias. The shades were drawn. Brian rang the bell and we stepped to one side. No answer.

"We could break the door down." I tapped it with my foot.

Brian gave me an admonishing look. "You know we can't until we get a warrant, Sam."

We found the old brown car parked behind the house. It was in mint condition, polished chrome on the dash, door handles gleaming. It wasn't locked and it was empty. The faded red barn in the field beyond it was like something out of an Andrew Wyeth. All that was missing was Christina, the semi-paralyzed girl who pined after Wyeth as he painted her crawling through the tall grass. Woods crept up to edge of the property. Gray clouds rolled in and the sunlit afternoon went dark.

Through the window in the back door I saw a kitchen table and chairs but no sign of anyone. I went over to a basement window and crouched down. Brian knelt next to me with a groan and said, "Remind me just say no to basketball." As we peered through the dust-filmed glass, there was a sharp *crack*. Thunder. The skies opened up, filling the silence with the desperate hush of rain. There was another *crack* and a bullet splintered the glass into a spider web. I whipped around to see a man racing from the woods toward the barn. We took off after him with the heavens crashing all around us. Brian fell in the mud yelling, "Goddamn knee."

The man disappeared into the barn. I ran after him, then stopped to peer through its weathered double doors. No sound except for rain tapping on the roof. There were stalls on either side, a loft, and an old pickup truck parked with its nose poking out of another set of double doors open at the other end of the barn. The smart thing would have been to wait for Brian, but I hadn't come this far to let this man slip through my fingers. I took one quiet step, then another, pausing at each stall to look inside with my gun raised. No sign of him. I inched along one side of the pickup truck. Another crash and lightning lit up the barn behind me. When I turned to look, someone darted out from in front of the truck and tackled me to the floor. My gun went flying. I tried to reach for it, but the man grabbed me by the throat and pressed the cold barrel of his gun against my temple. I looked into the holes in his ski mask and saw nothing but shiny, dark beetle eyes watching me. His grip was so tight I could barely breathe. I waited for the end of my life. But it couldn't end this way. Not with *him*. The trigger clicked. I braced myself, but he fired into the air, whipped the gun across my face and threw me back down. Pain exploded through my head. The man disappeared through the double doors. A few minutes later,

Brian hobbled into the barn. He helped me to my feet and asked if I was okay.

Blood ran into my eyes. "I'm fine," I said. "He was close as you are to me, and I lost him. Goddamn it."

"You're okay. That's what matters. You got a cut on your forehead. That's all." He eyed me. "I should have gotten him. Fucking knee. Did you see his face this time, Sam?"

"He was wearing a ski mask and his eyes were all dark, like he was wearing black contacts." I chewed on my lip. "He could have killed me. But he let me live, like the first time. I don't get it."

"We don't need to get it. We need to get him," he said.

We headed toward the house. The rain had stopped, and the meadow glistened in the setting sun. Woods and fields extended in every direction, no houses in sight, no sign of him.

"He can't have gotten far on foot," Brian said.

I glanced at the house. "He could be in there. He's a dangerous suspect who attacked me. We got probable cause." Brian nodded. I kicked the back door in and we stepped into a kitchen with oak cabinets, gray Formica counters, harvest gold appliances probably dating back to the seventies. The living room had all the charm of a cheap hotel room—ugly pallet-knife paintings, gray couch with spindle legs, matching wall-to-wall, and a rectangular glass coffee table.

I heard sirens, growing steadily louder, and then a stampede as backup officers swarmed in. Some of them scattered to search the woods and nearby homes. The rest searched the house with us. In a plain maple dresser in one of the bedrooms, we found a white leather album filled with neatly labeled butterflies. There was no Luzon Peacock Swallowtail, no Red Glider.

The finished basement had fake-wood paneling, a cracked gray linoleum floor, and wooden stools bellied up to an old wet bar. Models of boats lined steel shelves along the wall.

"Talk about your garden variety nerd." Brian said.

"A multitalented nerd." I pointed to the small paintings on the wall. Each depicted a young woman from a myth in the *Metamorphoses*, including Daphne, Leda, and Philomela. I was leaning in for a closer look when a tech called out, "You've got to see this."

He was in an adjoining room piled with boxes. One was open. Inside were photos of Bridget: smoking a cigarette with her blond bangs in her face, walking on the beach, laughing in the snow, sprawled half naked on a bed. I inhaled sharply as I held the one of her head in the leaves, *Goddess Transformed* written on the back in tight handwriting.

The next box held photos of Shannon, one as a toddler splashing in a wading pool, another at age six in a green sequined costume and tap shoes from when she had won her first competition, more through the years, including one in her Poker Face costume—the words *delicate, flower,* and *my sunshine* written on the back.

I turned to Brian. "He's been watching her since she was a kid."

"Jesus," he said.

There were too many boxes to go through right now, but I opened one more. It contained photos of the dance team—more of Shannon half naked in her high cut sequined purple costume, Nina on point in a white tutu, Megan straddling a chair, looking coyly seductive in her skimpy red fringed costume and patent leather boots. They were all photos from States. I stared at the ones of Nina and Megan—each of them trapped in the silent eternity of a glossy 5 by 7.

My hand shook as I showed Brian the one of Corinne in her sparkly "Paris in the Rain" costume. My mouth opened and an avalanche of garbled sounds escaped.

"Sam?" His brown eyes held mine.

I struggled to compose myself. "Corinne's having her birthday party at our house right now. I was supposed to bring the cake. It's still in the fridge at the station. I'm not there and he's out there."

He pressed his hands into my shoulders. "There's no way he knows about the party, but I'll send an officer to your place to check things out and send one to watch Shannon's house, too."

He stepped back. "We'll find this guy. Go on home."

Chapter
Twenty-Nine

I TOLD THE officer stationed in front of our house that he could leave, and I went inside. Corinne had invited the whole team, but Shannon, Beverly, and Lane were the only ones at her party. They all were staring at me with alarm, including Jeff.

"You're bleeding," Corinne said, looking up from behind the stack of presents on the dining room table.

My hand went to the bandage on my forehead. "It's nothing. I'm sorry I didn't get the cake."

Jeff gave me a distressed glance. "I bought a new one. It's right there." He pointed to it.

I thanked him and told Corinne to go ahead and blow out the candles. She eyed Jeff warily. Ever since she was little, he'd played this game where he'd reach his hand in front of her when she was about to blow them out. He'd do it over and over until she screamed in frustration, but tonight Jeff sat there frozen as she blew them all out. I handed around slices of the rainbow-sprinkled cake. As I dug my fork into mine, Corinne stared at me without taking a bite. She touched my bandage and said, "Mom, your forehead's purple. What happened to you?"

I put my fork down. "A suspect hit me with a gun but I'm okay. He got away but we'll get him. That's all I can tell you for now." Jeff's eyes widened in alarm.

When everyone finished their cake, I said half-heartedly, "Time for presents?"

I sipped my wine as Corinne did her best to act enthusiastic as she opened the eyelash curler from Lane, the velvet PJs from Shannon, and the aromatherapy lotions from Beverly. Jeff handed Corinne the present from us. He'd wrapped it expertly with sharp corners and curled ribbon. She feigned surprise when she lifted the flower-splashed halter dress from the box. Her eyes met mine. "Thanks, Mom. I love it."

She saved the present from my father for last. He never forgot her birthday. The small box contained a geode with violet crystals that he'd gilded with delicate gold leaf. The note on his birthday card said to *Find the fairy hiding in her purple castle.* She and her friends exclaimed in wonder as they peered into it as if they really expected to find her. I sighed; they might be sixteen, but they were also still children. I thought of the photos we'd found in Concannon's basement. *Children.* A few minutes later the bell rang and Barb Delaney bustled in followed by Linda Tran.

Without even saying hello, Barb said, "There's a police cruiser parked in front of our house. Max tells me a suspect in Nina's murder is on the loose and that he almost killed you, but you escaped. What's going on, Samantha? Are we all in danger?"

"We're keeping everyone safe." I took in their looks of horror.

Barb gave Shannon and Lane a nod. "Come on," she said, "we're leaving." She fastened her eyes on me. "I let Shannon come here because she felt sorry for Corinne. I feel sorry for her, too, but I can't put Shannon at risk anymore."

As Linda stood there helplessly, I went over to her. I'd called a few days ago and told her the portrait was done, that I'd give it to her discreetly on Corinne's birthday, and she could surprise Beverly with it later. But when I mentioned it now, she stepped back and said, "Barb told me what happened. This is too unsafe. I'm sorry, but I don't want the portrait. I just want to get out of here." Before I could answer, she and Beverly followed Shannon, Lane, and Barb out the door.

Corinne remained composed for all of a second before the tears spilled out. "Now I officially have no friends. Thank you for ruining my life, Mom. Great present I picked out for myself, by the way."

I reached for her, but she dashed out the door after them. Ginger went to the window barking. Jeff stared at me. "I'll get her," I said, grabbing my gun. I was only a minute or so behind her, but by the time I stepped outside, she was gone. I looked up at the cold stars, the space between them like those blank black eyes bearing down on me and called her phone. No answer. I left a message for her to please, please pick up, and called Barb.

"Corinne ran off and I can't find her," I said. She told me she'd just seen her walking toward the park at the end of our street. Her voice softened as she said she'd let me know if Shannon heard from her.

It was barely a park, just a few trees, a patch of flowers planted by the local garden club, and stone benches in memory of this or that person. I hurried along the gravel path that wound through it, reassuring myself that Corinne would stay away long enough to make her point and come home. That was her MO. But my heart still hammered in my chest.

It didn't take long to search the entire park. When I'd finished, I walked toward the train station, hoping she wasn't headed there. The street looked peaceful enough, but it wasn't safe at night. I'd gone about a block when I saw her rounding a corner, her face blotchy from crying. I sighed with relief as she came toward me and stopped beside the plaque that read: ANN HUTCHINSON TARRIED HERE. When she was in third grade, I had told her how Ann was exiled to Rhode Island for heresy. She was so impressed she'd written a paper titled, "My Favorite Heretic." I walked over to her now and asked, "Are you tarrying?"

Her face darkened. "Mom, why are you chasing after me like I'm five?"

"Things are different now. There's a dangerous suspect on the loose. You can't run off like that, Corinne."

"What are you going to do? Lock me in my room so he doesn't get me?"

I swallowed hard. "If you're careful everything will be fine."

Her eyes went wide. "Fine? Megan and Nina are dead, Anton's still in jail, all my friends hate me, and someone hit you with a gun."

"It wasn't just someone. It's the person we've been looking for all this time and I'm going to get him." I looked up at the sharp stars piercing the sky. This was too much for anyone to bear, let alone my own daughter. "I love the dress you picked out," I said in a softer voice. "You have great taste."

"It was on sale," she said.

I smiled. She always looked for a bargain. "I'm sorry I couldn't go with you."

"Beverly came," she said flatly.

My stomach fell. Linda wasn't going to let Beverly come over again anytime soon. I pressed my hands on her shoulders. "I'm sorry for ruining your birthday."

"It was already ruined. Hardly anyone showed up." She drew her brows together. "And when I ran outside Shannon's mom was parked out front. I went up to the car, and she wouldn't even look at me. Her mom drove off like I wasn't there."

I straightened. "That was mean. They're all scared right now, but I promise you everything will be okay. And if they're still mean to you, fight back. You're better than they are." I reached out for her, but she pulled away.

"You don't understand." She turned to me, eyes cold. "I wish we hadn't had the party here," she said, and we walked back to the house side by side, miles apart.

* * *

Corinne went upstairs without a word and slammed her bedroom door. Jeff sat on the couch with a defeated look on his face. I sat down beside him.

He pressed his hands on his knees. "That officer you put outside told me you could have been killed today, Sam."

"But that didn't happen. I almost had him. He escaped but we're close. We have his name," I said.

"First it was Anton, then Devon. Now this guy?" The concern in his dark eyes ate at me. "Next time it will be someone else."

"It won't. This is the guy. We found evidence in his house." I shouldn't have said more but I had to tell him, to make him understand. "He had photos of Shannon, of all the girls on the team ..." I paused. "Including Corinne."

"Corinne?" The color drained from Jeff's face. "She's not safe here. You know that don't you? Because sometimes I wonder." His words cut right through me. There was a long pause and then he said, "I can't sit back and wait for you or Corinne to be killed. I'm taking her up to my mom's place by the lake."

"She needs me, Jeff. I'm her mother." I stared at him in disbelief.

"Corinne does need you. But you're stuck in a loop, Sam, and Corinne and I need to get out of it before it turns deadly. We'll leave tomorrow. I can take time off, and my mom can stay with Corinne when I go into work. She will have all of our attention," he said in a tone that left no room for argument.

"I'll check in when I can," I said, as the reality sank in that I'd be farther away from her than ever—and it was probably for the best.

Chapter Thirty

I DID MY best to concentrate as Brian explained that Robert Michael Concannon was an only child who had grown up in Hough's Neck. He was twenty when Bridget was murdered. He moved to Portsmouth, New Hampshire, with his parents shortly after that. He enlisted in the army in 1996, later served in Afghanistan, almost lost his leg after stepping on an IED, and was honorably discharged in 2002. His parents died in a car accident a year later and left him the money he used to buy the house in Lakeville. He worked for an insurance company until 2007 when he quit.

"Then he falls off the grid," Brian said. "Never married. No girlfriend that we know of. No friends. No criminal record. No digital footprint. We got fingerprints and DNA from the house, but no matches. Officers canvassed his old neighborhood on the Neck. No one remembers him, but most people who lived there then have moved away."

George rubbed his clean-shaven jaw. "None of his neighbors in Lakeville got a good look at him. He kept to himself. He's basically the invisible man."

Brian nodded. "We found photos of Bridget, Shannon, the dance team, and of other victims in his basement, but the only photo we've found of Concannon is a license photo from 2008." He showed me it. "Is it familiar?"

My frustration rose as I stared at Concannon's jowls, broad forehead, curly brown hair, and bulging round eyes the license indicated were gray. "I don't recognize him."

"No one does." Brian wrote *blue rose*, *watch*, and *butterfly* on the whiteboard and stepped back. "But the missing blue rose from your shoe connects him to Bridget's murder. The watch connects him to Megan's and the butterfly he bought connects him to Nina's murder. We have enough evidence to convict him. We just have to find him. And we will." He turned to George. "See if Concannon has any army buddies who are still in touch with him. Sam and I will talk to Anton, Shannon, and her parents. We'll start with the Delaneys."

As George went to leave, Brian smiled. "I've been meaning to ask. How was your date?"

"Fun," George replied.

"Fun?" Brian said. "Here's an excuse to talk to her again. Tell Alice to get the paper to publish his name and photo. We'll release that info to the local television stations, too. That might bring someone forward." After George left, Brian said, "Fun, that's all George has to say?" and I smiled for what felt like the first time in forever.

As I made copies of the photos of Shannon to show her parents, I took a quick, heart-stopping look at the one of Corinne. Jeff had sent a brief text saying they were fine. But I felt sick thinking of them at the lake without me.

I reassured myself it would have been easy for Concannon to find the dance competition photos online, including the one of her. The candid ones of Shannon were a different story. I studied a recent one of her leaning against a boat railing. The boat was familiar, looked like Max's boat. I'd been on it once for a dance team cruise. I enlarged the photo and made out metal railings, polished wooden trim, a red stripe on the hull with a blue star on the tip. Someone stood next to her, but all you could see was part of an arm in a gray shirt printed with black anchors. Something sparkled on a gold chain around Shannon's neck but that wasn't what caught my eye. She was wearing pink earrings that could have been tiny dancers—like the ones Renee showed us in her store.

* * *

Max insisted we meet at Cyrano's, a trendy restaurant on the boardwalk in Starlight Bay. The restaurants were all decent, but if you wanted a quiet place with white tablecloths you went to Cyrano's. Max and Barb were seated at an outdoor table with a view of the sun setting over the marina. We sat down with them. I ordered an old-fashioned. Cyrano's made a damned good one with a cherry that was a delicious dark shade of burgundy and a fat, slow-melting ice cube. Brian got a gimlet, Barb a Campari cocktail, and Max scotch, and calamari and arancini for the table.

Brian turned his mirrored sunglasses to Barb. "We thought Shannon would be here."

She explained she was with Jay in New York, for the audition the *Wish Upon a Dancer* folks had promised her. "Opportunity of a lifetime," she said. "Plus, she's safer there." I wasn't so sure about that.

Max sampled his scotch and turned to Brian. "I thought you had the guy, but you had the wrong one, and now there's a suspect on the loose. What's going on?"

"Between us, it's only a matter of time before we apprehend him." He pushed the license photo toward them. "This guy's name is Robert Michael Concannon. He's a person of interest in Nina's murder, Megan's, and Bridget's, too. Do you recognize him?"

"I heard about him on the news." Max straightened his pink shirt cuff. "But I've never seen him before." He turned to Barb. She didn't recognize him, either.

"He had photos of Shannon in his house. We thought he might be a family friend," Brian said.

"Photos of Shannon?" Barb's lavender-shadowed eyes widened with alarm.

Brian nodded. "We found some going back to when she was a little girl. I'd say he's obsessed with her."

"Obsessed?" Barb stammered.

I spread more photos on the table. "I brought these for you to look at. Do you have any idea how he could have gotten these pictures?" The table descended into tense silence as they looked through them.

Max cast a sharp glance at Barb. "I told you not to share personal things on social media."

Her hand closed around the amethyst pendant at her throat. "I only share dance photos with my friends on Facebook. I don't know how he got these other pictures."

Max's face turned pinker than his shirt. "Barbara, a homicidal maniac has pictures of our little girl, pictures you took. There has to be a way he got them."

Barb picked at her nails. "I uploaded our photos to a site called Peek-a-boo. I was worried if we had a fire or a robbery, we'd lose all those memories."

"And now we could lose her." Max thrust himself back in disgust. "I told you not to use those sites, but you never listen." He raised his hand like he might strike her but lowered it to his drink.

"Anyone could make a mistake like that," I said. "Those sites claim to be secure, but none of them are, especially not Facebook." I handed them the photo of Shannon wearing the earrings. "What can you tell me about this picture?"

"I've never seen it before." Barb glanced at Max. "Have you?" He shook his head.

"Was it taken on your boat?" I asked.

Max pushed the photo back at me. "That's not my boat."

"You sure?" I said.

"I know my own boat." He set his steely eyes on me.

I smiled. "Then whose boat is it?"

"I have no idea." He turned to Barb. "Do you?"

"Might belong to someone on the team," she said.

"Was this photo taken on Shannon's birthday?" I asked.

"Why do you think that?" Barb asked.

"She's wearing her birthday present." I gave Barb a hopeful glance.

She looked at it more closely. "Right. Max gave her that necklace for her birthday, her first diamond. She was over the moon. Remember, hon?"

He managed a weak smile. "Jewelry is Barb's department. I just sign the checks around here."

Barb ran her tongue over her mauve lips. "I bought the necklace and showed it to you. You told me it was lovely and signed the card."

"Of course, I remember the necklace. It was a pear-shaped diamond like the one I gave you back in the day," Max said. The waitress brought the appetizers. Max helped himself to fried calamari. "This is the best thing on the menu."

I took a bite of a tasty tentacled one. "Did you give her those earrings for her birthday, too?"

Max squinted at the photo and turned to Barb. "Did I give her those?"

Barb took a look. "No. One of her friends must have."

I waited a beat. "Any idea which friend?" Barb shook her head.

Brian helped himself to an arancini. "Can you think of anyone who might have taken these photos of Shannon? A fan or maybe someone she met on the internet?"

Barb fingered the strap of her taupe spandex dress. Here I was in black jeans from Marshall's thinking I was chic. "I can't. But I'm very careful about who Shannon associates with."

"Could she have met someone through Jay? Maybe one of those talent scouts he knows took pictures of her," I said.

"Jay would never let them do that. He's as careful as I am." She cast a glance at Max. "He's like a second father to her."

Max's mouth twisted bitterly. "He dotes on her the way someone who doesn't have to pay the bills can." He turned to us. "My brother is softhearted, but he lacks common sense."

"Why do you say that?" I asked.

"Always encouraging those addicts' half-cocked schemes and

dreams. Jay doesn't understand. People aren't entitled to happiness. They have to work for it." He folded his manicured hands on the table. "He tells Shannon to shoot for the moon and her dreams will come true. But she wouldn't like the life of a dancer if she had to pay her own way."

Barb shot him a scorching look. "She's far too young to give up on her dreams." She sounded like someone whose own dreams had let her down. Given Max's reputation for chasing women, I wasn't surprised. There was a story floating around that Miranda Crowne and Barb were dining at some swanky restaurant when Max came in with a pretty girl on his arm. Barb ate her entire meal without ever looking his way—quite a change from the days when she used to brag to me and Bridget about her perfect dream house, perfect wedding, perfect Max.

"I'd like to see Shannon realize her dreams," Max said, "but she needs to be practical to get there." He eyed the people milling on the boardwalk like a man who has something better to do. "Are we done here?"

Brian speared another arancini. "Bring Shannon to the station when she gets back from New York. We'll chat more then."

Barb frowned. "Why does she have to go to the station like some criminal?"

"We're not treating her like a criminal," Brian said. "We're keeping her safe."

Max curled his sun-spotted hand around her smooth one. "We'll bring Shannon by, but that's your last chance to talk to her. I'm hiring my own security, someone who knows how to do their job." He gave us an imperious look, flagged down the waitress, and paid the check.

As they went to leave, Barb turned to me. "It's strange how you narrowly escaped being killed by Concannon."

"Strange?" I said.

She nodded. "You escaped him twice when no one else did. Makes me wonder why he keeps letting you go." I gave her a hard stare as Max hooked his arm in hers and they left.

"Don't listen to her," Brian said when they were out of sight. "How about another round?" I nodded. I wasn't ready to return to my empty house. And there was calamari left.

As I finished my third old-fashioned, I said, "I could have sworn Shannon is on Max's boat in the photo, but he says it's not his. Why lie about that?"

"You could be mistaken." Brian stroked his chin. "Or he might be lying for reasons that have nothing to do with the case. Maybe he had another woman on board and told Shannon to keep it secret." He stood up. "Let's go."

We walked down the boardwalk toward a club called Deja Blue, known for the shifting cones of blue light it sent out over the bay. Things were in full swing as we walked by. It attracted a young crowd, not much younger than I was, but they made me feel old. I thought Brian wanted to keep the party going, but he went past the club to the end of the boardwalk. I teetered as I stared at the glassy green water below. Usually I can handle a few drinks, but I'd eaten almost nothing that day apart from the fried squid.

He pointed to a wooden ladder with mossy rungs leading down to a pier extending into the harbor. "Think you can handle it?" I told him to shut up and clambered down, almost missing my footing. He followed me onto a wooden walkway. "I think Max moors his boat at this end of the marina," he said. "A white yacht called the *New Dawn*."

"*New Dawn*, new Quincy, maybe someday we'll get the New Barb." I smiled.

We scanned the crowded marina and finally spotted the *New Dawn* at the end of a pier perpendicular to the one we were on. We walked over. Up close, it was long, sleek, and beautiful as a blue-shadowed glacier. Brian ran his hand along the bow. "I'd like a boat like this, but only in my impractical dreams," he said.

I grabbed the cool damp railing and felt the sting of disappointment. "It's not the same boat. The one in the photo has metal railings, but this has wooden ones and the stripe on the hull is black. The one in the photo is red."

"You sure?" Brian leaned in for a look.

"I'm sure." As I climbed back up the ladder, I felt defeated. Max hadn't lied about the boat and once again I'd fixated on the wrong thing. "If it's not Max's boat in the picture then whose boat is it?" I asked.

"Shannon should know," Brian said.

As we walked along the boardwalk, David Bowie's "Let's Dance" spilled out from Deja Blue. My head pounded. I told Brian I felt woozy from my drinks, and we sat down on a bench. I pressed my hands on my knees and leaned forward. Bowie crooned, "Put on your red shoes," and everything went quiet. A familiar buzzing ran up the back of my head. The vision came as softly as the water kissing the edge of the pier.

A disembodied voice in the darkness said, "You must do this to survive." I thought Brian was saying this, but he wasn't. "Do it this way. Put the butterfly there and hold it," The voice was demanding, like I was some kind of apprentice. As I touched the repulsive creature, the voice wormed its way through my mind. "The black flowers unfold in swirls of India ink. My thoughts are yours. Yours are mine. I'm not telling you the whole story yet." I began sobbing.

"Hey there." Brian touched the back of my neck. I realized I really was sobbing.

"Those drinks were stronger than I thought," I said. I wiped my tears with my sleeve. "You need to forget you ever saw this." After I'd gotten home from the hospital all those years ago, sometimes I cried so hard in my room it was like I'd never stop. But once I had my own apartment I wouldn't let anyone see me—not my father, not my roommate. By the time I met Jeff, I almost never cried.

Brian's concerned look made me even more embarrassed. "We all lose it now and then."

"You don't understand." I hesitated. "What if Barb's right? What if I did something to help him, and that's why he let me go?"

"You remember something, Sam?" I shook my head, and he said, "Don't let that foolish woman get under your skin." He rested his arm behind me on the back of the bench. I smelled his spicy cologne, felt comfort from the soft rise and fall of his chest.

"It's not just her. I was sure it was Max's boat and it wasn't. I was sure about Devon and I was wrong. I was as close to the killer as you are to me, and he slipped through my fingers. I'm beginning to doubt my ability to do this job."

He leaned forward, staring at the wraiths of fog drifting over the marina. "When I started out as a detective it was my dream job. But I got worn down by seeing the awful things people went through every day, especially after I failed my brother. Finding Bridget's body was the worst moment of my life. It really broke me, Sam," he said, repeating what he'd told me before. Only this time tears filmed his eyes. He pushed them away. "Forget you saw *that*," he said and composed himself. "And now Nina. Jesus, Mary, and Joseph, it makes me wonder what the point of this world is. But when I found you, the way you looked at me, like you'd come back from something so terrible you were astonished to be alive, that was the best moment of my life. It changed me. I knew I had to keep doing this job because I could make a difference. We don't win them all or even most, but every victory matters." He squeezed my hand like for once he needed me. "How's Corinne holding up?" he said, and lit a cigarette.

"She's with Jeff at his mom's place by the lake for a while. I worry about them up there. The Chief's sending an officer to keep an eye on them." I swallowed hard. "It feels like it's really over between me and Jeff. Maybe it's for the best."

"He'll be back," he said. "That's the difference between us. When someone leaves me, it's because they know better. Even Finian didn't come back." Finian was his black cat who had headed out in a thunderstorm and never returned. It was a running joke that Quincy's lead detective couldn't find his own cat. When we were working a case, we even used the name as a safe word sometimes. "But Jeff won't be able to stay away and he's a fool if he does." He smiled and took a puff of his cigarette.

"You're going to kill yourself with those," I said for what felt like the hundredth time.

"You live, you die. I accept however it unfolds." He winked at me and tossed the burning ember into the drink.

Chapter
Thirty-One

GEORGE BROUGHT CINNAMON buns that Casey had made to the station the next morning. They were perfectly thick and doughy and glazed with orange-vanilla frosting. I envied his restraint as he carefully tore off a small piece.

"No decent leads from the photo we released yet," Brian said. "All we need is one person who remembers this man. One fucking person."

"I didn't get any leads from Concannon's army buddies, either," George said, "but I have a person for you. After Bobby was discharged, he spent time at a VA hospital in Portsmouth in rehab for his injured leg. He was also treated for heroin addiction, but left their substance abuse program for a rehab in Quincy called Hope for a New Day. Turns out someone we know was working there." He paused. "Jay Delaney."

"I thought Jay worked at Road to Redemption." I sank my teeth into my cinnamon roll. It was all I could do not to eat three or four of them—nothing between me and despair except a mouthful of orange-vanilla frosting.

"He did a stint in rehab at Hope for a New Day." Brian leaned back in his chair. "Found his way to sobriety, worked there a while, and started Road to Redemption." He smiled. "If he's still in touch with Concannon, he could help us find him."

George wrapped the rest of his cinnamon bun up in a napkin. "Unfortunately, I couldn't reach Jay."

Brian frowned. "He's in New York with Shannon, giving her the chance of a lifetime."

"'Chance of a lifetime'?" George raised an eyebrow.

I licked frosting off my fingers. "Jay wrangled her an audition with *Wish Upon a Dancer* without Anton. I suppose from their perspective it's a juicy story. If she gets past this round, it's on to the next level on her road to fame and fortune."

"Leaving us to figure out who killed her friends and stop her from becoming his next victim. Let's talk to Jay as soon as he gets back," Brian said.

I nodded. "We can talk to Anton while we're waiting and show him those photos of Shannon we found in Concannon's basement. If Concannon is his accomplice, they might convince Anton to turn on him."

* * *

We interviewed Anton at the house of corrections in a room with gray cinderblock walls, a gray table, and gray chairs. He'd only been there two weeks, but it was like a light had gone out inside him. He crossed his long legs awkwardly in the chair that was too small for him and said, "Why are you here again? I've told you everything I know."

Brian pushed a photo over to him. "This guy's name is Robert Michael Concannon. You know him?"

"No."

Brian cocked his head. "You sure? Because he murdered Nina Crowne. You want to see pictures of what your buddy did to her, I can show you."

Anton gave the dusty overhead light fixture an imploring glance. "He's not my buddy. I don't know who you're talking about."

Brian leaned closer. "I'm talking about the guy who has a basement full of pictures of your girlfriend."

"He had pictures of Shannon?" Anton's voice cracked.

I gave him a folder with the copies of them. He became sickly pale as he looked through it. I pushed the picture of Shannon on the boat toward him. "This one look familiar?"

He studied it. "I've never seen it before. Why are you asking me about this?"

"Concannon had that photo. He also had Megan's watch," Brian said.

Anton's eyes went wide. "He had her watch?"

"Yup. The Disney watch her mom gave her when she was a little girl. How do you explain that?"

"I can't."

"I can. He's your accomplice. He helped you kill Megan and he took the watch. Or you gave it to him," Brian said.

He gave me a distraught look. "He's not my accomplice and I didn't kill Megan."

Brian jammed his elbows into the table. "Are you even listening to me? Concannon murdered Nina and now he's stalking your girlfriend." Anton's gaze shifted away. "Look at me. I'm talking about Shannon here. The girl you say you love. The girl who, in case you haven't heard, has an audition with *Wish Upon a Dancer*. The girl who's got a bright future if this guy doesn't take it away."

"I'm happy for her." Anton rubbed the round burn scar on his wrist.

"You're happy for her?" Brian said. "Because the way you're acting, I think you'd rather see her die than succeed without you."

"That's not true. I love her." He pushed his hand through his hair.

Brian shook his head in disappointment. "I don't know what kind of hold he has over you, but if you love her, now is the time to tell us how to find him."

Anton rubbed the scar some more. "I want to help, but I don't know who you're talking about."

"I'm talking about the man who killed Nina. The man who helped you kill Megan. The man who gave you those scars." I pointed to the scars hidden among the tattoos going up his arm. It was a leap, but this killer left scars. He'd scarred me. If Anton knew him, this man may have scarred him, too.

His startled eyes met mine. "You're wrong," he said after a painful breath. "Shannon gave me those scars." His mouth twisted. "Sometimes she puts cigarettes out on me. She begged me not to tell, because she can't help it. She cuts herself, too, says someone in her life hurt her, and that's why she does it." What little color there was in his face left it. "Could this man you're talking about be the one who hurt her?"

I shifted in my chair, imagining Shannon pressing a lit cigarette into one of those roses or flames on his arm. If what Anton said was true and Concannon was the man who hurt her, that meant he was already part of her life, perhaps even someone she trusted. "It's possible," I said, "And that means she could be in grave danger." I leaned closer to him. "We believe Concannon is planning to kill her, and we need to find him before he does. Did she say anything else about the man who hurts her?"

"She told me he whispers poison in her ears. And . . ." His pasty face shone with sweat as he went on. "She said she heard his voice in her head telling her to set my bird free. I thought she was making it up because she felt guilty for leaving a window open. But what if she wasn't?" He gave me a desperate look. "You have to convince her to tell you who he is, Mrs. S., please."

* * *

"What was all that about the bird?" Brian said in the deli across from the house of corrections.

"Anton's bird went missing while Shannon had it. Maybe that was her way of admitting she let him fly the coop." I paused. "Or something worse."

"Or Anton's making things up." He stared at me. "Do you really think she gave him those cigarette burns? Doesn't make sense. She's pretty and talented. She has everything going for her."

I sliced my cheeseburger in half. Blood oozed out from the under-cooked meat. "Just because she's pretty and talented doesn't mean she isn't troubled. I could imagine her cutting herself and hurting Anton to deal with the pressure she's under."

"But he never mentioned it before. Why now?" Brian grumbled.

"She's his girlfriend. He didn't want to make her look bad. but now he realizes she's in danger, so he's speaking up."

Brian slathered a mound of mayo on his chicken sandwich. "Or he's lying to make it look like it's Concannon's fault to take the heat off himself."

"Or Anton really is innocent." I dipped a limp fry in ketchup. "Let's see what Shannon has to say."

"Fine. But don't ask about her hurting herself or Anton, unless you have a damn good reason. The Delaneys will be all over us if you do."

I frowned. "I'll only go there if I absolutely have to, like, you know, to save her life."

"Things don't always work out the way you expect when you try to save someone who doesn't want to be saved." Brian gave me a grim look, probably thinking about how his efforts to save his brother had gone so wrong.

Chapter
Thirty-Two

SHANNON QUALIFIED FOR the next level of *Wish Upon a Dancer* and was still in New York. Barb was staying with her, but Jay came back for a Road to Redemption meeting at the Our Lady of the Doves church on the Neck. We made plans to talk to him afterward. We parked opposite the church beneath a giant oak whose roots pushed up through the sidewalk. The church needed a new coat of paint. The blackbirds gathering in a half-dead tree on the lawn serenaded us as we walked up to the front door.

Jay greeted us with a smile as glowing as this place was bleak. We followed him downstairs through a familiar warren of halls painted a glossy shade of eggshell. My father was an atheist, my mother a lapsed Catholic. My experience of religion consisted entirely of Bridget taking me here with her, elbowing me when it was time to kneel, handing me the hymnal, then tugging me downstairs with her when the service was over to sample the baked goods, laughing as she said, "This is how I save you."

We passed the bulletin board with photos of smiling neighborhood girls who took dance lessons here (far more low-key than Elle's), notices about the domestic-violence support group that Bridget used to call the Wife Beaters Club, and a schedule of Road to Redemption meetings. I helped myself to coffee from a giant urn, avoided the plate of Oreos, and sat down in a metal chair. Jay leaned back, black shirt open at the neck, the gold RTR gleaming against the dark curls on his chest. "To what do I owe the pleasure?"

Brian filled him in on our concerns about Shannon and showed him a photo. "Do you know this guy? Name's Robert Michael Concannon."

"That's the guy who was on the news, right?" Brian nodded. Jay furrowed his brow as he leaned over it. "He seems familiar but I'm not sure why. Can you help me out here?"

"'He was a patient at Hope for a New Day same time you were working there," Brian said. "He served in Afghanistan, had a bum leg, was dealing with PTSD and substance abuse. Both parents died in a car accident."

Jay studied the photo more closely. "Now I remember. He looked different then but that's Bobby. He was a big guy with a sad soul, all alone in the world, zero personality. He used to sit in our rec room for hours making model boats and dollhouses. He paid attention to the smallest details, even painted the flowers on the teacups. He didn't tell me much about himself. I figured the war did a number on him." He scratched his head. "I pegged him for a lonely man living in his own little world."

"Did he have any friends in Quincy?" I asked.

"He told me he was looking for a friend named JP or TT or PJ, something like that. He thought I might know him, but I didn't. It was like there was a weight on his shoulders. I worried he might off himself, told him we could help with addiction, but he needed to talk to a counselor to straighten out his head."

"Did he get counseling?" I sipped my bitter coffee.

"I don't know. I lost track of him."

"Has he reached out to you since then?" I asked.

Jay shook his head. "He was odd but seemed harmless. You think Shannon is in danger from him?"

Brian frowned as he brushed a wet leaf from his shoe. "That's why we're here."

"Jesus, Barb told me you had a suspect, but when I saw that photo on the news I didn't realize it was the Bobby I knew." He hefted himself up from his chair. "I have to find him before he finds her."

"Leave that to us." Brian motioned Jay back down. "If anything else comes to you, let me know."

* * *

"Do you believe Jay's story about Concannon?" Brian asked as we sat parked up the street, waiting for him to leave.

"There might be more to it," I said. "But he has no reason to lie. He's not a suspect. He has an alibi for Megan's murder. He was at Barb's party with me when Devon's suicide was staged. And he cares about Shannon."

"He's so protective of her, he could try to handle this on his own." Brian's hand went to the ignition as Jay pulled his Mercedes out of the church driveway. "With any luck he'll lead us to Concannon."

We followed at a distance as Jay drove straight home. His pale orange town house in Starlight Bay had a view of the marina, but it was nothing compared to Max and Barb's mansion above the bay. Lights came on as he made his way past the fountain grass and tasteful plantings and went inside. Brian reached under the seat for a thermos, filled two plastic cups and handed me one. "It's gonna be a long night."

The coffee was laced with bourbon, strong and warm all the way down, just the way I liked it. "It would be nice to find that other counselor Concannon went to. They might know more than Jay," I said.

"Yeah." Brian's arm brushed softly against me as he grabbed a pack of cigarettes from the glove compartment and lit one up.

"You better roll the window," I said.

"Your wish is my command." As he leaned back, his knee touched mine. He let it stay there a beat too long, and I felt his touch all the way up through me. "Want some more coffee?" he said. I told him I'd had enough.

The smell of the sea came through the window. A bell buoy tolled in the distance until it was all I could hear. It was as if the sound was muffled in black petals. I could feel it inside me with each small breath I took. My leg hurt from when I'd been knocked down in the barn. I stretched it out and we sat there in silence for what felt like forever, watching the shut door of that orange town house.

"I bet he's snoring in front of the TV now," Brian finally said. He glanced in annoyance at his phone. "Shit. I'm late."

"You got someplace to be?" When I got home, I poured myself some more bourbon, my only salvation lately, making the world tolerable one sip at a time. I took a fortifying swallow, ignored the dirty dishes stacked by the sink, and called Corinne. She'd been dodging my texts and calls for the past couple of days, but this time she answered.

She told me they'd just gotten back from dinner at the White Tiger Inn, a fancy place offering expensive prix fixe dinners that left you hungry. I chased my sinking feeling with more bourbon. We always went there on vacation. She went on, "I got one of those dry ice mocktinis, you know, the ones that look like fog is coming out of them."

I knew and I was missing out. I pushed away the voice inside me that said I'd never go there again with her and told her about Shannon making it to the next level of *Wish Upon a Dancer*.

"I know. She's got twenty thousand likes on her Insta. I'm happy for her," she said.

"Does she always get so many likes?" I asked.

"She got almost as many on her birthday," she said.

"I hope she wins." I stared into the remains of my drink. "How's everything going?"

"Okay." She paused. "Dad and I made babka today." I took a long breath. Jeff and I usually made babka together on vacation. For a second I could smell the sweet scent and feel the satiny softness of the dough. "I wish you could have had some," she said.

"Me too." I paused and added, "I love you."

"I love you, too," she said. "You want me to put Dad on?" I told her sure.

Jeff and I shared an awkward hello. "So, how are things going?" I asked.

"As well as can be expected." After a painful silence he said, "How are *you* doing?"

"Working hard." I paused. "Heard you made babka, without me."

"Wish you were here," he said.

"Are you coming back anytime soon?" I asked.

More silence. He finally said, "I'll bring Corinne back for practices, but we're staying here for the rest of the summer. It's best for her."

My stomach tightened. "I miss her, Jeff. If you bring her back, please tell me."

"I will," he said. "And you can come up here whenever you want."

"I will when I have time," I replied, though I worried if I went up there, I might lead Concannon right to them. I paused. "We've got someone looking out for you but let me know immediately if anything doesn't feel right." He told me he would.

The Lean Cuisine I'd taken out of the freezer was sweating on the counter, but I wasn't hungry. I thought of all those likes Shannon got on her Instagram post about *Wish Upon a Dancer*. Maybe Concannon had liked it, too. I brought the post up on my phone and spent half the night searching through the users who'd liked it. No one named Bobby or Robert Concannon. He could have been using a different handle but there was no obvious way to tell if it was him. There were lots more posts. She'd chronicled her short existence in excruciating detail. Most were of her striking cute, inspiring, or suggestive poses. I scrolled until I found the birthday post with thousands of likes. She was standing on a beach as the wind blew her diaphanous cover-up against her, revealing the faint outline of her string bikini beneath it. The caption read, Every minute of the day, every second, I am reborn, happy infinite birthdays to me (heart emoji). No likes from anyone named Bobby or Robert. I was about to give up when I noticed a post near the birthday post.

I enlarged it to see it more clearly. There she was—wearing those pink earrings and leaning on the railing of a boat that looked like the one in the picture we'd found at Concannon's. It had been posted the day after her birthday. There were no suspicious likes or comments. I brought up the photo we'd found at Concannon's on my phone. Her Instagram picture looked just like it. He could have printed the photo from here. Or he could have taken the photo and shared it with her. My mouth went dry.

Chapter
Thirty-Three

SHANNON CAME TO the station two days later. We put her in the nice interview room with the plaid couch, matching chairs, and a vase of fake flowers on a pine table. Her blond hair glistened. She wore a red dress and matching patent leather stilettos. She hung her tiny red leather bag on the back of a chair, sat down next to Max and Barb and turned to us with a poised smile.

"I hear congratulations are in order," I said.

"I still can't believe it." She fluffed her hair. "Is there, like, a two-way mirror in here?"

Brian rolled his eyes. "No. We need to talk." She frowned, but he went on. "We have reason to believe you have information that would help us find Nina's killer."

Her green eyes went wide. "Me?"

Max gave her a sharp glance. "Do you know who they're talking about?"

"I have no idea, Daddy."

"This man's name is Robert Michael Concannon. Do you recognize him?" I showed her the photo.

She shook her head. "I don't know anyone named Robert Michael Concannon." She enunciated each syllable of his name. "Is he the killer?"

Brian stared straight into her bright eyes. "He's a person of interest. We found photos of you in his house."

"Mom told me. What a creeper." She frowned.

"We found more than photos. We found evidence indicating he may have murdered Megan, Nina, and other girls."

Shannon's mouth fell open. "You did?"

Brian nodded. "And evidence he could be targeting you as his next victim. You sure you don't remember him?"

"I swear, I don't," she said.

I took a breath. "The photo I showed you was from when he was younger. He probably looks different now. He might not call himself Robert. Could go by Bobby or another name. He might seem nice, but he's dangerous. Can you think of anyone?"

She told me no. Her phone buzzed. She wormed it out of her tiny patent leather bag. "Oh my goodness, I'm so sorry to interrupt, Mrs. S., but my *Wish Upon a Dancer* post hit fifty thousand likes."

"That's wonderful, but I'm not sure you appreciate the seriousness of this." I showed her the photo taken on the boat. "We found this in Concannon's house. Can you tell us anything about it?"

She let out a little huff. As she held it close her expression darkened. "I don't remember this, either. Lots of random people take pictures of me." She gave Barb an anxious glance and passed it to her. "Do you remember, Mom?"

Barb lowered her eyes. "No. Samantha already showed it to me."

I turned to Shannon. "Do you recognize where the photo was taken?"

"That could be Lane's dad's boat. He took us out on it once."

"When?"

"Sometime in July."

I smiled. "I love those earrings you're wearing in the picture. Where did you get them?"

She squinted at the photo again. "Those are my pink dancer earrings. This is kind of weird, but someone sent them to me. There was a card, but he didn't sign his name. I figured he was a fan."

"When did he send them to you?" I asked.

She touched her finger to her chin. "It must have been in July, too." She turned to Barb. "Do you remember?"

Barb inhaled sharply. "I don't remember them at all."

"Could the photo have been taken on your birthday?" I asked.

"I didn't go on a boat on my birthday. I went to the movies with Lane and Nina. I wanted to invite Corinne, but Mom said I could only bring two friends."

I gave Brian a careful glance. "Shannon, I have a problem. You said you never saw this photo before, but I found one like it on your Instagram." I brought it up and handed her my phone.

She studied it with concern. "Oh my gosh, I forgot about that. I post so many, they all kind of blur together . . ."

"How did you get the photo?" I asked.

She furrowed her brow as she stared at her nails. "Lane must have taken it with my phone."

"We'll ask her." I kept my voice calm as I went on. "In the photo there's someone next to you and it's not Lane. Can you tell me who that is?"

She tugged on her dress that was so short it left little to the imagination. "I don't remember."

"We'll ask Lane if she remembers." I narrowed my eyes at her. "You do realize withholding information from a murder investigation is a crime, don't you?"

Max leaned forward. "Shannon Ann, tell her everything you know. Now."

She twisted the studded red patent leather cuff on her wrist and glanced at her father. "Fine," she said. "I wasn't with Lane. Nina and I were goofing around down by the marina, going on other people's boats, pretending they were ours." The corner of her mouth turned down. "Some guy invited us to a party on his boat. Nina took the photo of me. He didn't tell us his name, but he didn't look like the guy you showed me. He was a fat, pervy old guy with wicked beer breath, but he didn't do anything to us. I didn't say anything because

I didn't want to get in trouble for drinking." An alarmed look crossed her face. "Oh my god, I was with Nina and now she's dead. And that Robert guy had the picture. Do you think he got it from my Insta?"

"It's possible," I said.

Max shot her a stern look. "You're getting off Instagram and everything else."

"Dad," she said. "I need my followers to vote for me when I'm on *Wish Upon a Dancer*."

"Your life is more important than that." He clenched his jaw.

She pouted at her red polished nails. "I'm not going to let some creeper who's drooling over my Insta ruin my life."

"He's not some creeper, Shannon. He's a killer." Brian set his penetrating gaze on her. "First you said you didn't remember the photo. Now you're telling us a different story. Which one is it? Because our prime suspect had that photo and he gave you the earrings you're wearing in it."

Her mouth fell open. "Oh my god. He did?"

"Tell us who gave you the earrings," Max said through gritted teeth.

"I can't. He never signed any of his cards." Her gaze shifted away.

Max lunged forward. "That wasn't the first time he contacted you?"

"He wrote me encouraging notes. When I was feeling down they made me feel better." She turned to him slowly. "But I swear to god I don't know his name. I thought he was just someone who actually cared about me as a dancer, you know, unlike you."

Brian pressed his arms on the table. "Sending you anonymous gifts and notes doesn't mean he cares about you. He's stalking you. If you know anything about him, you better tell us now so we can find him before he finds you." He gave her a hard stare. "And if I find out you withheld information from our investigation, I will arrest you because I want you to stay alive."

Shannon's eyes darted from Barb to Max. "I don't want to be arrested, but I don't know who he is." The gold studs gleamed as she twisted the patent leather cuff.

"I like that." I pointed to it.

She looked up. "You do?"

Brian cracked a smile. "Looks like something you'd put on a dog."

She frowned and I said, "Don't mind him. He doesn't know anything. Mind if I take a closer look?" She nodded cautiously. I saw the pale horizontal scars on her arm, barely visible beneath a layer of concealer. I exchanged a glance with Brian and turned to her. "Anton is worried about you. He says you hurt yourself, and that sometimes you hurt him."

"What? That's bullshit. I'd never hurt anyone."

I nodded. "Then why would Anton say that?"

She lowered her voice like she was sharing a secret. "Anton's father beats him. He's had a troubled life. And all this time you've made him stay in jail . . . I think he's losing it."

I held her green eyes in mine. "Anton believes you hurt yourself because someone is hurting you. You don't need to be afraid or ashamed to talk about it, if this man has harmed you in any way. He could be the same person who gave you the earrings."

Shannon sucked on her lower lip. "I'm sorry, but I don't know who you're talking about."

I pressed my palms on the table. "Anton told us you do."

Her eyes filled with tears. "Anton is imagining things. I still love him, but this is destroying us." She pressed her hand on her chest with an alarmed look. "My heart is beating way too fast, Mom. Can I go home now?"

Barb put an arm around her. "Of course." She gave me an accusing glance. "The fact they can't solve this crime isn't your fault. None of this is."

Max stood up. "You done, O'Neil?"

"For now," Brian said. "But don't leave the state."

As Shannon strutted out, her heel caught on the rubber mat, and I felt for her as she stumbled clumsily in her high heels. She was usually so graceful. Max followed her, but I asked Barb to stay a moment to talk to us alone. She gave me a querulous look. "What is it now?"

"Shannon *is* hurting herself," I said. "I saw the scars on her arm."

She knotted her hands together. "I am aware. She's under a lot of stress, like all the girls on the team."

I frowned. "Why didn't you tell us?"

She tensed. "It's private and it's not relevant."

I tried to sound sympathetic as I said, "It's nothing to be ashamed of. Lots of girls cut themselves when they're under pressure." I paused. "Shannon may not be comfortable discussing it with us. But she might open up to a professional."

"I don't need your advice. I'm handling it." She stared at me. "I'd appreciate it if you don't talk about this. If anyone at *Wish Upon a Dancer* found out, it could hurt her chances."

Brian shook his head. "Last thing we want to do is hurt her chances. We're trying to save her life."

I pushed the window up after she left. I felt like I was suffocating. I turned to Brian. "I had to bring it up." He nodded. Down below Max pulled his black Mercedes up in front of the station. The last thing I saw was Shannon drawing her slender leg into the car, the shine of her red patent leather shoe.

Chapter
Thirty-Four

GEORGE, BRIAN, AND I met for dinner at the Lazy Dog a few days later. It wasn't far from the station, and we needed a break. A band was already setting up on a makeshift stage when we arrived. I got the mac and cheese with buffalo chicken that I usually ordered when I came here with Jeff.

As we dug into our comfort food, Brian's phone buzzed. He took the call, let out a low whistle and turned to us. "That was Finny. He's dropping the charges against Anton. Concannon raises reasonable doubt." He took a steadying breath. "I bet he got pressure from the Delaneys."

George looked up from his enormous salad with arugula, pecans, and cranberries. Leave it to him to find the one healthy choice on the menu. "You'd think he'd want Anton in jail until we're sure he's not involved."

"Shannon must have demanded his release. She gets what she wants." I lifted a forkful of steaming macaroni to my mouth. "The Delaneys are paying for Anton's lawyer. They think he's innocent. You have to admit it's starting to look like he is."

"Maybe." Brian said.

I showed George the photo of Shannon on the boat. "We found that on Shannon's Instagram. I found the same photo in Concannon's basement. When I asked her about it, she said the boat belonged to Lane's dad, but then she changed her story and said Nina took the photo and they were drinking on some stranger's boat. That could be true. Maybe Concannon grabbed the photo from her Instagram. Or she has some connection to him she doesn't want us to know about."

He rubbed at a spot of dressing on his white shirt. "I'll see if my techs can track down who owns the boat."

Brian leaned in for a look as he cut into his tenderloin medallion. He always ordered the most expensive item on the menu. "Shannon's playing with fire, dressing like she does with that guy stalking her. I thought for sure the threat of arrest would get her to open up, but nope."

I frowned. "Let's not blame her for her fashion choices. It's not her fault a psychopath is obsessed with her. Lots of girls and women dress the way she does. Nothing wrong with that and you don't seem to mind."

George laughed. "She shoots. She scores."

Brian pushed his hand through his hair. "You know that's not what I meant, Sam. I'm just worried about her."

"I am, too," I said. "Maybe she's more afraid of Concannon than of being arrested, or she really doesn't know who he is," I said. "It's possible he writes to her and pretends to be a father figure or mentor, but she's never met him."

"Concannon told that store owner he was buying the earrings for his daughter. In his twisted mind he might see her that way." Brian downed some beer.

"Right," I said. "She doesn't have a great relationship with Max. Jay is more of a father to her. She told me at Barb's party that Jay shares inspiring thoughts with her. Maybe someone else does, too."

"Speaking of Jay." George kept fussing with the stain on his shirt. "When I staked out his house, he stopped at Adams Behavioral Services on his way to work the next morning. I went back there later. The woman at the front desk told me Jay asked her if Concannon had been seeing any of their counselors in 2003. She said she couldn't disclose that information to him or me. When I explained this was part of a murder investigation, she said she'd see what she could find out. She called today and told me Concannon was seeing a counselor named Susan Green. I haven't been able to reach her. She left the job years ago, but I'll keep trying."

"Thanks for saving the best for last, George," Brian said, and we got another round. I finished up what I could of my enormous meal. As the band launched into "Wagon Wheel," a comfort song to go with the comfort food, Brian said, "Come on, let's dance." I hesitated and he shook his head. "If you can sit this song out, you're not human."

I reluctantly followed him onto the dance floor. He was a much better dancer than I was, though I wasn't awful. I felt the heat of his hand on the small of my back as we danced to the song no one could resist. As he turned me around, Mary Ann came through the door and headed straight for us. Her cheeks were aflame and her dark hair was in beautiful disarray. She gave me a cold smile, Brian a withering glance, and said, "I got tired of waiting for you. This doesn't look like a working dinner to me."

I didn't wait to hear Brian's excuse. The last thing I wanted was to cause her any pain. I stood next to George and asked if he'd do me the honor. He politely declined. I sat down and said, "Then I guess you're not human."

He laughed. "You're not the first person to tell me that."

I clasped my hands on the table. "How's it going with Alice?"

He shrugged. "I don't know. We see each other now and then."

"And your sister?"

He was saying, "She's okay. We don't talk much," when Mary Ann stormed past and out the door.

A moment later Brian came back over. "Well, that didn't go well," he said. He turned to me. "I'm trying, Sam. I don't want to lose her, but I don't know . . ."

I smiled. "Just try harder." Another rousing song came on. He grabbed my hand and asked for another dance. I felt that familiar warmth but told him no. He insisted on another round, but I said I had to get home.

* * *

Shadowy figures moved on treadmills in the orange light of the gym in the new apartment building across the street. I quickened my step. Lighted windows in the bars and restaurants glowed against the darkness. I barely recognized this street anymore. It had only been a short time since Max's ground-breaking ceremony, but scaffolding was already rising in the old parking lot. The city was changing all around me—without me—and I still had one foot in the past.

The house felt especially dark and empty without Corinne and Jeff waiting for me, but it was just as well because I needed to think about the case. I lay awake for hours obsessing about it. If Robert had murdered Bridget, why didn't he kindle even a flicker of memory in me? Did he know Shannon or was he someone she didn't notice? Had he known Bridget? I had so many questions, but I couldn't face tomorrow with no sleep. I put a baking show on the bedroom TV. As a young woman kneaded sweet dough, like Jeff's babka dough only flavored with cardamom, I could almost taste the holiday bread sprinkled with sugar that Bridget and I used to love. I was drifting off to circles being cut in the dough when I was hit with the memory of the Crust and Crumb café that I'd shared with Brian. Only this time there was more.

Bridget and I cup our hands around wide mugs in the coffee shop. She talks about her love bunny with the breathless excitement of a new crush. We look inside our favorite house in the model of the Christmas village. And then Bridget tells me she knows the guy who made it. He's so talented, but she feels sorry for him because he has no friends. She says, "I told him you love the house as much as I do," and I feel a twinge of embarrassment, like she's trying to fix me up with this strange guy. She says she's seen the even bigger model he has in his parents' basement, and he showed her how he sands and varnishes the wood and rigs the sails for his model boats. He dreams of having his own boat and sailing around the world someday. He says he'll take her with him.

A shiver went through me. Barb had said someone named Bobby made the Christmas village and also made the model house Bridget planned to give her as a wedding present. Bridget said the man who made the Christmas village made model boats. Concannon made model boats, too. He and Bobby had to be the same person.

I googled the Crust and Crumb café, hoping to find a reference to Concannon. I found a *South Shore Sun* article from when it had closed five years ago that mentioned the Christmas model, but not who made it. Barb didn't remember Concannon, but there had to be someone in Quincy who did. I went to the Everyone Loves Quincy Facebook group. When they weren't arguing about politics or folks who didn't pick up their dog's poop, they liked to chat about the way things used to be.

I got right to it and posted, *Detective Star here. Anyone remember the Christmas village at the Crust and Crumb café?*

I'm still living in it, someone joked.

Musta been all the drugs, someone else shot back.

Now it's a cell phone store, someone said. *Like we haven't got enough of them.*

Least it's not another nail salon or Chinese restaurant.

I thought about snapping back. I saw racist comments like this on this board a lot. But I couldn't afford to alienate them right now. *Anyone know who made the village?*

Did he do something wrong? Cell phone store guy said.

Probably stole Santa's reindeer?

I stole the reindeer.

Sssh! PD *on board.*

I typed. *Just doing some research for a craft project.*

Someone whose handle was KerriS said, *Bobby Concannon made it.*

You know him? I asked.

He lived near me. He set up a bigger Christmas village in his basement every year, she texted. I bit my lip hard. Bridget had mentioned this, too.

Someone said, *Bobby was in my shop class at Quincy High. He could make anything, but was dull as library paste.*

You make library paste exciting, someone else said. *Didn't he sell drugs?*

Probably sold coke like the rest of you, someone typed.

I didn't sell coke, said library paste. *Quiet. She could arrest us.*

I typed a smiley face. *Not here for that.*

There was another pause and then, *Is he the Robert Concannon who's been in the papers?*

I typed, *Yeah.*

Is he the Butterfly Killer? someone asked.

"We're looking into that." I paused. *Have any of you seen Concannon recently or know someone who has?* The comments stopped. I'd scared them off. I typed in my work number and said to call if they thought of anything else. Then I messaged KerriS and asked if we could chat more.

About an hour later she messaged back saying she had a photo that might help with my investigation. She said she was sorry we didn't get to talk more after that horrible day at the Good Luck Shamrock. I realized she was Kerrilyn Sloane, Walter Blair's girlfriend. She went on. *I can't believe my friend Bobby is the same person as that Concannon guy in the paper. He didn't seem like the type to hurt anyone.* I asked if she was still in touch with him. She said she hadn't heard from him in years, but she did have a photo. She'd kept it because she thought he might be famous someday.

The photo showed him standing next to a blond girl in a green-and-black plaid jumper who had to be Kerrilyn. I zoomed in on his broad shoulders, soft mouth, pudgy cheeks, curly brown hair, and round gray eyes—those eyes.

My heart amped up. It was like I'd pulled that black hoodie back and there he was—the guy who picked up me and Bridget.

Chapter Thirty-Five

THE WIPERS COULDN'T keep up with the driving rain as we drove to Kerrilyn's house. "This is all being gentrified now," Brian said as he turned on to Sea Ave., the only way in and out of Hough's Neck. "Already too rich for my blood. But not sure how much it's really changed."

"Yeah, the people born and raised here still hate everyone who wasn't," I said.

"They're good salt-of-the-earth people being priced out of the place where they grew up. Can't blame them." He gave me an admonishing look.

I wasn't ready to feel bad for them. They were like so many Quincy folks who felt special because they'd lived here for generations. Nothing was as important as the football games they'd won, the beers they'd drunk, and fights they'd gotten into all over the city. Their eyes filled with incredulous astonishment when others didn't share their overblown opinions of themselves.

A wave heaved itself against the low seawall, sending a slick spray onto the street. "I hope we don't get cut off," Brian said.

The Neck became an island in storms. Maybe that's why the residents were so tight-knit and didn't like outsiders. With Bridget I'd often felt like one. It didn't help that she and Barb had played cruel pranks on me like the lipstick one and sometimes didn't speak to me for days, or that Bridget cut me out of her life for months after we'd gone to Nostalgia.

I gave the zipper to my rain jacket a tug. It got stuck and I fought the urge to tear it apart. "Goddamn it," I said, and Brian raised an eyebrow. I gave it another tug and it shot up.

We drove by block after block of year-round cottages with plastic awnings and postage-stamp size yards. Kerrilyn lived in one on a side street whose claim to fame was that neighborhood kids changed the sign from Frick Street to Prick Street so often the city put up a new sign in cursive. Dogs came to the windows barking and women pulled the curtains back to get a look at us as we walked past. We stepped over the obstacle course of toys and bikes on Kerrilyn's front walk and past the bucket of cigarette butts on her front step. Before ringing the bell, I put my hand on Brian's arm. "Just so you know, I remembered him."

"Him?"

"Concannon. He's the one who picked me and Bridget up that night. I recognized him in a photo Kerrilyn showed me. Only a memory, but it felt real."

"It's more than a memory." Brian shot me a glance and rang the bell.

Kerrilyn looked much the same as when I'd talked to her before, only this time she wore a sleeveless pink shirt with her jeans. As we shook off the rain in the front hall, she took our coats and said, "Sorry for the mess. I got home late from work. Just finished getting the girls to bed."

"You doing okay?" I asked.

She shrugged. "I miss Walter. One day at a time I guess."

We followed her into her cramped kitchen. As she filled our cups with coffee from a glass carafe on the counter she said, "My oldest is a fan of the dance team. She had her heart set on ballet before all this." Her gaze shifted away. "Do you really think Bobby had anything to do with Nina's murder?"

"He's a person of interest. Detective Star tells me you know him," Brian said.

"I grew up on Arbor Lane, a couple streets over from here. He lived across from me. He was a few years older. I loved the Christmas village he made. He showed me his other models in the basement. I liked watching him work on them. He was always nice to me, though a little boring. I haven't seen him since then."

"Do you know anyone who's still in touch with him?" I asked.

"No. I got the feeling he wasn't close with many people."

"Was he close to Bridget?"

She ran her hands up and down her creamy arms. "I used to look out the window at the kids hanging out down below, wishing I was with them. I saw Bridget go into his house sometimes. They might have been friends, much as you could be friends with him. He probably showed her his models, too."

Brian leaned forward. "Did Walter know Bobby?"

She looked at the flecks of gold in the worn linoleum and took a long breath. "They were friends. He liked Bobby because he didn't call him Wally the Whale like the other neighborhood boys did." I exchanged a glance with Brian. That was the name Vince had given us at the Hat Trick. "He and Walter went out on Saturday nights same as everyone did then. I went with them sometimes and saw you, Bridget, and Barb. The queens of the Neck. Those were the days, huh, Sam?" I nodded, surprised she saw me that way.

Brian pushed his arms forward on the kitchen table. "Kerrilyn, Devon Ford, the man who's been all over the news too, met with someone at the Hat Trick the night Detective Star and Bridget were abducted. We have reason to believe it was Walter."

Kerrilyn nearly choked on her coffee. "You do?"

"We do and we need to know why he was there," Brian said.

Her eyes darted around the room. "I won't get in trouble, will I?"

Brian smiled. "If Walter sold coke to Devon, you won't get in trouble."

"He wasn't selling coke." She twisted her hands. "Walter did favors for people."

"What kind of favors?" Brian asked.

She looked away. "You know, someone asks to you to unload some stuff from a truck. You do it. You don't ask questions. You take a TV for yourself. Someone asks you to sell some coke in return for a cut. Bobby offered Walter serious money to help him with a job that night. All they had to do was beat some guy up and trash his car. He might have said his name was Devon."

I leaned forward. "Why did Bobby want him to beat up Devon?"

"Bobby had a friend who was paying him to do it. He didn't say why."

"Does Bobby's friend have a name?" I asked.

"Walter never told me."

"So, Bobby's friend paid them to beat Devon up the night Bridget was killed. Have I got this straight?" Brian said.

"Yeah." She lowered her voice. "Walter was supposed to meet Devon at the Hat Trick, collect some money from him, tell him to keep his mouth shut, and rough him up to make the point. He said Devon was a pussy, didn't even fight back. Bobby wrote copycat in dog shit on his windshield and slashed his tires." She kept twisting her hands. "Does this have anything to do with what happened to you and Bridget?"

"It could," I said.

"God, I should have said something, but I thought it was the kind of mean prank people play on each other around here, you know?" I nodded. "Bobby had an edge, like most guys here. But it never occurred to me he'd have anything to do with something like that."

"Can you think of anyone who could help us find him, maybe a friend or someone he worked for?"

She kneaded her thighs with her fists. "There was one guy Bobby introduced me to. He said he was the smartest person he ever met and had this special power, that he gave him a purpose in life. The one time I met him he made an impression. He had blond hair like Billy Idol, wore skintight pants. I thought he was a rock star." She turned her claddagh ring round on her finger. "But he was an artist. He showed me a sketch he'd done of Bridget. It looked like she was carved from marble with sunbeams all around her and a butterfly on her forehead." Her eyes met mine. "It was wicked beautiful. He wanted to draw me, too, said I looked like a kitten in a basket. I had a little crush on him, but he scared me at the same time, you know the type?"

I tugged at my collar. I did. The kitchen felt unbearably close. "Do you know his name?"

"Bobby called him JP." She tugged on a springy curl.

"When did you meet him?" I asked.

"Not sure. Maybe in June."

I took a breath. "Did he mention Devon?"

She bit her lip. "No, but he was going on about how Bridget was messing around with some worthless piece of shit."

Brian leveled his eyes on her. "Do you know how we can find JP?"

"I never saw him again. He didn't draw my picture, either."

He shook his head and exhaled loudly. "I have a problem, Kerrilyn. If you saw a drawing Bobby's friend JP did of Bridget with a butterfly on her, why didn't you tell the police?"

She smoothed her pink shirt. "I didn't make the connection."

Brian drew himself up. "Bobby and Walter beat up Devon the night Bridget was killed. JP did a drawing of her with a butterfly like the one found on her body, and you didn't make a connection? Really?"

She stopped smoothing her shirt. "Walter told me he'd be killed if I said anything about any of this." She set her light hazel eyes on us. A toddler wandered in, clutching her blankie to her red cheek, and said, "I have bad thinkings, Mommy."

"Don't we all." Kerrilyn hoisted her up. "This is my littlest. Say night night." The child waved her pudgy hand. "Hope you don't mind, but I have to put her back to bed."

* * *

The rain had stopped but left a chill in the air. I looked down the dark wet street. We were close to where Bridget and I had waited that night. Brian tapped me on the arm. "JP," he said. "Same initials Jay gave us. It appears Concannon paid Walter to beat up Devon, but JP was behind the scenes pulling the strings. We don't know why, but it wasn't a prank. We can't find Concannon and all we have are JP's initials." He lit a cigarette.

My skin grew clammy, my mouth dry. I didn't want to talk about it, but I had to. "Remember what Kerrilyn said about 'kitten in a basket'? Some guy said the same thing to Bridget and me at Nostalgia one night."

Brian lifted a brow. "It's not exactly a unique expression."

"Yeah, but I can still see him—blond, tight jeans, just like Kerrilyn described. He gave me a drug, might have been ecstasy, so his face is kind of a blur, but he made an impression." My heart kicked up a notch. I remembered Bridget waking me up in her attic room after the night at Nostalgia, saying she'd saved me, and how lost I felt.

Brian cracked a smile. "It's scary, you and Kerrilyn having the same taste in men."

"Zip it." I took a slow breath. "Bridget was seeing someone all that winter and spring. I assumed it was the guy from Nostalgia. She never told me his name, but it must have been JP."

"And JP was angry at Bridget for hanging out with Devon. We could have a love triangle as a motive." Brian exhaled smoke into the damp air.

"May I?" I reached for his cigarette. He gave it to me with a smile, and I took a puff. "JP and Devon both did drawings of Bridget. Artistic jealousy could be involved, too."

I handed his cigarette back. He started toward the car, but I said, "Humor me. Let's go over to the end of the Neck." We walked to the spot where I'd waited for Bridget that night. I looked up at her old house, a little balcony tacked onto each floor to grab a view of the churning sea below. The steps leading down from her house were slicked with rain, same as they had been then. "Devon was supposed to pick me and Bridget up right here. Walter and Concannon made sure he couldn't make it. Concannon knew Devon wasn't going to show. He and Bridget were friends. He knew she'd accept a ride from him." I pointed to where the road curved around the end of the Neck. "The street where Concannon used to live is that way. The white car came from that direction."

Brian flicked his cigarette into the water. "How did he know you two would be waiting there?"

"Bridget must have told him. She had no reason to keep it secret and she wasn't exactly tight-lipped."

"And she got herself killed." He sighed. "Want to hash this out some more over Chinese food? There's a place down the street that's not awful."

I shook my head, thinking about the drawing of Bridget that Kerrilyn had mentioned. Appealing as his offer was, there was something I needed to check at home.

Chapter
Thirty-Six

Before

July 12, 1994

I WAS DIGGING into my chicken and mashed potatoes when Bridget showed her parents the photo of the painting Devon had done of her. Her mother gave her a swift, "Very nice, hon," but her father glared at the picture of Bridget as Daphne, her arms folded across her bare breasts, her see-through dress wrinkled up around her thighs.

His fist thundered on the table. "You're not going to a party with that pervert."

She straightened. "He's not a pervert. He's an artist. And you already told me I could go."

He fixed his smoke-colored eyes on her. "Only a pervert would paint you like that when you're only sixteen."

She gave him a look as hard as he was giving her. "He won a prize for that picture of me. Someday he'll make me famous."

He pushed his sleeves up over his muscled arms. "I don't call the whole world looking at my little girl half naked famous. All he's going to do is make you a famous slut."

Bridget looked at her mother. "Tell him I can go."

The corners of her soft mouth turned down. "You and Samantha can watch a movie in the family room. There's pizza rolls in the fridge if you want a snack later."

Bridget pounded up the stairs to her room and slammed the door. I sat next to her on her narrow bed with its nubby white quilt. She lit a joint.

"It's raining," I said. "It might not be the worst thing to stay in and watch *Edward Scissorhands*." I waved my long, black polished nails at her in a vain attempt to lighten her mood.

"We're going. It doesn't matter what my parents just said. Mom has her girls' night out with my aunt. Dad's already half in the bag. We'll leave when he falls asleep."

The reality that this was our last night together sank in. "But your parents will miss you. And if you go to New York with him, you won't even get to finish high school."

She threw me a fierce look. "Seriously, Sam? This is the biggest night of Devon's life and mine. I thought you'd be happy for me."

Happy? I smoothed out the wrinkled scatter rug I'd slipped on once after we'd made drinks from everything in her parents' liquor cabinet. She opened the door to the little balcony off her room, and we stepped outside. She passed me the joint. I inhaled deeply, hoping it would help me escape my miserable self. We often smoked here on summer nights. She'd point to boats sailing past and say that one is taking me to the Bahamas, that one to Tahiti, Los Angeles, Alaska. I'd point at boats, too, though the thing I feared most was being left behind by the people I loved. Tonight, she and Devon were leaving me behind for New York. Once she made up her mind, there was no changing it.

"I am happy for you." I smiled uncertainly.

She smiled back. "I have a feeling you're going to meet someone tonight."

"Hope so," I said, though Devon was the only person for me.

We went back inside, and I pulled my tank top over my head, shimmied out of my jeans, grabbed my blue dress from the back of a chair, and slid into it. The silky material felt nice beneath my palms. I stepped into my blue shoes with a rose on the toes and zipped Bridget into the silver sequined dress she'd gotten on sale at Wet Seal. She clicked over to her bureau in her red stilettos, turned to me and said, "Come on, let's get beautiful."

We leaned close to the mirror with the photos of her, me, and Barb, stuck on the frame. We put on black eyeliner and smoky gray shadow and flicked thick black mascara over our lashes. Bridget went for glossy red lipstick. I chose brick-brown. It was difficult, but I finally got the laurel crown pinned into her hair. She pulled mine back with blue butterfly clips, and we smiled at ourselves in the mirror. We'd achieved our signature drugged-out doll look. But as she tilted her face toward mine, she reminded me more of a blow-up doll, larger than life, something rattling around in the emptiness inside—something I didn't understand.

"I don't get why you have to leave and never come back," I said. "Are you that in love with Devon?"

She took a moment to answer. "I'm not in 'love' love with him. But I love that he's taking me away from here."

I stared at her in disbelief. She'd put me through all that heartbreak, for this? "You're using Devon to get out of Quincy. Really?" My voice rose to an uncomfortable pitch.

A flicker of doubt crossed her face. "I have to leave with him. He's the only one who can save me."

"From what?"

She pressed her lips together. "From myself. I did something terrible."

I gave her puzzled look. "Are you talking about what happened to Debbie?"

She averted her eyes. "No. What I did to you."

"You mean stealing the guy who meant everything to me just because you could?" My anger rose up inside me. It took all my self-control not to slap her.

"You don't understand," she said.

What I didn't understand was how she could have done this to me when we were friends. I waited for her apology, but it didn't come and I suddenly hated her with her big mouth, her big tits that got her so much attention, and her undeservedly big opinion of herself. But I plastered a smile on my face, and said, "Let's party," determined to tell Devon the truth about Bridget when I got there.

Her father sat slumped in a worn leather chair, eyes shut, chin on his chest, a hand clasped around his beer. He didn't move as we crept past him, pushed the front door open against the wind, and stepped out into the fine rain.

As I slid onto the white vinyl seat of the white car, I reminded myself about what Bridget had said about me meeting someone that night. Maybe she really did care about me. I hoped he wasn't a weirdo. The guy driving the car was weird. I hoped it wasn't him. I acted badass with my dark shadowed eyes and crow tattoo, but I kept my gaze straight ahead, afraid to look past the dark edge of his hood.

Chapter
Thirty-Seven

WHEN I GOT home, I went straight up to the attic. The techs had made copies of the drawings I'd found in Corinne's room and returned the portfolio to me. I dragged it down from the attic and unzipped it on my drafting table. This time I examined the sketches more closely. In the first black-and-white sketch in the portfolio, Bridget looked like she was carved from marble with smooth slender limbs and an idealized pretty face, like someone you might see in a Maxfield Parish painting. The butterfly was on her forehead and her head rested on a sunflower, like the sunbeams Kerrilyn mentioned to us. I compared this drawing to a photo I had of Devon's winning painting. Devon's style was heavy-handed. His women were mannish like the giant Grecian women from Picasso's neoclassic period. In his painting that had won the contest, Bridget had muscular arms and legs, the butterfly was on her throat not her forehead, and she was half naked in the diaphanous dress her father had hated.

The murder scene was more like Devon's painting. The black-and-white sketch of Bridget was different. Could it be the actual drawing JP had shown Kerrilyn? But if it was, then why was it here? There was one person who might know. I took a deep breath and called my father.

"Is something wrong?" he asked.

"No. Sorry to bother you, but I have a question." I tried to sound upbeat.

"I'm always glad to hear from you," he said.

I texted him a photo of the sketch. "Did Devon do this?"

"That's not his work," he said perfunctorily. "It's sappy."

"I found it in the portfolio with his other sketches. What was it doing there?"

"I don't know." He paused. "It's a shame about him."

"It is." I swiveled my stool. "Dad, identifying who did this drawing could help us figure out who killed Nina Crowne. You sure you don't know?" Frustration seeped into my voice. "We need to stop him from killing more girls. He could be stalking Corinne."

"Corinne?"

"She loves the geode you gave her for her birthday. She misses you," I said.

"I miss her, too." He cleared his throat. "After he won the contest, Devon showed me a drawing Bridget had given him a few weeks earlier. Of her as Daphne. A friend of hers had done it and she wanted to know what Devon thought of it. Devon told her to tell her friend it was amateurish and he should take some classes. It looked like the drawing you just texted to me." He paused. "Devon told me it had inspired his winning entry in the contest. He was worried people might think he'd copied it."

"He did copy it."

"Artists paint the same subject all the time. The difference lies in the execution. Devon's is a work of art. This drawing is amateurish and sentimental. It's not art," he said disdainfully.

"But Devon was worried enough to talk to you about it."

He let out an audible sigh. "The artist sent him a threatening letter. Said if he didn't disqualify himself, he'd tell the judges Devon copied him."

"Do you know how this drawing ended up in the portfolio?"

"I assume Devon didn't return it and kept it with his other drawings."

"What about the names JP or Robert Concannon? Do they mean anything to you?"

"They don't. But my memory's cloudy. Kind of like cataracts in the brain. It's awful growing old, Samantha."

"Dad, this man drew Bridget, made the murder scene look like Devon's painting, and sent a threatening letter to Devon." I struggled to remain calm. "You didn't go to the police? You never told me?"

There was another pause. "After Bridget was murdered, Devon got another letter. It said if he didn't keep quiet about the drawing and the letters he'd sent, we'd all die."

I fought my rising anger. "And you kept your mouth shut."

"I did it so no one else would be killed, Sam." He paused. "After Bridget was murdered, I was so grateful to get you back alive. All I wanted was to get you away from Quincy and keep you safe. I'd already lost your mother to that terrible city. I couldn't lose you. But I suppose I did anyway." His voice cracked with the emotion he'd rarely shown me.

I told him I'd visit and clicked off before I said something I'd regret. Devon was no murderer, but he had been an arrogant coward, so desperate for an idea for the contest that he'd copied the wrong person, rationalized it was okay because his own work was "art," and ended up inspiring a serial killer.

I looked through *my* paintings stacked against the wall. The one of Bridget holding the blue periwinkle, hoping for a better world than the one she found herself in, was more like who she really was than Devon's heavy-handed languishing Daphne. My pastel of Philomela as Degas's *Singer with a Glove*—only with a glove tattooed with her story—was as original as any of Devon's work. I swallowed hard at the painting of me trapped in the darkness at the bottom of the cliff—still unfinished. All these years my father thought he was protecting me by keeping his secret, but he'd trapped me in the black hole of a mystery. I was shaking with anger. Philomena used her art to reveal her secret when she had no voice. Now that my father had finally told me the truth, I would use it to trap JP.

* * *

The next morning, I ignored the drug-related conversation in front of the cake pops at Starbucks and ordered a Frappuccino. I'd been up half the night and I needed caffeine and sugar. I sipped my frozen coffee and dropped some change in the cup of the homeless man seated on the sidewalk out front.

Brian and George eyed my Frappuccino enviously when I sat down in the incident room. I told them, "Sorry, none for you," and filled them in on what I'd learned from my father. "Devon didn't just steal Bridget from JP," I said. "He copied JP's drawing and won the contest. That's why JP sent Walter and Concannon to write *copycat* on Devon's windshield and beat him up."

Brian nodded. "Then Concannon picks up you and Bridget. He and JP get their revenge by murdering her, but you escape. They threaten Devon and frame him, but it doesn't stick. Fast-forward, Megan is murdered. Has to be a connection, though I can't see it yet. Then they murder Nina and frame Devon again. Someone holds a hell of a grudge."

"Never underestimate the rage of a disgruntled artist," George said. "If the Beach Boys had given Charles Manson proper credit for the song he wrote for them, things might have turned out differently."

"Duly noted. But that doesn't help us find JP or Concannon." Brian chewed on his lip.

The plan I'd come up with the night before tugged at me. "If this all comes down to artistic jealousy, maybe we can flush the killer out by making him jealous again." I sucked up more sweet, slushy coffee. "Alice has been bugging me to let her write an article on me with one of my paintings in it. What if I give her a painting and tell her to write about how it's better than the killer's crime scene art? To add insult to injury, we give Concannon credit as the artist. That could make JP angry enough to turn on Concannon and come forward to claim credit. Or Concannon might turn on him."

George smiled. "Poking the dragon in his sore spot, I like it."

Brian gave me a dubious glance. "This makes you the bait, Sam. I don't like that."

"I don't, either. But as long as JP and Concannon are out there, I'm not safe and neither is Corinne or anyone else on the team. It's our best shot." I squeezed my coffee cup in my fist and hit the wastebasket with one try.

* * *

Finny announced Anton's release at a press conference later that afternoon. Jeff called me before I could call him. He'd heard the news. After a long pause he told me Elle was having a special practice for Regionals and Anton would be there. Corinne would be heartbroken to miss this one, but he had an early morning meeting so he couldn't take her to it. "I was hoping I could drop her with you tonight," he said. "You can take her to practice tomorrow, and I'll pick her up." I told him that would be fine.

Brian and I met Anton at the house of corrections when he got out an hour later. It had started raining and he stood on the front steps getting soaked and clutching a white plastic bag with his belongings. His parents weren't there. He agreed to let us drive him home.

"How do you feel?" I asked as he sat glumly in the back seat.

"I don't know." He gazed out the rain-splattered window.

"You should be feeling lucky. You're free now," Brian said.

"Lucky to have been falsely imprisoned when I'm innocent?"

"The DA released you because the case wasn't strong enough, not because you're innocent." Brian shot him a backward glance.

"Whatever." He pushed a hand through his wet hair and asked how Shannon was.

"She's fine," I said. "But she insisted no one was hurting her and that she wasn't hurting you."

"I guess I was wrong," he replied.

I kept my eyes on him. "She wouldn't tell us who he is, but she might tell you."

He frowned. "And then you'll arrest her for withholding evidence."

"We don't want to arrest her," Brian said sharply. "We're trying to keep her safe."

At the intersection with the Dunkin' Donuts where I'd gotten the surveillance tape of Megan's car, Brian went to turn left toward Anton's house, but Anton asked us to drop him at Shannon's instead. As we headed toward Starlight Bay, he wanted to stop at a fancy grocer by the marina so he could buy Shannon flowers. He came out with a bouquet of pink roses, took an envelope from his bag of belongings and set it among the flowers.

"What's that?" I asked.

"While I was in prison I wrote her love letters. She said they were so beautiful, she saved them under her window seat with her other special treasures. I didn't get to send this last one."

"Under her window seat?" I said.

"Some guy who did work around the house for her dad made it for her when she was a little girl. She told me she kept souvenirs of her happiest memories there." He smiled wistfully. I shook my head. He'd probably been subsisting on fantasies of her the whole time he was in jail.

The rain had tapered off and the Delaneys' peach-colored mansion glowed in the soft light as we pulled up outside it. Anton hesitated and then sprinted to the front door.

Chapter
Thirty-Eight

WHEN I GOT home, Jeff was sitting at the kitchen table cursing his laptop. Seeing him here with Corinne lifted a weight from me. She looked up and said, "I can't wait to see Anton at practice tomorrow. I knew he was innocent." Her voice had the high-flying ring of hope returning.

I gave her a faint nod. "But there's still a killer out there."

"Barb's paying for extra security at the studio," Jeff said. He turned to me with an uncertain smile. "Good to see you, Sammy."

"Good to see you, too." I returned his smile.

Corinne went outside to read in the backyard. I hesitated and said, "Want to stay for dinner?"

"Sure," he replied and resumed ranting at his laptop about some error he was getting.

As I sat down at my drafting table, my father's words about JP—sappy, amateurish, not real art—came back. An intelligent assessment? More likely the language he and Devon used to keep this man who wasn't part of their elite circle in his place. My father had said similar things to me, so I knew the frustration of that. But I hadn't killed anyone over it.

As I lifted my brush, it took all I had not to snap it in half. But I had to paint something new, something that would get under this man's skin. I took a steadying breath, laid down a pale green wash, and let the images appear. Bridget stood beside a splintered tree, a shattered sun next to it, raising up a knife in one hand, holding a man's head covered in blood in the other. There was no diaphanous gown twisted around her. She wore a short silver dress and red high heels. Her eyes were pure fire and there was a look of triumph on her upraised face.

I called Alice and told her about the article. When I texted her a photo of my painting, she said it reminded her of Caravaggio's *Judith Beheading Holofernes*. I hadn't thought of that, but I told her to mention it, that comparing my art to the work of a great master would really get under the killer's skin. I explained what I needed her to write, that this would help us find Robert Concannon and we needed the paper to run it as soon as possible. "The exact words are up to you," I said. "But stick it to him."

I ordered pizza and Greek salad for dinner and basked in the feeling of all of us being together again. When it grew dark, I took Ginger out to pee. She quickly anointed her favorite tree. I sat on the front porch, while she put her nose on her folded paws and rested beside me. As I sipped the glass of bourbon balanced precariously on the arm of my Adirondack chair, a faraway siren mixed with the chirping of crickets and the thumping of boys shooting hoops next door.

My phone rang. It was Alice. She'd pulled some strings. The article would run in the morning. I thanked her but couldn't shake my dread that I'd made things worse. The front door opened. Corinne stepped out, sat down next to me, and pulled Ginger onto her lap.

"I missed you," I said.

"I missed you, too," she replied quietly. As she ruffled Ginger's silky hair, her phone buzzed. After a moment she looked up and said, "Anton texted me. He broke up with Shannon."

"He broke up with her?" This didn't sound like the boy who'd bought her roses.

"They had a fight about their dance for Regionals and he dumped her. Now he's doing the dance with me." She couldn't stop smiling. I worried about her being close to Anton with the killer still out there. But it had been hard enough winning her trust back. This wasn't the time to say anything. She went inside. I held on to a feeling of hope as thin as the crescent moon in the sky for a moment, and then I went back inside, too.

Jeff was on the couch frowning at his laptop. I sat down beside him. "Are you working on the recursion error that messed up your production release?"

"Yup." His black-coffee eyes met mine. "When recursion doesn't work, it might seem like the universe is rigged against you. But you just have to keep searching until you find the problem. It's always there. The smallest thing you didn't see. I'm going to find it." He shut his laptop and smiled. "But I'm taking a break now."

Much as I didn't want to ruin the mood, I had to say something. I shifted in my seat and told him about the painting and Alice's article, how we were trying to provoke the killer to come forward. I explained that out of an abundance of caution I was putting a police detail outside the house. With any luck we'd finally get this guy.

His brow creased with worry as he said, "Finally get this guy?" I waited for him to tell me I'd told him this too many times before, but all he did was stare at me intently and say, "Your eyes are like blue smoke." I raised a brow, and he explained like the sky when there was a fire somewhere. He pulled the tie from my ponytail, so my hair fell soft on my shoulders, and asked if I wanted him to stay over. I told him sure.

When he came down to breakfast the next morning, I showed him Alice's article on my phone. He read it and handed it to Corinne with a cautious grin, saying, "Your mom is famous." As I read over her shoulder, I felt something between excitement and a knife twisting inside me.

Bridget McGann's killer called her murder scene a work of art, but his act of monstrous cruelty is anything but. In her most recent paint-ing, Daphne Reborn, *Detective Samantha Star creates a modern version of Caravaggio's* Judith Beheading Holofernes *from Bridget McGann's tragic murder. Her masterpiece literally tears apart the* Metamorphoses *myth by splintering the tree that imprisoned and silenced Daphne. She is not a passive victim. She's a strong woman getting her revenge, and this is only the beginning. Star plans more paintings that challenge the patriarchal hold these myths have on our collective imagination. In his crudely arranged murder scenes, the Butterfly Killer, who police suspect is Robert Concannon, reveals himself as the talentless hack that he is. He's no artist. Star's art rises in triumph from the ashes and pain. If you have information regarding the whereabouts of Robert Concannon, contact the Quincy Police Department immediately.*

Corinne studied the photo of my painting in the article and said, "Mom, this is fierce. She's really fighting back. I love it." Her praise warmed my heart.

As Jeff stood to go, he turned to her. "Text me when you're done with practice and I'll pick you up." He leaned over and kissed her forehead tenderly. "We'll come back here after," he said to me with a smile. "I'll cook tonight."

Corinne's phone buzzed. She looked down at it and then up at him and said, "Lane's having a party after practice. She says I can go home from practice with her, so you don't need to pick me up, Dad."

I inhaled hard. "You're not going to a party. It's not safe."

"Her parents will be there." She gave me a pleading look. "I haven't seen my friends in ages."

"I'm sorry, but the answer is no," I said.

* * *

I parked behind the police detail in front of Elle's and followed Corinne inside. I didn't care if she wanted me to watch her practice or not. I needed to. I stepped over the dance bags and shoes scattered all over the waiting room that stank of feet and stood by the door to the sunlit studio. As the rest of the team did fan kicks across the room, Shannon pressed herself against the wall scowling. Anton beckoned to her. If looks could kill he would have been dead. But Corinne whispered something to her, and she raised her chin and joined in. Corinne followed, her kicks as high and straight as Shannon's. I smiled. My girl was the best. As she did one last triumphant kick, I tried to catch her eye, but she wouldn't look at me.

*   *   *

"The national news picked up the article," Brian said.

George looked up from it. "This sounds like some kind of feminist diatribe. It's going to piss people off."

I shrugged. "Hopefully him. That splintered tree rips the whole patriarchal myth apart."

Brian frowned. "I hope it breaks the case open."

"About that," George said. "I finally reached Susan Green. She saw Concannon as a patient years ago but doesn't know how to reach him now. She doesn't recall him mentioning anyone named JP but she's reviewing transcripts of their sessions."

Brian tapped his fingers on his desk. "Now we wait."

As I checked social media for comments about the article, Brian peered over my shoulder and said, "Going viral?"

"Twenty likes isn't viral." I smiled. We got coffee. We got some wackos on the tipline. And then I got an email.

Dear Samantha,

Robert Concannon is no artist, never was and never will be.
The only place he stands out is in his own field.

Long grass surrounded the hole dug in the middle of Concannon's field. Inside the hole was a body. It didn't take long for search dogs to find it. The deceased was the same height as Concannon, had a leg fracture like the one he'd received in Afghanistan, and a gunshot wound to the head. We were still waiting for dental records, but it was him, and according to the techs he'd been dead for years. Brian brushed the dirt from his knees as he stood up with a groan. "This means he didn't kill Nina or Megan." He stared at the weathered red barn. "And he wasn't the guy who ran from us that day. The guy who did is our murderer and we got nothing but the initials JP, a drawing, and a photo of Shannon to help us find him." He took his phone from his pocket. "I'm letting the press know that Concannon is dead and we're looking for a person of interest who goes by JP. Maybe someone will finally come forward."

He made the call and we took another look around Concannon's house. I eyed the timid and meticulous paintings from the myths in *The Metamorphoses* on the wall, and said, "These look like JP's work." I studied the one of Philomela, the myth that inspired his third murder. It showed a pretty young woman seated in a clearing in the woods, flowers blooming in a tapestry around her, like an idyllic scene from a Disney cartoon, except for the black-and-white swallowtail where her tongue should have been. But something about it bothered me. I turned to Brian. "Does this look like the woods in New Hampshire where his third victim was found?"

"Yeah, but the actual scene was more gruesome. They suspected she was murdered elsewhere, but they never figured out where," he said.

I stepped back. "In spite of what my father thought, JP's not a bad artist, but he idealizes women when he paints them. In real life he tears them apart." I went over to the models on the shelves. "And Concannon made these." I examined the model boats and caught my breath when I saw it.

"You know what kind of boat this is?" I pointed to a sleek sailboat with a metal railing and a decorative red stripe with a blue star on the tip.

"I'm not a boating person, but it looks like a nice sloop that might set you back a few bucks," he said.

I took my phone out and brought up the photo of Shannon on the boat. "Like this one?"

"Jesus," he said.

"I thought the boat in the photo was familiar because it belonged to Max but turns out it was familiar because I'd seen it here." I paused, unable to shake the feeling I'd seen that boat somewhere else, too. "What if the boat belongs to JP, and he was on it with Shannon?"

Brian nodded. "We have to get her to tell us what she knows. It's time to save her from herself." His call to Barb started off calmly as he explained we needed to talk to Shannon about a man named JP and ended up with him shouting into the phone, "I don't care if she's resting up before Lane's party. She could be in danger. You either get her to talk to us or we arrest her. You decide. We're on our way."

Barb called about an hour later. I took the call. "I told her she couldn't go to the party and if she didn't talk to you she'd be arrested. Now I can't find her," she said. "I've searched everywhere. She's not answering her phone. Her car's still in the garage."

I inhaled slowly. "Was someone watching the house?"

"Jay was, but he went to get her takeout from her favorite restaurant. He just got back. She's not with him. She's missing. You need to get here now," she said. I assured her we were almost there.

Squad cars were already parked along the Delaneys' long driveway. Max was on his way home, and Jay was out looking for Shannon. George was doing his best to calm Barb down in his stiff way, but she wailed that she'd called Lane and Shannon wasn't at the party. She wasn't anywhere. The killer had her. She was sure of it.

"Could she be with Anton?" I asked. "They just broke up. Maybe they're working through things."

"I texted him. He hasn't seen her."

"She might have left a clue as to where she went. Mind if we take a look around?" I asked. Barb said fine and Brian followed me up to Shannon's room. Her bed was made, a remarkable thing for a teen, and there were no clothes scattered about—equally remarkable.

Brian lifted the bouquet of roses from her wastebasket. "That didn't go over well."

I put on gloves and gathered up the torn pieces of paper beneath it. "Neither did his love note." I put it back together on her desk. "I miss you," was repeated about ten times. "I want you," was repeated, too, and finally, "Do not worry I will make everything all right, my LOVE." I turned to Brian, "Maybe he revealed more in his other letters." I lifted the heavy polished lid of the window seat and found dance competition programs, a headband with blue sequined flowers, and shoeboxes. I figured the letters might be in a shoebox, opened one up and found a pair of old toe shoes with the satin heel pressed down. I opened another and then another, and then my breath left me. "Take a look at this," I handed Brian the box containing a parakeet in a Ziploc bag. Though the bird was decomposed the feathers were still celestial blue with a faint shimmer of lavender on the neck.

Brian gave me a sideways glance. "I guess she didn't set Percy free and lied to Anton about it." I exhaled a long painful sigh. We called an officer in to collect the evidence and went back downstairs.

"Find out anything?" Barb raised her red eyes to us. I told her no.

George eyed me cautiously, "I called most of the team. No one's seen Shannon since she left practice." He paused. "I figured you'd want to contact Jeff."

When I called him and explained what happened, there was a long pause. "Jeff?"

"Shannon's not missing. She stopped by. Corinne talked to her," he said.

Every muscle tensed. "Corinne talked to her?"

"She came in while I was working and told me Shannon was out front and she'd offered her a ride to Lane's party. I said she still couldn't go. She wasn't happy about that, but she didn't argue."

"Let me talk to her," I said.

Jeff was barely coherent when he returned a few minutes later. "I can't find her and she's not answering her phone."

An icy feeling clawed at my stomach. This was all over the news. Corinne would answer if she could. "Did you see the car Shannon was in?"

"I was so obsessed with debugging that damn code, I didn't think to look." His voice quavered as he went on. "But that officer you put out front just told me he didn't see one and didn't see Corinne come out."

My heart pounded so hard I thought it would explode. "I'll be right there."

When I spoke to the officer parked outside, he insisted he hadn't seen a car pull up. I went around to the backyard. Corinne's book was open, spine up on the lounge chair where she usually read. A low stone wall separated our yard from our neighbor's. Corinne could have easily cut through their yard to meet Shannon on the other side of the block. I fought to stay calm as I raced across their lawn. No cars were parked in front of their house. No sign of Corinne.

"It's my fault. I hate myself for not paying attention," Jeff said as we sat in the kitchen agonizing over which photos of Corinne to share with the press. I told him I blamed myself, too. But this wasn't our fault. As panic roared through me, I reassured him that officers were canvassing the area. We'd put out an Amber Alert and an APB, and techs were checking Shannon's computer, phone records, and social media. "We'll find them," I said, desperately wanting this to be true.

Brian texted. "Can you come back to the station?" My stomach lurched. I glanced at Jeff. "You going to be okay?" It was a stupid question. Neither of us was going to be okay.

*　*　*

As I walked into the incident room, Brian turned to me. "We got something." My chest tightened. "Fill her in, George."

"Susan Green called," he said, and I let out a small sigh—not the news I was dreading. "Concannon was looking for a friend named James Patrick Donovan. She doesn't know anything else about him, but we have JP's full name now."

We spent the afternoon looking for James Patrick Donovans in the system or living in the local area who could be suspects. When we came up empty, we expanded our search to include locations in Vermont and New Hampshire near where his other two victims were found. So far, we hadn't found any leads there, either. I thought again of how the peaceful wooded scene in the painting of Philomela had bothered me. I reread the myth on my phone. Buried in the gory details was something I'd missed. I turned to Brian and George. "His third victim was found in the woods in New Hampshire, but in the myth of Philomela she's attacked in a cabin. Maybe JP owns property near those woods."

We were eating burgers in exhausted silence when George punched the air and shouted, "Bingo. A James Patrick Donovan owns a cabin a few miles from where the third victim was found. It's been abandoned for years."

Brian turned to George. "Let's head there." He eyed me. "This is your daughter, Sam. Let us handle it."

"I'm coming with you," I said.

"You can't." His unflinching look said it all. He didn't trust me. I was too emotionally involved. Maybe he was right. I called Jeff and told him we had a good lead and I'd let him know as soon as I knew more. I felt guilty for hanging up, but talking to him made me too anxious to function.

My phone buzzed a little later. I almost jumped out of my skin, but it was Peter. He'd just heard the terrible news about Shannon and Corinne and read the article about Concannon and JP. "If you come by the office, I can give you some information on them," he said. I told him I'd be right there. I called Brian and filled him in.

"Peter has info? That's surprising," he said.

"Not really. He's been a therapist in Quincy for years. Everyone knows everyone here."

He paused. "We're almost at the cabin. I might not be able to talk soon, but if you learn any more about JP from Peter text me 'Finian' and I'll find a way." *Finian: his cat who disappeared.*

Chapter
Thirty-Nine

"THAT IS SO awful about Corinne and Shannon. I'll do anything I can to help," Peter said as he let me in the front door and led me through the dark reception area to his office. I shifted in the unfailingly uncomfortable ergonomic chair, set my phone on the table, told Peter I was recording our conversation, and asked him to tell me what he knew.

He pushed his hand through his messy hair. "Robert Concannon was seeing a therapist named Susan Green. I worked with her at a counseling center back then. I ran into him a few times in the coffee shop next door and we talked. He was quiet, talented in a mechanical way. Today he might have been diagnosed as on the spectrum. He was looking for a friend named JP, wanted to know if I knew him."

"Did you know him?"

He unrolled the sleeves of his tan shirt patterned with flowers. He was like George, only instead of a closet full of white shirts he had a closet full of tastefully patterned ones. "A few weeks after Robert left the counseling center, James Patrick Donovan became my patient. Robert had recommended me to him. Quite frankly, Donovan frightened me, but I did my best to help him. He still sees me once in a while."

I held back a gasp. "When did you last see him?"

He took a moment. "A few weeks ago."

"Why did he come to you?"

"He used to have violent urges he couldn't control, and he was getting them again." He gave me an anxious glance. "Is he the person who took Shannon and Corinne?"

"It's possible."

"Sorry for not saying anything sooner," he said, "but I didn't make the connection until now."

"I need his contact information, transcripts from his sessions, everything you have."

"That information is confidential," he said.

"I can get a subpoena, but we don't have time for that. Nobody's going to question your professional ethics for doing the right thing to save Shannon and Corinne."

"Of course, I'll give you whatever you need." He rubbed his forehead as if, in spite of his superhuman ability to remain calm, he was succumbing to stress. "The transcripts are in the back office. Might take a while, but I'll find them," he said and left the room.

I texted Brian that Peter was getting me information on JP. He replied, "*Got it. Going in now.*" I tensed. They could be close to finding Corinne and Shannon, and I was stuck here. I went over to Peter's desk. He said he had met with JP a few weeks ago. That was about the same time Nina was murdered. Had Peter also met with him around the time Megan was murdered? I tried his laptop, but the screen was locked. I leafed through his day planner. I didn't find any appointments with James, but I found some with Shannon and with Megan. Jesus, they both were seeing him. How had we missed that?

I glanced at my phone. No news from Brian. As I paced the room to quell the anxiety racing through me, I stopped in front of the peaceful photos of the ocean on the wall. Everything went still.

There it was: the photo of the elegant sailboat. When I looked closer, I saw the same wooden trim, same metal railings, same red decorative stripe on the hull, same boat as in the photo of Shannon, same boat as the model in Concannon's house. I had seen it somewhere else. I'd seen it here before any of this happened. I thought of the pattern of anchors on the shirt in the photo, the sort of shirt Peter would wear. As I took a photo of it, something creaked behind me. I turned. No one.

I texted Brian the photo. *"Finian. It's Peter's boat."*

"We found nothing here. Call for backup and get out," Brian answered. I was calling when the lights went off. I inched along the wall, gun raised, and peered into the darkened hall. The sound of muffled crying came from the far end of it. I edged toward the sound in a crouch, glancing back every few steps. The crying grew louder. Light leaked through a partly open door. I nudged it all the way open with both hands on my gun. The room was empty except for a video of a girl tied to a chair crying, playing on a laptop on a table. It was so grainy and dark I couldn't tell who she was or where she was. I reached for the paper beneath the laptop, read the words written on it:

Welcome to the black sea, my Persephone.

I huffed a breath. Stupid, get out now. I stepped back and something cold stung my shoulder. I turned and met the eye holes of a white porcelain mask bedazzled with green glitter. Everything blurred.

Chapter
Forty

"IF YOU BEHAVE, I'll untie you." Peter peered through a Mardi Gras mask. Much as it killed me to go along, I nodded. He pulled a hunting knife from inside his black jacket and cut the ropes. I reached for my gun and phone. They were gone, but I was still wearing my same clothes. Thank god.

"I had to drug you to get you out of there, but it should be wearing off." He slid the knife back in his jacket. "I have so much to show you," he said and extended his hand. I didn't take it and slid off the bed onto a soft rose-colored carpet. I flinched at his touch as he helped me up. I fought my dizziness as he led me down a curving staircase to a room with floor-to-ceiling windows, artwork on the walls, a rug patterned with dancing leopards, and a laptop on a black marble coffee table. He sat down on a black leather sofa.

I steadied myself on a leather and steel chair opposite him. "Are Corinne and Shannon here?"

"They're fine. I'll bring you to them after I confess. Isn't that what you want—a confession?"

"I didn't expect it from the therapist I've trusted all these years."

He leaned forward. "When did you know it was me?"

"When I saw that the boat in the photo on your wall was the same as the one in the photo of Shannon we found at Concannon's."

He pressed his hands together. "Shannon and I have a professional relationship."

"I'm sure you do."

He put a phone on the black marble table. "I'll record it on this. It will be enough to put me away for life, and I'll never claim another victim."

I read him his rights and said, "Start by taking off your mask, and telling me who you really are, Peter." He pushed it up over his head, revealing the calm face beneath. His features came slowly into focus. "Can't believe I never recognized you."

"I'm older. I've put on weight and used to dye my hair." He took off his jacket. His chest strained the buttons of a short-sleeved blue shirt printed with palm trees—not his usual style. "Remember me now?"

The smell came back first, sweat and weed. Then the Hawaiian shirt, the lazy curl on his forehead, eyes green as the grapes in his hand—the man Bridget met the day she saved that boy. I held his gaze. "You're not as pretty as you used to be. How long before you ditched the mother of that boy who almost drowned?"

"She was nothing to me. But Bridget was the real deal. I saw that right away." A wistful look crossed his face.

I inhaled. "I guess I can finish my painting now and put you at the top of that cliff."

The corner of his mouth turned up. "Wrong answer."

I gave him a sour look. "Are you going to confess, James, Peter, whoever you are?"

He pushed record. "I used to be James. I'm Peter Reynolds now." He gave me the names of the victims we already knew about along with Devon and Robert Concannon. "There are more," he said. "I'll tell you later. I'd like people to appreciate the full breadth of my work."

"Your work?"

"Devon claimed I lacked talent, but he was the one who copied me. I took my art further than he ever dared to go. My works aren't Devon's clumsy figures trapped in paint. They're works of art made from flesh and blood."

"Did Robert Concannon take part in any of the murders?"

"Bobby had no idea what he was getting into when he agreed to pick up you and Bridget. He really believed he was taking you to a party." He flexed his fingers. "He thought hurting people was a sin until I explained that the Greek myths were about transformation and transformation comes from pain. Persephone had to be dragged into the world of the dead, so she could emerge as the goddess of spring. Imagine a world without spring." His eyes lit up. "Bobby thought I was a genius."

"How did he help you?" I asked.

"He helped construct the crime scenes. He was a fine craftsman, but he lacked a creative spark. Those models he made aren't art. They're following directions. I can't believe that foolish journalist gave him credit for my work."

"You should write a letter to the editor." I frowned. "Did he do anything else for you?"

"He did the camera work for the film I made of you and Bridget."

"Film?"

"My crime scenes are only the final act. You must view the films to get the full impact of my art. I filmed all my murders." His soft mouth twisted into a smile. "When Bobby found me again after he was discharged from the Army, he helped convert my films into videos, but his role was strictly technical. He might be alive today, if he hadn't insisted we confess."

"You have videos of all the murders?"

He nodded. "Someday they'll get the recognition they deserve."

"If you give me them, you could get recognition right away."

"I have them in a secret location," he said. "They'll stay there for now."

"What about Anton? Was he your accomplice, too?"

"He had nothing to do with it, just an unlucky kid in the wrong place at the wrong time." He handed me a plastic bag from the end table beside him. It contained a knife with a curved blade and a pearl handle inlaid with lapis.

I leaned in for a better look. "That's the murder weapon?"

"I used it to inscribe Megan. But I killed her by hitting her over the head with a rock."

"How did you get the knife?" I asked.

"I stole it from Anton's dimwitted cousin Dmitry."

"How did you know he had those knives?"

He sighed like I was such a fool. "Shannon mentioned in a session that his knife collection frightened her."

"So you stole one?"

"He has a fine collection, and I am a connoisseur."

"You had Megan's watch and the knife. What about her phone?" I said.

He appeared puzzled. "It's somewhere here. But that's not important right now."

We'd found her smashed phone in the marsh. He was lying about it. I wondered why, but I went on. "You weren't a suspect. You had a career. Why throw that away by killing Megan?"

"She copied Shannon's dance the same way Devon copied my art. I couldn't let her deprive Shannon of her dreams."

"Why are you so interested in helping Shannon?"

"She's my patient. I care as deeply for her as I do for you."

"Really?" I said. "And Nina? Was she in the way of Shannon's dreams, too?"

He exhaled slowly. "Nina was unimaginative like Bobby. But people are ignorant and a timid dancer like her might have won Regionals. I couldn't let that happen."

"Did Shannon ask you to kill Nina?"

He gave his head a sharp shake. "How can you suggest that? She had nothing to do with any of this."

"Shannon lied to us about the photo on your boat and the earrings you gave her. She's involved."

"Once again you're drawing foolish conclusions from circumstantial evidence. You're not very good at your job, Samantha. A hack, missing clues for years."

I shook my head at his obvious attempt to trigger me by cutting me down the way my father had. "Megan was your patient, too, and you killed her so Shannon could realize her dreams. You call that being a good therapist?"

"I've told you all you need to know. My confession is done." He stopped recording.

"Then it's time to release the girls." I went to stand, but he glanced at his phone and motioned me down.

"We need to discuss something else first, off the record." He lowered his voice. "I don't have an unhealthy obsession with Shannon. She's my daughter."

I let that settle. "Her parents might disagree."

"Barb was married when we met. You know what her marriage was like. She reminded me a little of Bridget. One thing led to another." He tugged a curl onto his forehead and pressed his lips into a suggestive smile. "And then I left. A year later she called and told me I had a daughter. She said she was still in love with me, but she was staying with Max because he could provide a better life for Shannon. Over the next few years, she shared pictures and stories about Shannon with me so I could be part of her life. They inspired me to become a better father than Max. I turned my life around for Shannon, became a counselor, dedicated myself to helping people— the kind of father she could look up to. When she had rheumatic fever, I came back and helped her heal." He lifted his chin. "And then she won her first dance competition. I'll do everything I can to make her dreams come true."

"Spare me the Hallmark stuff," I said. "You made her dreams come true by killing innocent young women and then you kidnapped her. Real fatherly."

"Hear me out, Samantha. When I explain it, you'll understand."

I shook my head. "Barb would never let Shannon have anything to do with someone like you."

"All Barb knows is I'm Shannon's father and the best counselor she could hope for." He fixed his green eyes, so like Shannon's, on me.

"Does Shannon know you're her father?"

"Barb wanted to wait longer to tell her I was her father, but I couldn't wait. She was having issues. It was the only way to reach her."

"What sort of issues?" I asked.

"She likes pain and struggles with self-harm. Without my help it would only be a matter of time before she hurt someone else or took her own life. I told her I understood her impulses, because I was her father and I'd struggled with them. She and I were alike. Twin souls you might say."

I thought of the blue parakeet in the shoebox. "You mean Shannon's a killer, too?"

"Of course not," he snapped. "I told her we were alike, so she'd realize she isn't alone and not hate herself. But I misjudged the situation. I fear I've poisoned her with my own darkness."

"What do you mean by 'poisoned her'?"

"A drop of India ink in water taints the whole glass and black flowers blossom." He gave me a knowing look. "Like the ones in your painting." I winced at how he'd twisted my own ideas to make his point. "I should have treated the stress that made Shannon seek out pain. Instead, I poisoned her mind with praise about her dark side because I was intoxicated with how I saw myself in her. I even told her it made her a better dancer."

"Why are you telling me this?"

"So you'll understand she's done nothing wrong, that she only protected me because of the hold I had on her. I failed as her therapist and her father, but I'm being a good father now. If you promise you won't arrest her so that she has a chance for a good life, I'll release her and Corinne and turn myself in. I'll never kill again." He tipped his face to the side. "It's an easy decision."

"But once everyone knows her father is a serial killer, Shannon will never win another competition. You call that a chance for a good life?"

His jaw tightened. "That's not going to happen because you're not going to tell anyone I'm her father. Shannon won't say anything.

Barb won't, either. She's a weak woman who values appearances far too much. In the eyes of the world, I'll be a crazed killer who is obsessed with Shannon and your daughter, for reasons that will never be known."

I went over to one of the windows and pushed aside the gray velvet drapes. I could just barely make out a yard with woods beyond it. Peter was probably lying but I had no choice. "Let me get this straight. You're turning yourself in as long as I promise not to arrest Shannon or tell anyone you're her father. Am I right?" He nodded. "Fine," I said. "Take me to the girls now."

A slow smile crossed his face. "Be patient. You need to hear the rest of the story."

Chapter
Forty-One

There was a girl, a quiet one no one noticed with a face like the moon through fog, but she wanted the same things as any other girl, the same things as her beautiful friend who reached out her hand and said come.

But this wisp of a girl was not the same as the others. I planted the dark seed of myself inside her. When it was time, her beautiful friend led her below ground, and she sank down into darkness.

You shall dwell in my palace, I said, and always love me. She tasted the red fruit that stained her lips with blood. But the smell of soil and bone made her sad, and she cried to leave. I let her go but left the smallest black petal of myself in her heart so she would always return to me.

I closed the notebook Peter had handed me. "That's not my story. It's a bunch of crap."

He took it away. "It doesn't matter what you think. It is your story, Persephone. But I have more to show you." I peered over his shoulder as he rummaged through a carved chest by the wall and slid back a panel at the bottom of it.

"Is that a secret door?" I asked.

"You might call it that," he said. "I told you Bobby was no artist, but he was a skilled carpenter. I keep my special treasures in here."

Special treasures—the same words Shannon had used. He held up a green satin ribbon, smiled softly, "From Shannon's first pair of tap shoes." There were tears in his eyes.

He ran his fingers through a box of blue butterfly clips like they were jewels and said, "Remember?" I told him no. He pulled out a framed photo of Bridget in her silver dress, her glistening blond hair fluffed on top, her drugged-looking eyes smudged with mascara. "She was so beautiful that night," he mused.

My eyes fixed on the faint gleam on her arm—the bracelet I'd remembered all these years. My stomach twisted as the shadowy reality rose to the surface. She cowered in her shining dress, her eyes like black holes dragging me in. "Help me," she whimpered. I reached for her, and she screamed in terror.

"I still miss her," he said with a sad smile.

I stepped back. "Then why did you kill her?"

"I loved her, but when she cheated on me with Devon, and he copied my painting and won the contest, that was too much. I begged her to leave him, but she told me she was running away with him and would go to the cops if I tried to stop her." He shook his head. "It was sad, a beautiful, gifted girl like that, but the little fool couldn't keep her mouth shut."

"What was she going to the cops about?"

"You ask too many questions." He gave the photo a last loving glance, put it back in the chest, and took out a leather case that held decorative knives. "I use these to transform my girls."

Vomit came up my throat. "'Transform'? Like in the myths?"

"I turned Bridget into a tree so she couldn't talk anymore."

"And Megan?"

"She talked too much, too. Another Daphne."

"Nina?"

"She denied herself everything, never thin enough, never pure enough. But she had a big appetite. Her secret dream was to be a cow."

I wanted to tear him to shreds like a crazed maenad, but I steadied myself. "You're wrong. Daphne didn't talk too much. She was silenced by her rapist. Covered in bark so no one could ever touch her again. Frozen in that moment forever. That's what happens when you rape someone, Peter." I inhaled. "Did Megan talk too much to you on that burner phone. Is that why you silenced her?"

"Keep your voice down, you're shouting," he said.

"I'm not shouting. I'm speaking." It was best not to set him off right now, but I had to go on. "You're wrong about the myth of Io, too." I thought of the horrific scene in that greenhouse. "It's about a delusional man who transforms the young woman he raped into a nightmare creature—not her dream come true." I shook my head. "And what's the point of the butterflies? There aren't any in the myths."

"I'm a true Surrealist. I create my own myths and make them real." He took a knife from the case. "I place the butterflies on the girls after I cut them—a symbol that their transformation is complete." He ran his finger down the edge of the blade. "I like cutting. Perhaps I should have been a surgeon instead of a therapist, but I like cutting through the human mind even more. Especially yours."

He tipped his face to the side. "I noticed you right off in Nostalgia, Samantha Flynn, a dark-haired girl with a dark smile. Bridget talked too much, but you keep your secrets, like I do. That's not all we have in common."

I took a hard breath. "What are you talking about?"

"All these years, I was sure you'd remember, but you held the lid down tight. I never saw a person more afraid to know herself," he said. "You're my only girl who ever came back from the dead, Persephone. I let you go that night, but I didn't set you free. Now I'm giving you another chance."

He put the knife on the coffee table, opened the laptop, and brought up the video I'd seen in the room by his office, only there was more of it. The camera zoomed in on the blue dress, the roses on my shoes, my dark hair. How could I have not seen it was me?

A man's voice said, "You have a right to hate her, Samantha. She takes everything you want from you, because girls like Bridget always win and you never do."

I winced at my reply. "Boys always go for her and never notice me. But I don't hate her. She's my best friend."

The camera switched to Bridget in her silver dress. "She has the life I dream of, and she takes it for granted," she said in her husky voice. "She doesn't know what it's like to have a father who beats you. Makes me want to beat her, so she'd know how it feels. That little bitch has everything and all she does is whine."

The screen went black.

The man's voice said, "The choice is yours. Kill her and I'll let you go. If you don't, you both die. What do you say?"

A soft voice replied, "Yes."

The scene cut to Bridget cowering in her silver dress as she screamed, only now I knew why she was afraid. A pale arm raised a knife. The camera zoomed in on me plunging it into her chest. It wasn't over. A shadowy figure raised my hand holding the knife up again and shouted, "Do it like this. That's how you finish it," and we brought it down on her neck and across, together. The screen went black.

I couldn't move. "That's not real."

He stared at me calmly. "It is real."

"I don't remember any of that." I said, even as the puzzle pieces clicked into place as he knew they would. I chose to kill my friend. And why? Because a boy I imagined I loved chose her over me? I curled on the floor and hugged my knees. This was how he wanted me to see it, and though I didn't want to believe it, I couldn't stop myself from sobbing.

He knelt beside me. "Bridget was strong, but you were stronger. It was such a pleasant surprise, I had to let you live. All these years your mind protected you from the knowledge you needed to become the person you were meant to be. You might never have known, if it hadn't been for me. It's a hard truth to face, but someday you'll thank me."

He caressed the back of my neck. "I became a new person for Shannon. I'm willing to sacrifice my freedom for her. You're a new person like me, too—Persephone—my last transformation." He continued caressing me. "As long you don't tell anyone I'm Shannon's father and don't arrest her, your secret is safe with me. I'll turn myself in and release the girls. But if you pursue Shannon, I'll tell the world you're a murderer and that my confession was coerced. Everyone will know who you really are." He helped me to my feet. "Deal?"

"Deal." I choked on the word. "Now take me to the girls."

He frowned in irritation. "Be patient. I have to get rid of this video so O'Neil doesn't find it." He clicked some keys on his laptop and said, "Gone. But I have another copy. If you don't keep your side of the bargain, I'll release it."

He stared at me sadly. "One last dance, Samantha, before I give up my freedom." I nodded, doubting he had any intention of freeing me or the girls. He did something else on his laptop and picked up the knife as the booming opening of "Let's Dance" came on. I froze as he held the knife to my throat and said, "Dance, honey." Without letting go of the knife, he put his hands on my hips, humming to the music as he rubbed his rough cheek on mine. "You fucking whore," he whispered. He jammed his heels into the floor and sang, "Put on your red shoes," as he spun me around. As he stared at me and smiled, the sharp contours of JP's strained face showed beneath his and I remembered, though *remember* is too strong a word. I got flashes of him dragging a razor blade over my back again and again, indifferent to my screams.

I slid my hand slowly from his and went up to a painting on the wall of a girl with a pink-cheeked angelic face and a wreath of flowers in her blond hair. It looked like an idealized version of Shannon. "I thought you only painted in flesh and blood," I said.

"I still work in traditional media now and then." His cool gaze rested on me. "What do you think?"

I stepped closer. "This is timid, sappy, and sentimental. Like a cheesy painting you'd find in a hotel." I turned to face him. "The work of a man whose grandiose dreams exceed his limited abilities. Devon was right about you. He was the real artist." I smiled as I rocked back on my heels.

He slapped me across the face and sent me backward onto the floor. "You don't know anything, you stupid stuck-up bitch."

I got back on my feet. "You're just mad because it's true."

"You want the truth?" His voice shook with rage. "You're just like Devon, your father, and all those elite snobs who wouldn't know a real work of art if it was staring them in the face. You think you're better than me, but your art is shallow crap. You got the painting you did for that article all wrong. Bridget wasn't holding the knife." He sneered. "You've never done anything that matters."

"What have you done? Murdered Bridget and other innocent young girls and called that art. You're a hack who actually hacks people up, not an artist."

"You don't know what you're talking about." His mouth twitched. "The artistic journey I began in the Christmas house goes far beyond anything you can comprehend."

"Christmas house?" I remembered Bridget pressing her thumb on a snow-patterned window in the model at the Crust and Crumb. "You mean the place Bridget told me you were building for her?"

"I mean the place where I'll finish my artistic journey with a work of art that will shake your pathetic world." He shoved me into the wall and fixed his reptilian green eyes on me.

"I can't wait to see it." I brushed a curl from his forehead and forced a smile. He pulled me close. As he went to kiss me, I grabbed the vase on the table behind me and smashed it down on his head. The knife flew from his hand as I slammed him down on the floor and hit him with the vase again to make sure he was out cold. I tied him up with the ropes he had used on me. I wanted to kill him, but I left him alive because I might need his help finding Corinne and Shannon. I took the phone with his confession on it from the table and texted *Finian* to Brian along with my location near the Blue Hills. He replied, *On my way.*

Chapter Forty-Two

I SEARCHED THE house and backyard frantically, but there was no sign of the girls. When I stepped into the front yard, I realized to my horror I'd forgotten to take the knife. But there was no time to go back. I had to find the girls before it was too late.

Peter said his journey would end in the Christmas house. But the stately gray Colonial on a wooded lot where he'd held me captive was nothing like the tiny house he'd built in the woods for Bridget. That was just a half-finished cabin. A cabin. I caught my breath. The girls were in a cabin, just not the one in New Hampshire.

I glanced around. Nothing here was familiar but the dead-end street was. I started down it. The entrance to a dirt road, like the one Bridget led me down years ago to show me the Christmas house, was hidden by overhanging tree branches and there were fresh tire tracks in the muddy ground. I sprinted over stones and gnarled tree roots, splashed through puddles like black mirrors, and came to a clearing. The cabin Bridget had showed me on that winter day was now covered with vines and had fallen into disrepair. He'd never made the Christmas house beautiful. A cold tremor went through me when I saw Anton's van pulled into some underbrush beside it. I slid the door back. Empty. I climbed the moss-covered steps to the sagging porch, nudged open the screen door hanging off its hinges, and stepped onto a floor thick with leaves.

Moonlight poured through a hole in the roof, illuminating a small dirty kitchen with a rust-stained sink—and a dark shape in the corner. As I inched along the wall toward it, I couldn't stop the memory from coming. *Bridget's screams. A blade flashing through the air. Blood all over me. On the floor. A horrible coppery smell.*

I stepped back, reeling. It took a second to see Shannon tied up and crouching in the corner. "I thought you were him. Is he coming back, Mrs. S.?" she asked in a trembling voice. I told her I didn't think so and untied her. She didn't seem injured as I helped her up. She brushed at her mud-stained platform sandals and pouted. "These are my favorite shoes, and they're ruined."

I asked the question I dreaded asking. "Where are Corinne and Anton?" She chewed her lip. I took her hands in mine. "Tell me."

She let go a thin breath. "When Anton came to see me after you released him, I was so happy to be back together, but then he broke up with me. He said I had too many problems, that there was something wrong with me. I felt so bad I wanted to die. When my mom told me I couldn't go to the party because you were going to arrest me, I really wanted to die. I called Peter and he said he'd pick me up and take me to the party, but he didn't take me there. He brought me here and made me tell Anton to come so we could talk through things. I was too scared not to do what he said." Her voice cracked. "When he got here, Mr. Reynolds dragged him into the woods, and I don't know what happened to him."

I could barely hold myself together as I asked, "And Corinne?"

She sucked on the end of a polished nail. "He made me lie to her about going to the party. He took her into the woods, too."

I brushed a twig from her hair. "Can you show me where they went?"

She shook her head sharply. "I was drugged. I don't remember."

"If he made you do things you feel bad about, it's not your fault," I said. "He did the same to me. I won't let him hurt you anymore, but you need to help me find Corinne and Anton because they could still be alive."

Slipping and sliding in the sandals she insisted on wearing so she wouldn't look like crap, she led me along a trail through the woods that went down a little hill and leveled off at the top of another incline. When I saw the road below and lights in the distance, I texted Brian, *Near old crime scene.* He texted back, *There. Soon.*

A log stretched across the path ahead of us—more than a log, an uprooted tree. Something was shining on the ground. I motioned Shannon to stay back. As I moved closer the memory tore through me.

"Get over here. Now," he shouts.

Silver flecks everywhere. Blood.

I crawl on my hands and knees toward Bridget's body.

All the breath left me. Corinne was tied up in the fallen tree and covered with branches, leaves, and silver glitter. I felt a shiver of relief as her eyes met mine. She was alive.

"Oh my god." Shannon gasped as she stood beside me.

I untied the gag from around Corinne's mouth, and she burst into tears. "I thought he'd come back to kill me," she said.

"You're safe now," I told her. I fought to remain calm as I brushed leaves from what looked like a red gash on her throat, but it was just a butterfly—a red glider. I let it slide to the ground and fell on my knees, shaking as I untied the ropes wrapped around her like a cocoon.

"I'm so glad you're okay," Shannon said, as Corinne stood up unsteadily.

I checked to make sure Corinne really was okay. She seemed stunned but not injured. I hugged her for a few precious seconds and let her go. "Both of you, we have to get out of here now," I said, but Corinne froze.

"Was that on my neck?" She pointed at the red butterfly on the ground. I nodded and she screamed, "Get it away from me."

As I put the revolting red creature on a rock beside the log, I remembered more.

The butterfly sticks to my bloody fingers.
I can't shake it off without tearing it.
Heart gallops as I press it on her throat.
This is how you do it, he shouts and shoves me away.
Someone says run.

"Mom." Corinne pulled on my arm urgently.

I turned to see Peter step like a shadow from the dark woods. The gun shook as he pointed it at me. "Get over here," he said, in a clipped voice.

"You don't have to do this." I spoke calmly as I walked toward him and stopped about a foot away. "We had an understanding."

He swayed as sweat rolled down his bloodstained face. "I thought I could count on you, but you're not my Persephone. I don't know who you are anymore. You lied to me."

"I never was your Persephone," I said. "I'm Samantha. That's all I've ever been. I don't have to pretend to be some mythical being to feel important." He studied me coldly as I went on. "You lied to me for years. But I'm not lying now. I have backup coming any minute and they'll kill you. And when the shooting starts Shannon or Corinne could be killed, too. Turn yourself in like you said you would, and I'll make sure no one gets hurt."

He shook his head slowly. "You expect me to believe that?"

As he struggled to keep the gun aimed at me, I glanced toward the woods on my left. "They're coming now," I said. When he whipped around to look, I twisted his hand back so hard the gun fell in the grass. He took off as I dove for it. I told the girls to wait for me and chased him through the vines and briars I remembered from so long ago, all the way to the ravine.

As he staggered toward the edge, I raised the gun and shouted for him to stop. He stared down into the abyss and then back at me with an oddly sad expression on his face.

"It's over, Peter," I said. As he went to climb down into the ravine, I shot him in the leg. He fell to the ground.

"You're not going anywhere now. I'm taking you in," I said.

He looked up, all the color gone from his face. "That's not what you want to do. You want to kill me. You always have. Do it. Get your revenge. Then you'll be free. Free to be a good mother, a good wife. A good cop."

"I'm taking you in," I repeated.

"I don't think so." His mouth twisted into a delirious smile, and he gestured toward the ravine. "Not when you see what I've done."

I peered over the edge. Anton lay on a rock ledge above the brook where Brian had found me. It was like someone stepped on my heart. I whirled around and jammed the gun hard into Peter's head as he sat at my feet bleeding.

He tipped his face to the side, feigning contrition. "Come on, finish the job, Samantha."

I wanted to shoot him, to know he was gone from my life forever. But that would be doing what he was telling me to do, and I was done with that. "Lie down. Now," I said. He clasped his hands over his head and lay back dramatically as I held the gun on him. A few minutes later Brian pushed through the underbrush with Corinne and Shannon behind him.

He looked anxiously from Peter to me and asked if I was okay. I nodded. He cuffed Peter. We propped him against a rock away from the edge and Brian took me aside. "Backup will be here soon," he said, "but you need to get Corinne and Shannon out of here now. I'll stay with this asshole."

I gnawed on my lip. "There's something I have to do first."

I led him to the edge of the ravine and we looked down at Anton, lying eerily close to the place where Brian had found me. Corinne and Shannon crept up beside us before I could stop them. As I descended the steep slope, I slipped on the dry grass. My feet slid out from under me and my gun went flying into the brook. Anton looked like he was dead. But when I pressed the vein on his wrist, I felt a faint pulse. His eyes fluttered open. "He's alive," I called out.

From high above, Shannon screamed. I glanced up, only it wasn't her I saw. I saw myself standing there, sick with the guilt of having killed Bridget.

Anton's eyes widened with alarm as he stared at Shannon. "She pushed me," he said.

"She pushed you?" I repeated loud enough so everyone could hear.

"He's lying, it was an accident," Shannon shouted.

I went to help Anton up, but he cried out in pain. I told him I'd be back for him soon and scrambled up the side of the ravine. As I hoisted myself over the edge, I motioned for Corinne to step away.

Shannon set her eyes on me. "You have to believe me. He's lying."

Brian rested his hand on her shoulder and said, "You can tell us about what happened later. Right now, we have to get you, Corinne, and Anton out of here to keep you safe."

She twisted away. "You're not going to keep me safe. You're going to put me in jail. That's all you've ever wanted to do." She held herself erect, still head to foot a dancer, as she walked up to the edge and said, "I'd rather be dead than tell you anything." I tensed as she rocked forward in her ridiculously unstable sandals.

"You're the victim here, Shannon. No one's putting you in jail. Everything's going to be all right. You got your whole life ahead of you," Brian said calmly as he moved closer to her.

She stood still a moment before she turned to him, brushed away her tears, and said, "Please help me." As he reached his arm around her to guide her back from the edge, she grabbed the gun from his holster and aimed it at us.

She gave me a fierce glance. "Try anything and I'll kill all of you."

I whispered to Corinne to stay as far back as she could. As Shannon herded us toward Peter, I said, "Don't do this. Brian and I are police officers. They'll show you no mercy if you shoot us. Corinne's your friend. I know you care about her. It's not too late to fix this. Just put the gun down."

She went to lower it, but Peter called out, "She's lying. Don't listen to her." She raised the gun again.

I inhaled slowly. "He's the one you shouldn't listen to, the one who makes you do things you don't want to do. He's a monster."

"You're wrong. He's not a monster. He calls me all the time. I can tell him anything and he doesn't lie to me." Her voice quavered.

"That's not true." I spoke softly as I edged closer to her. "He lies all the time, Shannon." I thought of Megan's smashed phone, how Peter didn't know about it. "Remember when you called Megan's boyfriend?"

"I don't know what you're talking about."

"I'm talking about the call you made when you were practicing with Megan. She called him first, but then you called him."

She looked from Brian to me. "She was really upset after she talked to him. She locked herself in the bathroom. I was worried she might be taking drugs and trying to kill herself, so I called to tell him."

"Must have made you furious when Peter answered and you realized *he* was her boyfriend."

"That's a lie," she said. "He wasn't her boyfriend. He was her therapist."

"That's what you want to think. But the way she talked about him, obsessed over him, bragged about the beautiful blue earrings he gave her, makes me think he was."

She frowned. "What earrings?"

"Real sapphires." It looked like sparks were about to fly from her eyes. "It must have been hard to realize your therapist was having an affair with your best friend. Did you tell him to come and get Megan that day?"

"No, when I heard his voice I hung up." She pressed her lips together.

"I know how you feel," I said. "He was my therapist, too. I trusted him with my deepest secrets. It hurt to learn who he really was. It must have really hurt you to learn he was involved with Megan and encouraging her even though you're a better dancer." I paused to let my lie settle. "Is that why you smashed her phone?"

"I looked through it." She frowned. "She called him all the time.

He told me I had more talent than any dancer he'd ever seen." Her voice shook as she went on. "He was supposed to be helping me win, not her. I threw her phone against the wall."

"Nothing worse than when your friend takes the thing you want most from you," I said.

"She always took what wasn't hers. It was my idea to dance to Lady Gaga at States. I should have won, but she stole my idea, and she stole Peter."

"That would have made me mad, too," I said.

She raised her chin. "When I told her I'd get her disqualified from the *Wish Upon a Dancer* audition for copying me, she knocked me down and kept banging my head on the floor. I thought she was going to kill me. I shoved her off me and she fell over backward and hit her head on the coffee table. It was an accident. I didn't mean for her to die."

I motioned for Corinne to move farther away and turned back to Shannon. "What you've done doesn't define you," I said. "Only what you do from here on will. Trust me. I know how you feel. I've been there. If you do the right thing, you can move on. You're a gifted dancer. You can still have a chance to share your gift with the world." I reached out my hand. "Give me the gun. If it was an accident, we'll make sure you get the help you need."

"Don't listen to her," Peter said sharply from behind us. "Finish it before they put you in jail for the rest of your life."

She turned to him and then back to us—the pupils of her green eyes so wide and dark they sent a chill through me. A cold smile crossed her face as she pulled the trigger. Brian went down and I rushed over to him. Shannon aimed the gun at me, but Corinne kicked her and knocked her down. The gun went flying.

As I grabbed it, Shannon took off. My breath burned in my throat as I raced after her and tackled her to the ground. I raised the gun, so full of rage I could barely think. But as she cowered at my feet, I saw Bridget, pleading for her life and crying and I couldn't move. From a distance Peter shouted, "Get going, you clumsy oaf," and Shannon ran stumbling into the darkness. She let out an earsplitting scream as she fell into the ravine.

The world went still the way it does after an explosion. From a distance I glimpsed officers swarming the scene. I walked like a robot through the cottony silence to the edge. Shannon lay spread-eagled by the black twisted ribbon of the brook, her head at an odd angle, Anton on the ledge above her. For a moment I couldn't breathe. Corinne was coming toward me. I could barely hear my own voice as I hugged her tight and told her not to look.

Chapter Forty-Three

THE CRACKED WALKWAY in front of Our Lady of the Doves was freshly swept and lined with pots of pink roses. The blackbirds were gone. I put one foot in front of the other, took a seat at the back of the crowded church, and allowed myself a quick glance at the chestnut-colored coffin.

I was sitting in almost the same place where I'd sat with Brian for Bridget's funeral. I'd been afraid to go, but when he'd said he could use my help identifying her killer, I'd agreed. As I held myself still next to him, he'd nudge me and say, "Do you see anyone who looks like him?" Each time I told him no. Afterward as we'd stood outside in the impossibly bright sunlight, he'd smiled and said, "It's okay if you don't know who he is. Someday you will." I had felt nothing but emptiness then, but his words had given me a purpose. I couldn't bring her back, but I'd find the man who killed her.

Now as I inhaled the overpowering smell of the lilies arranged on the altar, I did my best to kneel at the right times, to sing the hymns I didn't know, and blinked back tears as the priest read scriptures I barely followed. Then it was over.

Jay Delaney kept his gaze straight ahead as he walked past, his dark polished shoes clicking on the floor while the organ droned mournfully. Barb leaned on Max, weeping as he tried to keep her from falling. She looked up just long enough to flash me a cold stare I did not return. It's terrible to lose a child, and I had no desire to make her pain worse.

The official story in the news was that I had apprehended Peter and rescued Corinne, Shannon, and Anton. In the chaos that followed, Shannon shot Brian. She'd been aiming for me when Corinne knocked the gun out of her hand. Shannon took off and fell into the ravine. Corinne and I were portrayed as heroes, Shannon as the victim of a man who manipulated her into what appeared to be a desperate suicidal act.

* * *

"They let you out of the hospital already?" I said, as Brian and George pulled up chairs next to my desk.

"This morning." Brian's jacket was over his shoulder, his arm in a sling.

"He made them so miserable, they couldn't wait to get rid of him," George said.

I glanced at the bluish tinge to Brian's freckled cheeks. "I'm impressed you're back to work. But you look a little pale."

"I'm fine. The doctor says I'll get full use of my arm back if I do my PT." He shook his head. "But if Mary Ann has a say in it, she'll keep me on house arrest for the next month."

"That's sweet," I said.

"There's such a thing as too much sweetness."

"This from a guy who puts four Equals in his coffee?" I smiled.

"Bring Casey's cupcakes over here," Brian said to George.

George set a box on my desk. I chose a chocolate frosted one with hints of cayenne. "This is amazing," I said.

He nodded. "It's a Mexican cupcake. She got a job at a bakery that just opened in Dorchester."

I looked from him to Brian. "So, what have you guys been doing all morning other than eating cupcakes?"

Brian's expression became serious. "While you were at the funeral, we talked to Finny."

"You couldn't wait for me?"

"Chief wanted it done that way."

"I see," I said.

"Peter will plead guilty to everything, including Megan's murder." He rubbed his arm. "He admitted to having an affair with her, said her death was his fault, not Shannon's. Shannon was his patient, she was fragile, and he pushed her too far. He'll cooperate fully if we keep Shannon's role in Megan's death out of the news."

"You believe him?"

He leaned back. "I find it hard to believe a pretty, talented girl like Shannon would have done the things she did, including shooting me, if Peter hadn't made her do them."

"Just because she was pretty doesn't mean she was nice. You know that." I had to say it.

"Yeah, but the Delaneys lost a child. If we drag Shannon through the mud, they'll lose her twice. There's no point digging any deeper now that she's dead." He stared at me intently.

"Right." I sighed. Things were better left this way for me, too. I leaned back with my arms behind my head. "So that's it—end of the story. Case closed?"

Brian nodded. He turned to George. "When are you out of here?"

"Still waiting for my marching orders."

"You're leaving us?" I said.

"All good things must come to an end." He chose a cupcake with white frosting sprinkled with coconut and said, "I learned some things about Peter. James Donovan became Peter Reynolds after he killed Bridget. Peter bought the boat from Concannon through an LLC. The cabin James called the Christmas house was actually an abandoned property owned by a man who lived out of state. Peter bought the cabin and the land he built the big house on through the same LLC years later. He covered his tracks well so he could become a new person, but James is still inside him. The crime scenes are where he sets that monster free." He peeled the paper from his cupcake. "His father was a serial rapist. He went to prison when James was a teenager. His mother died and James went into foster care." He shrugged. "Maybe the apple doesn't fall far from the tree."

"Having a father like that could have messed him up," Brian said. "But lots of people with fucked-up childhoods don't do what Peter did. It's a reason, but it's no excuse." His expression softened as he turned to me. "How's Corinne doing?"

I folded my hands on my desk. "I'm worried about her. She tends to close up and she's locked up real tight now." My cupcake was suddenly unappetizing.

"At least she wasn't injured." George set his dark eyes on me. "And there's no evidence of sexual assault."

I winced at his words. "But Peter held her captive for hours and she won't talk about it." My stomach seized. "I wish to god I'd recognized that bastard years ago."

Brian rested his hand on my shoulder. "He wore a mask, gave you ketamine, and he was your worst nightmare. Christ, I run into girls I dated and don't remember them. Don't blame yourself. You and Corinne are the heroes here."

I let out a slow breath. "I doubt Corinne feels like a hero. Neither do I. And people died because I didn't recognize him. It's hard not to blame myself for that." I failed to add, let alone for the other thing I'd done. I looked for the comfort in Brian's brown eyes, but I couldn't feel it anymore. I was facing a future of perpetual fear of being unmasked, and that was exactly what Peter intended.

* * *

As I scarfed down pasta and spongy meatballs soaked with the delicious sauce Jeff had made with tomatoes from the garden, all I wanted was a quiet night with just the three of us. I kept my voice cheerful as I asked if Corinne had spoken to any of her friends today. A shrug. Was she going to any practices this week? Another shrug.

And finally, did she want to talk about what happened? She caught my dismayed look and said, "I'm sorry, Mom. But I don't want to talk about it right now."

I swirled spaghetti half-heartedly around my fork. After dinner, Corinne went up to her room. As I helped Jeff clean up, I said, "I'm worried about her."

"I am, too. I hate myself for paying so much attention to a coding bug that this happened," he said.

I rinsed a plate and handed it to him. "We both failed her. Don't blame yourself for what you couldn't have foreseen."

He slid a plate into the dishwasher and stared at me. "Sam," he finally said, "I'm giving my notice on the apartment. It will be best for all of us."

I twisted the dishrag in my hand, feeling a rush of anxiety. "I guess so."

"I thought you'd be happy." He gave me an agonized look. "Is this about what I did, Sam? Because I'm going to tell you now whether you want to hear it or not. I went out drinking one night after the conference. Everyone from work was there having a good time but me." His dark eyes met mine. "It had been so long since I'd had a good time, Sam. You were always pushing me away and I couldn't figure out what I'd done wrong. When this woman from work, who I barely knew, kissed me, it was like I was someone again and it felt good." His voice faltered. "I let it go further than it should have, but I knew right away I'd made a mistake. You may tear the blue out of the sky sometimes, but you're the one who makes me feel alive. You always have." He shut the dishwasher and said, "Just give us a chance."

I wanted to, but as I leaned back against the counter, I felt the weight of what I couldn't tell him, and I didn't say anything. We watched Netflix for a while and I took Ginger out to pee. When I brought her back in, she raced upstairs and sat whimpering outside Corinne's door. I knocked softly.

"Oh, my baby," she said as the dog bounded into her room.

I sat down on the bed. Ginger made a running leap, failed, tried again, and landed next to me. Corinne went back to painting her nails with shimmering blue polish. She didn't say anything, but she also didn't tell me to leave. "What you did was really brave. I love you so much." I said. She kept painting her nails. It felt as if with each stroke, the moment was slipping away, but I had to say more. "Whenever you're ready to talk about what happened, I'm here for you. Don't hold it inside." Our eyes met and my chest tightened at the thought of the secret I was keeping from her and Jeff.

"I'll be fine, Mom." She waved her nails to dry them. Her phone buzzed and she stepped out of the room to take the call. When she came back she couldn't hide her excitement as she said, "That was Anton. He's getting released from the hospital tomorrow. He still wants to work on the dance with me." She paused. "And he wants to talk to you and Brian."

Chapter
Forty-Four

I SETTLED INTO a mildew-stained wicker chair on Anton's screened front porch. As Irina poured tea into glasses from a red enameled pot, Brian gave his tea a skeptical glance.

"Put a sugar cube in your mouth and sip through it. Is better that way." She eyed Brian's sling. "You okay?"

"I'm lucky Shannon missed any major arteries." He took a reluctant swallow. A cool breeze jangled the wind chimes hanging from the ceiling. Anton twisted uneasily in his chair. Brian turned to him. "You're lucky not to have been seriously injured. That was quite a fall."

"I have a concussion and a broken ankle." He pointed to the plastic boot on his foot. "I won't be dancing for a while." He glanced at me. "But I can still help Corinne."

Irina adjusted the worn red pillow behind his head. "Do the right thing like we talked about and you'll be fine." She gave his shoulder a firm squeeze and left.

"She has a tendency to hover." He smiled nervously. "You aren't going to arrest me, are you?"

Brian shook his head. "We have the right guy in jail. So what have you got for us?"

Anton exhaled slowly. "The day Megan died, Shannon called and told me Megan fell doing a backflip and hit her head on the floor in the practice room. She couldn't wake her up. When I got there, she was lying in a pool of blood. She had no pulse. I wanted to call 911, but Shannon said no one would believe it was an accident, and I had to help her cover it up." He looked from me to Brian.

"Then what happened?" I asked.

"We put her in the trunk of her car and Shannon drove it to the park on the other side of the creek. I met her there in the van. We hung out at the beach until dark and walked back to Megan's car, put her body in a little boat and rowed to the Sailors Home Cemetery." He gnawed on a nail. "We left her under the tree, rowed back, and went to Piney."

I shook my head. "There are easier ways to get rid of a body."

"Shannon wanted to do it that way. It was her idea for me to steal the butterfly and make it look like the guy who killed Bridget did it. She stole Dmitry's knife and used it to make the cuts in Megan's chest. When we were on Piney, she insisted I go back for Megan's watch and that I move the car. That's when I ran into Megan's brother and we had the fight I told you about. When I got to the graveyard, I took her watch and hugged her goodbye."

His shoulders fell. "I ditched her car by the marsh and went to talk to Corinne."

"Why did you want to talk to her?"

"I couldn't go home or to Dmitry's with blood all over my shirt. I knew Corinne would believe my story. She's always believed in me." He lowered his eyes. "She gave me a clean shirt, and I went to Dmitry's. I gave Shannon the watch the next day."

I leaned forward. "Why did she want it?"

"She liked to keep certain things." His gaze shifted away.

"What about Megan's bag and her phone?" I asked.

"She didn't want them. I threw them in the marsh."

"And the knife?"

"I offered to get rid of it, but she said she'd do it."

I pressed my hands on my knees. "And she gave it to Peter."

"I tried to convince her that we should tell the truth, but she said we'd ruin our lives over an accident if we did that." He stared at the distant ocean. "I loved her too much to do the right thing."

Brian shook his head. "What changed your mind?"

"When you said the killer had Megan's watch, I knew Shannon was in danger." He rubbed his forehead. "After you dropped me at her house, I told her she had to tell me who she had given the watch to, and we had to tell the police everything before he killed her or someone else. When she refused, I said we couldn't be together anymore. She said if I loved her like I'd written in the letter I gave her, I'd stop asking questions. I told her I wouldn't stop until she told me the truth. She tore the letter up and stormed out of the room." He gave me a grim look. "I looked under the window seat to see if she had any letters from that man in there but all I found was a shoebox with Percy in it. My little bird . . ."

"We know," I said.

He struggled to continue. "When she came back I showed her the shoebox and called her a horrible, sick person. She claimed that she was trying to set Percy free, like the man told her to do, and she killed him by accident. I begged her to tell me the man's name, but she still wouldn't do it." His voice faltered. "I started to cry, and she said, 'What's your problem? Your father can get you a new bird.' She had this look in her eyes—all black with a thin rim of green—like there was nothing in there but darkness, and I knew."

"You don't find the truth in people's eyes," Brian said.

"Maybe you don't," Anton said. "For me, everything she'd done came together when I looked in her eyes and saw what she was capable of." He went on. "I broke up with her and said I was going to tell you everything. She called the next day threatening to kill herself if I didn't come and talk to her at that house in the woods. When I got there, she kept trying to convince me not to go to the police, but I wouldn't agree. The last thing I remember is standing beside her at the edge of the ravine. I went to stop her from jumping, and she got that same look in her eyes and pushed me over the edge. When I hit the bottom, I lay still so she'd think I was dead. I heard noises and worried she'd come back. But it was you." He looked up at me. "She said Percy died by accident, Megan died by accident, and I fell into the ravine by accident. But none of it was an accident."

"Do you have proof that these weren't accidents?" Brian asked.

"Just a feeling." He sank back in his chair. "I had a feeling about what my father did when I had that accident when I was a little boy, too. My mother talked to me this morning and now I know I was right."

"What did she tell you?" I asked.

"That he yelled at me for dancing on the beach and threw me down. I hit a rock and was knocked unconscious. He lied and said it was an accident. My mom told me she's felt bad for going along with him ever since. My whole life he's pushed me away because I wouldn't be the person he wanted me to be. I embarrass him." He set his pale eyes on me. "All I wanted was for him to love me. That's all I wanted from Shannon, too." He raised his chin. "But I'm telling you this now because I am not a liar and I'm not going along with anyone's lies anymore."

Chapter
Forty-Five

I PRESSED MY hands on the wrought-iron railing of the balcony off Shannon's practice room overlooking the ocean. The velvet breeze was warm, the sky robin's egg blue. Come to Starlight Bay and live your best life, the brochures said. Barb and Max were living their worst nightmare at their vacation home on Cape Cod, furious that we were here searching their house. The techs didn't have to search hard to find a large quantity of blood between the raised dance floor in Shannon's practice room and the subfloor.

"We could be looking at a murder or an accident." Brian leaned his good arm on the railing. "But Megan died from a blow to her head from a sharp-edged object. That doesn't sound like falling and hitting her head by accident the way Shannon described it."

"Right, which means there could be a weapon here somewhere," I said.

"If she tossed it in there, it's long gone." He stared at the foam-flecked ocean. "The thing I don't understand is if Shannon killed Megan and tried to kill Anton, why would Peter take the blame for her? He was her therapist, not her lover. Or was he? If he was screwing around with her as well as Megan, all the more reason for Shannon to explode."

I took a steadying breath. Brian would tear away at this until he figured it out. "There's something you need to know. After Peter confessed, he told me he was Shannon's father."

"Her father? Are you fucking kidding me?"

"He claimed he had an affair with Barb and had dedicated his life to being a good father to Shannon."

"Jesus. Why didn't you tell me, Sam?" The disappointment in his eyes ate at me.

"Me not telling anyone and not implicating Shannon was a condition of his confession. He wanted to give her a chance at a good life." I paused. "It's too late for that, but he could still retract his confession."

"You could have told me in confidence. You trust me, don't you?" The way he shook his head made me feel even worse. "We have to run a DNA test. I'll get George to expedite it."

"Yeah," I said. "And we need to keep the results confidential."

"He doesn't have any basis for getting the confession thrown out, but if this is true it will rip the Delaneys apart." Brian eyed me. "Peter's in jail. Shannon's dead. Technically we don't have to find out whether Shannon is guilty of murder. We could stop this search right now. What do you think, Sam?"

That would be better for me, too, but I had to know the truth. "Let's do this," I said.

We went through the arched glass doors to Shannon's practice room. I stood at the end of the torn-up dance floor. "Push me," I said. Brian gave me a quizzical look and a shove. I fell backward but didn't come close to hitting the coffee table at the end of the room.

He shook his head as I stood up. "Why are we doing this, Sam?"

"Shannon claimed she shoved Megan from the end of the dance floor and she hit her head on the coffee table, but that's not physically possible. It's too far away. She made that up because she knew Megan died from a blow to the head and that would explain how it could have been an accident."

I stepped back. "All the blood was under the dance floor. That's probably where she was killed. Assuming she didn't plan this ahead and the phone call is what set her off, she must have grabbed the weapon from somewhere around here." I looked around the airy sunlit space.

The small sitting area with the coffee table was at one end. A glass display that held Shannon's trophies, DVDs, and framed photos from her competitions was at the other end. I ran my finger along the beveled edge of the marble base of a gold plastic winged victory trophy—First Place Solo Dance 2011. I held it up. "This is heavy enough to do damage."

"First place can be a dangerous thing," Brian said.

I examined the other trophies. "Second place is even more dangerous. Shannon's second place trophy from States is missing."

His eyes met mine. "If she was smart, she threw it away."

"Peter kept trophies from his murders. Shannon kept the bird. Maybe she kept the trophy as a literal trophy."

We went downstairs to her bedroom. Bedding was strewn all over a pink rug patterned with toe shoes. The doors to the gilt-trimmed white armoire stenciled with ballerinas were open. Elegant dance figurines lined bookshelves along one wall. Barb and Max had created a dream room for their talented daughter. But sleeping here knowing a creature you had killed was hidden away in it must have been a nightmare. I went over to the window seat.

"The techs already looked there," Brian said.

"I'm looking again." I opened it up. It was empty now.

Brian peered over my shoulder with a heavy sigh. "Peter will be in jail for life. We've gotten the real monster. That's good enough."

I wondered if he'd think I was a monster when he found out—if he found out. I shut the lid and ran my hand over the polished window seat, as beautifully crafted as the carved chest where Peter kept his special treasures.

I turned to Brian. "Anton said someone who worked for the Delaneys made this. It looks like Concannon's work. He made something like this for Peter. It had a sliding panel on the bottom."

I opened the window seat again and shined the flashlight from my phone from one end of it to the other. I ran my hand along the bottom, feeling for any irregularity in the wooden boards, and found grooves that formed a rectangle at the far end. I leaned in with the flashlight, made out the faint outline of what looked like a trapdoor, and used the screwdriver I kept on my belt to pry it open. I reached for the white box pressed against the pink fiberglass insulation in the wall.

The trophy was inside it—a scrim of dried blood and hair along the sharp marble edge.

Chapter
Forty-Six

IT'S NOT ALWAYS a good idea to open a box—just ask Pandora. We did our best to close this one. When we told the Chief what we'd found out about Shannon, he said sit on it for now. The future of Quincy depended on Max Delaney, and this would only cause him and Barb more pain. While I struggled to find sympathy for this golden girl Peter had twisted into a distorted reflection of himself, I was fine with leaving things that way. We let Anton know he wasn't being charged with anything, and we weren't going to take our investigation any further. He was fine with that. In spite of everything, he still loved her.

A few days later George dropped Peter's DNA test results on my desk and said, "When Brian let me know that Peter told you he was Shannon's father, I thought Peter was lying. But it turns out he wasn't." He rocked back on his heels. "Good job, but you should have told us about this sooner."

Brian stiffened. "She had no choice. He threatened to withdraw his confession if she told anyone."

George stared at me. "You didn't tell us about that, either."

I felt like I was shrinking in the glare of his dark eyes. "It won't happen again," I said. Contrition didn't come easily to me, but I needed all the good will I could muster before my entire world collapsed. "Do we tell Barb now?"

"No need. O'Neil and I already did." George said.

"It was better that way," Brian said in an infuriatingly calm voice. "She admitted to having an affair with Peter a few years after Bridget was murdered, said she was going through a rough time with Max, but they patched things up and Peter left. He came back when Shannon got sick. He and Barb became friends again, and she let Shannon get to know him without telling her he was her father. He was so good with her, it was like he brought Shannon back to life. He was a great therapist. She didn't want to mess with that, or her marriage. She claims she had no idea he was a murderer until she saw it in the papers."

George turned to us. "I told the Chief we have to get in front of this and make this new information public before it leaks on its own. The official story is Peter is Shannon's father, she was his victim, too, and we're investigating whether he manipulated her into playing a role in Megan's murder."

By the end of the day, it was breaking news. It didn't take long for the other shoe to drop.

* * *

Peter demanded Brian and I meet with him the next morning. I'd dressed like you might for a business meeting, tailored white shirt, black pencil skirt, low heels, my hair in a neat ponytail. His green-eyed gaze didn't waver as he pounded his fist on the table in the prison interview room and told us he was filing a complaint about me. His confession had been obtained illegally, I'd threatened to kill him if he didn't confess, and he'd taken my threat seriously because I'd done it before. He paused to savor the moment and in a calm methodical way told the story of how I'd killed my best friend, how I'd enjoyed it, how I'd always resented Bridget.

It was hard to decide which was worse, Peter's words, or the way Brian wouldn't look at me as he turned to him and said, "Do you have any evidence to support these allegations?"

He gave him a haughty nod. "Your officers didn't search very thoroughly. If you pull up the wall to wall in the living room in the house near the Blue Hills, you'll find a trapdoor in the floorboards and a DVD with a video you need to watch."

I folded my hands in front of me. "Who filmed that video?"

He eyed me with annoyance. "Bobby. I already told you that."

"Did he make the other videos, too?"

His lips parted in a slow smile. "There are no other videos. I lied about them."

"So, some things in your confession were true and some weren't. Have I got that straight?" I said.

He sneered. "It was all coerced." He leaned toward Brian, cupped his hand around his mouth and said, "She's a sick woman. I did my best, but no amount of therapy worked. She killed Bridget and now Shannon's dead because of her and Corinne." As he spat out the last part, it was all I could do not to reach across the table and grab him by the throat. He flashed me an imperious look. "I told you to run, and you've been running from your crime ever since. It's time to face the truth."

I inhaled slowly. "Here's a truth you need to face. Shannon wasn't running from me or Corinne that night. She was running from you and what you dragged her into. That's what you do. You drag people into your darkness, so you won't be alone in it. You did that to Bridget. You're trying to do that to me now. But it won't work, because you'll always be alone with the monster inside you." I fixed my eyes on him. "Make no mistake about it. The last thing you said to Shannon is what pushed her over the edge of the ravine."

He fought to stay composed as he staggered to his feet in his shackles and yelled for the guard to take him back to his cell.

* * *

Brian came by my desk a few hours later. The techs had found a DVD with one video on it. "Just one?" I asked.

He nodded. "They tore the place apart. That's all they found. Want to watch it now?" I told him I'd already seen it and didn't need to watch it again. But he insisted, so I pulled my chair over. It was no easier to watch the second time. The devastated look on his face said it all. He reassured me it wasn't so bad.

"You don't have to lie to me." I replied. "You think he can get the confession thrown out?"

"You read him his rights. You didn't coerce him. It's all on the record. No one's going to throw it out. He would have killed you, but you got the better of him and didn't kill him when you had the chance. You did the right thing and got enough for us to put him away forever." His eyes searched mine for an agonizing moment. "Do you remember any of what was in the video actually happening?"

"I got flashes of memories in the cabin." I twisted my hands together. "And there's something I never told you."

"I'm keeping a list," he said.

"Even before that night, I wanted Bridget to die. I whispered it under my breath when Devon chose her over me, when he and my father fawned all over her." I forged ahead. "Before we left for Devon's party, I asked Bridget if she was really in love with him. She told me she had to get away from Quincy, she'd done something terrible and Devon was the only one who could save her from it."

"Did she say what she'd done?" he asked.

"No, but I assumed it was breaking my heart by stealing Devon from me and using him to get out of Quincy. We fought about it. I was furious when we left for the party. Some of that anger had to still be there when Peter, or rather JP, told me to kill her. He exploited it, but I'm not blameless. I'm the one who did something really terrible."

He drew his brows together. "Sounds like she was desperate to get away from JP."

"Yeah, Peter said she threatened to go to the cops. He wouldn't tell me why."

He eyed me calmly. "We don't know the whole story, but a jealous spat with your friend when you were only sixteen doesn't make you guilty of murder."

"And if I am?" I asked.

He gave the ceiling a weary glance. "Don't get ahead of yourself."

It wasn't long before the Chief ordered us into his office. I sat down and the shouting began. IA would investigate. I was on leave until they finished. What the hell was wrong with me? Why hadn't I told anyone this? Now the whole case could fall apart because of me. But I was lucky. No one was going to say anything about this until it was determined whether the tape was edited. They still might not say anything because if we raised any doubt, Peter might walk, and the world was a better place with him in jail. But that didn't mean what I had done was right. I offered no excuses as I handed in my gun and my badge.

That night Brian and I stopped for a drink at Finnegan's. We were drinking in silence when George joined us. He stared at me and said, "I find this hard to believe, Samantha."

"I do, too," I said. "It doesn't even feel like me in that video. I don't remember any of it."

George ate the olive from his martini. Apparently, he liked them now. "But it is you." He turned to Brian. "I can't believe you're covering this up."

"We're not covering it up," Brian said. "The video is edited. If people find out about it before we can prove that, Sam's life could be ruined."

George licked the toothpick from his olive. "There's always a good reason for covering something up, until it's a bad reason. People covered for Junior for years because it was important to have him as an informant. If they hadn't done that, the little girl he killed would still be alive." He fastened his eyes on me. "The way it looks, you killed Bridget. Peter played a role but so did you. We're covering it up to save the case and protect you, Sam, but what if we have to protect people from you? Not saying that's true, but we need an independent investigation to find out. Bridget's family deserves to know the truth and it will be better for you to know, too."

I inhaled so hard my chest hurt. "You think you know everything, but you don't know me. A few facts don't tell the whole story. If you ever bothered to really get to know anyone, you'd know that's true. You probably don't even know anything about your own sister, except that she makes cupcakes. When you go home at night all you have is your rigid principles to keep you company. But go ahead with your investigation."

"I don't have to listen to this," he said and left.

Brian ran his thumb over his cocktail napkin. "That was not smart, Sam."

*　*　*

I waited a couple days to get my things, because when I brought them home, Jeff and Corinne would know I was on leave, and I'd have to tell them why. I was almost done slamming drawers and shoving my things into boxes when Brian came over to my desk. He held out his phone and said, "Did you see this?"

I swallowed hard. "Detective Tied to Crime She Spent Her Life Trying to Solve" was the headline. Alice went on to say new evidence had emerged that indicated I might have some connection to the murder of Bridget McGann and I was on leave pending an investigation. She didn't mention the video and cautioned people not to rush to judgment until all the facts were known.

Brian looked at me. "It could have been worse."

I sighed. "It's just the beginning and we have George to thank for it."

He straightened. "Don't let this get to you. You're going to beat this."

As I lifted the framed photo of Jeff and Corinne from my desk, he said, "Leave that. You'll be back soon." He added something about being there for me and I gave him a frosty glance, told him goodbye, and didn't hang around long enough for him to turn it into something I couldn't deal with right then.

* * *

Jeff must have said, "What the fuck, Sam," three times before I got in the door. He'd already heard the news. I forced myself to tell him that Peter was saying I killed Bridget, and it was possible that I had but didn't remember. I couldn't bring myself to mention the video. "If you hate me, just tell me," I blurted out.

His pained look tore through me as he said, "I don't hate you, Sam."

Corinne came home a few minutes later, grabbed a bottle of water from the fridge, and sat down on a kitchen chair. She took a careful swallow. "I heard the news, Mom. I'm so sorry this is happening to you."

I told her I'd be fine and tried to sound like I believed it. We ordered Chinese since no one felt like cooking. Jeff poured me a drink and one for himself. "How long will you be on leave?" he asked cautiously. I poked at a crab rangoon without appetite and told him I didn't know, but I'd probably lose my job.

"That's not fair," Corinne said. "You saved my life and Anton's. Peter's the killer. I don't care what anyone says about you."

The room became so quiet you could hear the refrigerator buzz. She expected me to defend myself, but I couldn't. I was relieved when Jeff raised his glass and said, "I don't care, either. Fuck them if they can't see you saved this whole city from Peter." I raised my glass half-heartedly. We finished eating in silence and each chose a fortune cookie as we always did.

Corinne broke hers open and sighed. "*A new adventure awaits.* Right." Her phone rang and her expression darkened as she took the call. "That's it. I'm quitting the team," she said when she hung up.

"What's going on?" I asked.

She stood up. "I don't want to talk about it."

I put my hand on her shoulder. "Tell me what's wrong."

She looked grimly from me to Jeff and sat back down. "Beverly says that Lane is talking about how strange it is that you killed Bridget and survived, and now Shannon's dead and you and I are the only ones who saw what happened." Her voice filled with tears. "I can't stay on the team knowing everyone's thinking that when they look at me."

"You saved me and Brian," I said. "You're a hero. If they can't understand that, it's their problem."

"But what if they're right? If Shannon hadn't run from me, she might still be alive."

My shoulders knotted. I couldn't let that broken girl hurt Corinne more than she already had. She needed to know who Shannon really was. "She wasn't running from you. She was trying to escape from Peter and the terrible things she'd done. She killed Megan, made Anton cover it up, and attempted to kill him to keep him from talking. Shannon would have killed you, me, and Brian if you hadn't stopped her. You didn't do anything wrong."

"She tried to kill Anton?"

"He didn't tell you?"

She shook her head. "He won't talk about her."

I took her hands in mine. "It hurts right now, but you will be able to move on from this and have a good life, because you're a good person. Don't let anyone make you doubt that." I fixed my eyes on her soft gray-green ones. "And don't give up on the team because of what other people are saying about you or me. You hear me? Believe in yourself. Tell them your story. They need to know the truth." Her gaze veered away. I went on. "You still thinking of quitting?"

"I'll figure it out." My heart sank as she gave me a defeated look, clipped Ginger's leash on her collar and took her out for a walk.

As the door banged behind her, my stomach lurched. Things were only going to get harder on Corinne. She and Jeff were defending me now, but I couldn't bear the thought of facing them when the video inevitably leaked. I turned to Jeff and said, "I think you should both go back to the apartment tomorrow."

"Why?" His concerned look was almost impossible to bear.

"You and Corinne are better off not being around me right now."

He touched my shoulder. "Don't do this, Sam."

"You don't understand." I pulled away. "I have to fix this, and I have to do it alone."

*   *   *

I wanted to stay in bed for hours, as I had the past few days, but Ginger would have none of that. Jeff was at work, Corinne had practices for Regionals all week, and I had the dog. I liked the company, and I was relieved that Corinne had decided to give the team another chance. Ginger thumped her tail on the floor and looked at me expectantly. I yanked on a pair of jeans. I only meant to take her to her favorite tree, but I kept walking. We ended up at the Dunkin's down the street.

I looped Ginger's leash around a dying sapling that was part of the Greener Quincy project. As I waited in line behind a man ordering a large iced with three creams and nine Equals, I braced myself for someone to recognize me and say something. But no one did, except for the scruffy guy sitting as always at a table by the door, who gave me his usual "Hi, hon."

When we got home, Ginger clanked her bowl around to get at every last bit of kibble. I was alone with my thoughts and my iced coffee when my phone rang. It was Linda. She wanted to know if I could bring Pia's portrait to Regionals. I asked what had changed her mind about it. After a long pause she said, "I'll be there. You'll be there. It makes sense."

"You don't think I'm a murderer?"

"We both know that's bullshit." She paused. "Corinne told the team what Shannon did to you and Brian and what she did to Anton. That girl had a problem. Not you." It made me smile that Corinne had done that. With kids it was so hard to know if you were actually getting through, but amazingly sometimes you did. She went on to say she was worried about ruining the surprise for Beverly if she saw the painting, so we arranged for a discreet handover in the parking lot. "Like a drug deal." She laughed.

I sat cross-legged on the thin, cheap rug in our third bedroom going through my paintings stacked against the wall, looking for the one of Pia. I swallowed hard as I pulled out my unfinished painting of me at the bottom of the ravine—the black flowers on the water covering me—the shadow person above. I had to make that person me as well, but not now. Maybe not ever.

I put the portrait of Pia on the drafting table. She looked back at me with her big dark eyes, a happy dog in a happy green world in a happier time. I struggled not to give in to self-pity as I wrapped it up in brown paper. Peter said when I remembered what happened, I would become a whole person, but he'd lied about that. He had lied about *everything*. I swiveled my stool back and forth. I had to live with what I'd done, but I didn't have to let him win.

I called Brian and filled him in on what I'd told Corinne. "Maybe I shouldn't have," I said, "but she needed to know who Shannon really was or she'd never be able to move on from what happened. It could haunt her for years."

There was a long silence. "Then it's for the better."

"Right." I wrapped my ponytail around my hand. "There's something else you need to know. Peter lied when he told us there are no more videos. He bragged about them when he confessed, said they were part of his art. There's definitely more of them than just the one of me."

"Then why would he deny they exist?" Brian said.

"Because the videos of the other murders could provide enough evidence to convict him even without his confession, and he knows that. We have to find them."

"We? Have you forgotten you're on leave?"

"You have to find them. Maybe they're in the cloud or in that run-down cabin he called the Christmas house. He mentioned revelatory art there. Don't let me down."

Chapter
Forty-Seven

JEFF PRESSED HIS hand on mine as I settled into my seat beside him at the Northeast Dance Team Regional Competition. We'd hardly talked since I told him and Corinne to leave, but we'd made sure to both be here. When the dance before hers ended, his warm breath brushed my ear as he said, "It's time."

It began with a few bell-like piano notes. Corinne stepped onto a stage strewn with white petals, wearing a loose sweater over a blue sequined top and black shorts. She flung off the sweater and whipped her long hair around. Spots of light swirled over her like snow, as she did a precise, elegant tap dance, arms outstretched, a smile fixed on her face as the clicking of her heels merged with the bells. Beverly came out and tapped beside her. Other members of the team came out one by one, leaping, turning, and dancing in every style—jazz, hip-hop, tap, ballet. As the last strains of the music melted into silence, they formed a circle and threw petals into the air saying, "For Nina, for Megan." I stood up and clapped hard, and then everyone stood.

Their dance placed first, but it was impossible for the Fearless Flyers to make it into nationals without Megan, Nina, Anton—or Shannon. Corinne came up to me and Jeff in the lobby afterward and handed him her costume. I touched her shoulder. "Your dance was the best. I'm so proud." She politely raised a brow. I was about to share my wisdom about how their dance for Megan and Nina was a bigger triumph than winning Regionals, when Anton came by, and my well-intentioned words slipped away.

He wore a threadbare T-shirt and jeans. As usual his parents weren't here. I told him he'd created a beautiful dance. He brushed a petal from Corinne's hair and said, "Most of it was her idea." He gave me a quick smile.

I said, "I hope you'll be dancing again soon."

He looked down at the boot on his foot. "I'll always be dancing. Don't know how to do anything else. I hope you keep on painting." His light eyes met mine.

I turned to Corinne. "I am so impressed with the dance that you two created."

She gave me an embarrassed smile, grabbed his arm, and said, "Come on. Everyone's going for pizza." As they walked away, she gave me a look that seemed to say, *I have no idea what I'm going to do with him.*

Linda came over as Jeff was putting Corinne's costume in the car. "You got the goods?" She grinned and looked over her shoulder. "Coast is clear. I let Beverly go for pizza."

I handed her the painting from the trunk. She insisted on unwrapping it in the parking lot and placed it on the hood of our car. I stepped back for a look. Pia looked at us expectantly from the portrait I'd done before I knew what I knew now—or rather when what I knew was like the black beetle, inching along a rose petal behind the dog.

Jeff pointed to the black dot. "Did you make a mistake?"

I frowned. "It's a bug, a literal bug."

* * *

Jeff and I had a quiet dinner after Regionals. The stew he made was a fragrant mélange of cinnamon, beef, sweet potatoes, and apricots—his own version of tzimmes, with red rich slices of garden tomatoes on the side. We shared a bottle of expensive bourbon someone had given us last Christmas and talked about how good Corinne's performance was, and how she was bouncing back from this. He asked how the investigation was going, and I told him I didn't know because I was still on leave. I asked if he'd solved his production problem yet.

"Recursion will be the death of me." He pushed his hand through his shaggy dark curls. "I've run through every possible scenario over and over again, but I still can't find the edge case that makes it go wrong." The line between his eyes deepened. "I wish we could all be together again, Sam." I imagined everything returning to some semblance of normal, while I still felt like the failed person he knew I was, and told him I wasn't ready.

As we cleaned up, I asked if there was anything he wanted me to do around the house. He said, "No pressure, but if you have time tomorrow, the garden could use some weeding."

I smiled. "I'll do my best not to kill anything."

I was in the living room drinking more bourbon and watching a *Law & Order* rerun when my phone rang. "Sam, I've got news," Brian said. "Meet me at the Lazy Dog."

* * *

I hurried to the table at the back where he was seated. He signaled the waitress, and I got a bourbon. He pushed his plate of cheese fries my way. "I can't possibly eat all of these. Help me out." Tempting as they were, I told him I'd already eaten.

His pale blue shirt looked good with his navy sling. The tip of a matching tie showed from the shirt pocket where he'd stuffed it, and his freckled cheeks were flushed with worry, excitement, or some combo of both.

"Aren't you pretty." I smiled.

He didn't smile back. "There was an event earlier today." I raised an eyebrow. "Baby shower. Don't mock me."

"Mary Ann?"

"Her niece. It was a test and I failed. Mary Ann caught me smoking on the back porch. I might have offered Nick a smoke, too. Poor kid has been through hell. She said I was setting a bad example for her son and that was it." He made a throat cutting motion on his neck. "I've never been a good example for anyone, Sam."

I clasped my hands on the table. "You didn't have me come here to tell me that."

He sipped his drink. "We found a flash drive with more videos, including ones of the other murders. Techs are still going through them, but I watched a couple. Not a pretty sight."

"Better you than me," I said.

"We have enough to nail Peter without his confession."

"That's good news. But you could have told me that over the phone."

"I could have. You sure you don't want some fries?" I shook my head, and he went on. "We found a little model of a house on a shelf in that cabin. It looked like the one you told me Bridget admired in the Christmas village." He held my gaze. "We took it apart. The flash drive was inside a miniature window seat."

"Concannon was a clever guy," I said.

Brian leaned forward. "The drive also had the raw footage used to make the video of you. It's bizarre that Peter left it there, but the techs used it to determine that your video was heavily edited."

I nodded. "And that means . . ."

"It's not valid evidence." He smiled. "IA cleared you. Welcome back."

I stiffened. "Good to know, but I'm not sure about coming back."

His smile faded. "I thought this would make you happy and we'd celebrate with a drink or two."

I sighed. "None of this changes what I did."

He shook his head with frustration. "Peter staged that video just like he staged Devon's suicide, and that calls everything on it into question. When the techs put together all the raw footage, what he edited out could tell a completely different story." He took a careful sip of his drink. "You don't know for sure what happened between you and Bridget."

"I do." I pressed my lips together.

"About that." He inhaled as if bracing to go on. "After Bridget's murder, a young woman came to us with a tip. The winter before, she was walking to the T when a pretty blonde asked her to go to a party with her and her boyfriend. She got into a car with them. They drugged her, raped her, and left her in a vacant lot in South Boston. She reported it to the local PD and submitted a rape kit, but it didn't match anyone in the system. The investigation went nowhere, but when she saw Bridget's photo in the paper, she thought she might be the blonde who had lured her into the car."

"And you never fucking told me." I fought to stay calm.

He tugged on his collar. "The rape kit had been lost. I read the police report. She said she got into a brown car. We were looking for a white one. She couldn't describe the guy except to say he was blond and handsome and she didn't think he was Devon. She couldn't even say for sure if it was Bridget. We had nothing to go on, so we let it go." He gave me a guilty glance. "I didn't want to make you feel worse than you already did by disillusioning you about Bridget over something that was probably a false lead."

A sickening feeling spread through me. "Why tell me now?"

"When you told me Bridget said she did something terrible and that Peter said she threatened to go to the police, it got me wondering if it really was Bridget and Peter who picked up that young woman and that's what Bridget threatened to go to the police about."

He ran a finger over his napkin. "It was just a hunch. I still didn't want to say anything, but when you told me how Corinne needed to know what Shannon really did so she could move on, I realized I was wrong. I had to tell you. If it's true, it puts Bridget in a new light." *A new light indeed.* He eyed me with concern. "It was around the same time she introduced you to JP at Nostalgia. She might have lured you in, too, Sam."

I pressed back against my chair. "She never would have done something like that."

"Maybe not, but I could use your help figuring this out."

"If you'd told me back then instead of protecting my delicate feelings, I might have remembered something that would help, but it's too late now." I swallowed the last of my bourbon and put the glass down. "Really lovely of you to finally let me know all this, but I've got to go."

"I'll email you the police report," he said. "Read it. Let me know if anything jumps out." I wanted to bolt out of the restaurant and never talk about this again, but I told him I would.

Chapter
Forty-Eight

WARM, LEMONY SUNLIGHT poured through the kitchen window. Brian's email arrived as I was about to take Ginger for a walk on the beach. I clicked on the police report, heart in my throat.

In late February, six months before Bridget and I were abducted, Jennifer Connor, a seventeen-year-old from South Boston, attended the memorial in Quincy for Debbie Duggan, Bridget's friend who overdosed. I wasn't there but Bridget was. Debbie was Jennifer's cousin. Jennifer's friends left early because it was snowing, but she stayed.

She was walking to the T when a car pulled over. A girl got out, said she'd been at the memorial, too, and offered Jennifer a ride. The snow was picking up. Jennifer worried the trains might stop running, so she got in. The guy driving was handsome with blond hair. The girl was blonde, too, and wearing green-and-black striped gloves. She invited Jennifer to a party, offered her a white pill and said, "You don't know what happiness is until you've tried this." Jennifer woke up in a vacant lot with a hazy memory of being raped.

My sunny kitchen felt suddenly cold. I wrapped my arms around myself but couldn't stop shaking. That night at Nostalgia, Bridget had said the same thing to me about a white pill. I saw the hard lumps of ice clinging to her green-and-black striped gloves, heard her laughter as we pelted each other with snowballs. The next morning, when I woke with a pounding headache in her attic room, the memory of what happened had been erased as surely as the world had been blotted out with snow—but in some part of myself I knew. When we reconnected that spring and Bridget told me she'd done something terrible, she had to be referring to Jennifer but also to me.

Ginger looked at me expectantly. A walk would do us both good. I pulled into a spot along the beach, snapped her leash on, and headed toward a great soft-serve place near the end of the boardwalk. She was perfectly happy to amble along beside me, stopping to sniff every few minutes. As I passed the spot where Bridget's lifeguard chair used to be, I gathered in a hard breath. I was trained to construct a story from the evidence. Now I ran through what I knew to come up with mine about her.

She met Peter the day she saved that boy, and Peter exploited her newfound love of saving people and turned it into its opposite. All these years I'd remembered him saying "kitten in a basket" at Nostalgia, but what he said after was more significant: she gets my seal of approval. He must have pressured Bridget to bring me there. When I opened my eyes in Bridget's bedroom, she seemed relieved I'd woken up at all and said she'd saved me, but now I knew better.

We barely spoke over the next few months. I thought she was in love. More likely she felt guilty for what she'd done and was afraid that I'd remember. But I didn't remember and by spring we were friends again. I introduced her to Devon, and she stole him from me, or that's how I saw it. She saw him as a way to escape Peter. She was relieved when she met Devon. I saw the change. But I attributed it to the power of love, and I was jealous.

Peter asked her to show his drawing to Devon. When Devon didn't like it, that was bad enough, but when Peter learned she was dating Devon, he became furious. When she and Peter fought at the beach, she must have told him she was leaving Quincy with Devon and threatened to tell the police about Jennifer Connor and me if he tried to stop her. The night of the party she was going to leave for New York with Devon, but Peter put a stop to that. He wasn't going to lose her to the man who'd copied his painting and won the contest, and he had to shut her up. He planned to kill her and make it look like Devon had done it. But I was there. He saw it as a chance to get rid of both of us. But he wanted one last thrill—to watch her kill me and then kill her. He had Concannon film it to preserve his masterpiece. But things didn't go as expected.

I crossed the street to the soft-serve place and ordered a vanilla-and-orange twist, my favorite, but I wasn't hungry. I took a few licks and held it out for Ginger. She devoured it right down to the tip of the cone. When we got back into the sweltering car, I pressed my face in my hands. "How could you?" I screamed as I pounded my fist on the steering wheel and tears rolled down my cheeks. All that winter when I lived in a fog not knowing why I felt so broken? Not a word from Bridget. I went to start the car and stopped. I took out my phone and brought up my copy of the video Peter had made of me. I paused it at the place where someone said, "Yes." Just a voice, no image. It wasn't an artistic choice. It was a deception. I turned up the volume and listened again. The voice was soft, low pitched, and husky. It wasn't me. It was Bridget saying yes. The whole video was a deception. I slammed my phone down on the seat. Brian was right. The truth lay in what was missing. I forced myself to watch the video again.

That first shot of someone holding a knife was her, not me. I caught the familiar gleam on her wrist—that bracelet. My breath came in quick gasps as I remembered more.

She attacked me and I fought back. That's how she ended up cowering on the floor. But she was my friend. I couldn't believe she'd done this. I reached out to help her up and she whipped the knife out from behind her back and sliced my arm open. She was going for my neck when I wrenched the knife from her and plunged it into her chest.

I zoomed in on the shot of me holding the knife, blood running down from the gaping wound above my elbow. As I leaned back against the hot vinyl seat, I ran my hand over the scar on my arm, the knowledge as painful now as it must have been then. Ginger stared at me with wide uncomprehending eyes. The air was so hot and still I felt like I was suffocating. I started the car, jacked up the AC, and breathed in and out slowly until I was calm enough to drive.

When I got home, I went out to work in the garden. There was weeding to do, tomatoes to pick, and radishes and carrots to dig up. Yank, shake, toss. Damp rich soil under my fingernails. I got into a rhythm as the sun beat down without mercy and sweat trickled down the back of my neck. After an hour or so in the heat I was woozy. I put my trowel on the ground and stood to get a cold drink. That's when the world stopped. My heart galloped and I broke into a cold sweat. I went to call out for help, but the words wouldn't form. My thoughts were as scattered and broken as the weeds around me.

Nothing could stop the rest of the memory from coming.

I am in the woods, dizzy, and the world is out of focus. I smell pine trees, feel moist soil beneath my palms. There is something on the ground in front of me. Flower petals and flecks of silver, a trail in the moonlight. The silver grows brighter, until there is a whole sheet of it, a dress. Bridget, her body still, is lying in the hollow of the fallen tree.

He shouts, "Do it or you'll end up like her."

The butterfly sticks to my fingers, won't let go. I'm finally able to set it down on her neck. I try to put the branches in her hair the way he tells me to, but he keeps yelling, "Not like that."

He shoves me away and kneels beside Bridget, removes the butterfly, curses as he places it again. He bends over her, rearranging the branches, too lost in his creation to notice me creep away. As I stand behind some trees, the reality pounds in my head. I killed my friend, and now he's going to kill me. But I can't move. Someone touches my shoulder and startles me. "Run," he whispers. I take in the glassy round eyes, the earnest plain face, the video camera in his hand. Concannon. "Now," he says. I take one step, then another, trying not to make a sound as things crunch beneath my feet, and break into a run. A branch cracks, vines and briars tear at me, and I stumble in my shoes. I pull them off and keep on running. Peter crashes through the woods after me. I tumble over an edge, down and down, head banging on stones. I reach for something but can't hold on. There's the hard, cold splash of me hitting the water below. Silence.

The memory, fragile as raindrops glistening on a spider's web, disappeared as the green yard came into focus. I went into the kitchen, scrubbed the dirt off my hands, gave Ginger some water, and poured myself a glass. The fact I hadn't remembered any of this must have been an unexpected gift to Peter. He was able to give me back the memory of that night that he wanted me to have. I thought of the last line of his Persephone story from his notebook. "I let her go but left the smallest black petal of myself in her heart so she would always return to me." But there was none of him in me. He was the one who took pleasure in pain. I didn't. We weren't alike. And he hadn't let me go. With help from Concannon, a man I barely knew, I had escaped.

I sank down on a chair. My tears overwhelmed me, receding and returning in waves. I'd never know whether Bridget had gone along with Peter because he forced her to or if she was a willing partner in their dance into darkness. She wasn't here to explain or exonerate herself. I choked back more sobs, thinking of how his twisted versions of the myths silenced Bridget and his other victims by replacing their stories with his. I couldn't give Peter the last word on me or any of us. There was so much I didn't know, but in the end I told my story the way I wanted to and filled in the blanks with my truth. Concannon and Bridget were as much Peter's victims as I was. Shannon was, too.

* * *

Brian stood by my desk as I unpacked my boxes. "It's good to have you back."

I swiveled my chair to face him. "I wish I was glad to be here."

"Stay positive." He smiled.

"Right," I took a pencil from my Fearless Flyers mug and tested the point with my thumb. "I remembered something." His eyes widened. "Peter didn't let me go. Concannon helped me escape." I paused. "And I believe he also put the raw footage on the flash drive so that someday I might find out the truth. Realizing there was some goodness in him makes me feel better."

He gave me a hesitant smile. "You read the police report?"

"Yeah." I dumped what was left in my water bottle onto my sickly jade plant and told him about the striped gloves and what Bridget had said about the white pill. "But I don't remember anything else."

"That's enough to confirm my suspicions." He eyed me uneasily. "I talked to Peter. He said Bridget invited Jennifer to a party and all they did was show her a good time. He admitted to showing you a good time that night at Nostalgia, too. He says Bridget did nothing wrong and neither did he. He denies being a rapist."

"A good time? Nothing wrong?" I had trouble swallowing, breathing, existing, I was so furious.

"We both know he's lying, Sam." He fiddled with his watch. "But it doesn't matter. Now that we have the videos of all the murders, he's agreed to plead guilty to everything. It will spare the Delaneys a trial and do less damage to Shannon's memory."

"That's good news for them." I glanced away.

"Good news for you, too. It will help you move on," Brian said.

I took a pile of papers from a box and frowned. "It's going to be hard to move on knowing what I did."

His brown eyes met mine. "Don't blame yourself for doing what you had to do to survive."

I tipped my face to the side. "Easy for you to say. You don't have to live with it."

"You are stubborn." He stacked the papers neatly on my desk. "I'm a methodical person. You, not so much. But you solved this case. This world is a better place with Peter in jail. Give yourself credit for that." I stared out the dusty window. He went on. "Chief is throwing you, me, and George a party. I'll be deeply hurt if you don't come."

I turned to him. "Fine. I'll go even if George will be there."

"Great. Seeing as he finally got reassigned, it will be nice to raise a glass together one last time."

I smiled. "I'd rather throw it at him."

He pressed his palm on my desk. "George thought he was doing the world a favor by not covering up the video. But he didn't consider the fact that he might not have the whole picture. I tried to protect you from what I knew, but I didn't have the whole picture, either. But thanks to him being misguided, he pushed us all into the truth we were afraid to face. And it's for the better."

His fingers brushed mine as he lifted my framed photo of Jeff and Corinne. "You're lucky to have this, you know," he said.

"I am aware," I replied.

* * *

Jeff was at the sink rinsing grit out of lettuce when I got home. He turned to me with a smile. "I dropped Corinne and Anton at the mall and stopped by here to say hello. I picked up your stuff outside. Figured you were done gardening. I'm making dinner with some of those fresh vegetables." I told him I'd just dropped my things off at the station. He raised an eyebrow. "You went back to work?"

"IA cleared me." I sampled some chopped pistachios on the cutting board.

"That's good news." He placed his hand over mine. "Those are for the salad."

"Don't worry, I'll leave plenty." I took a handful to the table and straddled a chair. "Peter's pleading guilty. Chief's throwing a party for me, Brian, and George. I don't feel like celebrating, but I'll go."

"I have something to celebrate, too." He stood there with an odd look on his face. "I solved my recursion problem. It was right there from the very beginning. I just didn't see it until I found the edge case."

I raised a brow. "Edge case?"

"Something you don't expect to happen but when it does it messes up everything. You end up looping forever unless you figure it out." He stared at me intently.

I thought of the snow-crusted green-and-black gloves and felt a glimmer of recognition.

"You need any help with dinner?" I said.

He smiled. "No."

"Good," I said. "Because there's something I have to do."

I went upstairs, took out the painting I'd never been able to finish, and looked down at the dark water covering the girl at the bottom of the ravine, willing it to reveal more. Slowly, the black flowers parted like a dissolving veil and periwinkle blue appeared in the lines I'd cut into my painting. I picked up a brush and filled in the blue dress that fit smoothly over her hips, the impossibly intricate roses on her shoes, and her blue eyes.

I held my breath and turned to the dark shadow on the cliff, that nameless person I'd been seeking all these years, gave her the same blue eyes, and painted her reaching out her hand.

* * *

Corinne came home after dinner and plopped down on the couch next to Ginger. When I asked if she had a good time at the mall with Anton, she said, "It was fine."

"Can you be more specific?" I asked.

"He bought a T-shirt. I got earrings at the Icing." She patted Ginger as she said, "Anton talked about how he feels about Shannon. He said she wasn't really a bad person. That it was hard to know who she really was because Peter made her do everything." She looked up from patting the dog. "Then he asked what happened to me. And I told him."

I leaned forward. "What did you say?"

"That Peter was nice at first. But then he drugged me. I vaguely remember him tying me up, and saying I'd be fine, that he had to go and when he got back, he'd set me free. But I didn't believe him. The way he looked at me like I didn't even exist . . ." She breathed in slowly. "I've never been so afraid in my life, Mom."

My stomach clenched at the thought of what she'd been through. "I am so sorry this happened to you," I said. "I know it's hard but it's good that you're talking about it."

She smoothed Ginger's silky hair. "Anton and I are working on a new dance. He says creating something from nothing helps you believe in yourself." She drew the dog closer. "He told me Shannon was able to control him because he didn't believe in his true self. She almost pulled him into the darkness with her, but he saved himself before it was too late." Her eyes met mine. "Is that like what Peter did to you?"

Here it was: the conversation I dreaded. I had to tell her, but fear clutched my throat. All I could manage was, "I don't want to talk about it right now."

"But I do," she said. "I told you my story, Mom. It's your turn."

I twisted my shirt button like I might rip it off. She kept patting the dog, waiting. Jeff came in from the kitchen, looked from me to her, and said, "Is something wrong?"

Corinne didn't answer. He gave me a bewildered glance. I wanted a drink, to vanish into a green oblivion, to stay silent forever, but I looked from Jeff to Corinne and said, "I'm just going to tell you. When I was abducted Peter turned Bridget and me against each other. She tried to kill me."

I felt like I was drowning but I went on. "I fought back. I killed her. I didn't remember it for a long time, but I know now I had to do it to save my own life." I forced down a breath. "It's not easy. But I have to accept what I did—so I can move on and be here for you." I took in their shocked silence. "I hope you don't hate me now."

Corinne gave me an incredulous look. "I love you, Mom."

Jeff shook his head slowly. "How could you think we'd hate you?"

As I let their words sink in, he pulled me close, rested his hands on my scars, and massaged my shoulders, reaching into all the parts of me that hurt.

After a moment he let me go and said, "Have you thought more about giving us a chance?" His eyes were like pools of black ink just before you're about to create something new.

"I'm going to keep being obsessive," I said.

He shrugged "I'm obsessive, too, though my obsessions are a little less dangerous."

"Then we can both obsess together." I smiled.

Chapter
Forty-Nine

THE PARTY WAS supposed to be at Finnegan's, but they had a bachelor party booked, so it was being held at Nostalgia. As I stepped out onto the lot with weeds sprouting from the cracks in the asphalt, Brian came up behind me and touched my shoulder. I rocked forward in my high heels. I'd resisted the urge to come in jeans and was wearing my hair down with a silky midnight blue dress and a lacy black sweater I'd borrowed from Corinne. I shot him a glance. "We're doing this here? Really?"

He ran a hand through his hair. "Not my choice. I suspect they got a good deal on the space because Nostalgia's closing for good in a few weeks."

"I heard it's going to be a sushi place." There wasn't any place in this city that didn't bear the sweaty print of memories. My lips parted in a smile. "There's something different about you."

"No sling." He grinned as we stepped inside. Even with all the balloons and streamers, Nostalgia was still dreary. There was talk about how much everyone was going to miss this place once known for its live bands and some of Quincy's scummiest bathrooms. But I doubted many people would feel nostalgic for it.

George stood at the bar, close enough to Alice that they could be a couple, but not so close you'd know for sure. I gave her a sharp glance. "This is not a story."

She tugged on her orange hoop earring. "It wasn't my intent to screw you. I broke your story to get the facts out before everyone else jumped in and twisted it." She paused. "I'm in touch with a gallery that wants to do an exhibit of your paintings of the murder victims."

"Good timing," I said. "I just finished the last one."

She smoothed the skirt of her vintage op-art dress. "They'd like me to do an interview with you to go along with it."

I told her maybe and ordered an old-fashioned. The warmth down my throat eased me, and I gave in to the revelry, the expected jibes from the other officers, and fended off the usual crap and went to share an intimate moment with the sheet cake. "A Job Well Done" was written in blue on the white (whipped I hoped) frosting. I cut the cake into neat squares. George stood politely waiting for a piece. I cut a slice for him, and one for me.

He took a bite, hesitated, and said, "I want to apologize for what I put you through. I thought I had all the facts, but I didn't. I never should have leaked that video to Alice. It's not her fault. It's mine."

I let him suffer a moment and said, "I never would have faced what was in that video if you hadn't leaked it. I would have gone on hiding it from everyone and myself. That's no way to live. So thank you for being a rigid know-it-all." He gave me a faint smile.

After several drinks, I found myself under the ancient disco ball that sent spots of light around the room. No one knew what had happened here except for me, and even I wasn't sure. This place had seemed enormous then, an easy place to lose yourself in. He'd stood against the far wall in his tight dark jeans, face in shadow as he cupped his hand around his mouth to light a cigarette. I remembered the feeling, part thrill, part terror, as his eyes snagged mine, and he said, "Come on," and I walked into the world of the dead and tasted the sweet, sour fruit, ensuring I would always return like an animal drawn back to worry an old wound. He was in some cell now. He'd have years to sort through his shit, though more likely he'd spend his time left on this earth feeling wronged.

All around me, people were dancing. I danced with Brian, who was, as always, exceptionally graceful. George joined us and we grabbed more food and drinks and sat down at an outside table beneath a green awning.

Brian leaned forward. "How come Jeff's not here? You two still separated?"

I hesitated and said, "We're back together. But this isn't his type of thing."

He sampled some of my fries. "I'm meeting Mary Ann later. This isn't her jam, either."

"I thought for sure after you messed up at the shower that you two were over," I said.

"Me too. But she forgave me. If that isn't love, I don't know what is." He gave me a quick smile. "We're looking for a place. She wants me to be that guy who comes home at five every night and throws a steak on the grill. She's got a lot of rules, starting with me quitting smoking. But it's what I need. How about you, George? Anything new?"

"Casey's full-time at the bakery. She's moving out."

Brian winked at him. "Now you can concentrate on Alice."

George almost spilled his drink. "She's a mystery to me." He leaned forward. "Speaking of mysteries, what's happening with the Delaneys?"

"For now, Max is standing bravely by Barb," Brian said. "With no trial, in time, the good folks here will forget it ever happened. The new Quincy will be built by Max, and everyone will sing his praises."

"Do you think Barb knew anything?" George asked.

"We'll never know. Chief's adamant we lay off the Delaneys. They've suffered enough. So there you go. Case closed." Brian stared at his foam-streaked glass. "It's possible Barb had no idea what Peter was up to. But when someone works that hard to seem perfect, you got to wonder what they're covering up."

"There's something for you to investigate," I said to George.

"No can do," he replied. "Working a double homicide in Southie. What are you up to?"

"The usual murder and mayhem." I licked ketchup from my thumb.

"I'm going to make time to do more painting, too. Get myself out there. Don't know where it will lead, but I have to give it a chance."

George looked up from his beer. "I wish you luck."

Brian raised a brow. "More dog portraits?"

"No." I set my jaw. "Whatever I want to do. I'll figure it out."

"I'm sure you will." He grinned. "Will you still talk to us when you're rich and famous?"

"No." I smiled.

He smiled back. Alice swung by and spirited George away. Brian stood up. "I need one last smoke. Want to join me?"

I followed him across the street. It was high tide and the blue-black ocean almost came up to the breakwater. Boston gleamed in the distance like beaten gold. Somehow, Brian managed to light his cigarette in the stiff breeze. I took a breath. We were in almost the same place where I'd first met Bridget.

That night, folding chairs had been set up all along this stretch of sidewalk. The sound equipment had been right about where I now stood. I shut my eyes and saw my mother seated on the breakwater, her long red-and-black skirt, wide belt studded with brass stars, the cigarette between her lips, the glow of her cheeks, the wind rustling her red hair. Somewhere, a traveling rock group was still putting down loud, bright chords, and my father was painting my mother as she had never been, her hand curved around a snow globe, just like Devon painted Bridget as she had never been. Somewhere, Bridget as she really was approached me with her guileless grin and strong stride, snapping her heels into the cement, demanding we dance, and so we did—two girls before the wind and the water, not knowing what was to come or hearing the lonely howl beneath the blue.

Brian flicked his cigarette into the sea. The red glow tailed off and disappeared.

"That really your last one?" I said.

"It is." He stood there awkwardly. "The techs finished putting together a video from the raw footage. It's clear you acted in self-defense. I can show it to you now on my phone."

I leaned my elbows on the breakwater. "No, thanks. I have everything I need." He gave me a puzzled look, and I said, "I remembered."

"Then I guess I'll be going. Mary Ann awaits." He winked at me, his hand soft against my back, and asked if I'd be all right. I said I would, but I needed a moment alone. I pulled my sweater close, the lacy weave delicate on my shoulders.

When he was gone, I told myself my own story.

You go deeper and deeper into the Black Sea. You find the things you left behind, the things you never left, and when you rise up your petals open and in the center of the flower is a black drop in which you can see everything that is and was, and you see yourself as you once were and as you will be, and you take her hand and say come with me. You will be all right.

I sucked in the salty air and forgave myself as much as I could. Seemed like a step in the right direction.

ACKNOWLEDGMENTS

Writing a novel can be a solitary journey but my book wouldn't be here without a lot of help from my friends.

I am incredibly grateful to Anjali Mitter Duva and Henriette Lazaridis of Galiot Press for believing in *Swallowtail* and giving it the chance to reach readers. Huge thanks to my editor, Henriette Lazaridis, whose sharp insights, vision, and encouragement helped me take this book to the next level.

Thank you to the Novel Incubator students, alums, and our amazing teacher Michelle Hoover. The inspiration and support I received from this wonderful community of writers lifted me up when I felt like giving up and motivated me to get this book done. Special thanks to Marc Foster, Mandy Syers, Nancy Crochiere, Stephanie Gayle, and Michelle Hoover who read drafts of my book and gave me the valuable feedback I needed to move forward. An enormous thank-you to my writing group—Kate Leary, Liz Kahrs, Leslie Teal, and Kathleen Gibson—who read my novel many times from the earliest drafts to the later ones and supported me every step of the way.

Thank you to my daughter, Julianne, whose keen editorial eye and love of language helped me make my novel and my writing better. Thank you to my son and story whisperer, Tom, who whenever I came to him saying, "I'm lost. I can't figure this out," was able to tell me what I needed to do to make my story work—usually in a matter of minutes.

Thank you to my husband, Dave, for answering my endless plot questions (often over breakfast), pointing out what didn't make sense, and patiently walking me through alternatives.

Many thanks to my sister, Susanna Burns, who suggested I take a look at the myths in Ovid's *Metamorphoses*, because she thought they might relate to my book. They definitely did!

Last, I want to thank my parents, the extraordinarily talented artists Irene and John Burns, for raising me in a home where I was surrounded by art and the creation of art. It was at the heart of their world, and I am very grateful to them for making it a part of mine.

🎩 galiot press

Galiot's first three books were made possible in part though the support of the following individuals:

Allison Cook & Jack Humphrey
Dena Enos
Marina Hatsopoulos
Bandita Joarder
Breanna Powers Kirk
Erin McKenna
Julia Sullivan
Justine Uhlenbrock

And 295 other contributors to
our crowdfunding campaign

For more about the author, additional content, and to look up or purchase additional Galiot books, visit **www.galiotpress.com**

Upcoming books:

SEX OF THE MIDWEST by Robyn Ryle In this group of linked stories set in the fictional town of Lanier, Indiana, things get rolling when everyone in town receives an email titled "Sexual Practices in a Small Midwestern Town." A link leads to an extensive survey, but why has Lanier been chosen? And by whom? Street by street and house by house, the email opens up the secret (and not-so-secret) lives of one small Midwestern town grappling with current issues in our post-pandemic world. (Fall 2025)

BACKSTITCH by Marian Donahue Set in an art gallery in the Washington, DC, area, and structured as a journey through the gallery's rooms, BACKSTITCH is the story of two sisters who reunite at a retrospective of their troubled mother's art and must confront the consequences of her ambition and the difficult, private truths behind the family's public narrative. The novel is an exploration of family ties, the gift and cost of artistic talent, and the legacy that the artist's children must carry. (Spring 2026)

THE DAYS OF MIRACLE AND WONDER by Irene Zabytko In 1992, just after the fall of the Soviet Union, a Ukrainian-American woman travels to Ukraine and boards a bus on an unlikely pilgrimage. In a manner reminiscent of the Canterbury Tales, the passengers—a swimmer, an artist, an interrogator, and more—tell extraordinary stories of ordinary people caught between Soviet realities and American dreams. THE DAYS OF MIRACLE AND WONDER is a timely glimpse into the complexities of balancing political pressures, collective responsibilities, and individual happiness. (Spring 2026)